i

"A fascinating world filled with danger, romance, humour, and wonderful discoveries."

*—Totally Addicted to Reading*

"An Epic Adventure!"

*—EnjoyMeSomeBooks*

**Praise for
The Gifted Ones Books**

"Full of danger, intrigue, and passion... I'm hooked!"

*—Reading in Pajamas*

"Dianne Duvall has delivered a gripping storyline with characters that stuck with me throughout the day... A must-read!"

*—Reading Between the Wines Book Club*

"Addictive, funny, and wrapped in swoons, you won't be able to set these audios down."

*—Caffeinated Book Reviewer*

"Medieval times, a kick-ass heroine, a protective hero, magic, and a dash of mayhem."

*—The Romance Reviews*

# TITLES BY DIANNE DUVALL

*Immortal Guardians*

DARKNESS DAWNS
NIGHT REIGNS
PHANTOM SHADOWS
IN STILL DARKNESS
DARKNESS RISES
NIGHT UNBOUND
PHANTOM EMBRACE
SHADOWS STRIKE
BLADE OF DARKNESS
AWAKEN THE DARKNESS
DEATH OF DARKNESS
BROKEN DAWN
CLIFF'S DESCENT
AN IMMORTAL GUARDIANS COMPANION

*Aldebarian Alliance*

THE LASARAN
THE SEGONIAN
THE PURVELI
THE AKSELI

*The Gifted Ones*

A SORCERESS OF HIS OWN
RENDEZVOUS WITH YESTERDAY

iii

DIANNE DUVALL

# ROGUE DARKNESS

## IMMORTAL GUARDIANS

*NEW YORK TIMES* BESTSELLING AUTHOR

# DIANNE DUVALL

*For my family*

# ACKNOWLEDGEMENTS

As always, I would like to thank Crystal. You're such a pleasure to work with. I don't know what I'd do without you. I also want to send my awesome Street Team big hugs. You all *rock*! I appreciate your support so much. Another big thank you goes to the members of my Dianne Duvall Books Group on Facebook. I have so much fun in there with you and can always count on you to make me laugh and smile, even when I'm stressing over deadlines. And more thanks go to the bloggers and book influencers who celebrate every new release with me, making them extra fun.

Thank you, Kirsten Potter, for your stellar narration. You have a true gift for giving characters unique and entertaining voices that continue to delight listeners. I love working with you.

And, of course, I want to thank the wonderful readers who have purchased copies of my books and audiobooks. You've made living my dream possible. I wish you all the best.

# PREFACE

*Don't skip if you're an Immortal Guardians fan!*

I ALWAYS ENDEAVOR TO write each book in my series so that new readers who haven't read the previous books can pick up the latest and enjoy it without feeling lost. To that end, I've included a Prologue in *Rogue Darkness* that reveals how the hero and heroine—Sean and Nicole—first met Tessa Hayes, a strong secondary character. If you're new to the series, the Prologue will let you experience that initial explosive meeting firsthand, which I thought would be far more effective than simply telling you about it later. It will also give you a glimpse of Sean and Nicole in action before their relationship changes.

**Immortal Guardians fans**: If you've read *Death of Darkness*, you can skip the Prologue. The only new addition is a little bit told from Nicole's point of view. The rest remains the same. Also, if you've read *An Immortal Guardians Companion*, you'll recognize the first scene in Chapter One. It appeared in the companion as one of the deleted scenes I cut from *Death of Darkness* to reduce the word count. But that scene is what made me want to give Sean and Nicole their own book, so I considered it the perfect beginning for their adventure.

I hope you'll enjoy *Rogue Darkness*!

Dianne Duvall

# PROLOGUE

*A few months earlier*

S EAN LINZ THREW A dagger that buried itself in a vampire's neck, then swung his katana at the opponent in front of him. Clangs, growls, grunts, and cries of pain disrupted the night's quiet as he, his sister—Krysta, and her husband—Étienne fought a large vampire crew that had descended upon UNC Chapel Hill's campus.

There must've been almost two dozen of them. If the enhanced sense of smell Sean had gained when he'd become immortal hadn't warned him otherwise, he would've thought they were frat boys out making mischief. But his nose had caught the scent of blood that clung to their clothing.

As Sean sliced up the vampire in front of him, another slipped around behind him and tried to hamstring him. Sean shifted at the last moment, grunting when the blade cut across his outer thigh. After decapitating the vampire in front of him with a swipe of his sword, he spun around to confront the asshole behind him.

These vampires all appeared to be newly turned. Most still retained enough sanity to look nervous when their companions began to fall beneath the Immortal Guardians' blades.

*Not so confident now, are you, dipshits?* Sean thought.

He spared his sister a glance to see how she fared.

Krysta was kicking ass, as usual, thanks to her ability to see auras and anticipate the vampires' next movements.

Étienne grunted as a gash opened on his cheek.

"Stop watching me, damn it," Krysta snapped. "Keep your eyes on your opponent."

"Watching you kick ass," Étienne called back, "is far more entertaining."

Both were holding their own.

1

The body of Sean's latest foe hit the ground and began to shrivel up at his feet.

"Sean?" Krysta called. "How you doing over there?"

"I'm good," he answered, opening the carotid artery of his next opponent.

Panic lit the vampire's glowing blue eyes as he stumbled backward, dropped his long bowie knife, and tried to stem the rapid blood flow. One of his fellow vampires didn't move out of the way fast enough and accidentally stabbed the vamp in the back.

Sean saluted him. "Thank you." He pivoted to face the vampire behind him.

The vampire's gray eyes lost their glow as they rolled back in his head. His bowie knives clattered to the pavement as he sank to the ground, a tranquilizer dart protruding from his chest.

Nicole. He should've known his Second would shadow them. Like Melanie, she had minor precognitive abilities and had warned him earlier that she *had a bad feeling* about tonight.

Something flew past Sean's left ear with a *thwit.*

He spun to find the vampire who had accidentally stabbed his friend lunging toward him with his blade raised high.

The vamp stopped short and frowned at the dart that now stuck out of his chest. Then his eyes rolled back, and he sank to the ground.

"Damn it!" Krysta shouted suddenly.

"They're running," Étienne announced, his French accent tinged with disgust. "Bloody cowards."

Sean looked around. Seven vampires streaked away with preternatural speed. One jerked to a halt and sank to the ground, thanks to another dart fired by Nicole. "Go," he told the couple. "I'll take care of these."

Krysta shook her head. "Seth said not to hunt alone, to—"

"I'm not alone. Nicole is backing me up." And Sean doubted Seth—the immensely powerful leader of the Immortal Guardians—would want this crew to live to kill another night.

A dart struck one of the four remaining vampires in the neck.

"See?" he added. "I'll be fine. Don't let those bastards get away."

Though both looked uncertain, Krysta and Étienne took off after the others, leaving his sight within seconds.

Two vampires struck Sean in tandem while the third—wearing a baseball cap—hung back and bided his time. Nicole took out one of the vamps Sean fought with a dart before the bastard could sneak around and attack his back. Sean wounded the second, then turned to face the third.

The vampire's head lifted, the bill of his cap rising to reveal his features.

Shock rippled through Sean, freezing him in place. It was a woman. A slender woman, who couldn't be more than twenty-two or twenty-three years old, wearing baggy clothes that concealed her feminine form.

Her eyes glowed green as rage darkened her pretty features.

"Oh shit," Nicole whispered somewhere behind him.

The woman's hands tightened around the hilts of the deadly katanas she wielded. Her fangs gleamed in the moonlight.

Sean stared in horror. A female vampire? He had never fought a female vampire before. He'd never even seen one. Insanity usually drove male vampires to kill the human women they captured long before the women could complete the transformation. But Gershom—the Immortal Guardians' vicious nemesis—had implanted commands in the local vampires' minds, compelling many to turn more humans. If a vampire who hadn't yet surrendered to the madness had caught this woman, he might have been sane enough to transform her instead of killing her.

Sean's stomach churned. The idea of decapitating this woman sickened him.

Could she be one of the missing immortals?

Gershom had kidnapped a dozen *gifted ones* and transformed them so he could build his own army of immortals. This woman's green eyes made it highly unlikely that she was one of them. Almost all *gifted ones*—individuals born with advanced DNA that lent them special gifts—had brown eyes that glowed amber once they became immortal. There had only been one exception in thousands of years.

3

The woman ducked to the side, dodging a tranquilizer dart. Then dodged another. And another.

He gaped. Holy shit! No way was this woman a vampire. "Call Seth!" he ordered.

The woman tossed her katana up in the air, drew a dagger, and threw it. Catching the katana as it fell, she leaped forward.

Behind him, Nicole grunted.

Sean hastily raised his weapons as the woman attacked. She was incredibly fast. So fast that he had to dedicate all of his attention to fending off her strikes.

A thud sounded behind him, like that caused by a body hitting the ground.

Shit! Had the dagger hit Nicole?

Worry rose as he deflected blow after blow of the woman's swords. "Nicole?" he called.

Silence.

One of the woman's blades carved a path across his chest as she took advantage of his distraction. Damn, she was strong. She *had* to be an immortal.

"Nicole!" he shouted, panic suffusing him when she didn't answer. Was she dead? Had this woman killed her?

His foe landed another strike. She fought like an elder Immortal Guardian. How the hell was that possible? At best, she should match Sean in speed and strength and be his equal. Instead, she was kicking his ass.

He parried every blow, but the sheer power behind them slowly drove him backward. Even if she slipped and gave him an opening, he couldn't strike a killing blow. Seth wanted the missing immortals taken alive. So how the hell was he going to get out of this? He couldn't fight her and contact Seth at the same time. He wasn't telepathic and had to use a phone.

Could he hold her here until Krysta and Étienne returned?

A moan sounded behind him.

Relief rushed through him, thickening his throat. Nicole wasn't dead.

He dug in his heels, not wanting the female immortal to get any closer to wherever Nicole lay, and kept her busy so she couldn't throw another dagger.

The long blade of her katana sank into his side and stayed there.

Agony engulfed him. Sean sucked in a breath, then drew his blade across her thigh.

She barely seemed to notice. "Immortal, my ass," she sneered, and yanked her sword out. "If you bleed, you can die."

It hurt so much that Sean nearly sank to his knees.

She renewed her assault. "The other vampires fear you." She scored another hit. "They think you're strong."

Pain lanced through him when she came damned close to severing his arm with another powerful strike. His sword fell from lax fingers, leaving him one weapon against her two.

"But you aren't. You're weak," she taunted in a voice full of hate. "Killing you will be easy."

Rapid *thwicks* reached his ears.

The woman danced backward as blood spurted from multiple bullet holes that opened in her chest.

The shooting stopped.

"He isn't weak, you stupid bitch," Nicole gritted.

Sean risked a glance over his shoulder.

His Second leaned against the corner of the nearest building, a dagger sticking out of her left shoulder. Blood stained her teeth and poured down one side of her face from a head wound as she aimed a 9mm equipped with a top-of-the-line suppressor and extended magazine at the woman. "He's honorable."

Grass shifted.

Sean hastily looked back at the female immortal as she took a step toward him.

Nicole shot her again. Twice. "Too honorable to *hit* a woman, let alone kill her."

The female immortal growled.

"Fortunately, I don't have that problem." Nicole shot her again, then again.

"Don't kill her," Sean huffed. Bending over, he grasped his injured arm. "Seth wants her taken alive."

No more shots ensued.

"Seth?" the woman snarled, blood spilling from her lips. Her eyes flashed even brighter as they met Sean's. "You tell that bastard I'm coming for him," she wheezed.

Sean shook his head. "Tell him yourself. I can have him here in two seconds."

Roaring in fury, she lunged forward.

*Thwick, thwick, thwick.*

More bullets struck home.

Staggering backward, the woman shook her head. Her weapons lowered as she fought for breath. "This isn't... over," she bit out. In the next instant, she spun around and dashed away in a blur even *he* could barely see. Her baseball cap tumbled to the grass at his feet, freeing long auburn hair.

*Shit.* That had not gone well.

Sean turned to face his Second. "Nicole?" He limped toward her.

She met his gaze. The hand holding the gun fell to her side. Her eyes closed. Her knees buckled.

Lunging forward with a growl, he caught her as she sank to the ground.

Pain wasn't new to Sean. He had absorbed Krysta's every time he'd healed her injuries during her six-year stint as the only successful mortal vampire hunter in history. But the immortal he'd just fought had wrought a *lot* of damage.

It took several seconds for him to find his breath. "Nicole?"

She didn't move or respond, neither when he spoke nor when he jostled her.

Sean wanted desperately to call upon his gift and heal her with his hands but knew from experience that his body was too beat-up to be of service.

Holding her in place with his good arm, he clenched his teeth and forced his injured arm to work long enough to drag her phone from her back pocket and dial Seth.

"Yes?" Seth answered.

"It's Sean. I just fought one of the missing immortals but couldn't hold her. She's on the run. Nicole's hurt. And I'm too injured to heal her."

"I have to go," Seth murmured, his voice distant as though he'd lowered the phone. "May I exit this way?"

"Yes," a woman said.

A door opened and shut.

"I'm on my way." Seth ended the call.

Sean closed his eyes. *Please hurry.* Nicole still breathed, but that dagger had come damned close to piercing her heart.

Seth appeared several yards away with his hand on Ami's shoulder.

Barefoot, the petite redhead Seth loved like a daughter wore only a nightgown that left her arms bare and stopped just above her knees.

Shrugging out of his long coat, Seth draped it around her shoulders to protect her from the chilly breeze. "One of the missing immortals was just here. See if you can lock down on her energy signal while I help Nicole." He zipped over to Sean and crouched before him. "Where are Krysta and Étienne?"

Sean gently lowered Nicole to the ground and withdrew his touch. "Chasing half a dozen vampires who made a run for it."

Seth removed the dagger from Nicole's shoulder and rested his hand on the wound.

"There are too many energy signatures here," Ami murmured. "I can't figure out which one is hers."

Ami fascinated Sean. Apparently, every individual produced an energy signal that was as unique as a fingerprint. And Ami was the only person in the world who could identify that signal and use it like a homing beacon to track people.

Seth caught Sean's gaze. "Which way did she go?"

He pointed in the direction the woman had fled.

Nodding, Seth rose. "I'll heal you when I return." Crossing to Ami, Seth lifted her into his arms and took off in a blur of motion.

Sean did his best to ignore the pain that pummeled him as he drew Nicole into his arms again.

Her head wound no longer bled. Like her shoulder wound, Seth had healed it. And if she were critically low on blood, Seth would've teleported her to network headquarters before he'd zipped away with Ami.

"She's okay," he whispered with a sigh of relief as he settled in to wait. "She's okay."

Nicole sighed as an arm drew her closer to a warm, muscled chest. Smiling, she snuggled her face into soft fabric... then grimaced. It was wet and sticky.

Her eyes flew open. Sean held her in his arms. Sort of. He cradled her on his lap, one arm supporting her back. The other hung limply at his side.

"Oh shit!" She sat up so quickly that she nearly rammed her head into his chin. "Are you okay?" After scrambling out of his lap, she knelt before him and gave him a quick once-over. He looked like crap but still lived and breathed. Nicole lunged for the 9mm she'd dropped, then palmed it, spun around, and aimed at... nothing. Her heart raced as she searched for the vampire who—

"It's okay," Sean said. "She's gone."

"Are you sure?" That hadn't been a vampire. The speed and strength the woman had displayed clearly labeled her one of the immortals their enemy had turned against them. For all Sean knew, the woman could be circling around to come up behind them.

Rotating, Nicole eyed the corner of the nearest building.

"She's gone," Sean repeated, every word belying his discomfort. "Seth and Ami are tracking her."

Now that her initial panic was subsiding, Nicole noticed that the agony in her head and shoulder had vanished. Fatigue pummeled her, but other than that... "Seth healed me?"

Sean nodded.

"He didn't heal you?"

"No time."

Seth must've worried Ami would lose the trail if he delayed further. He'd heal Sean when he returned.

Nicole rose and then crossed to the backpack she'd discarded when the battle had begun. "Where are Krysta and Étienne?"

"Still chasing down the others, I guess."

Grabbing the pack, she returned and settled on her knees before Sean. Most people who encountered her probably assumed the backpack was full of college textbooks and would be shocked to discover that instead it sported multiple pockets and compartments chock-full of ammunition, tranquilizer darts, autoinjectors full of the antidote to the only drug that affected immortals, a spare phone, an extensive first aid kit, and a chilly compartment stuffed with bags of blood. She dug one of the latter out and handed it to Sean.

He took it with a smile of gratitude and raised it to his mouth. As soon as his fangs descended, he sank them into the bag and started siphoning the blood directly into his veins.

Nicole caught a blur of motion approaching and hastily raised her weapon.

Krysta and Étienne skidded to a halt, raising their hands.

"It's okay," Krysta said. "It's just us."

Relieved, Nicole holstered her weapon.

Krysta frowned, her pretty face filling with concern as she took in her brother's haggard appearance. "What happened?"

When Sean would've lowered the bag, Nicole touched his hand to stay him and answered for him. "The shortest vampire ended up being one of the missing *gifted ones* Gershom transformed."

Both swore as their eyes widened.

"I don't know how or why," Nicole continued, "but she was as strong and fast as an ancient and would've killed Sean if I hadn't shot her repeatedly until she had no choice but to either surrender or run."

Étienne frowned at the fallen vampires that littered the ground. Their bodies shriveled up like mummies as the peculiar symbiotic virus that infected them devoured them from the inside out in a desperate bid to continue living. "I take it she ran?"

"Yeah. Seth and Ami are tracking her."

Krysta knelt and drew Nicole into a brief hug. "Thank you for having Sean's back."

She smiled. "It's my job."

"And you're damned good at it." Gingerly touching Nicole's bloody face, she frowned. "What about you? Are you okay?"

"I'm good. Seth healed me."

Sean lowered the empty blood bag. "She took a dagger in the shoulder and *still* saved my ass."

Pride and pleasure filled Nicole as she handed him another bag of blood. "According to the ladies," she quipped, "it's an ass well worth saving."

All laughed.

Krysta and Étienne began collecting the weapons the fallen vampires had dropped.

Nicole hovered near Sean, whose wounds began to mend as the virus within him went to work.

Seth abruptly reappeared with Ami in his arms.

Several beeps sounded as the tiny devices in Nicole, Sean, Krysta, and Étienne's pockets notified them of his return. Every Immortal Guardian and his or her Second had started carrying the devices when Gershom had demonstrated his incredible shape-shifting ability by assuming Seth's appearance. Seth carried a similar device in his pocket that automatically triggered the others to beep when he popped in so they would know it was him and not Gershom impersonating him.

He lowered Ami's feet to the ground. "Can you stay a little longer in case she doubles back?"

"Of course," Ami replied. "I'll stay as long as you need me to."

Nicole glanced at her.

Ami was barefoot and wore a short nightgown topped with a huge coat. Seth must have lent her his to protect her from the cool breeze. Since Ami was barely five feet tall and Seth was six feet eight, she looked like a fragile child wearing her daddy's overcoat. But that appearance was deceiving. Even though Ami wasn't an immortal, she fought like one.

Sean, Krysta, and Étienne regarded Seth grimly.

Her heart pounding a frantic beat, Nicole rose and faced him. Fear and dread soured her stomach. Seth wanted all the immortals Gershom led to be captured alive. He intended to help them see the truth—that they had been egregiously deceived—so he could induct them into the ranks of the Immortal Guardians. And Nicole had damned near emptied a mag into the one Sean had fought.

Sean lowered the now-empty blood bag. "Did you find her?"

"No." His face dark with fury, Seth approached them.

Nicole fought a sudden urge to retreat a step. Or two. Or three. Seth was the most powerful man on the planet. Pissing him off was exceptionally unwise.

Kneeling, Seth splayed a hand on Sean's chest. That hand acquired a faint golden glow as he healed the younger immortal's wounds.

The lines of pain that marred Sean's handsome face smoothed out as he released a relieved breath.

Clouds gathered overhead.

Everyone but Seth shared a wary look. The Immortal Guardian leader had spent thousands of years increasing his power and gaining new skills that no others possessed, such as the ability to control the weather. When his emotions ran high, however, that ability sometimes got away from him and reflected his inner turmoil.

As it did now.

Seth rose. "Étienne. Krysta."

The couple crossed to his side.

Krysta had emerged from the battle without a scratch, but Étienne was pretty banged up.

As Seth healed Étienne's wounds, thunder rumbled.

"Seth," Ami said softly, "it wasn't your fault."

Nicole held a hand out to Sean.

Grasping it, he let her tug him to his feet. "It was mine," he admitted. "I should've called you as soon as I saw her. But her eyes glowed green, so I thought she was a vampire. It caught me off guard."

Krysta frowned. "Are you sure she *wasn't* a vampire? I thought our eyes all glowed amber. Except for Seth's, Zach's, and Jared's, I mean." Almost all *gifted ones* and immortals sported dark hair and brown eyes that glowed amber. Seth's, Zach's, and Jared's glowed gold.

The wind picked up, whipping the trees into a fury

Seth shook his head. "Sarah's eyes are hazel and glow green."

"Oh. Right," Krysta said. "I forgot."

Sean shifted. "There's something else."

"Tell me," Seth ordered.

"She may be newly turned, but she fought like an elder immortal."

Nicole nodded. "She did. She was incredibly fast."

"And strong," Sean added. "She was kicking my ass and probably would've succeeded in killing me if the bullets hadn't slowed her down."

"I shot her," Nicole blurted, wringing her hands. Might as well get the truth out there. "A lot."

"No, she didn't." Sean stepped between her and Seth. "She's trying to cover for me. *I* shot her."

"Bullshit." Nicole moved to stand beside him and sent him a scowl before facing Seth. "She really *was* kicking his ass. And not just because she was stronger. Sean wouldn't take the offensive because he wasn't comfortable striking a woman."

Étienne frowned. "*Merde*. I didn't think of that. I wouldn't be comfortable hitting a woman either."

"Well, *I* didn't have a problem with it," Nicole snapped. "No way in hell was I going to let her kill Sean. I shot her all to hell and would've kept it up if Sean hadn't stopped me." Straightening her shoulders, she lifted her chin and looked Seth in the eye. "I know you want her and the others taken alive. But my first priority is to keep Sean safe, so... do whatever you have to do to punish me. I don't regret it." Holy crap, she was nervous though. Her hands even began to shake. Nicole was probably the only Second who had ever come this close to killing an immortal.

"Damn it, Nicole," Sean ground out.

Seth raised a hand to halt whatever else he intended to say. "There will be no punishment, Nicole. You kept Sean safe, and the woman didn't die. Next time, however, call me before you begin shooting."

She relaxed a little. "I was reaching for my phone when the bitch threw a dagger at me. It hit me so hard that I fell back into the building. The next thing I knew, I was waking up, and she looked like she was about to decapitate Sean."

Frowning, Sean touched the blood that coated the side of her face. "You must have hit your head on the side of the building."

Since she couldn't remember, she shrugged. "I guess so."

Sighing, he dropped his hand and turned back to Seth. "How could that woman be so strong if she's newly turned?"

Seth drew out his phone. After several taps and swipes, he held it out to Sean. "Which one was she?" he asked in lieu of answering.

Nicole glanced at it.

The photos app was open, displaying a woman's headshot.

Sean wiped his crimson-coated hands on his pants and swore when both came away more bloody.

"Here." Nicole turned away from him.

"Thanks." Sean rubbed both hands on the back of her jacket, then took the phone.

While Nicole and the others waited, he swiped through a few photos. "This is her." He glanced at Nicole. "Don't you think?"

Leaning closer, she studied the picture. "Yeah. That's her." The bitterness that had darkened the woman's features while she fought Sean was absent in the photo. Instead, she faced the camera with a friendly smile.

Some of the anger that had burned inside Nicole over Sean's close brush with death gave way to remorse as she looked up at Seth. "I'm sorry I called her a bitch. It isn't her fault Gershom is fucking with her head." That bastard was twisting the minds of his immortals with lies so they would help him defeat Seth.

Taking the phone, Seth studied the picture. "Tessa Hayes."

*Tessa Hayes.*

Committing the name and face to memory, Nicole hoped fervently that she and Sean wouldn't have to face the woman in battle again.

# CHAPTER ONE

*Present day*

S EAN FELT HIS SECOND'S stare boring into him as he wolfed down the lasagna she'd prepared for them. Thank goodness immortals weren't undead like the vampires in movies. If that had been the case, he would've missed *many* drool-worthy meals like this one.

Though it might seem like it should be pretty far down the list, one of his favorite perks of being an Immortal Guardian was the food. Incredibly enhanced speed, strength, and regenerative capabilities were awesome, of course. But he and Krysta had endured some lean times since leaving their parents' abode to pursue their respective goals as adults.

After surviving a vampire attack as a freshman in college, Krysta spent several years becoming the only mortal in history to hunt and slay vampires and live to tell the tale. That last part had largely been due to Sean, who had studied medicine at Duke University while he did his damnedest to keep her alive. Since her vampire-hunting treks had limited the hours they could work to pay the bills...

Yeah. They'd had some lean times.

Yet that hadn't bothered him nearly as much as having to sit on the sidelines night after night while she risked her life to protect those of future vampire victims. He had wanted to join her on the hunts. Unfortunately, Krysta had an edge over her opponents that he lacked. And Sean had barely survived the one night he'd hunted with her.

Both he and his sister had been born *gifted ones*. Krysta could see auras, something she had often bemoaned as useless until she'd realized that vampires' auras moved before they did, which provided her with enough warning of their swift actions to kick their asses. Sean had been born with the ability to heal others with a touch. So before his transformation, his only contributions to reducing the vampire population had been driving Krysta to her hunts, studying in the car while she kicked ass, and using his hands to heal any wounds she incurred.

Not anymore. Now *he* hunted psychotic vampires and kicked ass.

He also ate as many delicious meals as he wanted to because traveling and fighting at preternatural speeds burned a considerable amount of calories. And vampire hunting as an Immortal Guardian paid very well. It also came with a lovely house in the country and his choice of Seconds—or human guards—who... well... guarded him during the day, took care of business he couldn't during daylight hours because of his new photosensitivity, and rushed to his rescue if he needed backup during battle.

Seconds were pretty much today's version of Renfield.

Seated across the table from him, Sean's Second continued to study him with an expression he couldn't read. Chris Reordon, the head of the East Coast division of the human network that aided Immortal Guardians, had given Sean his choice of three network employees who were ready and eager to serve as a Second. Nicole had topped the list.

That had surprised Sean. Not because he didn't think women could perform the job. Krysta had kicked ass and taken names for six years *before* she became immortal. But every male Immortal Guardian Sean had met had a male Second.

"Nicole is the best of the lot," Chris had told him, "but I'm having a hard time placing her."

"Why?" Sean had asked curiously. Did she have an attitude problem or something?

"There are very few Immortal Guardian women," Chris explained. "Vampires tend to be particularly brutal with female victims, so women rarely live long enough to complete the transformation."

"That's messed up."

DIANNE DUVALL

"Yes, it is. *And* most Immortal Guardians were born hundreds or thousands of years ago, when men considered women the weaker sex in need of protecting."

"I'm sure Krysta, Lisette, and the other Immortal Guardian women would be happy to disabuse them of that notion."

Chris had laughed. "They already have, but old habits are hard to break. So I have a difficult time finding immortal males who don't resist the idea of a woman possibly sacrificing her life to protect them."

That had given Sean pause. "Does that happen often? Seconds dying while trying to protect their immortals?"

"Not as often as it used to. But it's always a possibility." He'd pointed to Nicole's profile. "Since you served as a Second of sorts for your sister before she transformed, and you're a healer, I thought you might be more amenable to the idea."

Honestly, Sean found the idea of Nicole sacrificing her life to protect him as unpleasant as the others. But he would've felt the same about any man dying to save him, too. So he'd chosen the best of the best.

It had been a little weird at first. Sean had moved into this house as soon as the network offered it to him, happy to escape Krysta and Étienne's home (as well as their constant flirtation). Nicole had arrived the next day and had resided with him ever since.

Sean hadn't lived in a dorm while in college. Since he and Krysta had rented a small house together, he had never had that *move-in-with-a-complete-stranger* experience. Fortunately, Nicole's personality resembled Krysta's, so they had gotten along from the beginning.

Could she be stubborn as a mule sometimes?

Yes.

Did he question her taste in music?

Often and loudly.

Did he like that she charged headlong into danger the way his sister did?

No, though he admired her courage.

Was he okay with the fact that she had already come damned close to dying at least once while serving as his Second?

16

Hell no.

But she was incredibly efficient at her job... and good company.

"So, what's up?" Nicole asked before she stuffed another forkful into her mouth. That her appetite rivaled his own never ceased to delight him. He'd had too many dates with women who picked at their food because others had made them feel self-conscious either about their weight or about eating what some might consider an indelicate amount in public.

Both were utter bullshit.

Nicole, however, ate as much as he did. She had to. She needed the extra carbs to fuel her training sessions with Darnell and the other Seconds. *And* him. It had taken Sean a long time to feel comfortable sparring with her. Because he hadn't been immortal long enough to know how much speed or force he could safely use without hurting her, he had panicked every time he'd knocked her down until she started to knock *him* on his ass.

"What do you mean?" he countered.

"You've been weirdly quiet and sullen lately. Why?"

"It's nothing," he muttered, unwilling to tell her. Sometimes Nicole could be a little too discerning.

"Come on. I'm your Second. You can tell me anything."

"Not anything."

"*Anything*," she insisted.

"Fine." He released a long-suffering sigh. "I need sex."

"Anything but that."

He laughed. "Well, you asked."

"I did, didn't I?" She was quiet for a moment as she tucked into her meal. "Yeah. I do, too."

"Do what?"

"Need sex," she confessed, surprising him. "I love this job. But it has put a serious dent in my love life."

He snorted. "At least you have a love life for it to dent." Not that he had ever seen her date.

He fought a frown. Wait. *Did* she date?

If so, how did she do it without him knowing? And why did the notion trouble him?

17

"Oh please," she scoffed. "As handsome as you are, I doubt you'd have trouble finding a woman interested in getting naked with you."

"Thank you. But one-night stands don't interest me." Sean had resorted to those a few times, when Krysta's vampire hunting had crimped his dating life, and hadn't liked it. He didn't just want sex, he wanted companionship. "Even if they did..."

"Yes?" she prompted.

"I can't keep my damn eyes from glowing when I'm turned on." Usually brown, his eyes glowed bright amber whenever strong emotion—like anger or lust—gripped him. It was an involuntary response he'd had no luck bringing under control.

"Oh." Her brown eyes met and held his with an almost clinical stare. "Right. I guess that would be a little hard to explain."

"Exactly."

She chewed another mouthful. "Maybe you could find someone who's into dominance and submission and blindfold her."

He smiled. "That's not really my thing."

Her lips twitched. "Me either. I hate being ordered to do shit."

"So I've learned," he retorted dryly.

She laughed. "And if any man spanked me, I would kick his ass."

An easy feat for her, thanks to her intensive training. "Since it took me so long to get used to sparring with you, I'm sure you know I wouldn't get off on spanking a woman. I would much rather have her climb all over me and ride me hard than submit to me."

She pointed her fork at him. "That's an image I could've done without."

He smiled.

"Well, if all else fails, you could always... take care of your own needs."

That had better not be a blush he felt creeping up his neck. Sean knew he was supposed to be able to discuss anything with his Second, but this? Really?

Hoping Nicole wouldn't notice, he shook his head. "Masturbation depresses me."

"Because you wouldn't have to do it if you had a woman?"

"Yes. And..." He hesitated, unsure if he should say it.

She raised her eyebrows. "Let me guess. Your hand can't compete with a warm, willing woman?"

"Exactly. In the end, it just makes me feel more lonely."

She chewed thoughtfully. "Yeah. I get that. Masturbation depresses me, too."

A statement that, of course, brought images to mind of her touching herself. Nicole was a very desirable woman, something he'd had a hard time ignoring. Standing five feet six to his six feet two, she had a toned, slender build with curves in all the right places. Imagining her naked and writhing on a bed while she touched herself, one hand cupping her breast as she slid the other down her pale, flat stomach and—

"Great," he grumbled as his body responded. "Thanks for that. Now I'm hard again."

Her face lit with surprise. "Because I mentioned masturbating?"

"Yes, damn it." That image was now burned into his brain and was *not* how he should think of his Second. They were friends and work colleagues. That was all. Chris Reordon had made it exceedingly clear that sex was not a duty he should expect his Second to perform. If Sean tried to pursue *anything* intimate with Nicole, Reordon would flip his lid.

Seth would, too. And Sean did *not* want to end up on the Immortal Guardian leader's shit list.

Nicole stared at him, something he couldn't quite pin down in her expression. Curiosity? Intrigue? "I see what you mean about your eyes."

He swore silently. "They're glowing, right?"

"Super bright amber."

"Wonderful."

She bit her lip. "I can't think of a way around that."

"Me either."

"What do other Immortal Guardians do?"

"You mean the ones who aren't married?"

"Yes."

"Based on everything I've heard, they abstain."

Her eyebrows flew up. "Really? They're all so hot."

He didn't know why that rankled, but it did. "Nevertheless."

"That sucks."

"Yes, it does." He hadn't thought about sex when he'd asked Étienne to transform him. He had instead been focusing on finally being able to contribute more to eradicating vampires and saving lives.

Now Sean could only hope he would meet his future wife soon. His father, born with precognitive abilities, had admitted Sean would marry an immortal woman. But when Sean had asked him who that woman was and when he'd meet her, his father had shrugged and said he didn't know, that he had only seen her in visions.

"You could always do it doggy style," Nicole suggested helpfully. "If she isn't facing you—"

"I already thought of that. But it's been so long that just kissing a woman and holding her close makes my eyes glow. Wouldn't you want to be held and kissed and stroked before a guy spun you around, bent you over, and took you from behind?"

"Definitely." She frowned. "And now *I'm* turned on."

A statement that merely increased his arousal. "That isn't helping."

"Sorry. Maybe you could wear contact lenses that—"

"I tried. They only change the color my eyes glow."

"That sucks," she said again.

Yes, it did.

The sound of an approaching vehicle reached his ears. "Are we expecting company?"

"No." She frowned. "Why? What do you hear?"

"A car, still a few miles out." On a road that led only to this house.

Nicole shoved her chair back and rose. "Sometimes I envy telepaths." Turning away, she headed up the hallway to the armory.

Sean had to agree with her. Being able to peek into the driver's mind and determine whether the approaching person was friend or foe would've been nice. But he was secretly glad Nicole couldn't delve into *his* mind. He doubted she'd appreciate the images that had flitted through it during the past few minutes. "It's probably just my mom and dad stopping by."

"Evelyn usually calls ahead first," she responded, out of sight.

True. And Krysta either texted or had Étienne send him a mental heads-up when they planned to visit.

Unwilling to abandon his meal, Sean tightened his grip on his fork and put on a burst of speed, determined to finish his lasagna in record time.

Head down, he heard Nicole return.

"Oh, for Pete's sake!" she blurted.

He glanced up.

Her face awash with exasperation, she fastened the bulletproof vest she'd donned. "I'm gearing up for war and you're in here stuffing your face?" She now wore a shoulder holster that housed two Glock 18s with thirty-three-round mags.

Laughing, Sean nearly choked on the last forkful.

Closing the distance between them, Nicole pounded Sean on the back.

"I can't help it," he protested once he swallowed. "It's too good to waste."

Her eyes went to her now-empty plate and narrowed. "Wait. Did you finish mine, too?"

He grinned.

Laughing, she gave him a shove. "Go arm up."

Sean rose, gathered the dishes in a heartbeat, conveyed them to the sink, and headed for the armory.

Shaking her head, she left the kitchen.

Nicole hadn't expected any immortal she served to contribute to the mundane household tasks. Kinda hard to imagine a powerful immortal being spending his nights hunting and slaying psychotic vampires to protect humanity, then heading home to do laundry or the like. Particularly since—in recent years—Immortal Guardians' duties had expanded to include preventing freaking Armageddon.

Yet, on numerous occasions, Sean had beaten her to the dishes.

"You know I'm supposed to do that for you, right?" she'd asked once.

He'd shrugged. "That doesn't mean you *should* when I can do it myself. Besides, you cook most of our meals."

He was a good guy. A good friend, too. She'd thought moving in with a man she didn't know from Adam would be awkward. And yet she'd ended up getting along far better with him than she had with her first college roommate. That girl could make a saint swear like a sailor.

Nicole grabbed the assault rifle she'd left by the stairs and crossed the foyer. Drawing the curtains back a bare inch, she peered outside.

Bright solar-powered floodlights illuminated the front yard. This house was parked in the middle of she-wasn't-sure-how-many acres of field and forest. By design, no trees obscured the view from the house on any side for the first fifty yards or so.

Immortals and their Seconds liked to see their enemies coming.

No headlights illuminated the meadows yet.

An unexpected visit like this usually wouldn't cause much of a stir. The network was incredibly efficient in its multitudinous efforts to keep the rest of society from knowing vampires, immortals, and *gifted ones* existed. But a lot had changed in the past decade. Groups had arisen that posed a real danger to Immortal Guardians and those who worked with them. Lives had been lost, both mortal and immortal. So as Nicole waited for the car to appear on the winding road, she mentally prepared for battle.

Unease infiltrated her, driving her to shift her feet restlessly.

"Anything?"

She jumped. Sean could move as quietly as a mouse. "Not yet."

"You getting any bad feelings?"

The precognitive abilities Nicole had been born with sometimes gave her "bad feelings" when something foul was about to go down. "Yes."

Swearing, he drew the curtains back and peered outside, exercising none of the caution she had.

"Subtle," she said dryly.

He grinned down at her. "Did you want to turn out all the lights and pretend no one's home? Maybe duck down behind the sofa so anyone peeking through a window would see an empty room?" Sean was a dive-right-in kind of guy.

Rolling her eyes, Nicole checked his weapons. Two shoto swords in sheaths hung on his back. A bandoleer full of throwing knives crossed his chest. Sheathed daggers adorned his thighs. And... "You might want to do something about that. You wouldn't want whoever's coming to get the wrong idea."

"Do something about what?" He followed her gaze to his pants, which failed to conceal his arousal. "Damn it."

He looked so comically chagrined that she couldn't help but laugh.

"Oh ha, ha. Laugh it up. This is *your* fault," he accused as headlights appeared in the distance outside. "Quick, help me think of something that will kill it."

She stared at him blankly, then blurted out, "Zombies!"

"What?"

"I watched a zombie movie the other day that was utterly revolting."

"Says the woman who has watched me decapitate countless vampires and helped me dispose of their remains."

"Fine. Gross zombies who are half-decayed and falling apart while feasting on the entrails of other gross zombies," she elaborated. "And vomiting."

He grimaced.

"Then eating the vomit."

He laughed. "Ugh! Okay! Okay! Thank you. That's disgusting. And it worked."

She grinned. "Always happy to be of assistance."

Levity soon morphed into pensive silence, however, while they waited.

A sleek car crept up the road.

Nicole frowned. That wasn't Evelyn and Martin's. Looking up at Sean, she mouthed, *Anything?*

He shook his head.

The car pulled into the driveway and parked. The headlights went dark. A minute passed. Then two. Three.

Impatience rose.

Nicole touched Sean's arm to get his attention and signed, *Who is it?* She couldn't make out much because shadows concealed the driver. Sean, however, could see clearly in complete darkness.

He used the sign language they'd learned at network headquarters to spell out T-E-S-S-A so the car's occupant wouldn't hear him.

Nicole's hackles rose.

Tessa? As in Tessa Hayes, the newly inducted immortal who—because of the lies fed her by Gershom—had tried to kill Sean? The same one who'd thrown a dagger that had impaled Nicole when she'd come to Sean's rescue? The one who had later attacked Leah, the woman Seth recently married?

Nicole tightened her hold on the rifle.

Sending her an admonishing look, Sean took the rifle and leaned it in the corner.

Nicole schooled her expression into one of exaggerated innocence and mouthed, *What?*

He signed his response: *It wasn't her fault.*

The rational part of Nicole knew as much. Yet she hadn't quite been able to get past it. She had thought Tessa was going to kill Sean that night. The other woman's glowing eyes had radiated fury. And such malice had laced her speech.

Seth had since swayed Tessa to their side. The woman now lived at network headquarters with some of the other immortals who had fallen under Gershom's spell and several vampires who had surrendered to the Immortal Guardians, hoping the network doctors could keep them from going insane.

The peculiar virus that infected vampires caused progressive brain damage in humans, rapidly eroding their impulse control and driving them toward insanity. But the advanced DNA that *gifted ones* were born with protected them from the more corrosive aspects of the virus, so they became Immortal Guardians and didn't suffer the madness.

Sean had been a med student at Duke University before he transformed and was continuing his studies with Dr. Melanie Lipton, one of the network's top viral researchers. So Nicole spent quite a bit of time at network headquarters. Sometimes she hung out with the special ops soldiers she'd worked with before becoming a Second. She also liked to play poker and video games with the vampires to ease their boredom. Either way, she couldn't help but notice that Tessa always disappeared when she and Sean were on the premises.

That hadn't exactly endeared the woman to her. It had instead roused suspicion.

Did Tessa still harbor ill will for them because they'd nearly killed her?

It was hard to tell because the woman avoided them.

At last, the driver's door opened.

Well, Tessa wasn't avoiding them now.

Nicole's fingers twitched, wanting to grab that rifle.

Sean must have caught her glancing at it, because he scowled and sent her a warning look.

The car door closed with a *thunk*. Footsteps approached.

Did Tessa choose not to conceal her approach because she bore them no ill will or because Gershom had transformed her with the blood of an ancient and she knew she could easily overpower Sean?

Sean displayed none of the uneasiness that prodded Nicole as he opened the front door. "Hi, Tessa." At least he didn't greet her with a cheery smile. Instead, his features reflected puzzlement. "What brings you out this way?"

Nicole tensed as she awaited the woman's response.

"Hi, Sean." Tessa's reply sounded more tentative than Nicole had expected. "Is Nicole here?"

"Yeah." Ignoring Nicole's frown, he backed up and motioned for the other woman to enter. "Come on in."

Tessa stepped inside, her gaze flitting to Nicole as Sean closed the door.

Tessa was about the same height as Nicole. The standard garb most Immortal Guardians and Seconds preferred hugged her slender form tonight. Long auburn hair flowed down her back in thick waves, complementing hazel eyes and pretty features. No unconcealed weapons adorned her. She also lacked the long coat immortals wore that tended to hide a small arsenal.

Tessa dipped her chin in a nod of greeting. Her gaze took in the vest and weapons adorning Nicole, then slid to the rifle leaning against the wall nearby. "I'm unarmed."

Perhaps. "You're also as fast and strong as an ancient."

"Nicole," Sean warned.

"No," Tessa said. "She's right to be wary." Clasping her hands in front of her, she shifted restively.

Nicole frowned. Was she nervous?

"That's actually why I'm here." Tessa straightened her shoulders and raised her chin, seeming to bolster herself. "I came to apologize for what happened... for what I did that night. I've wanted to apologize—to *both* of you—ever since I realized..." Closing her eyes, she sighed and shook her head. "Ever since I realized how wrong I'd been to trust Gershom."

His features softening, Sean rested a hand on Tessa's shoulder.

Nicole fought an urge to object.

"It wasn't your fault," he told her gently.

When Tessa opened her eyes, they sparkled with tears. "I wanted you dead that night, Sean. I wanted you to suffer. I wanted you *all* to suffer."

"Because Gershom made you think Seth killed your brother," Sean pointed out.

"He also told us to take you alive that night, but I would've decapitated you if Nicole hadn't stopped me." She turned to Nicole. "And that dagger I threw would've pierced your heart if you hadn't turned away quickly enough. I would've killed you both and felt no remorse." Her throat worked in a swallow. "That knowledge haunts me. It's why I avoid you every time you come to network headquarters. Because seeing you makes me face what I had become."

Well, hell. Now Nicole felt bad about expecting the worst.

"You became what Gershom made you, Tessa," Sean said without condemnation, "through no fault of your own. You were a pawn in his twisted plot to destroy Seth and kick-start Armageddon. That bastard wanted to watch the world burn and was exceptionally adept at fucking with people's heads. He even managed to pit Roland against Aidan. And Roland is almost a thousand years old. If Gershom could manipulate someone *his* age and with *his* experience, why do you think *you* should have been immune to it?"

Tessa stared at him, unspeaking.

Sean dropped his hand. "Look, we're good, Tessa. I don't hold what happened against you. The more time you spend with us, the faster you'll realize that the Immortal Guardians family is a forgiving lot. Hell, Krysta tried to *kill* Étienne when she first met him. Twice."

Her eyes widened. "Isn't Étienne her husband?"

"Yeah. And he doesn't hold it against her. One time when Richart lost consciousness, John wanted to shove his ass out into the sun."

"I thought Richart was John's stepdad."

"He is."

Her brow puckered. "They don't get along?"

"They do *now*. But at the time, John thought Richart was a vampire and wanted to protect Jenna."

"Oh."

Nicole relaxed a little, Sean's words even beginning to convince *her*.

"And let's not forget," he added, "that Nicole here shot the shit out of you that night."

Tessa looked at Nicole. "Do you feel remorse?"

"For shooting you? Hell no," she answered honestly.

A hint of amusement brightened Tessa's features. "I don't blame you."

"I *did*, however, feel remorse for calling you a bitch when I did it." Nicole glanced from Tessa to Sean and back. "Is that weird?"

"Yes," Tessa and Sean both responded, then laughed.

Why did that cause Nicole's unease to return with a vengeance?

"You see?" Sean said with a smile. "You fit right in."

"Thank you," Tessa said, her relief palpable. "Both of you. Especially you, Nicole. Thank you for preventing me from killing Sean."

Nicole shrugged. "No problem. It's my job. I'd do it again."

Tessa smiled.

Nicole schooled her features into a grim mask. "No, seriously." The words emerged heavy with warning. "I'd do it again."

All levity fled Tessa's features as her eyes widened with alarm.

Even Sean looked uncertain as his gaze flitted back and forth between them.

Nicole winked. "Gotcha," she said with a grin.

Both laughed, the tension melting from their forms.

"If anyone's going to kill Sean, it'll be me," Nicole declared as she narrowed her eyes at him. "He keeps eating all my food."

He groaned. "I'm sorry I ate your lasagna."

"Too little, too late, buddy."

Tessa laughed.

Shaking his head, Sean clasped his hands before him in a pleading position. "I'm going to study with Melanie after my hunt tonight. If I promise to bring you a pie from the network's kitchen, will you forgive me?"

Chris Reordon liked to keep network employees happy and always outfitted the cafeteria's kitchens with the best chefs. "Only if you don't eat it on your way home."

"Yes!" Grinning triumphantly, Sean turned to Tessa. "Speaking of hunting, I was just about to leave. Would you like to join me?"

Surprise lit her pretty features. "Really? You want to hunt together?"

"Sure. It'll give us a chance to get to know each other better and show there are no hard feelings."

Nicole bit back a protest. Sean knew her gift was filling her with foreboding tonight. This was *not* a good time to mix things up.

"I haven't started hunting vampires yet," Tessa confessed.

His smile faded. "Did Seth want you to wait?"

"No. I think he's worried I might feel conflicted about it since I used to hunt *with* vampires under Gershom's command."

Nicole studied her. "Do you?" If Tessa intended to interfere in Sean's hunt instead of aiding in it...

Tessa bit her lip. "A little. But it isn't because of Gershom. It's because of the vampires at network headquarters. They're good guys and are fighting with every fiber of their being to beat the madness." She shrugged. "I just don't want to kill any vampire who might be worth saving like they are."

"None of us do," Sean told her, his voice reassuring. "Cliff's long battle with the growing insanity—the way he clung to honor year after year despite the voices roaring in his head—touched all of us." Cliff was one of Sean's best friends. "But when you're out hunting, it's easy to tell who's fighting the madness and who's reveling in it. And I always keep an eye out for others like Cliff."

Drawing in a deep breath, she nodded. "Okay."

"So you'll hunt with me?"

"Yes," she agreed with a tentative smile.

"Good." He motioned to her. "You're going to need weapons."

"I don't have any. Reordon thought it best not to arm anyone living on sublevel five because we often leave our doors open, and he doesn't want to tempt the vampires."

"I suppose that's best. The last thing you need when a vampire experiences a psychotic break is for a plethora of weapons to be at his disposal."

Nicole knew that was only part of it. Some of Gershom's immortals had *not* embraced their new reality with enthusiasm. A few still struggled to accept the Immortal Guardians as the good guys, something that contributed heavily to the weapons ban.

"Come on." Sean guided Tessa up the hallway. "You can use some of mine."

Nicole retrieved the rifle and followed them, ostensibly to return it to the armory.

"Nicole, do you have a coat she can borrow?"

"Sure." Though she had spares, Nicole chose the coat she always wore while shadowing Sean. "This should fit her." Their clashes with Gershom had driven Reordon to add tracking devices to the hem of every coat the network provided Immortal Guardians and their Seconds with. If anyone went missing again and Seth couldn't find them, the network wanted an alternate method of locating them.

Nicole didn't think most immortals were aware of that.

When Sean reached for the coat, she ignored him and held it up for Tessa to slip into.

Tessa smiled as she donned it. "Thank you. It fits perfectly."

Returning her smile, Nicole bantered with Sean while she armed Tessa with the usual array of blades. Even vampires who had long since succumbed to insanity retained enough of a desire for self-preservation to know they should avoid using firearms that would draw unwanted attention. The last thing they needed was a mob of well-armed human vampire hunters chasing them when they already had to elude Immortal Guardians.

Once Tessa was armed to Sean's satisfaction, the two left in Tessa's car.

Nicole smiled and waved as they backed out of the driveway.

After the car left her sight, however, her friendly smile vanished. As soon as she closed the door, she returned to the armory and removed her shoulder holsters. A few quick tugs released the Velcro closures on her vest.

What the hell was Sean thinking? He knew Nicole had a bad feeling tonight.

After removing the vest, she set it aside.

Was Tessa showing up the same night a coincidence?

Perhaps. But Nicole didn't like coincidences.

She donned a stab-proof vest the network had provided after her run-in with Tessa. No daggers hurled at her tonight would pierce her flesh, even if thrown with preternatural strength. Over that, she added her shoulder holster, already outfitted with Glocks bearing suppressors. Grabbing a spare coat she hadn't used before, Nicole drew her fingers along the bottom hem until she found the tracker, then pressed and held it to activate it as Chris had instructed. A beep sounded.

Shrugging it on, she turned to the multitude of weapons displayed on one wall. Since Krysta, Étienne, and their Second, Cam, often dropped by, Nicole kept the room stocked with enough weaponry and ammo to outfit all of them and then some, so there were plenty of blades for her to slip into the loops and pockets hidden inside her coat. After those, she added a hip-holstered tranquilizer gun. Only one drug in existence could knock out vampires and immortals. And the network had designed a tranq gun that could shoot multiple darts bearing it.

A twinge of guilt pricked her as she headed through the kitchen to the garage. Tessa had seemed sincere when she'd apologized. But that uneasy feeling continued to roil inside Nicole as she ducked into her car and raised the garage door.

She was taking no chances tonight.

She would shadow Sean whether he liked it or not.

# CHAPTER TWO

"**N**ICOLE DOESN'T TRUST ME."

Sean glanced at Tessa as they strolled along a sidewalk on Duke University's campus. "What makes you say that?" He thought Nicole had hidden her unease rather well earlier. She had even joked and teased Tessa while arming her.

"I could feel it."

He frowned. "Are you an empath?" He hadn't thought to ask Tessa what ability she'd been born with. Immortal Guardians boasted a wide variety of them. Younger immortals like himself usually only bore one gift. Older immortals—those whose DNA hadn't been weakened by thousands of years of *gifted ones* marrying ordinary humans—sometimes had several. Seth, the Immortal Guardians' leader, possessed them all, along with a few no one else did.

"No," she said, "but I still sensed it."

He shook his head. "Nicole understands why you did what you did, Tessa. The timing of your visit was off. That's all. She would've reacted better if you'd picked a different night to drop by."

Her brow furrowed. "What do you mean? Did you two have plans?"

"No. Nothing like that. She's a *gifted one* with mild precognitive abilities like Melanie."

Her eyebrows flew up. "Dr. Lipton has precognitive abilities?"

"Sure. Haven't you ever seen her reach for the phone right before it rings? That sort of thing?"

She pondered it. "I guess so. I just assumed it was a coincidence—that she wanted to make a call and the phone rang before she could."

He smiled. "I think you'll find there isn't much serendipity in the Immortal Guardian world. Things you mistake for happenstance are rarely coincidences." As soon as the words left his lips, he frowned. Hadn't he blithely dismissed Tessa's sudden appearance occurring alongside Nicole's premonition as a coincidence?

He shook it off. "Like Melanie, Nicole often gets a bad feeling when something foul is about to go down. And she got one tonight."

Tessa bit her lip. "Are you sure she wasn't just anticipating my arrival?"

He waved a dismissive hand. "Yeah. It was something else. Something that hasn't happened yet. Usually, when she gets these feelings, I end up coming very close to having my ass handed to me." He smiled. "And since my ass is still intact, I'm going to assume it wasn't about you."

She chuckled.

"If you'd rather not hunt with me tonight, though, I'll understand. Things might get a little dicey."

"Honestly, that makes me want to hunt with you even more. If something's coming, I'd like to help you fight it off."

"You do have mad skills," he praised. "How'd you come to be so good with blades?"

Anxiety touched her features as she looked away. "I don't know. Gershom did something. He... meddled with my head and... I don't know. Mind-controlled me, I guess. One day I couldn't throw a proper punch, and the next I could kick ass."

How unsettling must it be for her to know that someone had manipulated her mind to such an extent without her knowledge. "Zach did that once."

Her head snapped around. "What?"

"Zach did something similar to that. To Dana."

"He did? Why? Did she ask him to?"

"No. She didn't find out until later."

Her brow furrowed. "I don't understand. Why would he do that? I thought Zach was a good guy, one of Seth's right-hand men."

"He is," Sean hastened to assure her. "But Lisette is *everything* to Zach. And Aidan is important to Lisette. So when Aidan fell in love with Dana and vampires started targeting her, Zach planted what he called a *How to Kick Ass* manual in her head to help keep her safe." He grinned. "And *boy*, did it work."

That didn't erase her frown. "Is that something Immortal Guardians do often? Manipulate people's minds without their permission?"

*Crap.* He shouldn't have mentioned it. He had wanted to make her feel better and instead had spawned... what? Suspicion? Disapproval? "No. They don't. They really don't. There were extenuating circumstances and—" He broke off when a whimper carried to his ears.

"Oh shit," a woman whispered.

The sounds of a struggle ensued as a breeze carried the sharp scent of pepper spray to his nose.

He and Tessa shared a look, then darted forward, running so fast that any human they passed would catch only a faint blur of motion.

The scuffling ceased. Silence fell, disrupted by snarled curses.

Sean's nose twitched as he and Tessa honed in on the source of the pepper and swung around the corner of a building.

Both skidded to a halt and drew shoto swords.

Five vampires who could easily pass as college students lurked in a dark patch the bright campus lights failed to illuminate. Two were bent over, frantically wiping glowing blue eyes. Two more knelt over a couple of unconscious young women, their fangs buried in the victims' wrists. The last vampire stood tall and held his victim like a lover, his face buried in the crook of her neck. Sean couldn't see the woman's face but could tell by her limp arms and the way her head lolled that the vampire had already sunk his teeth deep, the pressure of the bite releasing a GHB-like chemical from the glands above them.

If she wasn't already unconscious, she would be soon.

The two teary-eyed vamps spun around.

"What the hell?" one blurted upon sighting them.

"Immortal Guardians," the second sneered, eyes weeping, nose running.

The kneeling vampires leaped to their feet. All four drew big bowie knives.

One attacked Sean. Three attacked Tessa.

He swore. "Kill them. They aren't worth saving." When confronted by Immortal Guardians, salvageable vamps either panicked and ran or waited for the immortals to strike first. They didn't all attack the smaller and—in their minds—easier-to-kill female.

There was no honor in that. Even during Cliff's worst psychotic breaks at network headquarters, he had *never* harmed a woman. Neither had Stuart or Miguel.

Sean swung his swords with wicked precision, deflecting blades and scoring hits. Most vampires weren't well trained, having spent most of the time prior to their transformation sitting on their asses, playing video games, or perusing social media feeds.

This one was no different. Swinging wildly, the vampire left himself open enough for Sean to swipe his head from his shoulders.

Before the vamp's body hit the ground, Sean spun to aid Tessa.

Even though she bore mad skills, she had little experience battling multiple foes and had yet to learn how to fight one vampire without the other two circling around behind her.

Sean dove forward and barely kept a vamp from hamstringing her. As he did, the fifth vampire slung his victim over his shoulder and took off.

"He's getting away!" Tessa cried.

"Go," Sean ordered. "I've got this."

"Are you sure?"

"Yeah." Since Tessa had transformed with the blood of an elder, she would have a greater chance of catching him than Sean.

If she failed, the vampire's victim likely wouldn't survive the night.

Tessa zipped away in a burst of speed.

The three vampires left behind looked at each other, then started hacking frantically at Sean with their weapons. Sean jumped up, somersaulted over their heads, and landed behind them. A quick swing of a shoto sword deprived one of his head.

They rarely expected that move.

The other two—one sporting shaggy blond hair and the other sporting a dark buzz cut—fought even more savagely, neither wanting to be the next to fall. Sean struck, parried, and kept them both in front of him.

Mostly.

The faint rhythmic thuds of shoes hitting grass warned him that someone approached at a run. At first, he thought Tessa was returning. But the steps came from the wrong direction at human speeds.

He swore. The last thing he needed was for campus security or some other looky-loo to come along, see what was happening, and live stream it to the internet.

The shaggy blond vamp howled in pain when Sean nearly severed his arm.

Sean pushed forward, keeping up a barrage of strikes.

The vamp with the buzz cut darted around to his back.

The footsteps halted.

Spinning around, Sean blocked a blow that would've taken his head and delivered one of his own. Blood spurted from Buzz Cut's neck when Sean's blade opened his carotid artery. Eyes wide, the vampire dropped his weapons, gripped his neck, and stumbled back a step.

Sean turned to face his last opponent.

*Thwick. Thwick.*

His arm raised to strike, Shaggy jerked.

Sean dove to the side as blood sprayed from the vampire's chest, accompanied by misshapen bullets. Judging by their placement, those lumps of lead had likely pierced the vampire's heart and abdominal aorta, ensuring he would rapidly bleed out.

As the vamp sank to his knees, Sean searched the shadows. Relief swept through him when his gaze alighted upon a small figure half hidden by the corner of the building.

*Nicole.*

"You shadowed me?"

Striding forward, she kept her head on a swivel and looked stunningly fierce. "Of course I shadowed you. I told you I had a bad feeling tonight. Where's Tessa?"

36

He backed away in the direction Tessa had fled. "One of the vamps took off with a victim. Tessa followed him."

"Go." Nicole strode past Shaggy, shot him again almost as an afterthought, and knelt beside one of the young women. "I'll take care of this."

Nodding, Sean sped away.

The fleeing vampire might be fast, but he couldn't compete with Tessa. Gershom had transformed her using blood he'd siphoned from Aidan after rendering him unconscious. In recent years, Immortal Guardians had discovered that *gifted ones* transformed by immortals with healing abilities often matched them in speed and strength. Aidan was roughly three thousand years old and a healer. So Tessa was even stronger and faster than immortals who were hundreds of years older than her.

It made catching up to this vampire easy.

Stopping him without hurting the woman he carried, on the other hand, might not be. Instinct tempted her to tackle him. But the woman slung over his shoulder wouldn't survive a crash to the ground at this velocity. So Tessa darted around in front of him and blocked his path.

The vampire changed course at the last second and took off in a new direction.

Tessa headed him off again. And again. The fourth time, he swore and slowed to a halt, his blue eyes glowing with frustration.

When she finally got a good look at his face, shock rippled through her.

She knew him. "Reed?"

The anger in his features morphed into confusion as he peered at her. "Tina?"

"Tessa."

His brow cleared. "Right. I didn't recognize you. I thought you were an Immortal Guardian."

Cautiously, she approached him. Reed had been one of the many vampires in Gershom's army. Tessa had seen him around the compound several times but had only hunted with him once. "I thought you were dead."

"Why would you think that?"

"The only vampires who didn't return from hunts were those killed by Immortal Guardians. And the last I heard, you hadn't returned." He had disappeared the night before Gershom had tasked her with capturing Leah, something she had thankfully failed to do.

He shook his head. "There was something I had to take care of. It took longer than I expected. And when I texted Gershom for a pickup, he didn't come."

Gershom had insisted that no member of his army know the location of his primary base. *It's the only way*, he'd explained, *to keep treacherous Immortal Guardians from plucking the information from your minds.* When he had sent Tessa and the others out to hunt, he had teleported them to locations that changed nightly and then returned to teleport them back when they called for a pickup. To this day, Tessa had no idea where he'd kept them.

"I've tried every night since," Reed went on, "but he isn't answering my texts. Did the pickup number change?"

She stared at him. He thought Gershom was still in power? How could he not know? "Reed, the number didn't change—"

"Look, I really need to talk to Gershom. Would you text him for me before—"

"Gershom's dead," she blurted. Well, technically, he wasn't. But Seth had ensured that Gershom would never see the light of day again.

Reed's eyes widened. "What?"

"The Immortal Guardians defeated him. Gershom's gone. Has been for months."

He staggered back a step. "That can't be."

"It's true. Immortals cleared out the place we stayed in. And they destroyed a military base Gershom took control of. There's nothing left of it. It's another reason I thought you were dead."

Silence fell as she gave him a minute to absorb her words.

"Are you and that guy you're with the only ones who made it out?" He looked beyond her shoulder. "Why are you dressed like Immortal Guardians? And why did you fight us? Were you pissed because we attacked the girls or something?"

One of the vampires Gershom assigned Tessa to hunt with had once bragged about doing more than drinking from the women he bit. Sickened and horrified, Tessa had beaten the shit out of him until Reed summoned Gershom to pull her off him. When Tessa revealed what the man had done, Gershom read the vamp's mind to confirm his foul deeds and then killed him, warning the others that they would suffer the same fate if they ever did anything so heinous.

It had been yet another reason Tessa had trusted Gershom.

"No," she responded. "The man I was with isn't just dressed like an Immortal Guardian. He *is* one." She thought it best not to mention that she was, too. Not yet anyway. Reed looked pretty twitchy.

He took a step back. "What? Then why the hell are you with him? Did they capture you?"

"Yes, but—"

His expression darkened. "Did they hurt you?"

She held up her hands in a *calm-down* gesture. "No. They helped me, Reed. And they can help you, too. Gershom lied to us."

"Bullshit." Anger tightened his jaw. "Is that what they told you? Did they brainwash you or something?"

"No. That's what Gershom did," she stated, keeping her voice placid. "He was controlling us, Reed, in ways I never guessed possible until I was away from him."

"How do you know *they* aren't the ones lying to you and controlling you?"

"Because they can prove it. They *have* proven it. Without a doubt. And they can prove it to you, too."

He shook his head, but a hint of indecision entered his expression.

"Gershom had telepathic and empathic abilities he used to manipulate us," she explained, "to keep us from doubting him or questioning his orders." Pausing, she lowered her hands as uncertainty struck.

If Reed had been out from under Gershom's influence for months, shouldn't he have long since begun to question the wisdom of following Gershom's orders? Shouldn't doubt over past actions have crept in by now?

Her gaze shifted to the limp figure draped over his shoulder. "Why did you take the woman, Reed?" Sean had told her she'd be able to tell who was worth saving and who wasn't. Did Reed fall into the latter group?

His hold on the woman tightened. "I didn't want the other vampires to hurt her."

Some of her anxiety retreated. "You were protecting her?" That was a good sign, wasn't it?

"Yeah. Those vampires were crazy. You should've heard the sick shit they were bragging about."

"If they were crazy, why were you with them?"

He shifted his weight from one foot to the other. "I couldn't reach Gershom. Or find any of the rest of you. I knew Immortal Guardians were hunting us and figured... safety in numbers, you know?"

During her brief time with the immortals, she'd heard that hunting in packs—which used to be rare—was common among the vampire population now. "You said the other vampires were crazy. You don't want to end up like them, do you?"

He met her gaze. "No."

"Then let the Immortal Guardians help you like they're helping me."

The sound of someone swiftly approaching carried to their ears.

Stiffening, Reed glanced past her again. "He's coming." In one quick motion, he flipped the woman off his shoulder and hurled her at Tessa.

Surprised, Tessa fumbled to catch her as Reed raced away. Though Tessa could easily support the other woman's weight, they were almost the same size. And getting a good enough grip on the unconscious form to keep her from sliding out of Tessa's hold and hitting her head on the pavement was awkward as hell.

Sean skidded to a stop beside her. "You okay?"

"Yeah."

"Where's the vampire?"

She nodded in the direction Reed had fled. "He threw the woman at me and ran."

Sean shot off in a blur.

Guilt pricked Tessa as she shifted the woman and cradled her like a baby.

Should she have told him that Reed said he took the woman to save her from the others? She hadn't been able to discern whether he told the truth. And Sean might slay him on sight without asking questions.

Sticking to the shadows, she strode back the way she had come. Sean had no doubt left four dead vampires decaying beside two unconscious women.

When she reached the scene of their initial confrontation, Tessa stopped short.

Nicole stood with her feet braced apart, aiming a tranquilizer gun at her. Upon seeing Tessa, she relaxed her stance and lowered the weapon. "Where's Sean?"

"Chasing the vampire."

She frowned. "You couldn't catch him?"

"Sean?"

"No, the vampire. You're faster than Sean. Faster than the vampire. You should've been able to catch him."

"I did."

Nicole gave her a quick head-to-toe glance. "Are you injured?"

"No."

"Then how did he get away?"

Hesitant to admit she'd tried to recruit him, Tessa indicated the woman in her arms. "I couldn't attack him while he was holding her. I was afraid she'd get hurt. Then the vampire heard Sean coming, threw her at me, and took off."

Her face filling with concern, Nicole holstered the weapon and motioned for Tessa to set the woman down. "Is she dead?"

"No. She's still breathing, just unconscious." Tessa gently laid the woman down beside the other two. "Are the others okay?"

"Yeah. Looks like we got here before the vampires could take too much blood. They're both just out of it from the bite." And would have no memory of being attacked when they awoke.

Nicole knelt beside the third woman and touched her wrist. Checking her pulse, perhaps? "We'll have to call in a network cleanup crew to give the women a medical exam, confirm they're okay, and see them home."

"They also need to check the security cameras. We sped past at least two."

"You and the vampire?"

"Yes."

Nicole nodded. "Her pulse is strong, so he must not have taken much blood." The diligent Second proceeded to check the woman over for injuries, beginning with her wrists and the bends of her arms, popular targets for vampire bites.

"I didn't realize you were shadowing us," Tessa murmured.

"Neither did Sean."

Had Nicole shadowed them because of the bad feeling Sean mentioned her having or because she didn't trust Tessa?

If it was the latter, Tessa's next words would undoubtedly increase that distrust. "I knew him."

"Who?" Nicole asked absently.

"The vampire."

Nicole froze for several long seconds, then sat back on her heels and looked up at her. "What?"

"I knew him. He was a member of Gershom's army. I only hunted with him once and assumed he'd been killed, either when Seth and the others descended on home base or in the final battle."

All expression left Nicole's face. "You hunted Immortal Guardians with him?"

Tessa nodded. Would she ever rid herself of the shame that spawned? "He didn't know Gershom isn't around anymore. He said he took the woman to protect her from the other vampires, so I thought..." A long sigh escaped her. "I don't know. I thought he might be worth saving and was trying to talk him into surrendering when he heard Sean approaching."

"And then he threw the woman at you?"

Tessa nodded. "I think he was just scared."

Several heavy seconds passed. "Well, Sean should be able to catch him." Nicole went back to examining the woman.

Not knowing what else to do, Tessa started collecting the fallen vampires' weapons. All four vamps were shriveling up and would soon leave nothing behind save their clothing, watches, phones, and dental fillings.

"Oh shit," Nicole whispered.

Straightening, Tessa glanced at her. "What is it?"

Nicole brushed the woman's disheveled hair back from her face and stared at her in astonishment. "It's Becca."

"Who?"

"Becca. Kayla's daughter. She's a student here."

If Tessa remembered correctly, Kayla Dorman had fallen in love with Immortal Guardian Nick Belanger a few months ago and only recently transformed.

Reaching into her coat, Nicole withdrew a cell phone.

The crunch of grass beneath boots arose in the distance. "Someone's coming," Tessa warned.

Dropping the phone, Nicole stood and drew the tranq gun. "Is it Sean?"

"I can't tell. Whoever's coming is downwind." Tessa drew the shoto swords Sean had lent her and planted herself in front of the downed women—ready to defend them *and* Nicole—just in case.

A blurry figure shot around the corner of the building and slid to a halt.

Sean faced them, his hands up in surrender. "It's okay. It's just me."

Nicole glanced past him. "Where's the vampire? Did you kill him?"

"No." His features darkened with frustration. "I lost him on the other side of campus. I think he ducked into a car and left."

Nicole swiftly holstered her weapon and bent to retrieve her phone. "Well, we'll worry about that later. Right now we have a bigger problem." She motioned to the unconscious woman.

Sean's eyes widened with alarm. "Oh shit. Becca." Kneeling beside her, he touched his fingers to Becca's neck while Nicole

43

speed-dialed a number. His eyes closed with relief upon finding her pulse.

"*Oui?*" a Frenchman said on the other end of the call.

"Richart," Nicole said briskly, "we need you. Now." She quickly told him where to find them.

A dark figure appeared about five yards away. Spinning around, Richart strode toward them. "What happened?" When he followed their gazes to Becca, his face paled. "*Merde.* Is she okay?"

Nodding, Sean lifted Becca into his arms and rose. "A vampire attacked her and her friends. She's been bitten, but her pulse is strong." He passed her to Richart. "Get her to the network."

Brow furrowed, Richart cradled her close. "Warn Chris I'm coming so he'll turn off the alarm."

Reordon had outfitted network headquarters with an alarm that blared every time an immortal teleported inside without warning. Tessa had never asked why but assumed he had added that when Gershom had started shape-shifting into the forms of various Immortal Guardians and wreaking havoc.

"Reordon."

Tessa glanced at Nicole, who had already dialed the network's leader.

"It's Nicole. We need a cleanup crew at Duke."

"Who's we?"

"Me, Sean, and Tessa. Vampires attacked three women."

"What's their status?"

"They're alive, but they're all unconscious. And one of them is Becca Dorman."

He swore.

"Richart is going to teleport her to network headquarters now," Nicole told him.

"Okay. Tell him the alarm's off."

Richart vanished, his enhanced hearing having allowed him to hear both sides of the conversation.

A large dark figure abruptly appeared beside Tessa.

Jumping, she let out a little squeak of surprise and prepared to fight. Then she glanced up and relaxed.

Though Jared was an immortal as ancient as Seth, he had only recently joined the Immortal Guardians' ranks. Nearly seven feet tall, he exuded power and was intimidating as hell when angered. But he had always been kind to Tessa.

He gave her a quick visual inspection. "Are you all right?"

She nodded.

"No injuries?"

"None." Tessa fidgeted. "A vampire got away. The one who bit Becca. I chased him, but—"

"Did he hurt you?" he demanded, face darkening.

"No."

"Threaten you?"

"No. He threw Becca at me and took off."

"Which direction?"

Sean pointed. "I followed him but lost his scent at Flowers Drive. I think there may have been a car waiting for him. Or maybe it was his."

Jared dashed away.

Tessa looked at Sean.

He shrugged. "Ancient immortals can sometimes track people in vehicles."

She stared at him. "Their senses are that much sharper than ours?"

"Mine? Yes. Yours? I don't know."

Worry and self-doubt peppered Tessa as she and Sean collected the fallen vampires' weapons. She should've tackled Reed once he stopped. Or raced forward and plucked the woman from his arms, set her aside, and... she didn't know.

Every second ticked past like an hour.

Jared suddenly appeared again.

All jumped and then sighed.

"I lost him," he announced.

Nicole motioned to the other women. "Would you take these two to the network? I'd feel better if Melanie looked them over."

"Of course." Unlike Tessa, Jared had no trouble gathering both women into his arms and soon teleported away. Seconds later, he returned with three network soldiers. "Now, the rest of you. These men will guard the scene until the cleanup crew arrives."

Tessa started to ask why he hadn't brought the cleanup crew with him, then realized whatever vehicle they usually drove probably carried a host of equipment that would enable them to rid the scene of every speck of blood *and* hack into the university's security feeds.

Jared rested a hand on her shoulder, his touch almost tentative.

Sean took Nicole's arm and clapped a hand on Jared's shoulder.

Duke University's campus fell away, replaced by darkness. A peculiar feeling of weightlessness engulfed Tessa, making her stomach feel uncomfortably buoyant, as it sometimes did in an elevator. In the next instant, the brightly lit infirmary on sublevel five surrounded them.

The large room bustled with activity while Tessa's eyes adjusted to the sudden brightness. Anxiety hung heavily in the air. Dr. Melanie Lipton and her husband, Bastien, leaned over an exam bed upon which Becca now rested. The other two victims occupied beds nearby.

Three techs rushed toward them with bags of blood and IV paraphernalia. The handful of vampires who lived on sublevel five had all gathered to see what the fuss was about and huddled on the other side of the room.

Seth promptly appeared amidst the controlled chaos, his hands on the shoulders of Kayla and her husband, Nick. The younger immortals' eyes glowed bright amber with concern.

Kayla glanced around, a panicked look on her face, then spotted her daughter. Crying out, she dashed over to the bed in a blur. "Becca? Honey?"

Melanie started setting up the IV. "She's okay. She just needs a transfusion."

Nick looked murderous. "What happened?"

Sean and Nicole filled him in.

Tessa waited in anxious silence for them to condemn her for letting the vampire get away, but Nicole opted not to mention the conversation with Reed.

Had Tessa been wrong? Should she not have tried to sway Reed to their side?

Her gaze slid to Becca's still form. What if he had lied and only told her what he thought she wanted to hear? What if he'd intended to kill Becca?

Chris Reordon entered. "What happened?" Though he was human, Chris commanded thousands of network employees and was the mortal equivalent of Seth. He wielded so much authority that even immortals obeyed his rules.

Well, most of them did.

Sean and Nicole again recounted events for Chris.

"Okay. I'm on it," he declared.

*On what?* Tessa wondered. Searching for the vampire? How? He knew nothing about the man. Not his name. Not his face.

But *she* did. Her stomach roiled with nerves. "I knew him," she blurted.

Silence fell as all eyes focused on her.

"What?" Chris asked, his gaze piercing.

Fear and apprehension escalated until she wrung her hands. Would they believe she'd let him get away on purpose? Would they think her complicit?

A large hand touched Tessa's upper back, a welcome warmth against her shoulder blades. The anxiety that plagued her swiftly melted away, replaced by calm.

She glanced up at the man who towered beside her.

Jared dipped his chin in a nod, his dark eyes full of kindness and encouragement.

Straightening her shoulders, Tessa faced the others. "I knew the vampire who bit Becca." She described her brief conversation with him.

Nick scowled. "I thought we wiped out Gershom's entire army."

Seth's brow furrowed. "I did, too. When we blitzed his home base on Roanoke, the only survivors were the immortals we rescued. And no one survived our attack on the military base."

*Gershom's home base had been on Roanoke Island?*

Chris frowned. "Well, no vampires returned to Roanoke after you cleaned it out. There's been no sign of any at the remains of

47

the military base, either. My guys had surveillance cameras set up at both locations before the dust had even settled."

"Without Gershom, vampires *can't* return to home base," Tessa reminded them. "He never told us where it was. Gershom always teleported us there. He didn't want any Immortal Guardians to find its location in our thoughts." And she had known nothing about the military base until after the immortals defeated Gershom.

Chris drew a small notepad and stubby pencil from his front shirt pocket. "You said the vampire's name is Reed?"

"Yes. He disappeared right before Seth captured me. He said he's been trying to text Gershom ever since."

"Do you know his last name?"

"No," she said apologetically. "I only hunted with him once."

Seth frowned. "Gershom didn't have a cell phone on him when I defeated him."

Chris scribbled something in the notebook. "Well, if he dropped it while you were fighting, it was destroyed in the blast." He looked at Tessa. "Can you draw me a picture of Reed?"

She grimaced. "No. I'm sorry. When it comes to drawing people, smiley faces and stick figures are the best I can do."

Seth approached her. "If you'll allow me to access your memories of tonight's skirmish, I can draw him. Then Chris's contacts can use their agencies' facial recognition databases to learn his identity."

Anxiety returned with a vengeance. Tessa's heart pounded despite Jared's calming touch. Seth had been inordinately kind to her, considering she had nearly killed Sean and Nicole, then tried to kidnap Leah, whom Seth had married shortly thereafter. She trusted him and knew Seth was a good guy. And yet Tessa couldn't help but cringe at the idea of him wandering around inside her head. It actually made her panic a little inside. Not because she had anything nefarious to hide, but because...

Well, she supposed she feared it for the same reason someone whom wolves had attacked might not want to venture into the forest again. Having been mind-controlled once, she couldn't help but fear history would repeat itself.

"Sean saw the vampire," Jared said. "Search his memories instead."

That was kind of him. His empathic ability must have let him feel her apprehension.

After a moment's pause, Seth turned to Sean. "Did you get a good look at him?"

Sean nodded. "I think so. See if it's enough."

Seth stared at Sean's forehead for several long seconds, then blinked. "That will do. Thank you."

"You're welcome."

Seth crossed to the desk Melanie often used in the infirmary and picked up a pencil and a blank sheet of paper. Leaning down, he held the paper in place with his left hand and began to draw. His right hand and forearm blurred as streaks of gray rapidly filled the page.

After only a few seconds, he set the pencil down. Turning to Tessa, he held up the paper. "Is this a good likeness?"

Her eyes widened as she stared at it. He might as well have snapped a black-and-white photograph of Reed. It was *that* detailed. "Yes. That looks exactly like him."

Seth handed it to Chris.

"I want a copy of that," Nick growled, radiating fury.

Though Kayla half reclined on the bed next to her daughter, her expression was as murderous as her husband's. "I do, too."

Nodding, Seth returned his attention to Chris. "Send every immortal in North Carolina *and* their Seconds a copy. This Reed fellow didn't appear to know who Becca is—that she's a *gifted one* and the daughter of an Immortal Guardian—but I'd like to confirm that if we can."

Nick loosed a scoffing sound. "Are you serious? You think this was a coincidence?"

Standing beside Melanie, Bastien shrugged. "It could've been. You know universities are prime hunting grounds for vampires. Drunk college students make easy prey."

"Becca hasn't been drinking," Kayla protested, her expression stony. "We would smell it on her."

Unruffled by the rebuke, Bastien spoke calmly. "I know that, Kayla. I was going to say that eggheads staggering home after pulling all-nighters studying are easy prey, too. Neither are vigilant. And while trolling for those particular groups, vampires sometimes get sidetracked by pretty girls. Cliff and I have come to the rescue of many young women on our hunts, both students and employees, as have you and Nick, I'm sure.

"All of us have," Sean commented.

A rumble of agreement ensued.

"If this Reed fellow had targeted Becca," Seth said, "he wouldn't have needed to band together with other vampires. He could've simply waited until she was alone to take her. So yes, it's possible that she was just in the wrong place at the wrong time. Nevertheless, Chris, see what you can dig up on Reed."

Reordon nodded. "Give me twenty-four hours."

"Done." Seth met Kayla's gaze. "Becca will suffer no ill effects from the bite. But if the three of you would like to sleep at David's tonight, you are more than welcome."

She nodded. "Thank you. I don't want her returning to her dorm."

Chris looked up from whatever he was writing. "Her dorm is as secure as I could make it without stationing guards inside the halls and along the perimeter. I'll have my guys review the university's surveillance feeds for the past couple of weeks and see if Reed has been hanging around. I also had a crew add a few non-university-sanctioned hidden cameras of our own after you joined the Immortal Guardians family, Kayla. The cameras cover the entire exterior of the building and every interior hallway that leads from the entrances to Becca's room. And before you ask... no, I did not install cameras in her room."

She smiled. "Thank you."

"If Chris finds anything," Seth said, "I'll call a meeting. In the meantime... Sean, Tessa, you're done hunting for the night. Do either of you have any injuries you'd like me to heal before I go?"

Tessa shook her head. So did Sean.

"Good. I'll head over to Duke and check on the cleanup crew." He vanished.

Tessa looked at Sean. "I just realized I left my car at Duke. I can't give you a ride home."

Jared spoke. "I can teleport them home and retrieve your car from Duke."

Surprised by the offer, she looked up at him. "Really?"

He nodded.

Reaching into her pocket, she retrieved the keys and held them out.

He shook his head. "I don't need them."

She blinked. He could start a car without a key? "Well, now I kinda want to go with you to see how you'll do it."

He grinned. "Let me take Sean and Nicole home. Then I'll return for you."

At last, she found a smile. "Thank you."

He crossed to Sean and Nicole, then gripped their shoulders and the trio vanished.

# CHAPTER THREE

A S SHE HAD EVERY evening for the past week, Nicole donned a stab-proof vest. She had shadowed Sean compulsively ever since Becca's attack. So far, his hunts had been of the standard variety. He'd encounter one or two vampires, engage in a quick battle, and defeat them without incident. Reordon had found nothing to suggest that Reed had been stalking Becca. And no Immortal Guardian had caught so much as a glimpse of the elusive vampire.

With every uneventful night that passed, the "bad feeling" that had plagued Nicole retreated a little more. It still lingered, though, like a mosquito bite that wouldn't stop itching even as it shrank.

Tonight, she covered her vest with a black T-shirt that sported a giant bumblebee with the word "Kind" written in fancy script beneath it. A shoulder holster came next, already outfitted with a 9mm. After haphazardly tucking the T-shirt into the front of her pale blue well-worn jeans, she drew on a gray zip-up-the-front hoodie Sean never wore anymore.

Since he was about eight inches taller than her, broad-shouldered, and muscular, it swallowed her. Which was perfect. In addition to concealing the weapons she carried, it left her looking like a college student who had borrowed her boyfriend's jacket. Her artfully tousled ponytail should complete the look.

Nicole dragged a sleeve back and attached a knife to her wrist. After securing a second knife to the other one, she stuffed her feet into scuffed running shoes. She was bent over, tying the laces, when Sean spoke behind her.

"Is that my hoodie?"

Dropping her foot to the floor, she turned.

Sean stood in the armory's doorway, staring at her as if she sported a peculiar Halloween costume.

"Yes. You don't mind if I borrow it, do you?"

"No. Where's your coat?"

"I'm not wearing it tonight." Holding her arms out to either side, she struck a pose. "What do you think? Do I look like a college student?"

"Yeah. Why? You planning to troll Duke for some innocent young stud you can lure into carnal bliss?"

She laughed. "Yes, Sean. Because everyone knows that the best way to pick up a man is to wear another man's clothes."

He shook his head. "Any man who sees you in that is definitely going to want you to pick him up."

Surprised, she glanced down. "Really?" Since when were jeans, sneakers, and an oversized jacket considered alluring?

"Don't even try that. You know your ass looks amazing in those jeans."

When something warm and tingly fluttered in her chest, she hid it with an eye roll. "You can't even see my ass. Your hoodie covers it."

"And I will reward it for that later. But I don't *need* to see your ass, because I know those jeans. I recognize the tear in the knee. And your ass looks amazing in them."

"Wow. You're cataloging my jeans and ranking them according to how my ass looks? You *do* need to get laid, don't you?"

He laughed. "I really do."

For the first time since she had accepted the position as his Second, Nicole was tempted to... what? Lure *him* into carnal bliss?

No. It had taken her years to land this gig. She didn't want to muck it up by crossing a line Chris Reordon had made a point of drawing several times. Sean's sister was married to Étienne. Étienne and his sister, Lisette, were both telepathic and known to delve into the minds of others without asking permission. Étienne was, in fact, the one who had outed Tracy for having sex dreams about Sheldon. If Nicole and Sean pursued something more intimate, there would be no hiding or keeping it a secret.

And even if she and Sean *could* keep it a secret, what if one of them developed feelings that weren't reciprocated by the other?

She fought an inward shudder. No way would that end well. And who knew how long she would have to wait for another immortal to take her on as a Second *if* Reordon didn't fire her for having inappropriate sexual contact with the man she was supposed to guard? Reordon could be a total hard-ass when it came to keeping things on the straight and narrow. Hell, he still held grudges against Bastien and Aidan for breaking network rules, and they were Immortal Guardians.

Thus far, Sean had shown *no* interest in her, romantically speaking, and treated her like a sister. If he hadn't gone so long without sex, he wouldn't have given her ass a second glance.

"So, where are your combat clothes?" he asked, disrupting her thoughts. "Are you taking the night off?"

"No. Nick called. He thinks Becca could use an outing. He and Kayla have insisted she spend every night at David's place and be inside half an hour before sunset. She's feeling a little frustrated and cooped up."

Sean frowned. "She understands it's for her safety, though, doesn't she?"

"Yes. But Reordon hasn't found anything to indicate she wasn't simply in the wrong place at the wrong time. It's been a week, and nothing has happened."

"Because she's been safely tucked away at David's place."

"Exactly. I think the frustration Nick's picking up on isn't so much that Becca wants to go out and party with her friends. I think the waiting—the not knowing—is just starting to get to her." Nicole shrugged. "Being attacked and having no memory of it is creepy."

"I'm sure it is."

She sat on the bench. "You know what happened to Jenna, right? How Richart met her?"

"Yeah. John told me." John was Jenna's son. Since he and Sheldon—Richart's Second—were close in age to Sean, the three of them often hung out together.

"Like Becca," Nicole reminded him, "Jenna had no memory of the vampire attacking her. But she confronted him later with

Richart's help, and it helped her get past it. I think Becca may need to do the same." She considered it a moment. "Either that or she wants to know once and for all if someone *is* targeting her. It's the only way she'll ever feel safe again."

He sighed. "I can understand that. So what's the plan?"

"Nothing terribly interesting. I'm going to pose as her friend—"

He smiled. "You *are* her friend."

Yes, she was. Chris Reordon rarely recruited anyone younger than twenty-five, wanting to ensure they were past the party-your-ass-off-now-that-you're-no-longer-under-your-parents'-roof phase and could be counted on to perform their duties without getting drunk on weekends and spilling network secrets. But there were occasional exceptions. And Nicole had been one of them.

Nicole's parents had been of the push-her-as-far-and-fast-as-she-can-go sort. Not because they wanted her to have the brightest future possible, but so they could brag about it to their friends. And boy, had they bragged. Nicole had graduated from Harvard, summa cum laude, with a doctoral degree at the age of seventeen. She now had almost no contact with her parents. Nicole had been nothing more than another token of achievement for them. Another bauble to dangle in front of their friends to show them up because little Harrison III of the same age was barely passing eleventh-grade English.

She couldn't remember her parents ever hugging her, kissing her cheek, or offering any other gestures of affection. All they'd given her was stress, and who needed more of that? So she'd cut ties with them as soon as she legally could.

Chris Reordon had recruited her shortly thereafter. Consequently, even though Nicole was only six years Becca's senior, she felt far older and was protective of her friend.

"I am," she agreed belatedly. "That's why I'm taking her out tonight. Nothing daring. I figured we'd go to my favorite restaurant and bar, hang out for a while..."

"And see if Reed will attack her?"

"Pretty much," she admitted.

He was quiet for a moment, his expression inscrutable. "Nick and Kayla are on board with that?"

"They understand but aren't thrilled about it. That's why they want me with her."

His lips quirked up in a smile. "Because they know you can kick ass."

She loved the admiration that simple statement conveyed. "Yes, I can."

Straightening, he strolled toward her. "How many weapons are you carrying?"

Nicole stood. Gripping the lapels of the hoodie, she opened it wide enough to expose the 9mm. She would've carried a tranq gun, too, but it was bulkier than the other and harder to hide.

"What else?"

She peeled back both sleeves and showed him the wrist blades. "And?"

Turning away, she raised the back of the hoodie enough to display the extra mag she'd tucked in the back waistband of her jeans.

"Excellent."

She grinned at him over her shoulder. "The weapons or my ass?"

He laughed. "Both."

When she faced him once more, her stomach did a little flip. His eyes bore a faint amber glow. Nicole pointed at his face. "You'd better not look at Becca with that glow in your eyes, or Nick will wipe the floor with you. He might not have raised her, but he watched over Becca while she grew up and is now a very proud and protective papa."

He grinned. "I won't. Becca is just a friend."

Confirmation that he wasn't interested in Becca shouldn't affect Nicole, so why did she feel relieved?

Wait. Did his mentioning that his eyes wouldn't glow around Becca because she was just a friend mean he thought of Nicole as *more* than a friend?

She nearly growled with frustration. *Why* did her mind keep going in that direction?

Because of that damned talk they'd had a week ago when he'd mentioned needing sex and gotten turned on by her. Now she couldn't *stop* thinking of him that way.

"I'm going with you," he announced suddenly.

"What?"

"I'm going with you."

"No way. The whole point of doing this is to see if Reed will attack again."

"Exactly. That's why I'm going."

"No, you're not." She motioned to him. "Look at you. Even if Reed doesn't recognize you from the other night, he'll know you're an Immortal Guardian and keep his distance. The whole point of this is to see if the attack was a fluke. If it wasn't, two college girls will seem like easy targets and lure him into acting again, particularly if he thinks I'm drunk thanks to the beer I intend to *accidentally* spill on my shirt. If he sees *you*, he'll keep his distance."

Frowning, he glanced down. "I can change my clothes."

"It isn't just the clothes, Sean. It's your face and hair and... everything else." She shook her head. "Immortal Guardian males all look so much alike that you can pass for brothers."

"Hey, the males aren't the only ones. You and Becca could practically be twins."

"Oh please. We don't look *that* much alike." *Gifted ones* and Immortal Guardians *did* tend to resemble each other. Whatever genes determined one's physical characteristics must be more dominant in *gifted ones* than in humans because those traits had prevailed for millennia.

"But you look similar," he insisted. "Same height. Same slender build. Same dark hair, dark eyes, and annoyingly cute nose."

She laughed. "You are *so* weird. You think my nose is cute?"

"Yes, damn it. It's freakishly appealing."

Taking him by the shoulders, she turned him around and pushed him toward the door. "Go get laid, Sean."

Laughing, he dug in his heels and faced her. "I didn't say it turned me on." Assuming a thoughtful expression, he tilted his head to one side, narrowed his eyes, and stroked his chin. "Although..."

Nicole shook her head with a grin and checked her watch. "Ooh. I have to go, or I'll be late. Nick told me to pick Becca up at her dorm before sunset."

Abandoning his pose, Sean followed her from the armory. "Seriously, Nicole, I don't think you should go alone."

"Don't worry. I'm not one of those women you see in made-for-TV movies who receives death threats then—having no self-defense experience at all—refuses protection and goes for late-night walks alone. I have weapons. I know how to handle myself. And I have Richart on speed dial. If Nick and Kayla are okay with it, you should be, too."

"I wish you had put that a different way."

"Put what?"

"That you know how to *handle* yourself."

Again she laughed. "Get your mind out of the gutter."

"I'm trying," he said with amusing bafflement. "It just isn't cooperating."

She halted before the front door. "Where do you plan to hunt tonight?"

"Duke."

Nicole had already tucked her mini wallet in a back pocket, unwilling to carry a purse that might get in the way should Reed attack. So she grabbed her keys off the table by the door. "With Tessa?" she asked casually. The two had hunted together three or four times now.

"No. Alone."

She stared up at him. Relief and worry warred within her. She still didn't trust Tessa and would rather he not hunt with her. And yet, Nicole didn't want him to hunt alone and couldn't shadow him tonight. Not until after she returned Becca to her dorm, where Kayla would be waiting for her.

Should she suggest he hunt with Krysta and Étienne? That was a bit of a sore subject for Sean. He loved his sister but didn't like feeling as if he needed a babysitter after the years he'd spent sitting on the sidelines while she hunted vampires without him.

"What?" he asked when she said nothing. "Still have that bad feeling?"

"Yes," she admitted. "It's weaker but still there." Reaching out, she clasped his hand and stared down at it. Though she wasn't as petite as some of the other *gifted one* and immortal women, his hand was so much larger by comparison that it made hers look delicate.

Warmth engulfed her when he curled his fingers around hers. Quiet fell.

"Anything?" he asked softly.

She shook her head. "Just the same buzz in the background that I've had for days. I think it would get stronger if you were in danger, though, so you should be good tonight. Becca, too."

"And you," he said with a smile.

It didn't always work that way. Her gift had totally screwed her in the past by not offering a heads-up that *she* was in danger. But she forced a smile. "And me."

He gave her hand an affectionate squeeze, then released it. "Be safe. And call me if you need me."

"I will. Don't forget to take a tranq gun with you tonight."

"I won't."

"See you later." Nicole headed outside and skipped down the front steps. The wispy clouds above were already acquiring a coral hue as the sun approached the horizon. *Sheesh*. She'd better hurry, or she wouldn't reach Duke before the sun set. Nick and Kayla were probably antsy enough about this already. How much more so would they be if the woman they'd asked to guard their daughter was tardy?

Despite the crush of rush hour traffic, Nicole managed to reach Becca's dorm before the sky darkened enough for vampires to venture out.

Becca sat on the front steps, chatting with Kayla.

Most of the college students Nicole had known would've been horrified by the notion of their mom hanging out with them on campus. But these two had been best friends ever since Kayla had divorced Becca's adulterous father several years ago. And now that Kayla was immortal, she looked almost as young as her daughter. Nicole doubted anyone who saw them together would even guess they were mother and daughter.

Kayla waved. "Hi, Nicole."

Waving back, Nicole joined them. "You ready for a night out on the town?" she asked Becca.

Her friend responded with an enthusiastic, "Yes!"

Kayla's smile seemed a tad strained as she kissed her daughter's cheek and gave her a hug. "Well, I'll be on my way then. You girls be careful."

"We will," Becca promised. "Bye, Mom."

As Kayla walked away, Nicole asked loudly enough for her voice to carry, "So how many keggers are we hitting tonight?"

Kayla spun around, eyes wide, mouth open to protest. Then she caught Nicole's teasing expression and relaxed.

Becca burst out laughing.

Shaking her head, Kayla sent them a rueful smile. "Don't do anything I wouldn't do."

"Now that she's immortal," Becca murmured as her mother walked away, "I don't think there *is* anything she wouldn't do."

"I heard that!" Kayla called without looking back.

They chuckled.

"So, what *are* we doing tonight?" Becca asked as they strolled away from the dorm.

"Going to my favorite restaurant." Technically, it was a restaurant and bar that was popular with the college crowd. But Becca was too young to drink legally.

"One of the network's?"

The network owned and operated a few restaurants that immortals and their Seconds could frequent without worrying about their differences or conversations drawing attention from humans.

"Nope."

Becca smiled. "Good. All the eyes watching me are starting to get on my nerves."

"Well, it's just you and me tonight."

And they thoroughly enjoyed themselves. The bar was bustling with students determined to blow off steam after a long week. The food was excellent. The music rocked. And Becca seemed to enjoy herself as the night went on, though she didn't let loose enough to flirt with any of the guys who hit on her. Even the most charming of them received cold shoulders.

"Are you dating someone, Becca?" Nicole asked, wondering why her friend kept shutting down everyone who approached her. Immortal Guardians were notorious gossips, so Nicole was pretty sure someone would've mentioned it if Becca had a boyfriend.

"Not right now, no."

Nicole smiled. "Are Nick and Kayla chasing away all the guys?"

She laughed. "No. I've just been too busy studying my ass off to do anything else."

Nicole grunted. "I know what that's like."

"What about you?" Becca studied her curiously. "Are you dating anyone?"

"No."

"I've heard being a Second can make it pretty hard to have relationships."

"It does." So did lusting after the immortal she was supposed to be guarding.

"That sucks."

Before Nicole could respond, a deep voice spoke behind her. "Hey, babe. Sorry I'm late." A British accent colored his words.

Becca's eyes widened as they focused on someone behind her.

Nicole turned to see what had grabbed her attention... and gaped.

Sean strode toward her, a smile on his handsome face.

A very different Sean.

His combat blacks were gone, replaced by worn, faded blue jeans that molded themselves to muscled thighs. A white Henley T-shirt hugged eight-pack abs. Atop that, he wore a dark gray shirt, unbuttoned, with the long sleeves pushed back to his elbows. Dark tattoos now whorled and swirled up his muscled forearms. A watch adorned one wrist. Three black string bracelets circled the other. And his hair...

He had shorn his raven hair close to his head on the sides. The rest of his thick, wavy locks looked like he'd finger-combed them back from his face and sported so many pale golden streaks that he looked blond. A tattoo similar to those on his arms crept up one side of his neck, accenting his firm jaw.

*Holy hell.*

Butterflies fluttered in her belly.

Stopping beside her chair, Sean grinned down at her, looking jaw-droppingly gorgeous... a description that ended up being more accurate than she'd realized.

Tucking a finger beneath her chin, he closed her gaping mouth, then leaned down and pressed a kiss to her lips.

Nicole's heart began to slam against her ribs.

What was happening?

The stunned look on Nicole's beautiful face was absolutely priceless. Sean couldn't wipe the grin off his own. But his little plan almost backfired when the simple kiss he delivered heated his blood and nearly caused his eyes to glow.

His heart thumped harder as he straightened and glanced over at Becca, whose eyes danced with mirth.

"Looks like I missed dinner," Sean said with a faux British accent. "But I'm up for whatever comes next."

"I'll bet you are," Becca said with a gleeful grin.

Nicole made a choking sound and reached for her beer. "What are you doing here?" she asked after taking a hardy swig. "I thought you had to work late."

"I'm bunking off. So what would you two lovely ladies like to do tonight now that I'm free?"

Loosing a sigh of regret, Nicole rose. "Nothing actually. Becca's had a long week, so we were just about to head back to the dorm."

"Great. I'll come with."

Nicole started to set her beer down but fumbled it, spilling most of what remained on her shirt.

Becca hastily grabbed some napkins and shoved them toward her. But Nicole had already accomplished what she'd meant to do. She now reeked of alcohol.

Impressive. That had seemed one hundred percent real. Nicole could act. If she hadn't told him earlier that she'd planned to do it, he would've thought it an accident.

She scrubbed at her shirt for a few seconds, then gave up and tossed the napkins on the table. "Ready?"

Becca smiled. "I think you may have had too much to drink."

"Nah, I'm fine," Nicole insisted with a smile. When she turned away from the table, she staggered and seemed to lose her balance.

"Woah." Sean clasped one of her arms to steady her. "No way am I letting you get behind the wheel. Let me drive you both home."

"Hell no," Nicole grumbled. "You keep driving on the wrong side of the road. We're just gonna walk back to campus."

Becca nodded.

On their way to the door, Nicole lurched sideways and bumped into a guy sitting at the bar.

"Hey!" He swung around with a scowl that vanished the moment he saw who had bumped him.

"Oops," Nicole said with a crooked grin. "Sorry."

He sent her a leering smile as he admired the way her wet shirt clung to her breasts. "You look like you could use a ride home."

Sean wrapped an arm around her. "She already has one. Me."

"Are you sure she wouldn't rather leave with me? She'd love it if I gave her a ride."

Sean's hackles rose. "Bugger off. She's mine."

Beside him, the man's friend leaned in and mumbled something crude that made Sean want to wipe the floor with both of them.

Becca took his arm. "Let's just get her home before she pukes."

Sean committed both A-holes to memory so he could teach them some manners if he ran into them again.

A chilly breeze buffeted him as they stepped outside, clearing his head of the weird fog of fury that had gripped him.

No wonder Nick was so protective of Becca. Predators seemed to lurk *everywhere*.

Once they passed several groups loitering in front of the bar, the trio turned a corner and headed up a much quieter street.

"Way to overact," Nicole grumbled, her usually enticing gait still marred by the occasional stagger.

"I wasn't over*react*ing," he countered, ideally to remind her that Reed might be listening if he was out of sight somewhere, stalking Becca. But his mind lingered elsewhere. Those words—*she's* *mine*—had felt right, falling from his lips. A little *too* right. Dropping his arm, he took her hand and twined his fingers through hers. "Nice jacket, by the way. I was wondering where I left that."

"I didn't think you'd mind if I borrowed it."

"Not as long as you don't get sick on it."

Her lips quirked up. "You won't get in trouble for ditching work, will you?"

"Nah." Although Nicole might kick his ass later for ignoring her wishes and joining them. He just hadn't been willing to risk her or Becca coming to harm and was still a little surprised that Kayla and Nick had agreed to this.

"Well," Becca offered cheerfully, "I'm glad you could join us, George. I was a little nervous about going out tonight and feel safer with you here."

Nicole snorted a laugh at the fake name Becca bestowed upon him.

He grinned. "It's my pleasure."

Sean kept up a running conversation with them as they strolled back to Duke and made their way onto campus. He kept his senses peeled for any hint that someone followed them. His sharp gaze caught no movement in the shadows. His sense of smell failed to detect the aroma of blood that often accompanied vampires, but the cologne he'd applied to disguise his own scent hindered him. No stealthy tread echoed theirs. Even with base boom-boom-booming in the distance from what sounded like one hell of a party, he would've heard it if someone matched their steps.

The crisp breeze strengthened, dragging his shirttail back. Were he human, he would wish he had a jacket. As an Immortal Guardian, however, he could control his body temperature, often as an afterthought, so his hand kept Nicole's nice and warm.

She laughed at something Becca said, drawing a smile from him. He liked Nicole's laugh, the feel of her small hand in his, and the memory of her kiss.

That was going to stick with him.

"Thanks for walking us home," Becca said, jolting him from his thoughts.

He feigned disappointment. "I can't join you inside?"

Nicole shook her head. "We're having a girls' night, remember? That's why you were working late tonight. That and the deadline you have to meet next week."

"Bugger. I forgot." He released her hand. "Are we still on for tomorrow night, then?"

"Yep."

"Okay. See you around seven?"

"Sure."

Sean pressed a kiss to her cheek.

"Seriously?" Becca said dryly. "You can kiss her goodnight, George. Like a *real* kiss. I told you it won't make me feel like a third wheel as long as you don't start groping each other."

Nicole's eyes shot to his.

Sean sent her a cocky grin. "You heard her." Sliding an arm around her waist, he drew her up against him. When she made no objections, he dipped his chin and brushed his lips against hers. Once. Twice. Gentle explorations. Curious to see if the electric shock the first one had sparked had just been a fluke.

It hadn't.

When Nicole rested a hand on his chest and slid it up to cup the nape of his neck, lightning struck. Fire raced through him, speeding his pulse and driving his heartbeat to drum in his ears. His heightened hearing caught the rapid thumping of *her* heart, along with the slight catch of her breath.

Did she feel the spark, too?

Her lips parted. Sean slid his tongue inside to stroke hers. So unbelievably good. Nicole pressed closer, rising onto her toes as she wrapped her other arm around his neck. Her hips shifted against his. Her breasts brushed his chest.

Hard and aching for her, he clutched her tighter.

Becca laughed. "I said *not* to grope each other. You—"

*Thud.*

Sean jerked his head up in time to see a blur of motion streak away.

Becca no longer stood beside them.

"Oh shit!" Slipping behind him, Nicole leaped onto his back. "Go!"

Tucking his arms under her knees, he took off.

"Was it Reed?" she asked, holding on tight as he raced forward at speeds that made the buildings around them blur.

"I don't know." He'd been too busy losing himself in their good-night kiss, which was *supposed* to have been for show.

*Dumbass*, he chided himself.

The vampire only had a few seconds' head start but led them on quite a chase. They left Duke behind and flew through Durham, passing cars and pedestrians who would only notice a breeze. Sean tore around the side of a building in an area of town he wasn't familiar with and skidded to a halt in a narrow alley. The two buildings rose on either side of him, looking industrial in nature. No bystanders were visible and—

He gaped.

Becca fought the vampire.

"What the hell?" Nicole blurted.

Becca swung two sais she had hidden Sean-didn't-know-where.

Reed drew two bowies and stumbled backward as he parried the blows.

"Who are you?" Becca snapped. "Why do you want me?"

Sean released Nicole's legs. As soon as she slid down his back, he drew the daggers hidden beneath his shirt and started forward.

Becca must have been training with the Seconds, because she was actually holding her own.

"What the fuck?" Reed blurted, and actually took a step back.

No. She was *more* than holding her own.

"Tell me!" she shouted as one of her blades sliced into Reed's arm. Another carved a path across his stomach. "Why did you attack me?"

His face darkening with fury, Reed swung his bowie. "Fuck you!"

Becca blocked it despite his greater strength. "Fuck me?" she snarled. "Is that your answer?" She swung again, drawing blood.

Sean stared.

Gun drawn, Nicole kept pace with him, watching in awe as they approached the duo. "Damn. Becca has skills. Do you think she's like Krysta?"

Krysta's ability to see vampires' auras had helped her defeat vampires—with their enhanced speed and strength—long before she'd become immortal.

Sean shook his head. "I don't know." He didn't think Becca had ever mentioned her ability.

"Is that why you want me?" Becca's voice acquired a French accent as she cut Reed again. And again. And again. Then swept one of Reed's weapons from his grasp. After dropping one of her own, she grabbed him by the throat.

As Sean and Nicole watched in dumbfounded disbelief, Becca's form changed, growing taller, bulkier, her clothes straining to contain it, then tearing and falling away.

Nick now stood before Reed, his face twisted with fury.

Reed's eyes damned near popped out of his skull. Swearing, he swung his other bowie.

Nick yanked it from his hand and hurled it away.

Sean and Nicole ducked as it flew past.

Lifting Reed by the neck, Nick shoved him up against one of the buildings. While Reed kicked his feet and clawed at the hand that choked him, Nick leaned in close. "Is that why you took my daughter?" he demanded, his voice deep now and nearly vibrating with rage. "You wanted to fuck her?"

"Oh shit," Nicole whispered.

"I was... I wanted to save her," Reed wheezed.

"Bullshit!" Nick roared, and motioned with the sai in his other hand to a bloody patch on his neck. "You sank your teeth into her neck. Into *my* neck, thinking I was her. I still bear the marks."

"I... I just wanted to calm her," Reed sputtered as he squirmed, making no headway in securing his release.

"Don't lie to me!" Nick roared. He drew Reed away from the building, then slammed the vampire back into it hard enough to crack the brick. "If you wanted to save her or protect her, all you had to do was walk up to her and tell her so. Instead, you bit her and whisked her away. And this was the *second* time you did so!" He slammed the vampire into the wall again, the cracks in the brick lengthening.

"Fuck you!" Reed shot back, anger seeming to overcome fear. "Yeah, I took her." Or perhaps the madness that afflicted all vampires had begun to kick in. Because that dumb bastard started telling Nick in nauseating detail everything he'd wanted to do to Becca.

Nick dropped his sai and proceeded to beat the shit out of Reed.

Sean remained where he stood, allowing the elder immortal to vent his rage. It didn't really matter what condition the vamp was in when they questioned him. They would kill Reed anyway once they elicited the answers they sought. And Sean thought the vampire deserved an ass-kicking. If Reed had been sincere in his desire to protect Becca, he wouldn't have bitten her. Nor would he have spewed the vile things he'd said, even in bluster. Honorable men just didn't think that way.

Reed tried and failed to get in a few punches. Nick was hundreds of years older, far stronger, and couldn't care less that he fought naked.

Nick grabbed one of the fallen sais and prepared to strike what would surely be a killing blow.

"Wait!" Sean called, and took a step forward.

Nick glared over at him as Reed struggled to pick himself up off the ground. "What?"

"Don't kill him, Nick. We need to know for sure why he took her."

"He just told us why he took her," Nick growled, and turned back to Reed.

Weaving where he stood, Reed peered up at Nick through swollen eyes. "Nick? Did he say Nick?" he asked through swollen, bloody lips and staggered. "Are you Nick Belanger?"

The smile that curled Nick's lips was chilling. "Yes. And now you know the name of your executioner." He swung.

Sean and Nicole both lunged forward. "No!"

Reed's head tumbled from his shoulders and hit the ground. His body sank into a lifeless heap beside it.

Jerking to a halt, Sean stared at Nick.

No smile graced his face as he stood, chest heaving, glaring down at Reed as if he wanted nothing more than for the vampire to open his eyes and stand up so Nick could kill him again. His bare form splattered with Reed's blood, Nick turned to face them. "He can't hurt her now, can he?"

"No," Nicole said softly. "He can't hurt her." Glancing up at Sean, she caught and held his gaze. "Becca's safe now."

Sean nodded.

But was she?

# CHAPTER FOUR

N ICOLE DREW HER CELL phone out of her back pocket and dialed Seth.

"Yes?"

"We need you," she told him.

In the next instant, the Immortal Guardians' leader appeared beside her.

While Nicole floundered mentally and wondered how to explain what had happened, Seth studied Sean, arched a brow at his altered appearance, then glanced over at Nick, who stood over the decaying vampire's body, as naked as the day he was born, with rage painting his features alongside the blood.

Seth strode toward Nick. "Let's get you home before someone sees you." As soon as he touched Nick's shoulder, the two of them disappeared.

Nicole turned to Sean.

"We fucked up," they blurted in unison.

Swearing, Sean paced away a few steps. "We should've run this whole thing by Seth first."

She nodded. "I know. I just... It didn't occur to me that—"

"Something like this would happen. It didn't occur to me either."

"At most, I thought Reed would appear, play the good guy like he did with Tessa, and I'd tranq his ass."

"And I figured if I tagged along and pretended to be human, he wouldn't consider me a threat, and I could keep him from hurting you both if shit went sideways." He dragged a hand through his hair, then grimaced at the feel of the product that coated it. "Did you know Becca wasn't Becca?"

"No. Did you?"

"No."

Seth reappeared.

Nicole's stomach fluttered nervously. They had just lost their only lead in terms of discovering why Becca was being targeted. And based on Reed's last words, it seemed like she was definitely being targeted.

Seth again took in the scene. Nicole and Sean stood quietly with what she imagined were looks of both guilt and dread on their faces while the vampire shriveled up in a pool of blood. Tilting his head back, Seth looked up at the structures that bracketed them, turned, and scrutinized the building on the other side of the street at the end of the alley. That one, Nicole noticed, boasted several windows.

Seth closed his eyes.

Nicole glanced up at Sean.

He shrugged.

"There was a witness," Seth murmured.

*Oh crap.* "Should I call Reordon?" she asked hesitantly.

Seth opened his eyes. "No. I took care of it. The man is drunk, his mind easily manipulated. I commanded him to erase the pictures and video he captured on his phone and then buried his memories." He strode toward them. "What happened?"

She and Sean quickly recounted the events of the night.

His face impassive, Seth studied them. "You didn't think it strange that Nick would relax his vigil so quickly?"

Inwardly, Nicole winced. "I thought it was less that and more that he wanted to know if Becca was being targeted. Kayla, too, I'm sure."

Sean nodded. "I thought the same. And there really was no other way to know other than to put Becca out there."

Well, technically speaking, Nick had found a way. She just wished he would've clued her in first.

Seth sighed. "You had no inkling that Becca wasn't Becca?"

"None at all," Nicole admitted. "I didn't even know Nick could assume the appearance of other people. I thought he only shape-shifted into animal forms."

The elder immortal shook his head. "Most older immortal shape-shifters can assume another person's appearance but choose not to, believing it too great a deception."

"Well," Sean said, "Nick was spot-on in his impersonation of her. I'm impressed as hell. He even got her voice right."

Nicole nodded, understanding now why Becca had given all the men who'd tried to chat her up the cold shoulder.

"That doesn't surprise me," Seth offered absently. "Nick has watched over Becca ever since she and Kayla moved in next door to him when she was a child. He knows her every mannerism, every intonation in her voice." He shook his head. "Next time, consult me first before you launch what Reordon will no doubt deem a covert op."

"Yes, sir," they chorused.

Reordon would be pissed that they'd blown this opportunity. Information gathering was a huge part of his and the network's job. And he did *not* like anyone interfering in that and mucking it up.

"Let me get you home." Seth touched their shoulders.

The alley faded to black. That peculiar feeling of weightlessness engulfed Nicole. Then they stood in the foyer of Sean's house.

"I need to speak with Chris," Seth said, "and let him know what's happened."

As soon as they nodded, he teleported away.

Nicole stared up at Sean.

He looked as unsettled by the night's events as she was. "Reed knew Nick's name."

She nodded. "I think that confirms he was targeting Becca. Don't you?"

"Yes."

"To get to Nick?"

"Looks like it."

"How did he even know that she and Nick are related? They don't have the same last name. And Nick and Kayla just got married a couple of months ago."

He shook his head. "I was wondering the same thing."

Her mind raced, trying to connect the dots. "Do you think Reed was the only one targeting her? Or is this part of some greater scheme?"

"I don't know. There were other vampires with him the first time he attacked her, but this time he was alone."

And Nick had slain the only man who could've told them if more were involved.

She sighed. "We fucked up."

"Yeah. Big time."

Belatedly realizing she still held the 9mm, she shoved it into her shoulder holster. "This is my fault."

"No, it isn't. We all agreed to this. You, me, Nick, and Kayla."

She found a faint smile. "The only one who may *not* have agreed to it is Becca."

He smiled. "I doubt she even knew about it."

"If she had, she would've insisted on posing as bait herself."

"Yeah. She's as hardheaded as you are."

Nicole laughed. "And you *aren't* hardheaded? Remind me again... how many times did Seth have to pop in and save your ass when you refused to hunt with a partner while vampire populations were off the charts?"

His lips turned up in a sheepish grin. "Okay. We're *both* hardheaded. We're going to have to work on that in the future."

She grimaced. "If Reordon doesn't fire me."

Sean snorted. "Let him try it. I'll kick his ass."

Nicole knew he expected her to laugh, but Reordon's reaction was a genuine concern for her.

He sobered. "Wait. You aren't actually worried about that, are you? About Reordon firing you?"

"A little," she admitted. In the greater scheme of things, she was still new to the job.

"Well, don't. Chris won't fire you. He knows what an incredible asset you are, Nicole. You should've heard him singing your praises when he gave me my choice of Seconds."

Surprise coursed through her. "Really?"

"Hell yeah. You rock. And Reordon knows it."

Damned if that didn't give her a major case of the warm and fuzzies. *And* make her blush. She'd received so few compliments in her life that she didn't know how to accept them. "Thank you."

He grinned knowingly.

"You know what doesn't rock?" she asked before he could razz her about the color staining her cheeks.

"What?"

She pointed to his head. "That hair."

Eyebrows rising, he turned his head from side to side. "What? You don't like it?"

"The cut's fine." She liked the buzzed sides and would love to run her fingers across them to see if they were rough, like beard stubble, or soft. "It's the color I don't like. How did you bleach your hair so quickly?"

He laughed. "I didn't. It's some kind of fancy hair wax. Sheldon showed me how to use it."

"Really? I don't think I've ever seen him with blond hair."

"Me either. The yellow came with a set containing just about every color of the rainbow. He wanted me to go with blue, but I refused."

She laughed. "I could totally see Sheldon with blue hair."

Her cell phone rang.

After digging it out of her pocket, she checked the screen. Chris Reordon. Dread stole away her amusement as she took the call. "Yes?"

"It's Reordon," Chris said, his voice clipped. "I'm calling a meeting. Tomorrow night. David's place. An hour after sunset."

Nicole met Sean's gaze. "We'll be there."

Sean remained silent as she ended the call.

"I'd say he seemed pissed," she commented, "but that's how he usually sounds."

"True."

Quiet descended.

When it lingered, Nicole felt awkward for the first time since she'd moved in. Now that the adrenaline rush had receded and they'd dealt with the night's events, her thoughts returned to the goodnight kiss she and Sean had shared outside the dorm.

The kiss they *shouldn't* have shared.

The one that had made her body burn.

Sean cleared his throat. "I'd better go wash this crap out of my hair. Sheldon swore it wasn't permanent, but I'd rather not leave it on too long, just in case."

"Or," she suggested with false cheer, "you can leave it in, and I can start calling you Sunshine."

Laughing, he turned and strode up the hallway. "I'll be in the shower."

Gloriously naked, a thought that brought butterflies back to her belly.

Shaking her head at herself, Nicole headed for the armory and put her weapons away. Why, oh why couldn't Sean be more like Nick? Or rather, why couldn't her *reaction* to Sean be more like her reaction to Nick? Seeing Nick naked earlier had done absolutely nothing beyond catching her off guard.

But just imagining Sean naked steered her mind in directions it really shouldn't go.

And that kiss...

The way his body had crowded hers as his tongue stroked and teased and tantalized...

"I think I'll have a shower, too," Nicole muttered.

A very cold one.

Nicole had been around immortals long enough to know that living forever had its drawbacks, the greatest of which was watching the mortals you cared about grow old and die generation after generation.

Being denied the opportunity to fall in love, marry, and have children was another.

Immortals rarely pursued relationships with mortals because those never ended well. Often, the human would grow bitter when she aged and the immortal didn't, sometimes accusing the immortal of keeping a younger woman on the side. Then anger and resentment would sour the relationship.

Other times, the two never stopped loving each other, as was the case with Tomasso and Cassandra. Those two had been together for one hundred thirty-five years, thanks to Seth's ability to heal Cassandra and extend her life. But even Seth—with all of his immense power—couldn't stave off death forever, so Tomasso would lose his human wife to old age in another two or three decades.

Until recently, no *gifted ones* had been willing to transform and spend the rest of eternity with their immortals because they hadn't understood the difference between immortals and vampires and feared their condition resulted from a curse or the like that would damn them for eternity. Sarah Bingham had been the first *gifted one* in history to ask to be transformed.

Consequently, loneliness was pervasive among Immortal Guardians.

Almost as old as Seth, David had lived since biblical times and had been Seth's second in command for nearly as long. His home here in North Carolina was the hub of the Immortal Guardians world on the East Coast, a favorite gathering place of those who hunted in the area.

Seth and David maintained such homes all over the world and always opened their doors to Immortal Guardians and their Seconds. It was their way of easing the loneliness that could grip the mighty warriors.

It was also a way to help them feel more normal. Most of humanity had worked during the day and slept at night for millennia before electricity and all-night superstores appeared on the scene. So having a place where they could gather and socialize after a long night of vampire hunting made a difference and gave them all a family to spend time with since they had long since lost their own.

During her stint as a network special ops soldier, Nicole had heard rumors that Immortal Guardians were like one big, closely knit family. But she hadn't realized how accurate that description was until she became a Second and joined it.

Immortals treated Seconds like family, too, which meant the world to her. She'd had no siblings growing up. And her parents had sucked. Instead of greeting her with smiles or affectionate hugs when she came home from school and asking how her day had been, they had immediately demanded a description of the topics her teachers had covered before giving her a strict study schedule for the rest of the afternoon and night that allotted her twenty minutes to eat dinner, ten minutes to shower, and permitted no other breaks.

The only time she could remember looking forward to going home was when bullies had given her grief for being smart enough to skip several grade levels.

But as she and Sean strode up the walk to David's sprawling one-story home, Nicole found her spirits lightening as they often did. This place felt as much like home to her as Sean's house. Located in the country, it sat in the center of enough acres to ensure that the nearest neighbor lived miles away.

The grass in front was neatly mown. Tall evergreen trees formed a colosseum of sorts around the house and its lawns. Multiple cars lined the curved drive in front of it. Others occupied the large barn in the back, which served as a parking garage for those who stayed the night.

And more had been staying the night in recent years, wanting to provide additional protection to Ami—Seth's adopted daughter—and her baby, Adira, the first child ever fathered by an Immortal Guardian.

Though they'd eliminated the threat to Ami and Adira, many immortals still sought their beds here. Out of habit, perhaps. Or maybe they just enjoyed the family atmosphere as much as Nicole did.

A cacophony of voices met her ears when Sean opened the front door. Light and laughter spilled out to embrace them.

Nicole smiled as she stepped inside.

Sean followed and closed the door behind them.

Two or three dozen people—all clad in black—filled the large living room. Some occupied the many sofas, love seats, and wing-back chairs. Others loitered in groups. Most called a greeting.

After giving them all a cheery wave, she slipped behind Sean and helped him shrug out of his coat. The wall just inside the door bore multiple wooden pegs, most of which already supported long black coats. Nicole added Sean's—heavy from the weaponry within it—and committed the alphabet letter and number above it to memory so she'd know which one was his later.

"Nicole!"

Glancing around, she looked for whoever had called her name.

On the opposite side of the room, a hand waved. Then Becca's face appeared as she jumped up and down a couple times to see over the shoulders of the tall males that surrounded her.

Nicole laughed. Every immortal male present was at least six feet tall. Most of the male Seconds were, too. The women, however, ranged in height from five feet to Nicole and Becca's heights of five feet six.

Becca made her way through the throng. "Hey. I heard what happened last night." Upon reaching her side, she drew Nicole into a tight hug. "Are you okay?"

"Yeah. I didn't get so much as a scratch." Backing away, she squinted her eyes at her friend. "You *are* Becca, right?"

She grimaced. "Yes. I can't believe Nick did that."

"You didn't know?"

"Not until Seth popped in with Nick all bloody and naked, a sight I *definitely* could've done without now that he's my stepdad." Wrinkling her nose, she frowned. "If I'd known, I would've insisted on doing it myself."

Sean nudged Nicole with his elbow. "I told you she was as hard-headed as you."

Laughing, both women swatted him.

Then Becca swept them both with a dubious gaze. "You really thought Nick was me?"

"Yes," Nicole admitted. "He was very convincing."

Sean nodded. "He even sounded like you."

A look of consternation crinkled her features. "That's kinda creepy."

Nicole watched her carefully. "Are you mad?"

"At you?" Becca replied. "No, of course not. At Mom and Nick? Absolutely."

A sharp bark split the air. The immortals near the back hallway parted as a cat shot out of it, raced through the living room to the connecting dining room, and disappeared into the kitchen. A beagle followed, ears flapping and nails clicking on the floor as he took a turn too quickly and skidded sideways.

"Jax!" Susan called from somewhere on the other side of the living room. "Leave Slim alone!"

High-pitched giggles filled the room as a beautiful toddler burst out of the hallway. Her orange curls bounced and jounced as she ran after the dog and cat with that adorable run all toddlers seemed to have. The one that made it look as if they were barely in control. A second toddler followed closely on her heels, his short black hair blowing back as his laughter joined hers.

Every immortal present smiled fondly. All adored Marcus and Ami's daughter Adira and Roland and Sarah's adopted son Michael, doting on them endlessly... now that the warriors had grown accustomed to holding the little ones. Most of those present had not been around small children since they were children themselves hundreds or thousands of years ago, so they had been amusingly nervous when they'd held the fragile little ones for the first time.

As Nicole, Becca, and Sean made their way farther into the room, Krysta and Étienne joined them.

Krysta gave her brother a discerning look. "Rumor has it you were a hot blond with tattoos last night."

Sean glanced at Nicole.

She shrugged. "I didn't tell her that."

Étienne stepped up behind his wife and rested his hands on her hips. "I told her."

How had Étienne known? They hadn't seen him the previous night and—

Nicole scowled at him. "Wait. Did you read my thoughts?" She seriously doubted Sean would've described himself as *hot* in his head.

"Yes," the French immortal admitted without remorse. "But only because I heard something foul went down last night and was worried."

Krysta nodded with exaggerated solemnity. "And because he's nosy."

Étienne laughed.

Nicole turned to Sean. "Okay. So I *did* inadvertently tell them. But I did *not* mentally use the word *hot* to describe you."

"Yes, you did," Étienne corrected her. "Many times."

"Damn it," she grumbled.

Sean grinned.

Tracy, Lisette's Second, joined them. "Did I hear someone say tattoos?" Her gaze roved over Sean. "Where are they, and how much clothing will you have to remove to show me?"

"Dude!" Her boyfriend, Sheldon, called as he worked his way through the crowd. "I'm right here." The youngest Second present, Sheldon was often treated like the kid brother of the group.

"What?" Tracy asked innocently. "You might want to get a tattoo in the future, so I thought I should research some designs."

Laughing, Sean shook his head. "They were temporary tattoos and washed off in the shower."

"Okay, everyone," Darnell called as he emerged from the back hallway. "Time to get settled." Tall, broad-shouldered, and muscular, he crossed to the dining room. Darnell had no problem issuing orders to the immortals present, despite his being a mortal. He'd served as David's Second—*and* Seth's whenever the need arose—for quite a long time, though he looked like he was the same age as Nicole and Sean. His smooth brown head didn't appear to hide a receding hairline. Nor did his face bear any wrinkles. Nicole had no idea how old he was, if he'd been a young recruit like her and Sheldon, or if he was two or three decades their senior and aging very well, thanks to Seth.

Either way, Darnell wielded as much authority among the Seconds as Chris Reordon did. He even trained them whenever time allowed it.

"Immortals," he ordered, "take seats at the table. Seconds, you can hang in the living room and listen in."

Immortal Guardians flowed into the adjoining dining room like a black tide.

"Nicole," Darnell added as he caught her gaze, "you, Becca, and Cliff join the immortals."

She'd figured as much and was glad Cliff would join them. Nicole spent nearly as much time at network headquarters as Sean did, so she'd gotten to know Cliff well. It was wonderful to see him looking so happy after his years of struggling with insanity.

*And* buff. Cliff had packed on loads of muscle since regaining his mortality.

A table long enough to seat at least thirty graced David's dining room. The immortal family in North Carolina had grown significantly in recent years, necessitating the addition of multiple leaves.

The chair at the head of the table was reserved for David, and the one at the foot for Seth. Nicole had always believed that the best leaders were those who didn't feel the need to flaunt their power. And that described Seth to a T. Seth never unseated others in their homes or businesses. Here at David's house, he always insisted that David sit at the head of the table. And he did the same with Chris Reordon whenever they met at network headquarters.

Conversation resumed as the dining room filled.

Nicole and Sean found seats near the middle of the table with Krysta, Étienne, Richart, and Jenna. Becca sat across from them with Kayla and Nick. Darnell sat on what would be David's right once the elder arrived. Ami sat where she always did, on the opposite end, catty-corner to Seth, with Marcus at her side. Marcus plunked little Adira down in a booster seat attached to the table at his elbow. Roland settled Michael in a second booster seat next to Adira. Then he and Sarah claimed the chairs beside her.

Roland Warbrook was renowned for being the most antisocial of the Immortal Guardians. But one would never guess that by watching him now. Smiling fondly, he spread construction paper and crayons on the table in front of the children.

Zach and Lisette sat across from them, leaving the seat closest to Seth's vacant for Leah. In short order, the rest of the immortals found chairs.

Darnell retrieved his cell phone, tapped the screen a few times, and then held it to his ear. "We're ready."

David abruptly appeared beside his chair at the head of the table. Seth's second-in-command was an imposing figure. Six feet seven inches tall, he boasted broad shoulders, thick muscles, skin as dark as night, and masses of thin dreadlocks that were drawn back at the nape of his neck and fell to his hips.

"Abaye!" Adira cried with a big grin.

His striking features softening with a smile, he strolled along the table to drop a kiss atop her head. "Hello, poppet. Are you drawing us another pretty picture?" he asked with an Egyptian accent.

"Uh-huh."

He gave Michael's dark hair a gentle pat. "I see you are, too." As he returned to the head of the table, he murmured, "Jared."

Jared appeared seconds later, his hands on the shoulders of Tessa and Chris Reordon.

David sank into his chair. "Seth."

Seth appeared at the other end of the table.

Adira waved a crayon at him. "Hi, Baba!"

Like David, he bent and pressed a kiss to her russet curls, then offered Michael a friendly pat on the head. As he turned to his seat, his gaze strayed to the empty one adjacent to it. "Where's Leah?"

Darnel answered. "Healing Jules in Haiti."

Seth closed his eyes. A moment passed.

Leah appeared beside him. "Hi, babe. Did you miss me?"

He smiled. "As always. How did it go?"

Leah was gradually beginning to play a more prominent role in the Immortal Guardians family, answering some of the calls Seth, Zach, and David usually handled.

"It went well." She held up blood-smeared hands. "I'm a little messy though. Give me a minute to clean up. Then I'll come back and kiss you long enough to make everyone squirm."

He laughed as Leah ducked into the kitchen to scrub her hands and forearms.

Usually somber, Seth had smiled and laughed much more since she came into his life.

Nicole thought it sweet and heartwarming and hoped to experience a love like that herself one day.

True to her word, Leah returned and gave him one hell of a kiss.

Nicole grinned. Seth wielded more power than anyone else on the planet. And most immortals viewed him as a father figure. So the fact that Leah wasn't at all intimidated by him and treated "Daddy" like an ardent lover continued to stun the immortal world.

Though she was five feet ten, Leah still had to rise onto her toes to loop her arms around his neck. When she finally dropped her heels to the floor, she sent him a teasing smile. "How's your day going, handsome?"

A faint golden glow lit his eyes as he grinned down at her. "Things are definitely looking up."

"*Ba-dum-tish*," Sheldon said in the next room.

Everyone laughed.

Seth seated Leah, then himself. "All right. Let's begin. A situation has arisen that involves Becca."

All eyes went to the teenager, who did *not* look comfortable being the center of attention.

"Sean, Tessa," he continued, "fill everyone in on what happened last week."

Sean described their confrontation with the five vampires who attacked Becca and her friends. Tessa let him do most of the talking, only stepping in long enough to relate her brief conversation with Reed before his escape.

Marcus frowned. "Was this a coincidence, or was Becca targeted?"

Chris rested an elbow on the table. "That's what we wanted to find out. I had my guys review security footage covering that area in the two weeks leading up to the attack, and they found nothing to indicate that Reed had been hanging around Becca's residence hall, stalking her."

Cliff spoke. "As a vampire, he wouldn't *have* to hang around the building to stalk her. His enhanced eyesight would enable him to watch her from long distances."

Chris nodded. "That was my thought, too. I had them check the rest of Duke's security footage. There are over 1,300 cameras on that campus, so it took a while. And they *did* catch sight of Reed.

Twice. But it was nowhere near her dorm and late enough that she was already inside, asleep."

"Nicole," Seth said.

She sat up straighter. "Yes?"

"Tell us what happened last night."

As succinctly as possible, she cataloged the night's events... leaving out the heated kiss she and Sean had shared, of course.

Roland scowled at Sean. Or maybe he had already been scowling and she hadn't noticed. That seemed to be the surly immortal's go-to expression whenever he wasn't looking at his wife, Michael, or Adira. "You didn't see or hear him coming?"

Sean shifted uneasily. "I didn't. I was pretending I was about to leave and telling Becca and Nicole goodnight."

Heat crept into Nicole's cheeks. Damn her tendency to blush! "There was also a party raging in the distance," she added. "The music was pretty loud." A lame excuse.

Roland arched a brow.

"Even though I didn't hear him," Sean said, "he wouldn't have escaped this time. I was instantly on his heels, so he couldn't halt without confronting me. And once he did—if I couldn't find a way to safely extricate Becca—Nicole would've tranqed him."

She nodded. "Sean piggybacked me."

"Instead," Chris inserted with obvious displeasure, "Nick killed him."

A hush descended as all eyes went to the French immortal.

Unrepentant, Nick crossed his arms over his chest.

Beside him, Kayla remained tightlipped and looked as if she would tear into anyone who fussed at him.

Marcus cleared his throat. "I would've done the same."

When Adira heard her father's voice, she grinned up at him.

He winked and sent her a smile, then she returned to her joyful scribbling.

"I would have, too," Roland added.

"And I," Bastien said.

Chris loosed an exasperated sigh. "It doesn't surprise me that you would, Bastien. You kill *everyone*." A comment that inspired laughs all around. Bastien was notorious for his violent nature. "Look, I understand what motivated Nick, but we needed the information Reed could've given us. He knew Nick's full name, which indicates that Becca was likely targeted because of her association with him. Reed probably wanted to use her as bait to ensnare Nick."

"For what purpose?" Nick demanded. "I don't know him."

"That's what I'm trying to find out," Chris explained patiently. "And thanks to you, we're out of leads. This operation should never have been executed without consulting me first. Sean and Nicole are new enough not to have realized that. But Nick, you've been an immortal for hundreds of years and should've known better."

Nicole had to admit she felt relieved at being given an out. She would have to ensure she didn't repeat the mistake in the future.

When Nick and Chris launched into a heated argument, Seth held up a hand.

Silence fell.

He looked at Chris. "Where do you believe we should go from here?"

Chris leaned back in his chair. "If Reed was acting alone, then his death should end it. But if he worked with someone else or with a *group* of someone elses—we don't know if those other two vampires he hunted with the first time were in on it—then we need to get to the bottom of this. The cleanup crew checked his phone and found nothing to suggest that Reed was being tracked. Does anyone know if he was wearing a wire that night? My guys didn't find one."

Sean glanced at Nicole.

She shrugged. "I didn't see anything."

"I didn't either," Sean said.

Nick sighed. "He wasn't. I would've felt it when I was pummeling him."

"Then, if we're lucky," Chris said, "no one knows what happened to him, which provides us with an opportunity."

Nick nodded. "I'll continue to pose as Becca—"

"Hell no!" Chris and Becca both shouted, then looked at each other in surprise.

Chris addressed Nick first. "No way. Not you. You're too close to this, and I can't risk you killing our next lead."

Aidan, a nearly three-thousand-year-old Celtic immortal, spoke up. "I could do it. But I'd have to spend time with Becca first to get her mannerisms down."

Becca frowned. "*No one* should imitate me. *I* should be the one to do it. *I'm* the one being targeted, after all. And having a bunch of look-alikes running around posing as me is creepy."

Nick frowned at his stepdaughter. "If Reed had taken you the second time, he would've rendered you unconscious with a bite, just like he did before. You wouldn't have been able to stop him from stealing you away."

"I would've if I'd carried a tranquilizer gun."

"You aren't proficient with weapons."

"I'll *get* proficient with weapons," she countered.

Nicole admired Becca's courage and determination but agreed with the others that the teenager shouldn't be involved in this. Her lack of experience could very well get her killed or captured, leaving them with no way to find her. "I'll do it," she stated calmly.

Everyone turned to her.

Sean scowled. "What?"

"I'll do it. I'll pose as Becca and see if anyone takes the bait."

# CHAPTER FIVE

W HEN EVERYONE STARED AT her, Nicole shrugged. "Sean just mentioned the other day that she and I look like sisters, so I'm sure I can pass for her with the right haircut, makeup, and clothes. I know all of Becca's mannerisms because we hang out together. I'm also well-trained in combat and fighting vampires. And I already have experience with both."

"No," Sean protested.

Nicole continued as if she hadn't heard him. "I can move into her dorm. Becca no longer has a roommate and keeps a low profile, so I think I can get by without anyone noticing the switch. I'll go through her daily and nightly routines, and we'll see if anyone attacks."

"No way," Sean insisted.

She turned to him. "Why not? It's not like I'd be in danger. I'd be armed. And I'm sure you'd insist on shadowing me."

"Hell yes, I would."

She smiled. "Then there you go. We have a plan."

Frustration darkened his features. "That isn't what I—"

"Actually," Chris interrupted, "that's not a bad idea. They do look alike. And Nicole knows how to handle herself in combat."

"Which would help her *how* if one of Reed's vampire buddies takes her and bites her?" Sean demanded angrily.

Chris waved a hand in dismissal. "Nicole is excellent in a crisis. You should know that since she's saved your ass in the past. That's why she was special ops before she became your Second. If a vampire bit her, I'm confident Nicole could tranq him before she passed out."

"Not if he sees her draw the gun."

Melanie raised a finger. "I could load several autoinjectors with the tranquilizer and give them to Nicole. Anyone who takes her would be far less likely to notice those, particularly if Sean is chasing him."

But Sean continued to shake his head. "Why can't Zach or Jared pose as Becca instead? They're both shape-shifters."

Jared glanced at him. "I don't know Becca, so I doubt I could impersonate her believably."

Zach nodded. "Same. Impersonating specific humans is far more difficult than assuming the form of generic animals. You have to get the look, the voice, the walk, the laugh, and a hundred other things right to succeed. If I had to impersonate another male Immortal Guardian, it wouldn't be as much of a stretch. We bear similar appearances, builds, and voices, so I'd only have to tweak a little here and there and get the accent right. But posing as Becca would be a challenge. Nick could do it because he's known her for years. Nicole knows her almost as well. We don't know how long Becca has been targeted, how long she may have been watched. Nick and Nicole are the only obvious choices."

Chris leaned forward. "And I don't trust Nick to keep his temper in check. I want to know what the hell we're dealing with here."

Everyone looked at Seth.

"Could this be related to the troubles Nick and Kayla faced in Texas?" Seth asked.

Chris shook his head. "That occurred to me. But the network cleaned that up months ago and left no loose ends."

Ethan frowned. "What happened in Texas?"

"Kayla was in a car accident," Seth told him. "While at the hospital with her, Nick bumped into a man he hadn't seen since shortly before the war in Vietnam. The old man recognized him and wanted to know how Nick had managed to not age a day in the decades since their last encounter."

"He was tenacious, to say the least, and caused quite a few problems," Chris added. "But we took care of it and tied up all the loose ends."

Nicole looked back and forth between them. "Could someone have unburied his memories like what happened with that mercenary group?"

Seth shook his head. "He's dead. And his eldest son, the only other member of his family who encountered Nick, believed his father was confusing Nick with Nick's grandfather because the old man also suffered from dementia."

Chris nodded. "Henderson has been monitoring things in Texas and has seen no sign of new activity on that front. So I don't know what this is."

"Well," Nicole said, "the only way to find out is for me to pose as Becca."

Seth consulted David. "What are your thoughts?"

After a brief pause, David nodded. "It wouldn't extend too far outside the boundaries of Nicole's duties as a Second or former special ops soldier. If she's willing, I believe it's worth a try." When Becca opened her mouth to protest, David held up a finger. "I do, however, think it best that Nick and Kayla take Becca somewhere safe while we wait to see what happens."

"I agree." Seth turned to the family in question. "Pack some bags, and I'll teleport you to my castle in England. With no record of your travel, no one will trace you there, so the three of you will be safe."

Becca looked from Seth to Nick to Kayla. "What about my classes? I've got final exams in a few weeks and—"

"Don't worry about that," Chris said. "I'll take care of it."

Becca still looked unhappy with the outcome as she met Nicole's gaze. "I don't want you to get hurt."

"I won't," Nicole told her with a smile. "I kick ass, remember?"

Sheldon called from the living room, "She kicks *my* ass all the time when we train. Even if I were a vampire, I wouldn't want to go up against Nicole."

Nicole grinned. "You just earned yourself a pizza, buddy."

He laughed.

She lost her smile, however, when she turned back to Seth. "Seriously, though, I'm all in. But what will Sean do for a Second? Can you assign someone to watch over him in my absence?"

89

"I don't want another Second," Sean protested. *"You're* my Second."

"And I'm trying to protect you," she told him calmly. "You killed Reed's fellow vampires and chased him after his chat with Tessa. What if Nick's name isn't the only one he knows? What if he heard yours and told someone else? I don't want you hunting alone without a Second keeping tabs on you."

"I won't be hunting. I'll be shadowing you."

"While hunting."

Cliff leaned forward. "I can be his Second."

All eyes swung to the former vampire.

"What?" Bastien blurted, his face awash with surprise.

Cliff shrugged. "It would only be temporary, right?"

"Yes," Chris answered.

"Then I'll do it."

Melanie glanced at Bastien, then addressed Cliff. "Don't you think you should talk to Emma about this first? Considering everything you two have been through, I don't know if she'd want you taking that kind of risk."

"I take a risk every time I go to network headquarters," he pointed out. "Seth managed to convince the other vampires that I was unexpectedly *cured* by the darts I was hit with at the military base. But you haven't been able to *reproduce the serum,*" he said, making finger quotes. "In their lucid moments, Stuart and the others don't blame me for being cured while they still suffer. They envy me. But during their psychotic breaks, that can shift pretty quickly to resentment if I try to step in and calm them. Emma knows spending time with the vampires is a risk. But she also knows those guys are my friends and how much it means to me to help them.

"Sean and Nicole are my friends, too. And the risk here is minimal. I'd just be performing the usual duties of a Second and keeping track of Sean. Emma won't mind."

Bastien arched a brow. "Even if it means temporarily moving in with Sean?"

Cliff smiled. "That part will suck. But she can come over every night and hang out with me while he hunts." He glanced at Sean. "Can't she?"

After a long pause, Sean sighed in defeat. "Yes. And she can stay at our place for the duration if we end up doing this."

Nicole smiled when he referred to the house as *their* place rather than his.

"All right," Seth announced. "We have a plan. Nick, Kayla, Nicole, Sean, Cliff, and Becca, remain here so we can work out the details. The rest of you may begin your hunt. But be vigilant. Telepaths, search the thoughts of every vampire you encounter for any mention of Becca or Nick, tranq any whom you suspect may be involved, then summon me or David."

"What about those of us who *aren't* telepaths?" Ethan asked.

"If you've time, call Zach, Aidan, or Jared and have them read the vampires' minds before you dispatch them."

Murmurs of agreement filled the air before most of those present rose and took their leave.

A tinny version of Skillet's "Monster" broke the tension-filled silence that fell in their wake. When Seth drew his phone out of a pocket, Leah plucked it from his hand.

"Seth's phone," she answered brightly. "Leah speaking. How may I help you?"

Seth grinned.

Nicole fought a laugh.

Leah sounded like an employee at a hotel's front desk, waiting to take a room reservation. She listened for a moment. "Sure. I'll be right there." She pressed a quick kiss to Seth's lips. "Love you."

"Love you, too."

She disappeared.

Still smiling, Seth turned to the rest of them. "Now. Let's work out the details."

Sean paced the length of Nicole's bedroom while she packed a duffle bag.

"Sean," she said without looking up, "you are working my last nerve. Either sit down or leave."

He sat on the foot of the bed beside the open bag. "How soon did Melanie say she could have the autoinjectors ready?"

"Later tonight." She dumped an armful of bras and bikini panties into the bag.

More of those were lacy than he'd expected. For some reason, he'd assumed she preferred utilitarian sports bras. "Do you know how to use them?"

"Flip the cap open, then jab the vamp. Easy-peasy lemon-squeezy."

"Not if he bites you."

"I'll still have time to jab him before I get loopy. And if he *does* bite me, he'll probably go for my neck. I could always wear a turtleneck and tuck one of the stab-proof guards inside it."

"Something that would instantly tell him you aren't who he thinks you are. And what if he isn't alone when he grabs you?"

"*If* he grabs me. We don't even know if someone is still out to get Becca." She sighed. "You're overthinking this, Sean."

"When it comes to your safety, there *is* no such thing as over-thinking it."

Pausing, she smiled. "Awww. That's so sweet."

He frowned.

She pointed at his forehead. "Keep doing that, and people will believe you're as antisocial as Roland."

He attempted to smooth his brow. "I still think one of the shape-shifters should do this."

Nicole added socks to the bag, then headed into the bath-room. "There's no way any of those guys could pass for an eigh-teen-year-old girl from this century. You know how out of touch they are. The only thing most of them can do on a smartphone is make a call. Stanislav can't even download audiobooks. If Susan isn't around, Alexei has to do it for him."

Immortal Guardians did tend to be behind the times when it came to electronic devices, slang, and the like.

Upon returning, she added a hairbrush, comb, and various other toiletries to the bag. "Besides, I'm fully capable of doing this. Re-ordon and Seth wouldn't have okayed it otherwise. Neither would David." Grabbing the bag, she left the room.

Sean followed her to the armory and sat on a bench while she added a multitude of weapons to the duffle. "It isn't that I don't think you're capable. I'm just worried."

Sighing, Nicole sat beside him and took his hand.

His heartbeat picked up a little as he twined his long fingers through hers.

"I know," she said softly. "But I'm the best one for the job. Becca is gutsy. I'll give her that. But she's only eighteen and has lived a pretty sheltered life. She's new to this vampire-hunting world. *Very* new. You and I, on the other hand, have been at this for a while now. Years, if you count the time you and Krysta hunted vampires before you transformed. If something happens, I'm more likely to think on my feet and less likely to be traumatized. Plus..." She gave his shoulder an affectionate punch with her free hand. "I'll have *you* at my back."

Nodding, he met her pretty brown eyes. "Always."

Nicole was his best friend. He would always be there for her. And even if this mission didn't carry an element of danger, Sean still wouldn't want her to go simply because he'd miss her.

She blinked. And the moment passed. "Well." Releasing his hand, she stood up and grabbed the bag's handles. "I think that's everything."

Sean rose. "Seriously? All you packed was underwear and weapons."

"Not true. I also packed my toothbrush." When he continued to stare at her, she laughed. "I'm not going to run around campus in my bra and panties, Sean. I'll be wearing Becca's clothes. Remember?"

"Oh. Right." He smiled. "Actually, I'd have more fun shadowing you if you stuck to the bra and panties."

She laughed again, and his spirits lightened. "I bet you would. Should I pack the jeans with the hole in the knee?" The ones her ass looked fantastic in?

He threw out his hands in feigned dismay. "No!"

Shaking her head, she chuckled and left the armory.

Sean strode along beside her. "I'm going to miss you," he admitted.

She sent him a sly smile. "Will you miss my music?"

"Hell no."

She laughed, unoffended. "Don't worry. I'm sure you and Cliff will have loads of fun. You two can pretend this is your bachelor pad."

"Did you forget Emma will be staying with us?"

"Yes, I did. That was very nice of you, by the way, inviting her to join you."

He shrugged. "They're newlyweds. They shouldn't have to be apart, especially after everything they went through."

"So, so sweet," she said with a smile.

Sean sighed. "Why do I always cringe when women say I'm sweet?"

"I don't know, because it's a good thing. I was only attracted to bad boys until I tried to date them."

He studied her curiously. "It didn't pan out?"

"No. They might make great eye candy, but they suck as boyfriends."

"I think Melanie would disagree."

She grinned. "Yeah. Bastien appears to be the exception."

"And Zach."

"Zach, too. *Hmm.*" Her look turned thoughtful. "Maybe I should've tried dating *immortal* bad boys. They seem a lot less a-holish."

He shook his head.

Retrieving her phone from the counter in the kitchen, she headed for the front door. "You want to give me a ride to network headquarters? Reordon's crew plans to give me a makeover, so I'll look more like Becca."

"Sure. I'm glad you won't have to cut much off the length of your hair," he commented as he grabbed his keys.

She shrugged as she stepped onto the front porch. "It's just hair. It would've grown back."

Closing the door behind them, Sean already dreaded returning home without her.

Two weeks passed. Every night, Nicole put herself out there as Becca, walking to restaurants and bars, going to the library, and even attending a few parties.

Parties weren't really her scene. Because the students in her classes had always been older than she was, they had never invited Nicole to any. Nor had the other students ever pressured her to join them and get wasted. She had only ever gotten drunk once, curious to learn the appeal, and had *not* liked it. She'd hated the pounding headache and vomiting the next day even more. So the only beverage she consumed at the parties she attended now was club soda she brought herself.

More cognizant of what happened on college campuses, Becca had issued several dire warnings before Nicole assumed her new role. "If you go to a party, don't drink anything someone else prepared. Never leave your drink unattended. And limit yourself to one drink so you won't have to go to the bathroom. *Never* go to the bathroom at parties."

If Sean had heard the other things Becca had told her, he would've freaked out and insisted Nicole avoid parties altogether.

No vampires had attacked yet. Other than drunken revelers, no one approached her at all. Tessa had hunted with Sean several times and confided via text that she'd had to hold Sean back a few times when drunk guys had hit on Nicole.

Nicole thought it sweet that he'd wanted to kick their asses on her behalf.

Some *had* come on to her pretty aggressively—more than once in pairs—especially when she pretended to be inebriated. But any who seemed disinclined to take no for an answer got their butts kicked. Not by Sean. By Nicole.

Becca would have quite the reputation as a badass by the time this ended and she returned to school.

The network had nailed Nicole's makeover. Sean had admitted that even he couldn't tell she wasn't Becca from a distance. Nicole didn't know what Chris had done regarding Becca's academic schedule, but that man had a hand in everything. So Nicole thankfully didn't have to contend with putting herself out there as bait all night *and* getting up early to attend biology, psychology, and other classes the following morning.

She did, however, follow some of Becca's other routines that didn't include class time. Nicole figured it would seem suspicious if she stayed in the dorm room all day and emerged only at night. So she ventured out for lunch and went for a jog every afternoon.

Much to her surprise, none of the dorm residents she passed on her excursions seemed to notice she wasn't Becca. While Nicole was relieved not to have her cover blown, she thought it sad that Becca had formed no friendships there in the residence hall.

Fortunately, Becca had friends who lived in other dorms and off-campus. Nicole had been successful, thus far, in ducking those. Though Becca was safely ensconced in Seth's castle overseas, she could still text and call her friends to make excuses for not meeting them.

Nicole skipped down the steps in front of the dorm. Night had fallen. Again. If she were at Sean's house, she would be laughing right now over the vast amount of food he consumed, then gearing him up for a hunt. She missed that. Missed their routine.

Missed *him*.

The isolation of this little impersonation was starting to grate on her nerves. She texted Sean every morning before dawn to make sure he made it home before sunrise. But she couldn't call him and hear his voice. If a vampire were eluding them and surveilling her, she didn't want him to overhear anything that would link her to Sean and the Immortal Guardians and blow her Becca guise.

She talked to Nick and Kayla, though, calling them every other night and chatting about her day. Nicole remembered enough about college to invent study- and class-related stories. She had recounted enough of them to her parents when she was in school. But *her* mom and dad had never responded as warmly as Becca's did, offering encouragement, praising her accomplishments, and teasing smiles and laughter from her.

She really envied Becca that.

Her cell phone pinged loudly, making her jump.

A student walking past with her arms full of books glanced over at her.

Smiling ruefully, Nicole pulled the phone from her back pocket. "I must have been thinking too hard. That startled the crap out of me."

The student smiled back.

Unlocking the phone, Nicole read the text.

**Sean:** You had to wear those jeans.

She grinned. Sure enough, she wore the jeans with a tear in the knee, one of Becca's snug-fitting sweaters, a jacket, and a purse.

**Nicole:** Thought they would make a good lure. Worked last time.

He responded with a frowning emoji that made her laugh.

Her spirits lighter, she strolled along the sidewalk. Tired of the parties, she planned to enjoy a delicious meal at her favorite restaurant and hang out at the bar until it closed.

**Nicole:** Is Tessa with you?

**Sean:** Yes.

She still had mixed feelings over that and would have to find some way to get past the Tessa-almost-killing-Sean thing.

**Sean:** Jealous?

**Nicole:** Hell no. She'll keep you from stealing my snacks.

When he texted a drooling emoji, she laughed.

The restaurant was packed, so she ate at the bar and read an ebook.

"Hey," a man said behind her. Leaning in on her right, he rested a hand on the bar. "Whatcha readin'?"

"How *not* to get picked up in a bar," she responded without looking up.

He laughed. "Doesn't sound very interestin'. Can I—?"

"Nope."

"You didn't let me—"

"Nope."

Muttering something derogatory under his breath, he left.

Sean texted her a laughing emoji.

Smiling, she finished her meal and spent the next hour sipping club soda.

Another man approached her and received a similar "Nope." Then another.

Sighing, she texted Sean again.

**Nicole:** I think I may be antisocial.

**Sean:** I'm OK with that.

She laughed.

"Hi, Becca," a woman said cheerfully behind her.

*Oh crap.* Nicole tensed. Though she had avoided Becca's friends for the past couple of weeks, she supposed running into one at a popular hangout had been inevitable.

Hoping she could pull this off, she swiveled on her stool.

Tessa grinned and gave her a little wave.

Nicole relaxed. *Thank goodness.* "Hi. What are you doing here? I thought you had to work tonight."

Tessa claimed the stool beside her. She wore a bulky hoodie she'd borrowed from Sean over hunting blacks. She had also unbraided her dark hair and let it flow down her back in pretty waves. "Business was slow, so they let me leave early."

Happy to have company for a change, Nicole smiled. "Awesome."

"What's good here?"

"Drinks or food?"

"Food."

"Are you looking for a snack or a meal?"

"A snack."

"Then you should try the spicy nachos. They're totally addictive."

"Excellent."

While Tessa placed her order, Nicole's phone dinged with a new message.

**Sean:** Save me some!

Nicole laughed and showed it to Tessa.

The two ended up eating all the nachos while they chatted, meandering from topic to topic, so they ordered extra to go. When they left, Tessa carried the container in a bag bearing the restaurant's logo.

Nicole shivered. Another cold front must be rolling in. The temperature had dropped enough for her to envy Tessa and Sean's ability to regulate their body temperature.

Nicole's phone dinged as they strolled onto campus.

**Sean:** Walk faster. Those smell delicious.

Another drooling emoji followed.

She grinned.

**Nicole:** `Change of plans. I'm eating them as soon as I reach the—`

A heavy weight slammed into Nicole, knocking the breath out of her and sweeping her off her feet. Campus buildings blurred as arms clamped around her in a clumsy cradle. Her phone tumbled from her fingers. Wind whipped her, much colder as her abductor raced forward at inhuman speeds.

Momentarily stunned, she fought to regain her breath. Had the bastard broken her ribs?

Pain shot through her neck as fangs pierced her flesh.

*Crap.* Gritting her teeth, Nicole hastily fumbled in her pocket and withdrew an autoinjector. Her head started to swim as if she'd had too many drinks. Flipping the cap off, she jabbed the bastard in the side, the only part of him she could reach with his tight hold restricting her movements.

Grunting, he jerked his head back and cursed.

Nicole cried out as his fangs tore her flesh. Warmth poured down her front.

"What—?" The vampire's hold loosened. Still running at preternatural speeds, he stumbled.

Nicole flew out of his arms and hit something hard.

Pain exploded in her head.

Darkness.

Sean smiled as he awaited Nicole's next text. Her spirits seemed lighter now than they had earlier.

Good. All teasing aside, he could tell the long wait and the continued restrictions induced by her Becca disguise were aggravating her. Sean had Cliff and Emma to keep him company during the day and still got to hang with his other friends at David's place once he finished hunting at night. Nicole didn't. Chris had told her to refrain from heading to her usual hangouts—namely, Sean's house, the network, or David's place—at night or during the day until they knew what or whom they were dealing with. The only people Chris wanted her to have verbal contact with over the phone or FaceTime was Kayla and Nick.

Hence the texts Sean had sent to make her laugh.

From his perch on the roof of a building near her dorm, he watched her smile and start to text something that would undoubtedly make him grin.

Walking beside her, Tessa frowned suddenly and glanced toward the west.

A second later, Nicole was gone, swept away by a figure who ran so fast he blurred.

*Shit!*

Her phone clattered to the sidewalk.

Gasping, Tessa dropped the bag of nachos and raced after them.

Sean leaped off the four-story building and landed safely in a crouch. Taking off like a rocket, he chased the others at top speed. *Please, don't let him hurt her. Please, don't let him hurt her*, he chanted in his head.

Tessa was fast. She would catch whoever had taken Nicole and—

Up ahead, Tessa swore.

A thud sounded, followed by a rustle.

Sean's heart thudded wildly in his chest. There!

A man lay facedown on the sidewalk, unmoving, one arm bent at an unnatural angle.

Several yards away, Tessa bent over a figure crumpled at the base of a tree.

His heart sank.

Nicole lay on her stomach, as still as death, and made no sound as Tessa gently took her by the shoulders.

"No!" Skidding to a halt beside them, he sank to one knee and brushed Tessa's hands aside. "Don't move her. Not until we assess her injuries."

"She tranqed him." Tessa clenched her hands into fists on her thighs. "He went down, and she kept going. I couldn't reach her before she hit the tree."

Hands shaking, Sean leaned over Nicole and brushed her hair back. "What hit first? Her head? Her back? Her neck?" Her face appeared unmarred.

"I don't know," Tessa said, her voice thick with tears. "But I heard a crack."

"Call Seth." Icy fear filled him. If Nicole had broken her neck...

The sounds of a number being dialed accompanied his jagged breaths.

Sean had healed many of his sister's injuries over the years. But Krysta had never suffered damage to her neck or spinal cord.

He swiftly ran through everything Melanie had taught him regarding neck injuries. A broken neck didn't necessarily mean death. But if the spinal cord was damaged, it could disrupt the signals from the brain that controlled breathing.

He silenced his harsh breaths so he could listen for hers. Tears of relief filled his eyes when he caught the sounds of both her breathing and her heartbeat.

Then he noticed the blood pooling on the ground beneath her.

His eyes widened. There was so much of it! The damned vamp must have ripped open her carotid artery.

Hoping he wouldn't exacerbate any damage to her spinal cord, he carefully slid his fingers across her neck until he found the gaping wound. Warm blood pulsed over his fingers as Sean called on his gift. Healing warmth swelled in his chest and rushed down his arm through his hand into Nicole. Sean concentrated on mending the artery the vamp had torn, viewing it as the most immediate threat. The edges drew together while he carefully monitored her breathing.

The blood flow slowed from a gush to a trickle, finally ceasing as the wound healed.

"Yes?" Seth answered on the second ring.

"Come now!" Sean blurted before Tessa could speak.

Seth appeared beside him.

Sean gave him no time to take in the scene. "She's still breathing but has lost a lot of blood and may have broken bones. I didn't move her in case her neck or spine are damaged. And all I've healed so far is the torn artery."

101

"Oh shit!" a woman said in the distance. "What happened? Is she okay?"

Sean didn't even glance up, knowing Seth would seize control of the woman's mind, bury the memory of whatever she'd seen, and send her on her way.

A second later, the Immortal Guardian leader knelt beside him. "Back away."

Sean didn't hesitate, scooting back to give him room.

Seth rested one hand on Nicole's neck and the other on her head. Soon those hands acquired a golden glow as the elder employed his healing gift.

Sean wanted to pepper Seth with questions. Was Nicole okay? How severe were her injuries? Usually, Seth's hands didn't glow unless he was mending substantial damage. Could he heal them all? Was there brain damage?

Instead, Sean glanced over at Tessa. "Go get her phone."

Nodding, she zipped away.

If Nicole had hit that tree at preternatural speeds...

Sean wiped his bloody hand on his pants. Rising, he crossed to the unconscious vampire. Though he wanted to tear that bastard apart for hurting Nicole, he quelled the impulse and grabbed him by the wrist, dragging his sorry ass over to Seth.

The glow left Seth's hands. "She needs blood."

"But otherwise, she's okay?"

"Yes."

The relief that one word inspired made his head spin.

Tessa returned with Nicole's phone and the bag of nachos she'd dropped.

When Sean cast her a questioning look, she shrugged. "We usually don't leave anything behind after a battle." She shifted her feet. "And I tend to tidy when I'm nervous or anxious." As if to prove it, she collected Nicole's purse.

Seth stood. "Give me a moment. Then I'll take you all to the network." He vanished.

Kneeling beside Nicole, Sean slipped his arms beneath her back and knees. Her head lolled as he lifted her against him. One slender

102

arm slid to the side and dangled limply, her fingers brushing the grass.

Tessa moved forward and gently repositioned Nicole so her face rested against Sean's chest and both arms lay in her lap.

"Thank you."

Her expression darkened with remorse. "I'm sorry I wasn't faster."

Sean shook his head as he rose. "Once the vamp sank his fangs into her neck, there was no easy way to safely extricate her." That was why he hadn't wanted her to pose as bait.

"I didn't smell him coming." Tessa seemed as determined to hold herself responsible as he was.

"I didn't either. He was downwind."

"And by the time I heard him…"

It was too late. The vamp was already on her.

If the vampire had been sitting around for however long, waiting for "Becca" to return, the only way he would've drawn Sean's notice was if he had made little effort to hide, stood upwind, or chosen an area bereft of people, making his heartbeat stand out.

Since the bastard hadn't done any of those things, he must not have been a vampire for very long and still retained most of his cognitive faculties.

Nevertheless, Sean cursed himself mentally for missing it. He should've parked his ass on campus and waited to see if anyone would show up instead of following Nicole and lingering outside the restaurant. But without knowing where the next attack might take place *if* there was one, he hadn't wanted to let her out of his sight.

Seth reappeared, his hand on the shoulder of Imhotep, an ancient immortal warrior Sean didn't know well.

Imhotep nodded to them and glanced around.

Seth pointed to the vampire. "See how far you can trace this one."

Born with postcognitive abilities that allowed him to see recent events unfold as clearly as rewinding a video, Imhotep studied the scene for a few seconds and then took off, his dark skin helping him blend in with the shadows.

Multiple footsteps approached at a jog.

*Now what?*

Seth, Sean, and Tessa turned to face the group advancing toward them.

Sean frowned. Even though the newcomers were upwind, he couldn't detect any of the usual scents humans carried. Soap. Deodorant. Body odor. Hair products. Flowery laundry detergent. Perfume. Cologne.

That was weird.

Three men and three women charged around the corner of a nearby building. All wore jeans, casual shirts, and jackets of various colors.

Were they students eager to snap pics of the "carnage" they could post online?

Ire rose.

One man touched a walkie on his shoulder that Sean hadn't noticed. "Cancel the code 12. We're on the scene with Seth and two other immortals."

"Anyone injured?" Reordon asked over the walkie.

"Looks like *Becca* is injured, and one vamp has been tranqed," the man answered.

Sean relaxed. Of course, Reordon would install special ops teams on campus.

Seth touched Sean's shoulder as he addressed the soldiers. "Imhotep is here as well, retracing the vampire's steps. Don't shoot or tranq him when he returns."

"Yes, sir."

Once Seth reached out to clasp Tessa's shoulder, the campus dissolved into darkness.

# CHAPTER SIX

S EAN CLUTCHED NICOLE TIGHTER as the darkness gave way to network headquarters' brightly lit infirmary on sublevel five.

Masculine laughter met his ears but shut off abruptly at their sudden appearance.

Several feet away, Melanie withdrew a syringe needle from Stuart's arm and looked up. The vampire's eyes blazed brightly, belying his worsening struggle with madness. But the glow began to fade as he glanced over at them.

She must have given him a mild dose of the sedative to calm him.

Brow furrowing, Melanie discarded the syringe in a hazardous waste bin and hurried forward. "What happened?"

"Nicole needs blood," Seth said. "She lost quite a lot after a vampire tore open her carotid artery. She also suffered a severe concussion and several broken bones. I healed the broken bones and did what I could for the concussion."

*Did what he could?* Sean's alarm spiked as he tightened his hold on Nicole. "What does that mean? Will there be lasting damage?"

Seth patted his shoulder. "She may not remember the attack or the events that led up to it. Other than that… no." Dropping his hand, he addressed Melanie. "I have to get back to Duke." Seth vanished before she could respond.

Melanie motioned to a treatment bed. "Place her over there."

Stuart followed them. "What happened?"

Miguel, another of the vampires who resided on sublevel five, tagged along. "Shit. Did Becca get attacked *again*?"

"This isn't Becca." Sean lowered her to the bed. "It's Nicole."

"What?" Miguel and Stuart crowded closer.

Stuart's eyes lost their glow. "It *is* Nicole. I couldn't see her face for her hair." He drew in a deep breath. "And she smells different."

Miguel nodded.

Jordan Moore and Liora Duran, two newly turned immortals who also lived at the network, joined them. Seth had sent the other immortal newbies who had been under Gershom's influence to elder Immortal Guardians for training and mentoring.

Melanie shouldered her way through them all and started setting up an IV.

Sean repositioned Nicole so she lay more comfortably, then tugged the sheet at the foot of the bed up to her waist. "She's been posing as Becca to help us determine if someone was targeting Becca, or if the last attack was random."

Rapid footsteps drew his attention to the doorway.

The other vampires crowded inside.

"Nicole's hurt?" one said.

Murmurs of concern flowed together as the vamps gathered around.

Sean hadn't realized the guys knew Nicole so well. Studying with Melanie usually distracted him when he was there. But he supposed it shouldn't surprise him. Nicole could befriend a badger. A few vampires prone to psychotic breaks wouldn't have given her a moment's pause.

"All right. All right," Bastien spoke behind him. "Give her some room, boys. Nicole is okay. But she'll be out of it for a while since she was bitten."

Stuart and Miguel only backed away as far as the treadmills Chris's tech guys had modified to support immortal speeds. Everyone else except for Tessa reluctantly filed from the room.

Standing on the opposite side of the bed, Bastien stared down at Nicole. "I guess this means it wasn't a coincidence."

Sean nodded.

Jared abruptly appeared beside Tessa and looked her up and down. "No injuries?"

She shook her head. "Only Nicole."

Sean sat on the side of the bed and held Nicole's icy hand while blood slithered down a tube into her arm. Though voices floated around him, he paid them little heed and doubted he would've been able to concentrate on the conversation even if he'd tried.

He needed Nicole to open her eyes and tell him she was okay.

Duckwrth & Shaboozey's "Start a Riot" swam out of his back pocket. Sean retrieved his phone and glanced at the screen. *Cliff.*

"Yeah?"

"Is everyone okay?" Cliff asked.

Sean frowned. "How did you know something happened?"

"Nicole tagged the lining of your coat so I could track you." Of course she had, because Nicole was the most efficient Second ever. "In the past few minutes, you've gone from moving at a mortal's pace to shooting across a few hundred yards of campus to popping up in network headquarters."

Sean swiftly filled him in.

"Sounds like she'll be out of it for the rest of the night," Cliff said. "Why don't you bring her home so she can rest in her own bed?"

Sean glanced at Melanie.

She shrugged. "I'm fine with that. But I'd run it past Chris first."

As though summoned by his name, Reordon strode through the door. "Well, this confirms it. Someone is definitely targeting Becca. I wish to hell we could've found out another way though."

Sean did, too. "Can I take Nicole home now?"

He nodded. "Have a teleporter take you. I'm sure Seth wouldn't mind doing it. He should drop by shortly with the unconscious vampire."

"I'll do it," Jared offered.

Sean gave the elder immortal a grateful nod. "Thank you."

"Has Seth read the vamp's mind yet?" Bastien asked.

Chris shook his head. "They ran into some trouble at Duke. A student saw enough from a window to misinterpret the scene and texted his family that there'd been a shooting. Seth had to bury his memory of it, then go to his parents' house and his sister's apartment and bury their memories of it, too, while my team erased the texts and made sure he didn't post anything on social media."

Bastien grimaced. "I hate cell phones."

Most of the older immortals did, claiming vampire hunting had been a lot less complicated before the advent of smartphones that enabled accidental bystanders to instantly post pictures and videos of vampires and immortals online, reaching thousands in seconds. It made it much harder to keep the existence of vampires and immortals a secret.

"Well, I don't," Sean said. "If I hadn't had a cell phone, Nicole might've died before I could finish healing her." Though he had more stamina as an Immortal Guardian, his healing ability didn't work much faster than it had when he'd been mortal. And he still had much to learn regarding the intricacies of healing brain, spinal cord, and organ damage.

Melanie withdrew the IV and placed a small bandage over the transfusion site. "Okay. She's good. Let her sleep late tomorrow. Her wounds have healed, but her body still suffered trauma, so she needs to rest."

"Okay."

"If she wakes up in the next two or three hours," Melanie continued, "she'll be pretty loopy. So you should watch over her and make sure she doesn't hurt herself getting up to go to the bathroom or something."

He wouldn't take his eyes off her for a moment.

"She may also be confused when she wakes up. According to Seth, she suffered a severe concussion. Since he quickly mended the damage and this was her first one, she shouldn't experience recurring long-term or short-term memory issues."

"This wasn't her first. Or rather, it isn't the first time she's suffered a traumatic brain injury. Gershom—"

"Oh. Right." Melanie thought about it a moment, then shook her head. "I still think she won't have any lingering issues."

"Will she remember the attack?"

She winced. "Probably not, but that has less to do with the concussion and more with the chemical released into her blood when the vampire bit her. I have no memory of Bastien biting me." Her lips twitched. "Evidently, I said some things while under the influence in front of Roland and the twins that Bastien wishes I hadn't." The twins being Richart and Étienne. "So if Nicole says anything she shouldn't, be nice about it."

"Of course." He was sure Cliff and Emma would, too.

"Don't worry. The effects of the bite should wear off by morning."

Nodding, he motioned to Nicole. "Can we go now?" He would rather not have an audience while he watched over her, especially if she might awaken and say or do something that would later embarrass her.

Melanie smiled. "Sure. If you have any questions or concerns, call me."

"Thank you." Once more, he gathered Nicole into his arms.

Jared rested a hand on his shoulder. "Ready?"

He nodded.

Seconds later, he stood on his front porch. Sean blinked. He was so used to Seth and Richart teleporting him home that he'd expected to end up in his living room.

He frowned as a thought occurred to him. "How did you know where I live?" Jared hadn't plucked the information from Sean's thoughts, had he? Like many others in the Immortal Guardians world, Sean did *not* like telepaths scouring his thoughts at will. And since Jared was as old as Seth and boasted almost as many gifts, such would be a simple task for him.

Stepping back, Jared shrugged. "I followed Tessa here when she came to apologize."

Sean studied him. "Why?"

"I felt her anxiety and was worried about her."

"Oh." He could think of nothing to say to that. "Okay."

The front door opened. Cliff and Emma peered out at them.

"How's Nicole?" Cliff asked as the couple stepped back.

"She's okay," Sean told them. "Seth healed her, and Melanie gave her a transfusion. But she'll be loopy for a while and needs to rest." He turned to thank Jared, only to find the porch empty.

That guy was so weird.

Cliff seemed unsurprised, probably because he'd spent so much time around Jared at network headquarters that he was immune to the ancient immortal's idiosyncrasies.

Emma offered Sean a kind smile and touched his arm. "Let's get her settled."

Nodding, he carried Nicole to her bedroom.

As soon as he laid Nicole on the bed, Emma booted him and Cliff from the room so she could clean Nicole up and put some comfortable PJs on her.

Sean took a quick shower while he waited. He would've preferred to pad around barefoot, wearing only boxer briefs and a T-shirt afterward. Nicole always encouraged him to wear whatever he would've worn if he'd lived alone, adding that she wanted him to be comfortable as long as he *kept his goods covered*, which made him smile. But he donned sweatpants in deference to Cliff's and Emma's presence and topped them with a soft, well-worn T-shirt.

Since Emma wasn't immortal, it took her a while to tidy Nicole and get her settled. Cliff distracted Sean as best he could. But even a pizza the size of a freaking wagon wheel couldn't halt Sean's pacing.

At last, Emma opened Nicole's bedroom door.

Sean darted in, nearly bowling her over.

Emma smiled. "She'll be okay, Sean. She's just sleeping."

Even though the logical part of him knew that, the rest was shaken by how close he'd come to losing her and wouldn't relax until she opened her eyes and made some smart-ass crack that made him laugh. "Thanks, Emma."

"Would you like me to stay with her?" she asked tentatively. "I'm not sure how loopy she'll be when she wakes up. If she needs to go to the bathroom..."

"No. We're good. Thank you though."

Cliff nodded. "We're going to head to bed early then. Yell if you need anything."

"I will. Would you hit the light on your way out?"

"Sure." Cliff switched off the overhead light. "Goodnight." He and Emma headed up the hallway to the spare bedroom. A moment later, their door closed.

A light in the adjoining bathroom kept Nicole's room from falling into complete darkness, not that Sean needed it to see as he wandered around the room he rarely entered. Nicole kept it as tidy as the rest of the house. Like Sean, she disliked having to waste time looking for things when she needed them, so everything had its place. He closed the bedroom door when he came abreast of it and dragged her favorite reading chair closer to the bed. Sinking into the cushions, he took her hand in his.

Almost childlike by comparison, it was still tan from the long hours she'd spent in the sun during the summer and felt disturbingly fragile. She kept her nails trimmed short so they wouldn't interfere with computer work or combat training. Unlike the women Sean had dated in the past, she never painted them. Nor did she wear makeup. He had always liked that about her. With Nicole, what you saw was what you got. No surprises. No pretense.

He drew his thumb across the back of her hand in a soft caress. Sean had only held her hand once before, when he'd posed as her British boyfriend. And she had intertwined their fingers in a comfortable grip that had tightened whenever she laughed.

Now her slender fingers remained limp in his grasp.

Nicole sighed in her sleep and turned onto her side, facing him.

She looked so sweet. And innocent. Vulnerable. Not at all like she could kick his ass, he thought with some amusement. But damn, she was tough. And stubborn. So much so that she would probably insist on continuing her Becca ruse after she awoke.

"Hardheaded," he murmured with affection, the criticism lacking any heat. It was difficult to blame her for doing something he would do himself if he could.

"Who is?" she murmured.

Sean sat up straighter. "You are."

Her lids fluttered and lifted. Her eyes rolled around like a drunk's, then focused on his face. Both pupils were dilated, the chemical in the vampire's bite still coursing through her veins. Seth might be able to heal injuries, but he couldn't—as far as Sean knew—remove chemical substances from someone's blood.

"I'm what?" she asked, her voice a little slurred.

"Hardheaded," he replied with a grin, happy to see those pretty brown eyes open again. "*Very* hardheaded. And beautiful."

"Awww." She reached toward him with her free hand. "That's so sweet."

Chuckling, Sean abandoned the chair and sat on the side of the bed, his hip pressing against hers.

Nicole touched her fingers to his cheek. "Come closer."

He leaned down so she wouldn't have to reach up so far.

She gave his jaw a gentle stroke, then drew her hand over his hair, shorn shorter than usual on the sides. "Handsome."

He smiled. "You think so?"

"Absolutely," she said with the smile of a siren. "Always have."

His heartbeat picked up as he fought the urge to lean into her touch and rub against her like a cat. Her touch should *not* affect him the way it did.

Energy waning, her hand slipped from his face and came to rest on her stomach. "I smell pizza." Her jaw cracked with a yawn she ordinarily would've covered. "D'you eat it all?"

"Yep."

She snorted. "Figures." Again, she yawned. "Why'm I so tired?"

Sean brought the hand he still held to his lips and kissed the back of it. "You had a big night. Go back to sleep." The fear that had clamped around his heart like a vice eased.

She was going to be okay.

When he tried to release her hand, Nicole wouldn't let go. Instead, she yawned again and rolled away from him onto her other side, tucking his hand against her breasts.

Sean froze. *Hmm.* He would wiggle his fingers in an attempt to break free but didn't want her to think he was trying to cop a feel.

After sitting there for a moment, bent at an awkward angle, Sean opted to take the path of least resistance and gave in to temptation. Lying down on the bed, he spooned up behind her.

They were a good fit. On any other night, if he'd snuggled up to her like this, he might've focused on how fantastic her slender, toned body felt against his. Tonight, however, he was so relieved that she hadn't died and was still in his life that nothing else mattered.

Her hair tickled his nose as he rested his head beside hers on the pillow. Some strands were damp from Emma's ministrations.

As stress gradually released its grip on him, he sighed.

"Night," Nicole mumbled, sounding more asleep than awake.

He kissed a shoulder bared by the thin strap of her pajama tank top, confident that she wouldn't remember it. "Goodnight."

Gradually, her hold on his hand loosened.

Sean closed his eyes. Peace descended, luring a smile from him. *What a night.*

"Love you."

His eyes flew open at the barely audible murmur. His heartbeat picked up, and fatigue fell away as he stared at the back of Nicole's head. "What?" Rising onto an elbow, he peered down at her.

Had Nicole just said what he thought she said?

Long lashes rested upon smooth cheeks. Her lovely lips parted a bit as her chest rose and fell with slow breaths.

"What?" he asked again, tempted to jostle her a little.

No response.

Heart pounding, he settled behind her once more.

Had she been talking in her sleep? Or had she spoken just *before* she'd fallen asleep?

His mind raced as question after question barreled through it.

Had Nicole even been talking to *him*?

Melanie had warned him she'd be loopy for a while. But *how* loopy?

Was she so out of it that she thought he was someone else? She hadn't, after all, said *I love you, Sean.*

Though he'd been an immortal for a couple of years now, Sean didn't have that much experience with women who had been bitten. Usually, those he rescued from vampires were already unconscious when he reached them. The few who had clung to consciousness had been incoherent and barely aware of where they were, let alone who they were with.

When he realized tension tightened every muscle in his body, he forced himself to relax.

Even if Nicole had been conscious, in her right mind, and had said it to his face, she wouldn't necessarily have meant it romantically. They were friends. *Best* friends. How many times had he heard her jokingly tell Cliff—also her friend—*I am so in love with you right now* when he brought her and the vampires she played poker with pizza, donuts, or cookies?

And why was he getting so... rattled, he decided after determinedly nixing the word *excited*... over this, anyway?

Sighing, he closed his eyes.

Deep down, he already knew the answer to that.

He was rattled because Nicole meant more to him than a Second should. And those words coming from her lips had changed something deep inside him.

Something that would keep him from ever thinking of her the same way again.

Sprawled on her back, Tessa stared up at the ceiling.

Though the room was dark, she could see the faint edge of every paint stroke made by the roller some network employee had used to coat it.

She glanced at the kitchen, only partially visible through the open door to her bedroom, and could read the fine text on the bottom of the pita chip bag she'd left on the counter.

Was this what cats saw when they prowled around at night? Was their vision as sharp as hers?

Rolling onto her side, she stared at the art that adorned her wall. It still felt odd to see so clearly. And not only in darkness. Before Gershom had transformed her, she had been extremely nearsighted with astigmatism and had worn glasses since she was five years old. She'd tried contact lenses once she reached her teens, but frequent bouts of insomnia and late nights spent studying had left her eyes so dry that she'd quickly given up and switched back to glasses.

Usually, once she took those glasses off and went to bed, the ceiling above her would be a blur and the kitchen would be indiscernible shades of darkness. But the virus that had transformed her had also healed her eyes and corrected her vision more efficiently than a LASIK surgeon.

A long sigh escaped her. Sometimes she found the novelty of being able to see so clearly as great a sleep deterrent as the bouts of insomnia.

Will, her twin brother, had also worn glasses. How would he have reacted to suddenly regaining perfect vision?

As always, the thought of her brother brought tears to Tessa's eyes and a lump to her throat.

When she was in high school, her best friend's cat had been hit by a car and badly injured. Courtney had found the little tabby, which had died before she and her parents could get it to the animal hospital. And Courtney had later told Tessa that she wished one of her parents had found it instead because whenever she thought of her pet, she saw again the pain in its bloody face and the wounds it had suffered.

It was the same with Will. Tessa's brother had been with her when Gershom had posed as Seth and attacked. Defenseless against such strength and power, she had been gravely wounded and forced to witness every excruciating injury Gershom had inflicted upon Will, listening to her brother's cries of agony until he breathed his last breath.

Moisture welled in her eyes and spilled down her cheeks.

Sniffling, she wiped them away.

How she wished she could un-see that and remember Will the way he had been before that night.

*Don't think about it. Think about something else.* Anything *else.*

Rolling to her other side, she concentrated on the multitude of sounds that filled the building around and above her.

Tessa wasn't sure how many employees worked at network headquarters. Hundreds surely, maybe more. Few ventured down to sublevel five. Employees had to have the highest clearance to take the elevator this far. But the four other subterranean floors, coupled with the ground floor, hosted a hell of a lot of people who held a wide variety of occupations and specialties: physical trainers and physical therapists who worked with all employees—even those with desk jobs—to help them gain and maintain physical strength; hand-to-hand combat instructors who taught every employee how to use that strength in the event of another attack; physicians who provided free healthcare to all employees; weapons developers who provided the network and immortals with everything they needed on both a small and large scale; viral researchers like Melanie who sought a cure for the vampiric virus or a way to prevent humans infected with it from going insane; accountants and investors who kept the network and immortals wealthy and ensured that every employee earned a very healthy salary; hackers capable of providing immortals with new identities periodically so no one would realize they didn't age; hackers who could erase any immortal- or vampire-related information that popped up on the internet; actors who could step in and pose as witnesses, firemen, or even DEA or FBI agents in emergency situations to discourage looky-loos and gain control of the situation until Seth could arrive; chefs for the network's top-of-the-line cafeterias; auto repairmen who kept the network special ops vehicles in excellent condition; handlers who kept tabs on *gifted ones* so the network could step in if anyone discovered their advanced DNA and caused problems...

The list went on and on.

And Tessa could hear them all.

She listened in on an acting class in which the instructor pretended to be a police officer arriving on the scene of a vampire attack. Tessa hunted with Sean periodically, so she should probably learn how to handle witnesses if no telepaths were around to aid them.

Alas, the class wrapped up fifteen minutes later.

Grumbling, she rolled back onto her other side, then gave up trying to sleep and slid out of bed.

Immortal Guardians were supposed to have enormous control over their bodies, enabling them to sleep whenever and however long they wanted to.

For Tessa? Not so much. She couldn't seem to get her mind to shut off.

Padding into her living room, she crossed to the sizeable faux window one wall sported.

Chris Reordon was a good guy. Even in the face of her initial hostility and distrust, he had been nothing but kind to her and the other new immortals who had unwisely given Gershom their loyalty. When the Immortal Guardians had *captured* them, for lack of a better word, Reordon could've put Tessa and the others in holding cells until they'd calmed down and come to grips with their situation. Instead, he had given them lovely apartments filled with luxuries such as this window.

Longing rose within her as she stared at it. It wasn't an actual window, of course. She was five stories underground. Instead, it was a high-definition flat-screen television that broadcast a live view of the meadow outside the building.

Sunlight bathed tall grasses peppered with colorful wildflowers.

Every once in a while, a breeze would set all into motion, causing the grasses to ripple like ocean waves that had flowers bobbing on the surface. It was beautiful. And wonderfully hypnotic. Tessa wished she could be out there, feel the wind tug at her hair and replace the network's recycled air with the scent of those blossoms.

She glanced at the classic corded phone on the kitchen bar. Its keypad bore only one button.

Taking a deep breath, she crossed to it, lifted the receiver, and pressed the button.

"Reordon," Chris answered after just one ring.

"It's Tessa."

"Hi, Tessa." A creak carried to her ears, and she imagined him leaning back in his desk chair. "What can I do for you?"

"I could really use some chocolate." It was a code he'd given her the night she'd met him to let him know she wanted to talk without the vampires or other immortals overhearing them.

"No problem. I'll have Todd bring you some in a few."

"Thank you."

The call ended.

Tessa dashed back into the bedroom and exchanged her cross-back tank top and sleep shorts for jeans and a T-shirt. As she slipped on a pair of sneakers, a knock sounded on her door. Tessa swiftly combed her fingers through her hair to tidy it then tugged the door—as thick and heavy as that on a bank vault—open.

Todd, the highest-ranking guard on sublevel five, smiled at her as he held up a paper bag. "Mr. Reordon said you wanted some chocolate."

Smiling, she took it. "Thank you."

He glanced up and down the hallway, then jerked his head to one side.

Nodding, Tessa set the bag on a nearby table. As soon as she stepped out into the hallway and closed her door, Todd led her to the only elevator this level boasted.

A dozen guards with automatic rifles and tranquilizer guns loitered in front of it. Some stood. Some sat behind a large desk.

Among those standing, Jared stopped chatting with the guards and offered her a nod as she approached.

Tessa nodded back and forced a smile.

The elevator doors closed, sealing her inside with Todd.

Neither spoke as they ascended to the ground floor. More guards greeted them as they exited and headed down a long hallway to Chris Reordon's office.

His assistant's office preceded his and offered ample seating for anyone forced to wait. The large desk that presided over it sat empty. The door that connected Kate's office to Chris's stood open.

Todd only took Tessa as far as the doorway and rapped on the frame.

Reordon stood by his desk, shoulder to shoulder with Kate, as they went over some papers she held up for his consideration. Both looked over and smiled.

Tucking the papers into a file folder, Kate offered Tessa a silent wave and left.

Todd struck up a conversation with Kate while Reordon motioned for Tessa to follow him into an adjoining room.

Tessa entered a large swanky boardroom and waited for him to close the door.

Absolute silence fell when he did. There was so much soundproofing packed into this room's walls, floor, and ceiling that even Seth couldn't eavesdrop upon whatever took place within. And the only way anyone in the swanky boardroom could hear what happened outside it was if Reordon flipped a switch that let speakers play sound wired in from his office.

Though many considered Reordon a hard-ass, he turned to Tessa with a friendly smile. "What can I do for you?"

She shifted her feet. "I'd like to go outside." Having to ask permission still galled her. But she was new to this world and—after all they'd done for her—should play by their rules. At least for a time.

He glanced at the door he'd just closed as if it were a window with a view of the building's exterior. "It's nine a.m. And there isn't a cloud in the sky."

"I know," she said, "but I'm as fast as an elder and can reach the shade trees before the sun burns me."

Face sobering, he studied her with a piercing gaze. "Everything okay?"

"Yes." She forced a smile. "I just get insomnia from time to time. Always have. And becoming an immortal doesn't seem to have eradicated that."

"Well, that sucks," he responded with a commiserating smile. Tessa suspected, however, that he knew there was more to it than that. Reordon was a very discerning man.

"It really does. I thought maybe some fresh air would help."

"No problem. I'm sure Jared wouldn't mind accompanying you." Amusement sparkled in his eyes. "And the guards could probably use a break."

She laughed. The ancient immortal was well known for talking the guards' ears off. "I wouldn't want to bother him."

He waved her concern away. "It won't bother him." Before she could protest—couldn't she even go for a walk by herself?—he opened the door and poked his head out. "Jared."

He didn't yell the name, just spoke it as if the ancient were waiting in his office.

Jared appeared just outside the doorway and joined them.

Chris closed the door. "Would you escort Tessa outside? She'd like to get some fresh air."

Jared turned to her and issued a slight bow. "It would be my pleasure."

She doubted that. She wasn't exactly in a chatty mood.

Chris reached for the door. "Give me a minute to put sublevel five's *windows* on a loop. All the vamps are sleeping right now. But

119

if they wake up, I don't want them to see you out there and get jealous. Most of them miss daylight."

Vampires couldn't leave sublevel five unless Bastien accompanied them. And—in moments when the encroaching madness drove them into darker thoughts—they sometimes resented that the immortals could.

A couple of minutes later, she and Jared strode through the network's lobby.

The guards all greeted Jared like a friend and coworker. She would've thought they would be more in awe of him. He was, after all, as old and nearly as powerful as Seth. But his tendency to pester them with questions must have eroded that.

She and the ancient immortal had to pass through a glass vestibule positioned just inside the entrance. At least it looked like glass. According to rumor, whatever it was made from could survive a blast from a freaking bunker-busting missile.

Then they stepped outside.

Tessa squinted against the bright sunlight.

A narrow, tattered awning provided just enough shade for her and Jared to shelter in, not that he needed it. The older the immortal, the more sunlight he or she could tolerate.

A parking lot full of vehicles stretched before them.

She glanced to the right. Large trees provided shade for several picnic tables. In three hours, employees would gather at those tables and engage in laughter and enviable camaraderie while they ate lunch and enjoyed the cool weather.

Jared touched her shoulder. Half a second later, she stood beside those tables, safely ensconced in shade.

Tessa glanced up at him. "I could've made it on my own without burning," she said softly enough that the vampires wouldn't hear if any roused. "Gershom transformed me with Aidan's blood, so I can withstand more exposure to daylight than other young immortals."

"Apologies." He offered her another of those slight bows. "I forgot and didn't wish to see you harmed."

Nodding, she sat backward on one of the picnic benches, facing away from the table. Tessa was so used to the high-quality *everything* inside network headquarters that the tired, rundown exterior always surprised her. The one-story structure boasted no windows, just a nondescript wooden door. It looked like something a warehouse delivery service might use to sort and store packages.

When she'd commented on it once, Cliff had explained that Reordon wanted to make sure the place appeared so uninteresting that anyone who inadvertently got lost or wandered out this way would have no desire to investigate it.

Mission accomplished. The place looked boring as hell.

Tessa tried to relax now that she was outside. But Reordon's insistence that she not venture out alone continued to irritate her.

"It isn't distrust," Jared mentioned softly. "It's concern."

"What is?"

"Chris's reason for wanting me to accompany you."

She frowned at him. "Are you reading my thoughts?" After all the damage Gershom had done up there, she did *not* want telepathic immortals to ramble around inside her head.

"No," he responded, unperturbed by the heated accusation. "It's simply what I would think in your position, that he wanted someone to watch over me because he doesn't trust me."

"Oh." She pondered his words. "How do you know it isn't distrust?"

He shrugged. "I know." Coming from someone else, the response would've made her roll her eyes. But Jared had lived thousands of years and seen so much that the claim carried weight.

"What's there to be concerned about?"

He hesitated. "The sun is high in the sky. Accidents happen."

She wondered if Chris might be more worried about *non*-accidents happening. Did he think her so troubled that she might walk into the sun and let the light sear away both her troubles and her immortality?

Tessa shook off the unsettling thought, determined to enjoy herself. She hadn't been outside during the day in...

Well, she couldn't remember how long it had been. Not since the morning after she'd transformed, she supposed. Doubting Gershom's claims that the sunlight would harm her, she had stepped into it and learned—to her pain and eternal dismay—that it would.

A cool breeze buffeted her, tugging her hair back from her face. Closing her eyes, she drew in several deep breaths.

So nice.

When Jared sat on the other end of the bench, her end rose minutely.

She smiled. He was a big man. Two or three inches short of seven feet tall, he carried enough muscle to ensure he weighed at least twice what she did.

For once, he didn't speak.

She had noticed that about him. With everyone else, Jared talked incessantly, always asking questions, perpetually curious about the lives he had watched from afar while he'd remained in seclusion with the rest of the Others.

Tessa thought it sad that—for thousands of years—he'd had no contact with humanity and no interaction with anyone other than the dozen or so powerful males like himself who believed that interacting with mankind and influencing them in any way would kick-start Armageddon. He seemed perpetually hungry for new experiences and was as eager as a teenager to discover what a "normal" unencumbered life could entail.

And yet, he was often quiet in her presence.

"I know Chris does everything he can to provide employees with clean, healthy air," she murmured, "but it just can't compete with this."

"No, it can't," he concurred, his voice a deep rumble. Several minutes passed. "I wish you could've experienced what Earth looked and smelled like in the early days of civilization, long before the industrial revolution."

Opening her eyes, she turned and found him studying her.

He looked away, focusing on the meadow she had admired from the faux window in her apartment. "Even here, surrounded by so many trees that filter the air, it isn't the same."

She nodded, sharing the same wish. With her gift, it would've seemed like a Utopia.

Another breeze encouraged the blossoms to dance.

"Mortals often can't detect the fragrance of each individual wildflower," he disclosed conversationally.

"I could," she said, "even before I transformed."

He cast her a curious look. "Because of your gift?"

She nodded. Tessa had been born with the ability to make plants grow and flourish with a touch. And even though she'd lacked the hyperacute senses of an immortal, she had always been able to detect more floral scents than her peers.

Will had been the same way.

Flashes of her brother lying several feet away in a pool of blood, screaming in pain, erased the beauty of the meadow.

Tessa squeezed her eyes shut, as if that could banish the horrific memory. Curling her hands into fists, she clenched her teeth. Tears rose, but she ruthlessly forced them back.

How long would this continue? How much time would have to pass for her to stop seeing her brother's suffering every time she thought of him and instead remember the happy times they'd shared?

Opening her eyes, she rose and toed off her shoes. The grass was soft and cool beneath her feet as she strode toward the edge of the shade.

Behind her, Jared rose.

Halting, Tessa stared at the grasses and sporadic flowers that waved at her.

Her parents' home rested in the center of several acres of land. And from spring through fall, she and Will had kept the rolling hills covered with a wealth of fragrant blossoms.

More images of Will's last moments bombarded her.

More tears welled.

Kneeling, she buried her hands in the grass, wiggling her fingers until they reached the soil. It was still moist from recent rains and cold to the touch as she burrowed her fingertips into its depths. Energy thrummed through her as Tessa called upon her gift. Building in her chest, it flowed down her arms and entered the soft earth. Wildflowers in the meadow burst with new blossoms. Seeds dropped by the plants sprouted, the roots driving deep as stalks emerged, grew, and produced a wealth of fresh blooms. Dozens and dozens, then hundreds arose, rippling across the meadow like the white froth carried to the beach by ocean waves until they formed a dense, colorful, fragrant carpet.

Tessa's heart beat harder as her energy faltered, but she didn't stop, pouring everything she had into the ground beneath her. Tears spilled over her lashes and trailed down her cheeks. The warmth her gift always generated slipped away, leaving her cold and spent.

Exhaustion replaced it, so intense that her head hung low.

Her elbows buckled. Tessa toppled sideways.

Strong arms caught her before her head could hit the ground.

Her eyelids growing heavier by the second, she looked up and caught the concern that darkened Jared's expression as he drew her against his chest.

Sighing, she closed her eyes.

Perhaps now she could finally seek oblivion in sleep.

# CHAPTER SEVEN

I NSIDE A HOLDING ROOM on sublevel five of network headquarters, Seth frowned down at the vampire Nicole had tranqed. Gary was a mere twenty-two years old. Seth would pity him for the future that awaited him if the boy hadn't already had a history of violence before he'd transformed.

Having gleaned everything he could from perusing the young vampire's twisted mind, Seth touched a hand to Gary's chest. The heart housed within it ceased beating. A moment later, the vampire's body began to shrivel up. It was a painless death. More than the boy deserved after the suffering he had spawned in his victims. Gary had killed none of them, per Gershom's orders, but he had delighted in hurting and terrifying them.

Seth's lip curled with disgust. "Coward." The vampire had enjoyed picking fights with humans who were significantly weaker than he was, yet he hadn't hesitated to run when faced with the prospect of battling an Immortal Guardian who could match his strength.

Typical bully.

Turning, Seth opened the heavy door to the hallway. Sound flooded in, his enhanced hearing carrying it to him from every floor of the building. Reordon had thought it best to soundproof this holding room to keep vampires they couldn't persuade to join them from listening to the inner workings of the organization.

Normally, Seth wouldn't consider that an issue. Any vampires who didn't join them met the same fate Reed and Gary had. Since they couldn't be saved, a quick, merciful death seemed the only way to ensure they wouldn't harm or kill anyone else. So there was little chance the vampires would escape and share knowledge of the network with others. But there had been too many *How the hell could this have happened?* incidences in recent years. And Reordon liked to cover all bases.

Leaving the door to the holding room open, Seth headed up the long hallway. Perhaps he would pay each of the slumbering vampires who lived at network quarters a visit first and see what damage he could heal in their deteriorating young minds before leaving. Once the madness began to kick in, the vampires who sought refuge here became increasingly uncomfortable around the powerful Immortal Guardian leader because they knew he could see and hear every twisted thought and impulse they did their damnedest to suppress. So he often did it without their knowledge.

Seth was just about to visit Stuart, who seemed to struggle the most, when the elevator doors at the end of the hallway opened.

Jared emerged, an unconscious woman cradled in his arms.

"Oh shit," Todd blurted. "What happened?"

"Tessa's all right," Jared murmured. "She's just sleeping." But his eyes, when they met Seth's, said otherwise.

Seth met him at the door to Tessa's room and opened it. Once Jared carried the newly turned immortal inside, Seth entered and closed the door behind them. "What happened?"

Jared crossed the living room and entered her bedroom. "Are all the vampires sleeping?"

Seth listened for sounds of movement in the neighboring apartments, found none, and searched each vampire's mind. "Yes."

"What of the immortals?" Jared placed Tessa on her bed.

"Melanie and Bastien won't return until tonight. And Jordan and Liora are both asleep."

Straightening, Jared headed into the adjoining bathroom.

A cabinet opened, and water ran as Seth studied the young woman on the bed.

Dark circles painted the skin beneath her eyes. As long as Immortal Guardians transfused themselves often enough with the network's donated blood, they could go days—even weeks—without sleep before they manifested any physical symptoms of fatigue. And yet Tessa resembled a human who suffered from sleep deprivation.

His gaze traveled over her. She wore no shoes or socks. Dark soil coated her fingers and thumbs as though she had been digging in the dirt.

Jared returned with a dry towel in one hand and a wet one in the other.

While Seth watched in bemusement, Jared gently bathed the dirt from her hands.

"What happened?" Seth asked again. He could easily pull the information from Tessa's thoughts but refused to do so. Gershom had toyed with her mind enough. Seth wouldn't betray her trust by invading it without permission.

"She can't sleep," Jared murmured. "Tessa has suffered insomnia on and off throughout her brief life, and becoming immortal doesn't seem to have remedied it."

"She told you that?"

The Other shook his head. "I heard her tell Stuart once when she joined him for an afternoon run on the treadmills."

Sometimes the vampires ran themselves into exhaustion on the network's specially designed treadmills—not an easy thing to do when one has their strength and stamina—in an attempt to suppress the violent impulses spawned by the madness.

"Grief for her brother seems to have compounded it," Jared added.

Seth frowned. "You haven't been combing through her thoughts, have you?"

Jared looked at him from the corner of his eye as he dried Tessa's hands. "Only once. Today."

Anger rose. "Damn it, Jared—"

"I know." His brows drawing down in a scowl, Jared ceased his ministrations and faced him. "After what she's been through, it was a betrayal of her trust. But I was worried."

Seth's anger evaporated, replaced by surprise.

Drawing a hand over his short hair, Jared sighed with apparent frustration. "Tessa wanted to go outside. Something about fresh air helping her sleep. Chris asked me to accompany her. I could feel his concern and..." He shook his head. "If you had seen her, Seth... the grief she wrestled with as she stared at that field..." He paced away from the bed and back. "For a moment, I shared Chris's fear that she would walk into the sun and try to end it."

"Chris said that? That he thought she might—"

"No. I read it in his thoughts."

Seth frowned again. "If Chris finds out you ramble around in his head without him knowing, he's going to kick your ass." The last thing he needed was for those two to butt heads. This was the first period of peace the Immortal Guardians had enjoyed in some time. They had battled one enemy uprising after another for several years now. And they could all use a break.

Unconcerned by the warning, Jared stared down at Tessa. "We were sitting at one of the picnic benches. When she rose and walked toward the sunlight, I grew concerned and delved into her thoughts." He met Seth's gaze. "Grief for her brother is eating her up inside."

Once more, regret that he had failed to keep both Tessa and Will safe from his enemy gnawed at Seth. He watched over *gifted ones* as assiduously as he did Immortal Guardians. Gershom knew that and had killed Will, then recruited Tessa specifically because he knew how much those actions would hurt him.

Seth's inability to save those Gershom had slain haunted him.

"It isn't just that he died," Jared continued. "It's *how* he died. Tessa can't think of him without seeing it over and over again."

Seth sighed as the grief he'd harbored for thousands of years resurfaced. "It was the same with my wife and children." For so long, he had not been able to think of them without remembering the way he'd found them after enemies had taken their lives. The pain on their beloved faces still haunted him. "But I can remember them now with joy. It will be the same for Tessa once the wound is not so raw. Until then, there is little we can do other than be here for her and support her as you did today."

Jared studied him for a long moment. "There *is* something we could do that would help her." He slid Tessa a glance. "We could remove the memory of her brother's suffering and—"

"No," Seth snapped, the word an order, not a mere expression of disagreement. "You will *not* alter her memories, Jared. None of us will. We will *not* betray her trust."

Jared grimaced. "Even suggesting it felt like a betrayal. I just..." His shoulders rose and fell with a dejected shrug. "I don't want her to suffer."

Closing the distance between them, Seth clapped a hand on his shoulder. "None of us do. But Tessa knows what we are capable of. If she wishes us to bury the memory, she will ask us."

He nodded.

"And tampering with the minds of others—their thoughts, their memories, or even their *dreams*—is tricky... as you learned first-hand."

Jared winced. His earliest attempts to alter minds had nearly resulted in Heather's death. "True."

Seth dropped his hand. "What happened when she walked toward the sunlight? Did she intend to... end it?" He hated to even verbalize it.

"No. She stopped at the edge of the shade, buried her hands in the soil, and poured every bit of energy she had into filling the field with more flowers. Once done, she collapsed." Again, he stared down at her. "Her last thought was that now, perhaps, she would sleep."

Seth's heart went out to her. Losing a loved one was always hard. Knowing they suffered before dying—and witnessing that suffering firsthand—only made it harder.

"Why are *you* here?" Jared asked suddenly. "You usually spend your days teleporting to the other side of the globe to help Immortal Guardians in need." It was always night *somewhere*.

"Zach and David are fielding my calls." Seth motioned to the hallway. "I was scouring the mind of the vampire Nicole tranqed."

"What did you find?"

"We may have a greater problem than we believed."

Jared studied him. "You think Reed and this other vampire weren't working alone?"

"Correct."

Leah abruptly appeared beside Seth. "Hi, babe." Rising onto her toes, she pressed a kiss to his lips.

Seth smiled and slid an arm around her waist to keep her close, warmth and affection filling him as they always did in her presence. "What are you doing here?"

She studied him intently. "I sensed something was up. You okay?"

Had she felt his turmoil from so far away?

Pride filled him. Leah's power was growing. They often communicated telepathically while apart, much like Zach and Lisette. And shortly before he'd come to network headquarters, she had teleported to Nigeria to heal an injured immortal.

"Reed and the other vampire weren't working alone," he told her, keeping an arm around her.

Her brow furrowed. "Were you able to see who else is involved?"

"No. But I have my suspicions and want to look into a few things."

Giving his waist a little squeeze, she smiled up at him. "Want me to tag along?"

He grinned "Absolutely." After nodding to Jared, he teleported them to Texas.

Slumber slowly slipped away. Since Nicole had assumed her Becca guise, she'd been sleeping later than usual. There wasn't much to set her alarm and get up for. Chris had worked his magic to ensure she wouldn't have to attend Becca's classes.

Normally, Nicole would rise earlier and take care of business for Sean, which didn't require as many daylight hours as she'd initially thought. The most strenuous task she performed was mowing the lawn, something Sean had objected to until she'd convinced him she enjoyed it. It was a task she'd seen many kids do at their parents' bidding in television shows and movies, and one she'd heard her high school classmates complain about. But Nicole had always been too inundated with schoolwork to perform that chore, so she viewed it as yet another bit of normalcy she'd missed out on.

*Who's mowing the lawn now?* she wondered. They'd had enough warm spells that the grass still grew despite approaching winter.

Maybe Cliff was mowing the lawn and watering her plants. If so, he probably reveled in the normalcy of it as much as she did.

She sighed as discontent with her current circumstances crept in. For years, her life had revolved around working as either a network special ops soldier or Sean's Second. But she couldn't perform any of the duties those positions required in case someone was monitoring her.

Unaccustomed to this level of inactivity, Nicole was bored off her ass. Perhaps if her parents had given her enough free time to find a hobby or something to occupy herself with when she wasn't studying or working...

Determined to slip back into slumber, she snuggled into the covers and hugged the hand she held to her chest.

She stiffened.

The hand she held?

Instantly alert, she belatedly registered the big warm body behind her.

Her eyes flew open. "Oh shit." She wasn't in Becca's dorm room. She was in *her* room at Sean's house. Which meant the big body curled up against her was... "Sean?"

A sigh ruffled her hair as the muscled arm wrapped around her tightened. "Hmm?"

What the hell had happened? Why was she home? And why was Sean snuggling up to her as if they were lovers?

Wait. They weren't lovers, were they?

A quick glance down revealed she wore a tank top and pajama bottoms.

Oddly, Nicole alternated between feeling relieved and disappointed.

She peeked over her shoulder.

Sean slept on top of the covers in a T-shirt and sweatpants.

Nope. They were definitely not lovers. So why was he in her bed, holding her so tightly?

Her mind raced.

Something must have happened.

No. Something must've happened to *her*.

Nicole's gaze strayed to the blinds around which bright sunlight peeked.

It was daytime. So whatever occurred must have taken place last night.

She struggled to recall the events of the previous evening and could dredge up nothing. Vaguely, she remembered heading to her favorite restaurant for dinner but had no memory of reaching it.

*Had* she reached it?

Nicole frowned as a foggy memory of Tessa tried to force its way through the haze.

Had she seen Tessa last night?

Several moments of contemplation merely yielded more frustration. She couldn't remember.

*Okay, don't panic. Stay calm.* She had been injured in the line of duty before. When the Immortal Guardians had blitzed that huge mercenary base, and she and the rest of the network's special ops soldiers backed them up, she'd been shot. It had hurt like hell *and* had pissed her off because Richart had teleported her away to network headquarters for triage, so she'd missed the rest of the battle.

Nicole had no difficulty remembering that.

Then there'd been the night Tessa had impaled her with a dagger. That memory was clear as day. And Nicole had suffered brain damage once, thanks to Gershom's sorry ass. As with last night, though, she had no memory of the last. She'd been Sean's Second by then and new to the job. Sean had suffered injuries of his own and had been furious when he'd learned what had happened to her. For days, he had hovered over her—worried that she'd suffer permanent damage—until she'd finally convinced him she was okay.

He had *hovered*.

He hadn't *clung*.

And right now, Sean was clinging to her as if he thought she would fall off a cliff if he let go.

"Sean?" she said softly, dread pooling in her stomach.

"Mmm?" Shifting in his sleep, he snuggled closer.

Even with concern crowding her, she felt her pulse pick up at the contact. But now wasn't the time. "Sean," she repeated a little louder, not wanting to startle him, yet eager to get some answers.

His muscles tensed. "Nicole?"

"Yeah. What happened?"

A long moment passed. Then he hugged her even closer, nearly cutting off her breath. "You almost died," he whispered, his voice hoarse.

A chill skittered through her. "Tell me."

Without relinquishing his grip, he relayed the events of the previous night.

Nicole had to admit it unnerved her. She *had* almost died. She'd hoped Sean was exaggerating, but when he went into medic mode and started talking about a possible broken neck, her spinal cord, and excessive blood loss...

Yeah. It unnerved her. She swallowed hard. "Well. That didn't exactly go according to plan, did it?"

"No." And still, he held her.

"Was Seth pissed?"

"Only at Gary."

"I assume Gary was the vampire?"

"Yeah."

"Where's Gary now?"

"Dead. Seth killed him after reading his mind." The tone of his voice left no doubt in her mind that Sean wished *he* had been the one to kill him.

"You brought me home after Seth healed me?"

He nodded, his chin brushing the back of her head. "Melanie said you'd be loopy for a while. And I wanted you to be comfortable."

He'd also apparently felt quite clingy.

She frowned. Or had *she* felt clingy? Melanie had admitted to saying some pretty personal things to Bastien in front of several other immortals while she'd been under the influence of a bite. Nicole bit her lip as a new concern rose. "I didn't do anything I should feel embarrassed about, did I?" A vampire's bite didn't just leave victims loopy. It could also lower inhibitions.

"Other than ravishing me and stealing my innocence, then farting in your sleep? No."

She laughed. "I did not!"

"Okay. You didn't fart in your sleep."

She grinned. "But I did steal your innocence?"

"No," he said, injecting his response with amusing petulance. "I kept waiting for you to, but noOo. All *you* wanted to do was sleep."

Again she laughed. "I'm serious."

"You didn't do anything," he divulged softly, his voice gaining a somber edge. "You just slept. So deeply I worried that..."

She wouldn't wake up?

Affection filled her as she patted the hand still cradled against her chest. "I'm okay. I don't even have a headache."

A sigh ruffled her hair. "Thank goodness your head is so hard."

She chuckled.

A long moment passed.

He didn't move.

"So," she broached conversationally and struggled to keep her heart from beating harder at his nearness.

*Damn*, he felt good.

"So?" he parroted.

"You want to tell me why you're still holding me?"

"Well, if you must know...?"

"I must."

He sighed. "Cliff made pizza last night after we came home, and I'm afraid you'll kick my ass when you find out I ate it all."

She laughed.

At last, Sean slid his arm from around her and sat up. As she turned to face him, he rolled out of bed and sat in the reading chair now positioned close to it. "Yeah," he called, looking at the door. "She's awake."

The door opened, and Cliff poked his head in. A wide smile lit his handsome features when he saw her. "Hey. How are you feeling?"

Sitting up, she shrugged. "Other than being a little weirded out over not remembering what happened, I feel fine."

His lips turned up in a smile of commiseration. "I know how that is." When the encroaching madness had spawned psychotic breaks, Cliff had often retained no memory of what he had done afterward. "Any dizziness or nausea?"

"None."

"How many fingers am I holding up?"

She studied the hand he raised. "Three."

"No double or blurred vision?"

"None." Her stomach rumbled loudly enough to be heard in the next room.

Cliff grinned and opened the door wider as Emma appeared beside him. "Sounds like you could use some of the pizza we made last night."

Nicole glanced at Sean. "I thought you said you ate it all."

Cliff snorted. "Are you kidding? Sean hasn't put a thing in his mouth since he brought you home. He was too worried about you."

She grinned when the immortal in question shifted uncomfortably, a tinge of pink creeping into his cheeks. "Awww. That's so sweet."

"Oh brother," he grumbled, and rose. "I'm going to shower and change."

"No hunting tonight," Cliff said as Sean approached. "Seth's orders. I guess he figures you could use a break after last night."

"I could." His stomach growled as loudly as hers had.

Nicole laughed. "I'd better see how much of that pizza I can devour before you get out."

Sending her a grin, he put on a burst of speed and swept past Cliff and Emma in a blink.

Cliff shook his head. "I'd better make some sandwiches, too."

# CHAPTER EIGHT

S EAN DIDN'T EAT ALL the pizza. He was too content, watching Nicole scarf down a warrior's portion. She looked good. Almost good enough to make him forget how pale and bloody and—though he hated to think it—dead she'd looked, crumpled at the base of that tree.

The night Tessa had thrown a dagger at Nicole had scared him.

This time had shaken him so deeply that he didn't want to let her out of his sight.

Fortunately, he didn't have to. Not yet anyway. Cliff and Emma left after lunch, something about heading home to water their plants and feed the dog. Sean was so happy to have Nicole home again that he hadn't really been paying attention.

After Sean told Nicole that Melanie said she should take it easy today, they parked their butts on the sofa and spent the afternoon playing video games while they razzed and teased each other. They were just about to start binge-watching *The Mandalorian* again when Cliff and Emma returned.

"Time to go," Cliff announced with a smile.

"Go where?" he asked. "Did Seth call a meeting?" Sean had hoped to spend the evening relaxing with Nicole. She was stubborn enough to insist on resuming her role as Becca. So, for all he knew, she might leave again tomorrow.

"No. We're going to our place." Cliff curled an arm around Emma, who leaned into his side with a smile. "I thought I'd make burgers for dinner, and your grill sucks. Plus, our backyard rocks. You can relax by the fish pond, stretch out on the sofas and stargaze, or even dance under the moonlight."

Emma smiled up at him. "I love dancing with you under the moonlight."

The two shared an affectionate kiss.

Sean looked at Nicole.

Her eyes twinkled.

Both turned to Cliff with big grins. "You had us at burgers."

An hour later, Sean slouched on one of the cushy chairs on Cliff and Emma's back deck.

The relative newlyweds lived in an isolated country home with a large meadow in the back surrounded by multiple acres of forest. It was nice. Quiet. No neighbors around for miles. And the couple had worked hard in recent years to turn it into their dream home.

The sleek back deck Cliff had added was large enough for a sizable social gathering. But he didn't stop there. Cliff had many friends in the Immortal Guardians' world and made a habit of inviting them over. So after he finished the deck, Cliff added a limestone path that led to a large outdoor living space twenty yards away that he and Emma designed together.

It was awesome. Just looking at it eased Sean's stress so much that he was seriously considering adding something similar to *his* home.

The same limestone Cliff had used in the path made up the floor of the circular living area. An enormous fireplace with attached stone benches dominated one side of the space. Since the air tonight carried a brisk breeze, a fire crackled merrily in the hearth. Two sofas, a couple of armchairs, and an ottoman large enough for him to sleep on provided additional seating for the other guests Cliff invited to tonight's barbecue. All the furniture bore sleek, modern lines and thick, comfortable cushions. A pergola stretched above it, the retractable awning tucked away to reveal the bright stars above.

Beyond that rested a smaller limestone circle that supported a large table with half a dozen chairs and what looked to Sean like an entire outdoor kitchen: a grill, an oven, a refrigerator, a sink, and a couple of things that remained a mystery to him. Pretty solar-powered lights illuminated it all.

Bastien and Melanie arrived shortly after Sean and Nicole. Then Sheldon—Richart's Second—showed up with his girlfriend Tracy—Lisette's Second—and several bags of groceries. Those two rarely left each other's side, often carrying out their duties together. And Sheldon was renowned for feeding hungry immortals, always aiding Darnell and other Seconds in preparing lavish meals for the Immortal Guardian crew and keeping piles of sandwiches on hand for Seth and David to grab between calls.

Of course, Lisette arrived, curious to see what her Second was up to. Much to Sean's surprise, Roland and Sarah joined the growing crowd, along with their adopted son, Michael. The most antisocial of the lot, Roland wasn't as beloved as his brethren. But he *had* helped Cliff with the backyard construction, so Sean assumed that had netted him an invitation.

Naturally, Marcus and Ami brought little Adira to the gathering. Marcus and Roland had been best friends for eight centuries. And their children adored each other. The toddlers now alternated between chasing each other around the flower-filled meadow and marveling over the fish in the pond.

After years of believing that everyone with retractable fangs and preternatural speed was a bad guy, it still tripped Sean out sometimes to see the close family bond these immortals shared.

How lucky was he to be a part of it?

Cliff and Sheldon manned the grill while their friends and makeshift family stood or lounged in little groups throughout the backyard, laughing and talking, teasing and enjoying the cool night air, anticipating a scrumptious meal before they embarked upon their nightly hunts.

Sean wasn't getting as much one-on-one time with Nicole as he would've liked. Right now, she stood across the yard with Tracy and Emma while he sprawled in his chair and shot the breeze with Bastien.

If Sean and Krysta had thought their entrance into the Immortal Guardians' world had been hair-raising, it had been nothing compared to Bastien's. Sebastien Newcombe was the proverbial black sheep. He had somehow eluded Seth's detection when he transformed and had spent the next two hundred years believing

138

he was a vampire. Not only that, he'd thought Roland had killed his sister. Determined to exact his revenge, Bastien had spent most of his immortal years trying to track Roland down, then had raised an impressive vampire army—the first successful one in history—and pitted it against the Immortal Guardians in an attempt to slay them all. So most of the immortals had loathed him when Seth had brought him on board.

Sean, however, hadn't been invested in the Immortal Guardians' past when he'd met Bastien. And he had appreciated the Brit's honesty and enjoyed his sometimes dark sense of humor. Sean also admired Bastien's dedication to helping Cliff and the other vampires fight the insanity that clawed at them. He now considered Bastien and Cliff his other *besties*, as Nicole would say.

Sheldon nudged Cliff aside at the barbecue and held out a hand.

Smiling, Cliff removed his apron, which sported a cartoon gladiator, and handed it to Sheldon. The two bickered for a moment over who could produce the best burgers. Sheldon was sure *he* was the barbecue king. Cliff laughingly ceded him the title and headed toward the house.

After pausing a moment to drop a kiss on his wife's lips, he continued on to the deck.

Bastien scooted over so Cliff could sit beside him on a love seat next to Sean's chair.

"Vegans Do It Like Gladiators?" Sean said, quoting the apron. "Are you a vegan now, Cliff?"

He grinned. "Hell yeah. How do you think I bulked up so fast?"

Sean studied him. Cliff wore a pale blue T-shirt that left his brown arms bare. And those arms bore biceps the size of bowling balls. His shoulders were broader, too. And if his thigh muscles got any bigger, he'd have to go up a size in pants. "You *are* sporting more muscle than you used to." A *lot* more.

Bastien grunted. "I bet I could still beat you at arm wrestling."

Laughing, Cliff gave him a shove.

Bastien smiled.

For many long moments, the men watched their friends and loved ones mingle. Every face wore a smile. Laughter abounded. They really were like one big, happy family despite the dark existence they sometimes led. Seth and David had done a phenomenal job helping the immortals they shepherded find contentment and happiness in this existence.

Nicole suddenly threw her head back and laughed at something Tracy said then reached over and gave the other Second a playful shove. Sean grinned, happy to have her with him for an evening, even if she was across the lawn.

From the corner of his eye, he caught Cliff studying him.

Sean glanced at him. "What?"

"What's with you and Nicole?" Cliff asked.

"What do you mean?"

"What's going on?"

Shrugging, Sean returned to watching his Second. "I don't know. We're waiting to see if Seth is going to want her to continue posing as Becca or if—"

"I already know that. I mean, what's *going on* between the two of you?"

Sean kept his face impassive. "Nothing. We're just friends."

"Bollocks," Bastien drawled.

"What?" he asked, all innocence. Neither Cliff nor Bastien were telepathic, so they couldn't possibly know the illicit fantasies Sean had woven around her.

"I see the way you look at her when she isn't paying attention," Cliff imparted with a sly smile.

Bastien smirked. "As if you're starving and she's a steak."

Sean frowned. "Oh, come on. I do not." At least, not when anyone else was around.

Did he?

"Sure you do," Bastien countered, all amusement. "You also smile every time she does and grin whenever she laughs. Just like this poor besotted chap here." He jerked a thumb toward Cliff.

Cliff snorted. "Like you don't do the same with Melanie."

"Of course I do, which is why I know Sean here is telling porkies when he says nothing is going on between him and Nicole."

*Crap.* He hadn't thought he was that easy to read. Sean forced a casual shrug. "She almost died. I'm just happy to see her alive and well."

"Bollocks," Bastien protested again. "You're in love with her."

Sean had begun to think the same thing. "You realize every immortal here can hear you."

"Yes." Bastien examined those present. "Why? Are you worried there may be tattlers in their midst?"

Sean opted not to answer that. "Nicole is my Second. Are you saying you wouldn't be happy to see Tanner alive and well after he suffered a close brush with death?"

"I would be *very* happy to see Tanner alive and well after a brush with death," he responded, "as I was after you immortals attacked my lair and destroyed my army. But I wouldn't also be picturing Tanner naked."

Cliff burst out laughing.

Sean hadn't been picturing Nicole naked. Not at that particular moment. But he'd done it often enough lately that he had to fight the urge to squirm. "You're not a telepath. You don't know what I'm picturing."

"I do," Zach said, his smile rife with amusement as he climbed the steps to the deck and joined them.

Sean scowled. "Stay out of my head, damn it." As soon the words left his lips, he swore. That had sounded too much like an admission of guilt. "Look, nothing can happen between Nicole and me. She's my Second. It's forbidden."

"Forbidden?" Bastien rolled his eyes. "Why should that stop you?"

Cliff grinned. "Says the black sheep of the Immortal Guardians family."

"Well, if we're talking forbidden love," Bastien countered. "What about Ami? She was about as forbidden as you can get. Seth loves her like a daughter. But Marcus didn't let that stop him."

"Although," Cliff inserted, "Seth *did* kick his ass once. Sort of."

"He did?" Surprised, Sean glanced at Marcus, who lingered near Ami over by the fireplace.

Marcus turned toward them and nodded with a sheepish grin.

"And it *still* didn't stop him," Cliff finished.

Bastien motioned to Zach. "What about Zach and Lisette?"

All whistled.

Zach leaned back against the deck railing and crossed his arms over his chest. "Seth specifically warned me away from her *and* warned her to stay away from me, yet she pursued me anyway."

"Boinking Seth's enemy was ballsy as hell," Cliff stated with admiration.

Across the yard, Lisette laughed. "And totally worth it!"

Sean laughed.

"Face it," Bastien said. "We're all rule breakers at heart."

Sean wished someone would change the damn subject. Shouldn't they be bickering over sports or something? "It's different for you all," he pointed out. "You've been part of this world for a long time. But I'm the new guy. And so is Nicole."

"Technically," Zach commented, "I *haven't* been part of this Immortal Guardians world for a long time. I just joined it two or three years ago."

"But you've known Seth forever."

He pursed his lips. "True."

Sean shook his head. "It took Nicole years to land a gig as a Second."

"Why?" Bastien asked. "Is she difficult to work with?"

"No!" Sean instantly jumped to her defense. "That's the thing. She's freaking awesome. But most Immortal Guardians are male, and Chris couldn't find any who didn't instantly balk at the idea of a woman risking her life for them. I thought that was bullshit and not fair to her, so I chose her to be my Second. And when I did, Reordon made it very clear—*multiple* times—that sex is not part of her job."

"Is it part of her personal life?" Zach asked.

Sean frowned. "Chris wouldn't differentiate between the two. And I don't want to risk Nicole's professional future."

Bastien glanced at his wife. "I suppose I can understand that. I thought having any kind of relationship with me—even friendship—would cost Melanie her job. But it didn't. Reordon got over it."

Frustration built within Sean. These guys just weren't getting it. "Melanie leads the viral research division at network headquarters. Her work is invaluable, and she's one of only two doctors who are willing to work hands-on with the vampires who surrendered to the Immortal Guardians. She's essentially irreplaceable. Nicole isn't. There are dozens of other network employees who would love to step in and serve as a Second. Probably hundreds. And that's just on the East Coast."

Bastien waved his words away. "I wouldn't worry about Reordon. If he can get over me breaking his nose, violating safety protocols at network headquarters, and injuring countless guards, he can get over you diddling your Second."

Zach laughed.

Sean sent him a pointed look. "And how many years did it take Reordon to get over that?"

Cliff snorted. "He still brings it up occasionally."

"Exactly. And if any of the guys passed over for the job as Second made one snide comment about Nicole sleeping with me, I would have to kick his ass. Then Reordon would call Seth in to heal him and—"

"I doubt that," Cliff cut in. "Reordon doesn't tolerate that kind of crap from his employees. If any guy badmouthed Nicole for sleeping with you, Reordon would probably *watch* you kick his ass, make the guy heal the slow way, then either fire him or transfer him to a desk job elsewhere."

Sean stared at him. "Really?"

"Yeah."

"But Seth would still hear about it."

Zach sighed. "Immortal Guardians do love to gossip."

"And how do you think that would go over?" Sean continued. "Seth is as protective of *gifted ones* as Reordon is."

Bastien's eyebrows rose. "Nicole is a *gifted one*?"

"Yeah. She has minor precognitive abilities like Melanie."

He smiled. "Well, that's perfect." Because *gifted ones* could safely transform and become immortals without losing their minds.

Zach nodded. "Don't worry about Seth. I sure as hell don't."

Sean snorted. "Because you're as old as he is. If Seth gets mad at you, he won't kick your ass."

"What are you talking about?" Zach countered. "He *did* get mad at me, and he totally kicked my ass."

Oh. Right. He had.

They all laughed.

A thoughtful expression crossed Cliff's face. "I don't know that Reordon would actually object to you two pursuing a relationship. Look at me. You know how many people I injured during my psychotic breaks. You saw some of it firsthand and know how dangerous I was to be around. And yet Chris looked the other way when he found out I was secretly seeing Emma, one of the many *gifted ones* under his protection. He even called her in to calm me down on some of my worst days. So you wouldn't be the only one to tread where you've been told you shouldn't."

That actually gave Sean pause. Was he overthinking this?

A little ember of excitement flared to life when he let himself consider crossing the line and pursuing more than friendship with Nicole.

Cliff motioned to the barbecue's gathering. "Look around you, Sean. I didn't just do this because I know Nicole misses her friends and you both need a break after what happened last night. I did it because we've all been where you are. We've all wanted something or some*one* we thought we couldn't have."

Bastien nodded. "In other words, we have your back, brother."

*Wow.* Sean couldn't help but feel a little choked up over that vow. For years, Krysta had been the only one he could count on to have his back. His parents loved him. He didn't doubt that. But they had kept their distance for a time so they wouldn't inadvertently influence Krysta and Étienne's meeting and falling in love after his dad foresaw it. Now, these guys were all saying they would stand up to Seth—the most powerful being on Earth—if need be to ensure Sean's happiness?

"Thanks, guys. That means a lot to me."

Zach's lips turned up in a sardonic half smile. "Don't get *too* choked up. *We have your back* was just code for *get your head out of your ass.*"

Sean laughed. "I'll think about it."

While Sean changed the subject, apparently not yet ready to take the plunge and say he was all in where Nicole was concerned, Bastien let his gaze wander over the men and women who'd come to Cliff's barbecue, as well as the two children who watched raptly as Ami made them wildflower crowns.

It was weird being part of it.

Bastien hadn't just burned a few bridges when he'd burst onto the immortal scene. He had blown them to smithereens. And yet not only was he invited to these get-togethers, he also felt comfortable in them now and—dare he say—welcome?

Contentment settled within him. He still marveled over the peace Melanie and her brethren had brought him after two hundred years of strife. For the first time in centuries, he was happy. Only one thing troubled him, and it kept peck-peck-pecking at him like that crazy rooster in the *Moana* movie Adira and Michael loved so much.

Bastien studied Cliff from the corner of his eye.

A smile curled the former vampire's lips as he watched Emma. As Bastien had pointed out, Cliff's smile grew every time his wife laughed. And there was an air of peace about him that Bastien had never seen before.

Yet, one doubt continued to plague him.

"Are you happy?" Bastien asked softly.

Cliff's smile broadened. "Happier than I've ever been in my life."

He deserved it after the years he'd struggled. Cliff had held out longer than any other vampire and had tenaciously clung to his deep-seated honor until the very end, when he'd decided to end his struggle by sacrificing his life to save others.

Thank goodness that hadn't worked out the way Cliff had expected.

"No regrets?" Bastien couldn't resist asking.

Emma chose that moment to wave.

Grinning, Cliff waved back. "No regrets."

Bastien fought a strange urge to fidget.

"What's on your mind, Bastien?" Cliff asked without looking at him. "I can practically hear the wheels turning."

"Melanie," he quipped lightly. "Naked. Always."

Cliff laughed. "Aside from that."

He shrugged. "It's kind of hard to think about anything else when Melanie is up in my head, tempting me by—"

"Don't you dare say it!" she shouted across the clearing.

All the immortals present laughed while the mortals—who lacked their hyperacute hearing and weren't aware of the conversation—looked puzzled.

Once everyone returned to their conversations, Cliff looked at Bastien. "I know you better than anyone other than Melanie. Something's troubling you. Tell me what it is."

For a moment, he considered lying. But Bastien needed to know. "Don't you wish you could've become immortal instead of human again?"

"No." No hesitation tinged Cliff's response, nothing to indicate he held even a tiny shred of doubt. His tone turned gentle, coaxing, maybe even a little apologetic. "I'm not like you, Bastien." He nodded toward the immortals milling about his backyard. "I'm not like any of you immortals. I wasn't born with special gifts I had to hide. I didn't have to isolate myself from others to keep them from realizing I was different so they wouldn't hunt me, capture me, or try to kill me. I was born human. I had an ordinary childhood. Lots of friends and adventures. Lots of long summer days spent bike riding; going to the beach; and playing baseball, basketball, or soccer until my mom or dad called me in for supper. I had two parents who loved each other as much as I love Emma and you love Melanie. Parents whose love shaped my dreams for the future."

His gaze fastened on Emma. "I may not have been ready to settle down when I went away to college, but I knew what I wanted. I wanted to marry a woman who would be my best friend. Someone who would share the highs, the lows, and everything in between. Buy a house in the burbs or in the country. Raise children together. Have grandchildren. Spoil them rotten. Live happily ever after. And the vampire who transformed me took that away from me in an instant. All I've wanted since then was for life to go back to normal."

Bastien had heard him say as much too many times to count during their years of friendship.

Cliff's smile faded. "I admit, the idea of never growing old and of spending the rest of eternity with Emma sounds phenomenal. But I would've had to sacrifice the rest of my dream. A dream she and I both share. We want children. I want to watch her stomach get so big that she looks like she swallowed a beach ball. I want to rub her feet and her aching back and be there for her when she goes into labor. I want to hold our tiny newborn in my arms. Teach our children to walk. Take them to the playground on sunny afternoons. Spend the day at the zoo. Picnic on the beach and build sandcastles. All the things my parents did with me."

Bastien wanted that, too. Not being able to father children with Melanie was one of his deepest regrets. And while he knew they could adopt, what kind of life could they offer a child? He couldn't do the things Cliff mentioned, the things Bastien would want to if he were a father. He couldn't go outside during daylight hours because of his damned photosensitivity. And he'd seen how Roland and Marcus looked each time they sent their little ones to the playground with Sheldon during the day because they couldn't go themselves.

"If I had turned immortal," Cliff continued, "Emma would've had to choose between growing old while I didn't or transforming to stay forever young with me. And once she transformed, she would've had to miss out on all of those things."

Bastien knew Emma would've transformed for Cliff and understood well the sacrifices she would've had to make. They were the same ones Melanie had made. But there had been no other choice in Melanie's case.

"And..." Uncertainty crept into Cliff's expression, stealing his smile.

"And?" Bastien prodded.

Cliff sighed. "If I were an Immortal Guardian, I would have to spend the rest of my nights hunting and slaying vampires, especially since Gershom left so damn many behind." Tension crept into his posture as he shook his head and stared off into the distance. "Do you know how fucked up that would've been for me?"

He did. Cliff had been so disturbed by hunting other vampires that he had insisted on sneaking back into network headquarters

147

so the other vampires housed there wouldn't see or smell the blood that stained his clothing. He wouldn't have hunted vampires at all if he hadn't desperately needed an outlet for the violence the insanity incited. "Yes."

Cliff motioned to the other Immortal Guardians present. "*They* don't. You and Melanie do, but the rest of them? They don't know what it's like to be a vampire. To lose a little piece of yourself every day, no matter how hard you fight to keep it as the madness grows inside you. To struggle with every breath of your being to hold on to who you are while everything inside urges you to become a monster."

Cliff's struggle had been heartbreaking to watch.

"Most of the vampires out there didn't ask to be turned. They didn't ask to lose all sense of right and wrong. Some are like I was. They don't kill their victims. Not yet. They just infuse themselves and move along. Or they do like you had us do back when you raised your vampire army. They choose the worst of society to kill if they have to, assuaging those violent impulses while ridding the world of pedophiles, rapists, and murderers. They *fight* the madness."

Bastien looked at his fellow immortals. "They know that."

"But they ignore that, skip ahead to what the vampires will ultimately become, and kill them without feeling any remorse. Because they've never experienced it themselves. It's different when you do. And hunting other vampires, killing them night after night for hundreds of years..." His throat worked in a swallow. "I think that would've chipped away at me as efficiently as the virus did."

Sighing, Bastien wrapped an arm around his friend. "I know it would. I'm just selfish enough to want to keep you by my side for the next however-many centuries or millennia. Other than Melanie and Sean, you're the only friend I have."

Cliff chuckled. "I don't know about that. Aren't you and Zach best buddies now?"

Zach's lips twitched.

"Besides," Cliff added, "Seth said he could use his healing gift to extend our lives so Emma and I can have an extra century or more together."

Bastien smiled. "Think of all the children and grandchildren you could produce in that time."

"And great-grandchildren and great-great-grandchildren." His whole being lighting up, Cliff grinned, clearly thrilled by the prospect.

Bastien's heart lightened. "So you really are living the dream."

"I'm living the dream."

And Bastien's gift confirmed that Cliff was indeed exceedingly happy with the way things had turned out and had no regrets.

He had sensed no regrets in Emma either. The couple was blissfully happy.

Dropping his arm, he nudged Cliff with his shoulder. "You know I'm going to call you Grandpa as soon as your hair starts to gray."

Cliff laughed. "I figured you would."

Zach shook his head. "Immortality *does* have its downsides."

Bastien grunted. "If anyone would know, I suppose it would be you."

"And Seth, Jared, and David," Cliff added.

Zach made a sound of assent. "It's hard to live as long as we have and watch mankind make the same damned mistakes over and over again, ignoring the past and learning nothing from it. To see thousands of years of needless suffering as a result." He stared into the distance. "I admit I understand a bit the anger and frustration that motivated Gershom to want to watch humanity die out. But unlike Gershom, I clung to my hope that a generation would eventually come along who would be different."

"Has that happened yet?" Cliff asked.

"Hell no. Mankind still does the stupidest shit."

Bastien laughed. "Yeah. We're pretty flawed."

"You more than anyone," Roland Warbrook drawled loudly enough for his voice to carry.

Chuckles circulated the yard.

Bastien gave him the finger.

"Damn it, Bastien," Marcus snapped.

Surprised, Bastien glanced at Marcus, who scowled at him and looked pointedly at the two toddlers playing in the grass in front of him. Both sported flowery crowns and smiled proudly as they gave everyone the finger.

Standing beside Marcus, Ami sighed. "Marcus, honey…"

"What?" He glanced at her, then winced. "Oh. Right. Adira, sweetie, don't say 'Damn it.'"

Still giving everyone the finger, the toddler smiled. "Okay, Daddy."

When Marcus turned another frown on him, Bastien pasted an innocent look on his face and pointed at Roland. "What? He started it."

All laughed as Roland bit back a curse.

Discordant buzzes abruptly filled the air as multiple cell phones alerted their owners to incoming texts. Bastien's cell vibrated in his pocket.

Frowning, he shared a look with Zach as both retrieved their phones.

"Seth is calling a meeting," Sheldon announced before Bastien could read his text. "Tomorrow night, an hour after sunset."

He didn't have to say the meeting would take place at David's house. Unless there were extenuating circumstances, they always gathered at David's home to discuss strategy.

Clutching her phone, Nicole turned and met Sean's gaze.

Bastien didn't have to touch Sean to read his emotions, nor did he have to be a telepath to discern his thoughts.

Sean feared that Seth would put Nicole back into play as Becca.

And the last time she had acted as bait, Sean had almost lost her.

# CHAPTER NINE

EVERY IMMORTAL GUARDIAN STATIONED in North Carolina found a seat around the long table in David's dining room. There were so many now, thanks to recent marriages and transformations, that their Seconds had to sit behind them in folding chairs instead of taking a seat at the table. Though Tessa had not yet officially begun to hunt, she joined the immortal crew with Jared at her side. Once more, Seth sat at the foot of the table while David occupied the chair at the head of the table with Chris Reordon at one elbow and Darnell at the other.

Nicole sat between Sean and Tessa. Sean's knee bobbed up and down, betraying his agitation. And when she risked looking at him, his expression was grim as hell.

Nick, Kayla, and Becca sat across from them again.

"Is everyone settled?" Seth asked.

Nods all around.

"All right. Let's begin." Though the Immortal Guardian grapevine had spread word of the second vampire's capture and Nicole's injuries to most ears, Seth gave everyone a brief rundown.

When all eyes shifted to Nicole, she smiled. "I'm fine. Seth healed me."

More nods.

"After reading the vampire's thoughts," Seth continued, "and investigating the suspicions they spawned, I have come to believe that we are dealing with a larger problem than we initially thought."

Nicole studied him. "What did you see in his mind?"

Seth looked at Stanislav and Susan. "His thoughts were disturbingly similar to those of the men who hunted *you*."

Stanislav's brow furrowed. "In what way?"

"The vampires who attacked Becca and her friends with Reed were grunts. So was Gary. Reed led the group and only told them what they needed to know and—according to Gary—answered to an unnamed person with deep pockets."

Susan glanced at Stanislav, then Seth. "What did they need to know?"

"That Nick Belanger is an Immortal Guardian their... *buyer*, I suppose we'll call him... wants to get his hands on so his scientists can create a fountain of youth elixir he can sell to his billionaire cronies for a vast fortune. One that *won't* result in them succumbing to the same insanity that grips vampires. Word that had passed down through a shadowy chain of command suggested that Reed and the others could use Becca to lure Nick out of hiding."

"What the hell, Seth?" Nick blurted furiously. "How can anyone even know that? We tied up *every* loose end when that shit went down with Roubal."

Seth held up a hand in a calming gesture. "Such was my thought, so David and I—with the help of Chris Reordon and Scott Henderson in Houston—have spent the past twenty-four hours retracing our steps to see if we missed anything."

David nodded. "We've scoured every mind we altered during the cleanup."

"And?" Nick prodded.

Seth shook his head. "We found nothing."

Quiet descended.

Nicole studied the grim faces around her. "Could it be unrelated? I mean, Oliver told me what happened." Nick and Kayla's Second had been spending time here in North Carolina so he could watch over the newlyweds while Kayla completed her training as an immortal. "Could one of Nick's neighbors have seen something? Someone with the connections—"

Nick shook his head. "No one in my neighborhood would have those connections."

Kayla nodded. "It's all middle-class families. Anyone with the kind of funds Seth referenced would live in one of the more upscale neighborhoods."

Roland crossed his arms over his chest. "Perhaps one of the network employees in Texas has been whispering in someone's ear."

Chris slammed a hand down on the table. "Damn it, Roland. I'm tired of you trying to pin all the bad shit that happens in the Immortal Guardians world on network employees. Every man and woman we hire has been thoroughly vetted—"

"How recently?" Roland interrupted. "Situations change. I could name at least a dozen reasons someone might find himself in desperate need of an influx of cash. And if said individual wished to leak the identity of an Immortal Guardian for financial gain, now would be the perfect time to do it because everyone's mind would instantly veer in the direction it has: wondering what—if anything—Seth and the network might have missed while cleaning up the Roubal incident."

Silence fell.

Bastien spoke. "I hate to admit it, but he's right."

Chris glared at them both, then looked at Seth.

The Immortal Guardian leader sighed. "I believe it more likely that we did indeed miss something."

Leah nodded. "Someone Roubal's age would probably write himself reminders like Chris here does—with a pencil and paper—instead of typing it into his computer or phone. He might also have mailed a letter to someone instead of texting them so he wouldn't leave an electronic trail his snooping sons could follow. Seth said Roubal had little love for them."

Curses flowed freely.

Nicole didn't know how they could find out whom the old man might've told if he'd done it via snail mail.

Kayla's brow furrowed. "So, where does that leave us?"

No one spoke.

Nicole shrugged. "The same place we were before. I'll continue to pose as Becca and see what happens."

"Damn it, Nicole," Sean snapped.

She threw her hands up. "Well, what other choice do we have?"

"Let Nick pose as Becca," he flung back.

Chris shook his head. "Right now, Nick is the only immortal they appear to know by name. I don't want him involved."

Sean frowned. "You're just saying that because he screwed up."

"Actually, yes," Chris acknowledged without hesitation. "If he hadn't, we might know more than we do now."

"Not necessarily," Kayla tossed in, eager to defend Nick. "What makes you think Reed would've revealed more than Gary?"

Chris turned to Tessa. "Was Gary one of Gershom's vampires?"

She thought about it a moment. "I can't say with certainty, but I don't recall ever having seen him before he snatched Nicole."

Chris motioned to Tessa as he met Nick's gaze. "Then if nothing else, Reed could've at least told us if this is Gershom's Plan B."

An uneasy hush descended.

Seth studied Chris. "You think Gershom could've instigated this before we neutralized him?"

Chris shook his head. "Isn't that what we've all been waiting for—the other shoe to drop?"

Zach looked at Seth. "Gershom might have been off his nut, but he was a fucking brilliant strategist."

David nodded. "And every time we thwarted him and prevented him from kick-starting Armageddon, he enacted a new plan. One that he clearly had already set into motion. Otherwise, it would've taken him years to regroup after the defeats we delivered."

Nicole's stomach sank. She had hoped this would turn out to be a relatively small endeavor. The brainchild of some egomaniac whose greed knew no boundaries. Someone who wouldn't want to cut anyone else in on the action and, thus, keep their numbers low.

But if Gershom were involved in any way...

He didn't go small. He went big, upping the ante every time.

Tessa shifted restlessly. "I think it odd that Reed wasn't at our home base the night you came after me and the other missing immortals. Gershom gave us a strict curfew and a precise window of time in which we were to transfuse ourselves and hunt the Immortal Guardians we thought were our enemy. So we all returned by the same hour. And Gershom didn't tolerate disobedience."

Roland's expression darkened. "Something Veronica learned firsthand."

Tessa swallowed hard, her face full of remorse. "I didn't know about that. We were told..."

"That Immortal Guardians killed her," Seth said.

She nodded.

Nicole studied her thoughtfully. "Could Gershom have sent Reed on an errand?"

"The more I think about it, the more I think he must have," Tessa said. "Anyone who didn't return on time was... retrieved. Gershom teleported us to and from home base. And the few who missed curfew never missed it again after Gershom caught up with them. If Reed wasn't there, it must have been because Gershom wanted him elsewhere. Especially since Reed expressed no fear when he told me he needed to see Gershom."

Sean spoke. "Maybe Gershom tasked Reed with contacting the buyer's representative."

David nodded. "A buyer in whose ear Gershom had already been whispering."

Zach grunted. "We all know greed is a powerful motivator."

"If it weren't," Seth said, "we wouldn't have had so much trouble with mercenaries in recent years."

"And," David added, "this is an avenue Gershom knew we wouldn't suspect."

Nicole's gaze ping-ponged between them. "A drive in the private sector to be the first to create an immortality serum that actually works?"

Cliff nodded. "And works for *everyone*."

Sean motioned toward Becca. "Reed must have struck a deal with the buyer. Otherwise, he wouldn't have tried to nab Becca."

Tessa nodded. "He also seemed determined to carry out his last orders, whatever they were. He was pretty desperate to contact Gershom."

Seth sighed. "That was likely a result of mind control. Gershom excelled at such."

Tessa nibbled her bottom lip. "I don't know about that. Gershom was mind-controlling me, and it wore off pretty quickly once I was away from him."

Jared spoke softly. "Because hating and harming others is not your nature."

Nick scowled, his hands curling into fists. "It sure as hell was Reed's."

"And Gary's," Seth added.

Kayla clasped one of Nick's hands and twined her fingers through his.

Some of the darkness in his expression eased.

"Well," Nicole said again, "I'm willing to continue posing as Becca. I don't think the goal here is to hurt her. It's to use her as bait so they can get their hands on Nick. I probably wouldn't have been injured when Gary took me if I hadn't tranqed him."

"Not necessarily," Zach responded. "If those who want him know Nick is immortal and are aware of all he's capable of—"

"*Do* they know what he's capable of?" Becca asked. "Remaining forever young doesn't mean he has superior strength, speed, or other special abilities."

Cliff shook his head. "If they're working with vampires, they know about his enhanced speed and strength."

"What about his ability to shape-shift?" she pressed.

All eyes returned to Cliff.

"Most vampires don't know about immortals' special gifts, because they rarely survive encounters with you all."

Tessa nodded. "I didn't know anyone else in Gershom's army had gifts. We never talked about it."

Nicole studied her curiously. "Why?"

She shrugged. "Habit, I suppose. Plus, Gershom always exuded so much power that the little things we could do seemed inconsequential."

Seth sighed. "At least we may have that in our favor. If they thought capturing an immortal would enable them to gain eternal youth *and* special powers..."

Zach grunted. "They'd cause as much trouble as the mercenary outfits did."

And the mercenary outfits had caused *mountains* of trouble, all in a quest to create an invincible army they could hire out to the highest bidder for billions.

"Our primary lead," Seth continued, "is Becca."

And Chris seemed set against Nick posing as her.

"Then I'll continue my ruse," Nicole said.

"No," Sean insisted. "If Nick can't do it, let another shape-shifter do it."

Though she was loath to admit it, Nicole didn't trust Nick not to screw up again and kill their only lead. That had completely caught them off guard.

"I can do it," Aidan volunteered. "But I'll need to spend a week with Becca first to get her appearance, voice, and mannerisms down."

*A week?* Nicole glanced around the table. "Can we afford that kind of delay? If the vampires go missing for a few days, the bad guys might blame it on insanity. But if Becca disappears for a week, they may suspect we're onto them and become even more covert in their actions. If we can't identify and track them now, how much harder will it be if they go dark?"

"I agree," Seth said.

"As do I," David added. "But if Nicole continues to pose as Becca, she should only do so until Aidan can replace her."

"Why can't Aidan replace her now?" Sean protested, and glanced at the Celtic immortal. "You're an ancient. Would it really be that hard for you to pretend to be Becca?"

"Harder than you might think," Aidan responded honestly. "I usually shift into the form of animals. I haven't assumed the form of another person in"—he thought on it a moment—"at least a couple thousand years."

Seth nodded. "If Becca were a man, it would be easier. Aidan wouldn't have to alter his height as much. Adopting and maintaining a smaller form for long periods is always more challenging than going bigger. He also wouldn't have to speak in a higher voice, conceal his accent, or walk like a woman."

Sean's brow furrowed. "Could *you* do it? Or Zach?"

Seth shook his head. "We're needed elsewhere too often."

Leah chimed in. "I would do it if I were better at shape-shifting. I wouldn't have to change my accent or my walk. And speaking in a higher voice wouldn't be a stretch. But this is all still new to me, and I haven't had enough practice. Most of my attempts to impersonate others are hilarious."

Seth grinned. "She has difficulty holding the shape, so her features often fluctuate."

Leah laughed. "It's creepy as hell. Like something out of a horror movie."

"Then I'll do it," Nicole repeated. "I'll pose as Becca again." When Sean immediately opened his mouth, she turned to him and held up a hand. "It's just temporary. Last time, it took two weeks for them to attempt another snatch-and-grab. So I doubt anything will happen before Aidan replaces me."

Tight-lipped, he stared at her for a long moment before turning to Seth. "She's not doing it unless I pose as her boyfriend."

Nicole scowled at him. "What?"

Sean didn't care. She had just volunteered to place herself in danger. Again. "You heard me."

"How can you pose as Becca's boyfriend? You already pretended to be *mine* the night I took Becca to the bar."

"And Reed was the only one who saw me with you."

"That you know of."

"I don't care. I'm not letting you do this alone, even if I have to dye my hair blond and get real tattoos this time."

Melanie held up a finger. "Just a note. Immortals can't get tattoos. The virus views the ink as a chemical foreign to the body and pushes it back out."

Everyone stared at her.

"Seriously?" Sean asked.

"Yes."

"She's right," Aidan inserted. "I learned that firsthand. The only time the virus doesn't rid you of tattoos is if you already have them when you transform."

Melanie nodded. "It's the same with dental fillings."

"Fine," Sean stated. "I'll just buy more temporary tattoos."

158

Tessa leaned forward. "Sean can be her boyfriend, and I can be Becca's new roommate. That way, we can keep Nicole safe until Aidan's ready."

Sean could go with that. Two protectors would be better than one. And Tessa fought with the speed and strength of an elder.

But Nicole frowned. "Now, wait a minute. Seth didn't even say *Sean* could do it with me." She sent Sean a narrow-eyed look. "And don't say *ba-dum-tish.*"

He laughed. How did she do that—aggravate him one second and make him laugh the next?

Nicole merely arched a brow. "And when Aidan takes my place? Are you going to make out with him, too?"

*Ummm...*

Sheldon perked up. "You two made out?"

"No," Sean and Nicole quickly denied.

Aidan grinned. "I'll just dump him the day I take over."

Nick shook his head, his frustration palpable. "This is about me. Not Becca. They want *me*, so *I* should do it. I fucked up when I killed Reed. I won't make the same mistake twice. There's too much at stake."

"Actually," Chris said, "I think Aidan should do it." When Nick opened his mouth to fire back a response, Chris held up a hand. "For a different reason. He's a telepath. He wouldn't have to wait for them to capture him and cart him off to wherever they intend to do their research so we can find out what we need to know. He can pluck the information straight from their minds when they attack and instantly convey it to Seth."

Seth visually consulted David.

David nodded. "I agree. If those who attempt to capture him lack the information we need, Aidan can allow them to take him and provide us with live updates. The more of this group that he encounters, the more minds he can scour, which should lead us to the man in charge."

"We have a course of action then," Seth said. "Aidan, I want you and Dana to stay with Nick, Kayla, and Becca in my castle in England so you can have as much time with Becca as you need."

Becca slid Aidan a look of dread. "This is going to be so weird."

He grinned. "At least you know the man impersonating you won't run around killing people or kidnapping *gifted ones* whilst in your guise."

The teenager stared at him. "What?"

Laughing, Aidan shook his head. "It's a long story. I'll tell it to you in England."

"Nicole?" Seth asked. "Are you sure you're willing to risk posing as Becca in the interim?"

"Yes." She studied the somber faces around her. "It's not like I'm hoping to get captured or anything. One brush with death is enough for me, thank you. But I don't want whoever is behind this to think Becca and her family have gone into hiding. Roubal didn't know about vampires. This buyer does. What if greed isn't his only motivation? What if he's sick or dying? If he's as desperate as Roubal was and thinks he's lost his one shot at getting his hands on a genuine immortal, who's to say he won't start infecting himself and others with the virus and hope they'll be able to beat back the madness later on?"

*Damn it.* She would have to make a valid point.

Marcus groaned. "The last thing we need is another vampire uprising. We're still trying to stamp out the leftovers from the last one."

"Plus," Nicole added, "I trust Sean to protect me. And I can always restrict my movements at night to reduce the risk and buy some time for Aidan to replace me."

Sean took her hand beneath the table and rested it on his thigh. "I'll have her back," he vowed. "Becca, your dorm is coed, isn't it?"

"Yes."

"Are guys allowed to stay in girls' rooms overnight?"

"Only if she doesn't have a roommate. And you have to get permission from the RA first."

Kayla arched a brow. "And you know this how, young lady?"

Becca rolled her eyes. "My former roommate wanted her A-hole boyfriend to spend the night, but the RA nixed it."

Sean issued a decisive nod. "Then I'm staying in the dorm with her."

Chris drew a small notepad and pencil from his pocket and started jotting down notes. "I'll take care of it. I may need your help with that, Seth."

"Call me if you do."

Fortunately, mind control didn't cause brain damage. Erasing all traces of it would, but Seth needn't do that for this.

Melanie again held up a finger. "If you'd like a little extra protection, I can implant a tracking device that will allow us to locate Nicole if she's captured."

Sean frowned. "Won't they find that if they scan her?"

"*Would* they scan her?" Zach asked. "We've only seen vampires thus far and don't seem to be dealing with the kind of tech-savvy mercenaries we've faced in the past."

Kayla swiveled in her seat to address Nick's Second. "Did Roubal's goons scan us when they took us, Oliver? You woke up before I did."

"I don't know. I was still unconscious when we got there."

"Oh." Facing the table once more, she gave an apologetic shrug. "Sorry."

Bastien draped an arm across the back of Melanie's chair. "Could you put the tracker somewhere they wouldn't expect to find it?"

Sean bristled. "She could stick it up your ass. They wouldn't find it there."

Laughter erupted.

Unoffended, Bastien grinned. "I didn't mean someplace intimate. I meant somewhere they might miss it."

Melanie tilted her head to one side. "I could put it in her wrist, the one she wears her smartwatch on. If they run a scanner across it, they'll assume the signal is coming from the watch. I doubt they'll scan her wrist again after removing it."

Chris pointed at her. "That's not a bad idea. I think that'll work."

Sean tightened his hold on Nicole's hand. "I still go where she goes."

Seth inclined his head. "As you will."

"There's one more detail we need to discuss," she said and sent Sean a wary glance. "If they try to abduct me again before Aidan takes over, I think I should let them take me."

"What?" he practically bellowed.

Nicole ignored him. "If I do, you'll be able to track me, thanks to Melanie. And I doubt Sean will stray far, so he'll be right on their heels."

"Hell yes, I will," he snapped.

Chris tapped his pencil on the table, drawing Sean's attention. "And you *won't* stop them unless her life is in danger. We need to reach their hub and find out if we're only dealing with one buyer or if Gershom told others."

"Again," Seth reminded them, "we don't know that Gershom is behind this. Roubal could've told a friend or colleague about it. Chris, have your people find out who his cronies are and investigate anyone he maintained an amicable relationship with."

"Will do." More scribbling. "I'll also keep a special ops presence on campus and have a team member sneak into Becca's room and do a quick scan for listening devices, just in case."

Seth arched his brows as he met David's gaze. "Care to add anything?"

David leaned forward. "Everyone else should hunt in pairs and remain vigilant. We hope their focus will remain on obtaining Nick, but if they grow frustrated with their inability to secure Becca as bait, they may look for other immortals. Text your Seconds at the top of every hour and keep them apprised of your location and activities. If Gershom is involved, the group we're dealing with may have the sedative." The only sedative on the planet that could incapacitate an immortal or vampire. "Seconds, track your immortals. If they fail to check in, call me immediately."

A chorus of *Yes, sir* filled the room.

Seth caught Aidan's eye. "Work swiftly."

"I will."

Seth turned his attention to Nicole. "If you change your mind—"

"I won't."

"Then we're done here. Good hunting to you all."

A mass exodus began as everyone headed out to begin their hunts.

Sean seethed while Jared teleported him, Nicole, and Cliff home. The ancient Other immediately returned to David's place.

Emma emerged from the kitchen with a smile that faltered when she saw Sean's expression.

Well, he was too furious to don a poker face.

She sent Cliff an inquiring look. "Everything okay?"

"Yeah." Cliff closed the distance between them and pressed a kiss to her lips. "Nicole is returning to Duke tonight."

"Oh."

Nicole forced a smile. "Sean's pissed."

Emma nodded. "So I see."

Releasing Nicole's hand, Sean strode up the hallway. "I'm going to pack."

Low murmurs followed him as Nicole and Cliff caught Emma up on the situation. Sean paid little attention to it as he entered his bedroom. Grabbing a duffle from his closet, he started stuffing it with clothes.

Nicole already had everything she needed at the dorm, so she chatted with Emma as if it were just another night and she didn't intend to spend the next week *risking her damned life.*

Well, screw that. Sean was going to stick to her like glue.

"Let them take her, my ass," he grumbled.

Cliff entered, carrying a second duffle. Judging by the way his biceps bulged, the bag was heavy. "I packed you some weapons."

"Thanks."

"Emma's helping Nicole raid the fridge. Is there anything else I can do?"

Pausing, Sean struggled to calm his chaotic thoughts. "Would you drop by every other day and water Nicole's plants for her while we're gone? I'd really appreciate it." Sean had been taking care of them in her absence.

"Sure. That's a given. As far as this op goes, though... if something foul goes down and you need me, I'm just a call away."

He forced a smile. "Emma would tear me limb from limb if you got hurt coming to my rescue."

"Probably." Cliff grinned. "Then she'd fuss over me and kiss it to make it better."

Sean laughed. "No doubt."

Cliff's expression turned somber. "Seriously. Remember what Bastien said yesterday. We have your back, Sean. Every one of us." He smiled. "Even us mere mortals."

Lucky to have such loyal friends, Sean pulled him into a man-hug and clapped him on the back. "Thank you."

For some reason, heading to the kitchen and seeing Nicole laughing and talking as if she didn't have a care in the world resurrected the anger that had faded. Stewing in silence, Sean waited impatiently for Reordon to call and give them the go-ahead. When he did, Reordon said they hadn't found any listening devices in Becca's room.

Seth appeared shortly thereafter and teleported them directly to Becca's dorm room. "The special ops team is in place here on campus, and Tessa will hunt nearby with a partner."

Nicole smiled. "Okay. Thanks."

Seth teleported away.

Sean dropped the smile he'd forced.

Silence filled the room, growing heavier with every moment it took Nicole to pack Becca's mini-fridge with all the food she'd brought from home. As soon as she finished, Nicole spun around and threw up her hands. "What, Sean? What? Why are you so angry? You know this is the smart thing to do. Everyone agreed to it and—"

"The *smart* thing to do," he growled as he took a step toward her, "would be to wait and let Aidan put himself out there as bait next week."

"We already covered that. If Becca just disappears—"

"I don't care!" he shouted. "I don't care if a week's delay might make it harder to find out who's behind this. I don't care if Nick screws up again if he takes your place. I care about *you*! I care about your *safety*! I care about your *life*! And you almost died two nights ago! Do you not get that? *You almost died!*" Unable to stand still, he paced the small room. "Do you have any idea what seeing you crumpled at the base of that tree was like for me? It wasn't just that the vampire had severed your artery. It wasn't just the horrifying amount of blood gushing out of you. I thought you'd broken your neck! And yeah, I'm a healer. But the wounds I healed on Krysta always involved simple things like a broken arm or cuts and gashes. Do you know how complicated healing damage to a spinal cord is? It's like fixing fucking brain damage!"

Nicole watched him mutely.

"I'm not as powerful as the elder healers, Nicole. Like most *gifted ones* born in the past century, I'm fortunate to have any healing ability at all. When I lay hands on you, I don't always see what needs to be fixed and know exactly how to fix it the way elders do. I have to know *everything* about anatomy first. I have to know how a surgeon would repair the damage in an operating room so I can consciously mimic that with my healing gift. I'm learning everything I can from Melanie as quickly as possible, but I *still* didn't know *enough*. If you'd stopped breathing, I didn't know if performing CPR until Seth arrived would help you or kill you. I didn't know if I'd be able to make your heart continue to beat if it faltered. And Seth's healing abilities don't extend to fucking *resurrection!*" he ended in a roar.

Breathing hard, frustration coursing through him, he stopped a foot away from her.

Nicole continued to stare up at him, unspeaking. And as she did, tears welled in her eyes.

"Oh hell." Remorse filling him, he closed the distance between them and drew her into a hug. "I'm sorry. I'm sorry. I didn't mean to yell. I just..."

"Care about me," she finished for him.

"Yes."

Sliding her arms around his waist, she hugged him tight. Tears dampened the front of his shirt. "You care about me," she whispered.

Something about the way she said it made him wonder: Was he the first person who had ever told her that?

Cradling her close, Sean cupped one hand over her soft hair. "Yes," he confessed. "I care about you." His heart began to pound as he decided to take the leap. "I care for you far more than an immortal *should* care for his Second."

# CHAPTER TEN

N ICOLE'S EYES, WHICH SHE'D closed as she rested her head against Sean's chest, flew open.

*I care for you far more than an immortal* should *care for his Second.*
Was he saying...?

He stroked her hair, every movement conveying affection.

Tilting her head back, she stared up at him.

Sean's eyes glowed vibrant amber, as they had since he'd begun his rant. Anger tended to do that. But did something else illuminate them as well? *Another* strong emotion perhaps?

"I don't want to lose you," he said softly.

She drew her tongue across suddenly dry lips. "You won't."

He shook his head, unwilling to be drawn back into an argument. Good. She wasn't either.

When his gaze dropped to her mouth, excitement skittered through her.

His eyes brightened. His head dipped.

*Oh crap.* Nicole's breath caught as Sean's lips brushed hers. Considering how angry he'd been moments ago, she would've thought any kiss he'd deliver would be rough, almost punishing. But it wasn't. It was gentle. Almost tentative, as if he were waiting to see whether she would rear back and object.

When she didn't, he deepened the contact, those soft lips tempting and tantalizing hers, awakening hidden desires until she fisted her hands in the back of his shirt and tried to urge him closer.

Sean didn't comply. He retreated instead, enough that she had to relinquish her hold on him.

In the absence of his touch, cold seeped in, along with fear that he regretted the brief intimacy.

Reluctantly, Nicole looked up at him.

Luminous amber caught and held her gaze. Much to her relief, neither anger nor regret lingered in his beautiful eyes. Only desire blazed in them now.

Cupping her face in both hands, he stared down at her with an intensity that heightened her awareness of him. "Do you have any idea how long I've wanted to do that?"

She shook her head. He'd kissed her twice in recent weeks. Once in the bar, and again when he'd said goodnight outside Becca's residence hall, when he'd pretended to be her boyfriend.

But he made it sound as if he'd wanted to kiss her *before* that.

Unable to deny the impulse, Nicole tucked her index fingers through the belt loops on his cargo pants to keep him close. "Why didn't you?" she asked softly.

Much to her surprise, he didn't hesitate to respond. "Because I knew with you, one kiss would never be enough. I would always want more."

The confession made her burn. *With her*, he'd said. He would always want more *with her*.

The words hinted at a longing for something deeper than friendship.

A longing she shared.

Her heartbeat quickened even more. "*Do* you? Want more?"

After a last, affectionate brush of his thumbs against her cheeks, he dropped his hands to her hips. His heated gaze traveled slowly down her body, as arousing as a touch, then returned to meet hers. "I want it all," he proclaimed, his voice hoarse with need.

A sensual shiver shook her. The hunger conveyed by those four short syllables fueled her own and silenced any doubts the stringent rule-follower inside her tried to raise. *Nothing* was more important than this. Not her job with the network. Not staying in Reordon and Seth's good graces.

*Nothing* was more important to her than *Sean*.

Rising on her toes, Nicole slid her arms around his neck and leaned into him. "I do, too." She combed her fingers through his hair, her nails lightly raking his scalp. His breath caught when she pressed her hips to his, delighting in the hard bulge that strained against his zipper. "So let's take it."

His eyes flared brighter. Then he dipped his head and claimed her lips in a kiss so carnal she gasped. Locking a hard arm around her, he slid his hand down over her ass and urged her tighter against his erection as his tongue stroked and teased hers, flooding her with heat. He was so hard, his touch bold and aggressive, firing her need.

Fisting his free hand around her ponytail, he tugged her head back. Nicole moaned when he abandoned her lips and trailed a path of hungry kisses along her neck.

He drew in a deep breath. "I love your scent." Even his voice turned her on, so deep and hungry. Capturing her earlobe between his teeth, he gave it a little nip. "It's even better when you want me."

Nicole had never wanted anyone more. "Sean."

Releasing her ponytail, he drew his hand down her back, around to her front, and palmed her breast. Sensation shot through her when he teased the stiff peak through the fabric of her shirt and bra, skimming his thumb across it and delivering a delicious pinch.

She moaned and rocked against him, wishing no clothing separated them.

"Tell me you want me," he all but growled.

"I want you," she said breathlessly, practically climbing him in an attempt to get closer.

Stepping back, he yanked the tail of her shirt out of her pants. "I want to see you."

Nodding eagerly, she held her arms up and helped him rid her of the shirt. She would've regretted wearing the plain sports bra if he'd paid any attention to it but didn't think he even noticed as he tugged it off.

Nicole stood before him, bare from the waist up, pulse thumping in her ear.

"You're beautiful," he told her hoarsely.

Warmth suffused her. Sean had an amazing body. She'd seen him in his underwear enough times to know that every muscle was honed to mouthwatering perfection. That he found her trim, athletic form and modest breasts equally appealing pleased her immensely.

Sean cupped her breasts and drew his thumbs across the sensitive pink peaks. "So beautiful."

Need rose. "Take your shirt off," Nicole ordered, and started tugging at the fabric.

"Hell yes." The shirt was gone in a blink. Then his hands returned to her breasts as she admired him.

Dark hair coated his muscled pecs, trailing down washboard abs. Holy crap, he was ripped. She rested her hands on his pecs, caressed, and explored. When she toyed with his nipples and delivered light pinches, Sean groaned and tweaked hers again.

He tried to draw her closer, but Nicole resisted. Smiling, she slid one hand down his stomach, admiring and fondling his eight-pack abs. When she reached the waistband of his cargo pants, she kept going, molding her hand to the large bulge below.

"You're so hard for me," she whispered.

He groaned, pushing into her touch. "Yes."

He was big, too. She stroked him through his pants.

His breath whooshing out, he took her lips in another ardent kiss, devouring her hungrily as he stroked her breasts. Fire thrummed through Nicole. Releasing him, she drew a knee up and draped it over his hip. Both moaned when her core came into contact with his hard cock.

Sean slid both hands down to her ass. "Wrap your legs around me." As soon as he lifted her, she did so. More moans and hungry kisses followed as she rocked against him. He felt so good, his hard body pressed to hers. Nicole wanted him so badly that she was already close to coming.

Sean moved forward, hands hungrily roving her back. Tearing his lips from hers, he glanced over her head... and stopped short. "What the hell is that?" he blurted.

Startled by the dismay in his voice, she looked behind her and found nothing amiss. "What's what?"

"That." Holding her with one arm, he motioned toward the corner.

She frowned. "The bed?"

"*That's* a bed?" he asked with so much consternation that she laughed.

"Yes."

It was a single bed, typical of those found in many dorm rooms. And to a sizeable person like Sean, who was accustomed to sleeping on a significantly larger Alaskan King mattress, it must seem miniscule.

It was also high enough off the ground to accommodate dresser drawers beneath it. Nicole had to use a little footstool Becca kept beside it to get up on it.

He stared at it a long moment, then shrugged. "Fuck it. I'll make it work."

And make it work he did. Taking the remaining step to the foot of the bed, he set Nicole on the edge of the mattress. "Lie back."

Heart hammering against her ribs, Nicole reclined as he unfastened the button at the waist of her pants and drew down the zipper. In short order, he removed the cargo pants. Beneath, she wore lacy black bikini panties, which she hoped were more enticing than her sports bra had been.

Sean made a rumbling sound that resembled a growl as he stared down at her and slowly slid his hands up her thighs. Her breath caught when he brushed a thumb over her clit. "Now every time I see you, I'm going to picture you like this, wearing these."

She swallowed. "Are they better than the jeans with the tear in the knee?"

A devilish smile curled his lips. "Way better." He stroked her again, sending lightning bolts of pleasure through her.

Nicole shifted restlessly, pressing up into his touch.

"Scoot back a little," he ordered.

Raising onto her elbows, she eased back.

At the same time, he hooked his fingers into the delicate sides of the panties and drew them down her legs, tossing them to the floor. "That's good."

She stopped.

Sean took her left foot in his hand and propped it on the edge of the mattress. Taking her right foot, he did the same, splaying her legs wide. "Yeah," he murmured, staring at her center. "This'll work."

In the next instant, he slid his arms beneath her knees, leaned down, and took her with his mouth.

Moaning, Nicole threw her head back and fisted her hands in the covers. The things he did. Licking and stroking and teasing her clit. Over and over, he worked the little bundle of nerves. Pleasure overwhelmed her, rising and intensifying as he slipped two fingers inside her.

"Sean," she moaned.

One big hand held her hips in place while he ravished her. Just when she thought she would scream if she didn't come soon, he moved his tongue with preternatural speed, the sensation as mind-blowing as that of a vibrator.

Bucking against him, Nicole cried out as ecstasy filled her.

Sean moaned when Nicole's inner muscles clamped down around his fingers, his tongue unrelenting until he'd wrung the last ripple of pleasure from her. Lust pounded through him as he straightened.

Nicole lay spread out before him, her beautiful body bare, her taste still on his tongue.

And she tasted soooo good.

A slight sheen of moisture glistened on her skin. Her breasts rose and fell as she tried to catch her breath. Just the feel of her inner muscles squeezing his fingers had nearly made him come. But Sean had held on, wanting to be balls-deep inside her first.

He doffed his pants and boxer briefs in a blink. "Move back until your head's on the pillow," he ordered.

Bracing her feet on the bed, she pushed herself back until her hair nearly reached the headboard. Though the mattress was higher off the ground than her bed at home, Sean was tall enough not to have a problem getting a knee on it.

Her brown eyes gleamed with appreciation as he crawled toward her.

Sean braced his hands on either side of her to keep his weight off her and settled himself between her thighs, his hard cock nudging her slick entrance. She felt so small compared to his bulk. So delicate that he felt a moment's qualm.

Her look turned watchful. "What is it?" Resting her hands on his forearms, she gave them a sweet stroke.

"Tell me if I hurt you." He hadn't been with a woman since he'd gained immortal strength and wasn't sure...

Understanding dawned on her pretty features. "I will." Sliding her hands up his arms, she cupped his face and drew him down for a kiss. "But don't hold back unless I say something. Okay?"

He kissed her. "Okay."

Smiling, she wrapped her arms around him. "Now take me. I want to feel you inside me."

*Hell* yes.

Both moaned as he pressed forward. She was warm and wet, squeezing him so tightly he would've wondered if she was a virgin if he didn't know better. Sean wanted to go slow, to ease into her passage inch by inch and give her time to adjust, but it felt too good. *She* felt too good.

He thrust deep, burying himself to the hilt.

Nicole gasped. Her hands clenched on his back, her short nails pricking his skin.

Sean stiffened, afraid he'd hurt her. "Too hard?" He'd never had the guts to ask one of the married immortals if he'd ever lost sight of his super strength during sex and accidentally hurt his wife when she'd still been mortal.

Nicole's lips twitched. "*Ba-dum-tish*," she said breathlessly.

Sean laughed, then groaned when the action made his cock jump inside her.

Her laugh turned into a moan. Rotating her hips, she took him deeper and ground her clit against him. "Not too hard," she purred. "Too good."

So hungry for her that he shook, Sean withdrew almost to the crown and pushed deep.

She moaned. "Yes."

No longer fearing he'd hurt her, he repeated the motion, thrusting deep, pounding into her. It was incredible. Like nothing he'd ever experienced before. Now that he was immortal, he felt everything more. His enhanced senses overloaded him with her scent, her taste, every touch and brush of her flesh against his. She felt so good, her small hands roving his back as she arched up against him, urging him on as he drove into her again and again.

Sean altered the angle of his hips, stimulating her clit with every thrust. Her breath shortened when he toyed with her breast.

"Yes. More, Sean. Please."

*Oh yeah.* His balls tightened. She felt so fucking good. Her body writhing beneath him. Little moans of pleasure driving him wild until she threw her head back and cried out with another climax.

He groaned as her warmth clamped down around him, squeezing rhythmically until he could hold back his release no longer. Shouting her name, Sean poured his heat inside her and didn't think he had ever come so hard in his life.

Heart racing, he braced his elbows on the bed and let her take a little more of his weight while he lowered his head to the pillow beside hers.

Nicole's hold loosened as her muscles relaxed. Her breath came fast. And her heart raced beneath her breast. Every once in a while, a residual ripple from her orgasm would tighten her inner muscles around him in the most delicious way.

Warmth and affection welled up within him. Burrowing his arms beneath her, Sean hugged her close and pressed a loving kiss to her shoulder.

Her slender arms came around him. One hand stroked his back while she buried the other in his hair and massaged his scalp. He smiled. No other woman could make him feel this way.

Only Nicole.

Gradually, their breathing slowed. Calmed. Their skin cooled.

Resting a hand on her bottom to keep their bodies joined, he rolled them to their sides... and nearly fell off the damned bed. "Whoa!"

DIANNE DUVALL

Letting out a little shriek, Nicole tightened her hold on him until he could shift them closer to the wall on the narrow mattress.

Sean shook his head. "This bed is *not* working for me."

Laughing, she draped a leg over his hip and snuggled closer. "There's a second bed against the other wall. We can push them together."

He smiled. She'd lost her hair tie at some point. He had a vague recollection of tugging it off when he'd fisted her ponytail. Between him running his hands through the long locks and her tossing her head against the covers, her hair was now adorably mussed.

Peace and contentment suffused him, as did the certainty that this was where he was meant to be. Here. In Nicole's arms. In this ridiculously tiny bed that left his feet hanging off the end. Exchanging soft kisses and caresses as they sank back to earth.

"That was amazing," she whispered.

He smiled. "I was thinking the same thing."

Her pretty brown eyes held such warmth as she closed the minimal distance between them and kissed him, a slow exploration that increased the peace inside him... until she teased him with her tongue.

His cock instantly hardened. *Hello, awesome Immortal Guardian perk number seven.* Sliding a hand down over her beautiful ass, he gently thrust deeper.

Drawing back, she arched a brow. "Wow. I'd heard immortals didn't need recovery time, but you're hard again already?"

He offered her a sheepish grin. "Actually, I've been like this around you ever since you mentioned masturbating."

"Really?" The notion seemed to intrigue her.

"Does this feel like I'm exaggerating?" He thrust again.

Her breath hitched with a gasp of pleasure. "Not at all." Then something new entered her expression. Something that made his pulse pick up. "So you like to imagine me touching myself?"

If possible, he hardened even more. "Yes."

Flattening her hand on his chest, she pushed him onto his back—careful not to land him on the floor—and straddled him with his cock still buried deep inside her.

Sean's breath caught. *Oh yeah.* He liked where this was going.

Her lips—pink and plump from his kisses—curled up in a provocative smile. "So, seeing this might turn you on?" She curled the fingers of one delicate hand over her shoulder, the touch innocent, yet alluring. Then she slowly drew those fingers down, dipping into the hollow above her collarbone to give it a stroke, and continued on.

Sean clamped his hands over her hips as she brought her other hand up.

Tilting her head to one side, she cupped both breasts and played with the tight pink buds. He heard her pulse pick up as she flexed the muscles in her thighs and rose, his long hard length nearly slipping from her warmth before she sank back down.

"Again," he growled. And she repeated the motion, rising and falling, riding him slowly as she played with her breasts. But it felt too good. And the temptation was too great. Brushing her hands aside, Sean took over, caressing and teasing her breasts. "You're so fucking beautiful."

Her face flushed—with pleasure or passion, he couldn't tell. Bracing her hands on his chest, she rode him faster. Harder. Sean groaned when she gave the hair on his chest a tug and pinched his nipples. "Yeah," he urged. "More."

She rotated her hips. Picked up the pace. Her breath coming quicker.

He slid a hand down her stomach and stroked her clit as he thrust up into her, heat rising, pleasure intensifying, climbing higher and higher.

Nicole called his name as she came, her inner muscles squeezing his cock again and again until he joined her with a shout.

Sean's heart slammed against his ribs as she sank limply onto his chest. As the last ripples of release teased them, he wrapped his arms around her and cuddled her.

Yes. This was definitely where he belonged.

Smiling, he clung to the thought as they both succumbed to slumber.

Nicole awoke, feeling as if she had never slept better. Sean lay sprawled on his back with one muscled arm wrapped around her. She was snuggled up to his side, her legs tangled with his and one arm resting on his broad chest. Smiling, Nicole drew her fingers through the coarse hair there. Sean had kept her up until dawn, exploring her body and making her moan with pleasure. She'd had no idea sex could be so...

Well, she couldn't seem to find the right word for it, but she had never in her life felt this close to someone.

Her stomach growled.

Though his eyes remained closed, Sean's chest rumbled with a chuckle. "Sounds like you worked up an appetite."

She laughed. "And slept through lunch."

Tiling his chin down, he opened his eyes and studied her. "No regrets?" He drew the back of one finger down her cheek in a soft caress.

Nicole caught his hand and pressed a kiss to it. "No regrets."

His gaze sharpened. "No anxiety?"

She opened her mouth, intending to say no, but this was Sean. He was her best friend. She could tell him anything. "Maybe a little."

"What's worrying you?"

"Reordon."

"Forget Reordon. He can't dictate your private life. And how will he even know?"

She rolled her eyes. "Chris knows everything."

He laughed. "Not if we don't tell him. And I don't think any of the telepaths are going to tattle. Not unless you're only sleeping with me because you feel obligated." He narrowed his eyes and pursed his lips playfully. "You aren't, are you?"

"Well, *yeah*," she said with a distinct *duh* inflection. "I mean, if *I* don't sleep with you, who will? Look at you. All those muscles. That chiseled jaw. Those gorgeous brown eyes. And you're smart, too? What woman would possibly want that?"

He grinned. "You?"

"Damn!" she exclaimed in mock frustration. "I thought I was hiding it better than that."

Dipping his head, he pressed an exuberant kiss to her lips. His brown eyes were somber, however, when they met hers. "All kidding aside…"

Her heart flip-flopped in her chest.

"I *do* have a lot of muscles, a chiseled jaw, and gorgeous brown eyes."

Laughing, she gave him a hard shove. "Not so smart, though, are you? Clearly, I was wrong about that."

When she tried to clamber over him to get out of bed, he locked his arms around her. "Oh no, you don't. You can't leave now. I want more compliments." He tickled her ribs. Helpless giggles poured forth as she squirmed and tried to keep his fingers from finding ticklish spots, but he was merciless. "Give me more compliments!"

"No!" she refused with a laugh. "Let me go, you egomaniac!"

"Never," he declared with a grin, tickling more giggles from her. When he finally stopped, she sprawled on top of him, gasping for air.

A warm smile bathed his face as he watched her. Reaching up, he brushed her mussed hair back from her face. "Never," he whispered.

Nicole stared at him. Did he mean…?

Was that love she saw in his eyes? More than the love one felt for a friend?

Her heart began to beat faster.

Then *his* stomach growled.

She grinned. "As much as I'd like to spend the whole day in bed—"

"That's music to my ears," he proclaimed, resting his hands on her hips.

"I'm sure it is." His arousal was prodding her in the stomach. "But I need to go for my daily run. I'll pick up some lunch for us while I'm out." With much reluctance, she slid off of him, then stood beside the bed.

Sitting up, he glanced at the window. Beyond the curtains, bright sunlight shone. "Let me tank up on blood, and I'll go with you."

She frowned. "You can't. You have *no* tolerance for sunlight, Sean." He was one of the youngest immortals in the area and had not been turned by an ancient, so he lacked older immortals' limited endurance. "You'd have to carry a couple of blood bags with you to keep your skin from blistering when the first infusion wore off."

He slid out of bed and stood before her. "Then I'll carry a couple of bags with me."

"Seriously? You don't think people will freak out if they see you holding a bag of blood to your fangs?"

Scowling, he stepped closer. "Then don't go jogging."

"I have to," she reminded him patiently. "I'm supposed to be Becca and need to adhere to at least *some* of her normal schedule. *She* jogs every day after class, so *I* jog every day. Besides, vampires can't attack me when the sun's up. They're even more photosensitive than you are."

"I still don't like it."

She stared up at him. The moment stretched. "I'm sorry. I can't concentrate when you're standing there looking so irresistibly rumpled and poking me in the stomach. I'm not used to having naked conversations."

He glanced down at his erection and laughed. "I can't help it. It's just what you do to me. And I not only *enjoy* having naked conversations with you—even though you're currently aggravating me—I hope to have many more in the future."

Nicole grinned as some of her initial self-consciousness fell away. "That may take some getting used to." She had little experience with this kind of intimacy and familiarity. "But we can give it a try. For now, though, I have to go." Since they had showered last night before finally falling into an exhausted slumber, she grabbed a bra and panties from the top dresser drawer and donned them. "I'll take my phone so you can track me and pester me with texts."

"You aren't leaving campus, are you?"

"No. I'll just jog a couple of miles and then get us some goodies from one of my favorite lunch trucks."

"I still don't think you should go alone. Let me call Cliff. Or better yet, Aidan."

"I won't be alone, Sean. Did you forget Chris has stationed a special ops team on campus?"

His frown eased a bit. "Actually, I did."

"They work eight-hour shifts and cover us night *and* day. I'll have eyes on me the whole time I'm gone." She dug a pair of sweatpants out and pulled them on. "Plus, no one is going to try anything in broad daylight with over fifteen thousand students on campus, ready to witness it and record it on their phones."

"Okay." He sat on the side of the bed. "I still wish I could go with you."

Something in his voice compelled Nicole to pause and study him. She'd expected Sean to look worried. But a hint of wistfulness had entered his expression.

Did he miss being able to go out during the day and feel warm sunlight on his skin?

Though he had transformed voluntarily, she suspected his answer would be yes if she asked him.

Odd that she hadn't noticed that before, perhaps because he usually slept while she ran errands during the day.

She forced a rueful smile. "Well, I don't. You would insist on carrying the food for me and eat it all before we got back."

He laughed. "True."

Happy to have lifted his spirits, she drew a Blue Devils sweatshirt over her head and stuffed her feet into her favorite running shoes. "It's Taco Tuesday. Do you want tacos, quesadillas, or burritos?"

"Yes," he answered promptly.

She grinned. "Want me to get enough for dinner, too, so we can eat in?"

"No." Rising, he loosed a beleaguered sigh. "You're Becca. As you keep reminding me, you're supposed to be seen." Closing the distance between them, he looped his arms around her and pressed his forehead to hers. "I don't like this. I don't like you taking risks." He had made that abundantly clear the previous night.

Resting her hands on his chest, Nicole toyed with the hair there. "Want to know a little secret?"

He nodded.

"That feeling you're having right now? That feeling in here?" She tapped his chest.

"Yeah?"

"That's how I feel every night when you leave to hunt."

He regarded her with surprise. "It is?"

She rolled her eyes. "Yes, Sean."

"You worry about me?"

"Of course I do."

"But I'm immortal."

"You're *mostly* immortal. And you've almost died twice during my time as your Second."

"So have you," he pointed out.

"Yeah." She faked a frown. "We're going to have to stop doing that."

Smiling, he hugged her a little tighter. "I tell you what. I don't get many nights off, so I may as well enjoy it while I can, especially since Tessa intends to watch over us."

"Who is she partnering with?"

"I don't know. I forgot to ask," he answered absently. "Let's have a date night and eat at your favorite restaurant tonight."

A little flutter of anticipation filled her. "Because you're supposed to be Becca's boyfriend?"

He shook his head, rubbing noses with her. "Because I want more than friendship with you."

Her heart beat faster. "You do?" she whispered. More than friends with benefits? She'd feared it was too soon to clarify that, so she hadn't asked.

"Yes." Smiling, he pressed a tender kiss to her lips. "Be safe."

"I will."

# CHAPTER ELEVEN

Nicole's jog ended up being as uneventful as all the previous runs she'd embarked upon as Becca. She didn't wear earbuds, though many runners did. It was kinda hard to hear someone coming up behind you when you had music in your ears. And her belief that no one would try to kidnap Becca in broad daylight did *not* reduce her vigilance. The network had trained her well.

Without acknowledging it, she spied at least five special ops soldiers hidden among the student body. Six, if that flicker of light on the roof of one building was what she thought it was—the sun reflecting off the lens of a scope.

They blended in well. Anyone lacking her training would remain oblivious, especially since many students she encountered were looking at their phones, reading, or fooling around with friends.

As soon as Nicole returned to the dorm, Sean hugged the stuffing out of her, then dove into the food with amusing enthusiasm. She expected him to take her to bed afterward, but he seemed content to sit and chat with her, laughing and teasing the way they did at home.

Boy, she'd missed that. She hadn't realized how much non-work time they spent together until this assignment had separated them.

When the sun set, Sean applied the temporary tattoos and showed her the hair wax that made him look blond.

She stared at him. "That's amazing." He even added a little to his eyebrows to lighten them. "You really look blond." Then she grinned. "Once all this is over, can I talk you into trying the blue?"

Smiling, he stole a quick kiss. "You can talk me into just about anything, beautiful."

Pleasure brought a warm flush to her cheeks as they left the dorm. When they exited the building and descended the steps, he took her hand.

An unseasonably warm breeze caressed them, drawing her hair back.

This was nice, strolling along the sidewalk with Sean's fingers twined through hers.

A tall, absolutely stunning woman walked toward them, drawing Nicole's gaze. If anyone were to look up the term *sexy librarian*, they would surely find a picture of this woman. Every man within viewing distance took notice. With her dark hair twisted up in a disheveled bun, she wore black-rimmed glasses. Her white blouse boasted a conservative cut that offered not a glimpse of cleavage, yet left no doubt that she was full-breasted. She shifted the strap of a briefcase looped over one shoulder, wrinkling her black business suit jacket. Matching slacks followed the lines of her long, long legs and ended in... sneakers?

Nicole smiled. She'd heard that Leah was self-conscious about her height. Of course she would wear sneaks instead of heels. And yet, the casual shoes failed to reduce her sex appeal.

As Leah drew even with them, she smiled. "Evening, Becca."

"Hi, Professor."

"Great job on that biology exam."

She grinned. "Thank you."

Leah kept walking.

Sean nudged Nicole. "I knew you'd ace it," he said, adopting a British accent once more.

She laughed.

A short while later, they encountered Roland and Marcus.

Nicole stared. She couldn't recall ever seeing them outside their hunting togs before.

Both now sported black tracksuits that hugged muscular forms. They approached at a loose jog with white earbuds tucked in their ears. Nodding, as though to a stranger, the powerful immortals kept going.

It took considerable effort to suppress the desire to look back at them.

A block away from the restaurant, she and Sean turned a corner and bumped into Krysta and Étienne. Like Roland and Marcus, Sean's sister and her husband had abandoned their hunting garb in favor of jeans and dark sweaters.

"Excuse us," Krysta murmured absently, stepped past them, then addressed Étienne in aggravated tones. "That woman is not staying in our house. She hates me."

"That woman," Étienne replied testily, "is my mother. And I will *not* make her stay in a hotel after spending ten hours flying here from France."

As their faux bickering faded away, Nicole blinked back tears.

Were they all there to watch over *her*? Even curmudgeonly Roland?

That was so sweet.

And thus began a ritual. Every day, Nicole would go for a jog, grab some lunch, and return to spend the rest of the afternoon with Sean in the dorm. Then they'd head to the restaurant for dinner and spot several casually dressed immortals along the way. Almost every immortal in the area appeared at some point. Even David found time to check up on them.

It seemed to go a long way toward easing Sean's concerns. After that first night, he relaxed into the boyfriend role, and the two of them simply enjoyed themselves. They dined out every night, sometimes went clubbing and dancing, then returned to the dorm, where they fell into each other's arms. Sometimes their lovemaking was slow and sweet. Sometimes it was fiery and passionate. And sometimes it was playful, sparking as many laughs and chuckles as it did moans.

Even though everyone kept waiting for that other shoe to drop—for more vampires to whisk *Becca* away again—it was one of the best weeks of Nicole's life. Her college experience had been so different from this one. For most of her existence, she had lacked friends and family who cared about her enough to have her back. And Sean...

Sean was perfect. She had worried that sleeping with him might change things, and it had. Just not in the way she'd thought. There was no awkwardness. No tension. No uncertainty.

They simply grew closer. And closer.

*I'm falling in love with him,* she thought as her sneakers pounded the pavement. It felt so right that she had to wonder why she'd ever questioned the wisdom of it.

She almost hated for her Becca ruse to end. But soon, it would. Cliff texted them regularly, updating them on Aidan's progress. According to the last message she'd received, Aidan would take over as Becca tomorrow. Things would get back to business as usual. And she would no longer be able to spend all day and night with Sean.

She sighed. Naturally, Sean was all smiles. Not because it was Taco Tuesday again, but because he was glad Nicole would no longer be in danger.

Her lips twitched.

Okay, *partly* because it was Taco Tuesday. That man's appetite was unmatched. She didn't know if it resulted from the lean years he'd endured before joining the Immortal Guardians or because he burned so many calories now, but he was *always* hungry.

Bright sunlight filtered down through the trees, dappling the grass and pavement. There weren't as many students out and about today. A cold front had swept through the previous night, driving those who disliked nippy temps inside.

She snorted. Nicole had spent much of her life in Connecticut and upstate New York. North Carolina's winters were mild by comparison.

A squirrel wandered onto the sidewalk ahead of her. Consumed by its collection of acorns, it refused to budge, so she had to go around it.

Shaking her head with a grin, she admitted she would miss this, too: jogging outside on a pretty path. She usually just joined the vampires on the treadmills at network headquarters. And there wasn't much scenery to enjoy on sublevel five.

Two guys standing twenty or thirty yards apart tossed a football back and forth while their girlfriends sat together on the grass, their heads bent over their phones. Up ahead, a woman lounged on a bench, reading a paperback, a big bookbag tucked against her side. One of the network's special ops soldiers loped toward her in joggers, his breath forming white puffs in front of his face. As usual, he nodded cordially and kept going. Another quarter mile or so and Nicole would pass the special ops soldiers who posed as a couple and drank coffee while they debated politics, movies, or some other topic. Sometimes they occupied a bench. Other times, they ambled along the same path she did or sprawled on the lawn.

Pain suddenly exploded in the back of Nicole's head as something hard slammed into it. Stumbling forward, she lost her balance. Pavement abraded the skin on her palms as she threw her hands out to break her fall. What the hell?

Reaching up, she touched a hand to the back of her head as a pounding ache erupted and raced through her skull. When she glanced at her fingers, the tips were red with blood.

Was that from scraping her hand when she fell or from whatever the hell had hit her?

Her heart began to slam against her ribs.

Was this it? Was this the attack they'd been waiting for? Right here? In plain view?

If so, it couldn't be vampires. Vampires couldn't tolerate any sunlight at all.

Nicole swiftly flipped over onto her butt. Her head swam.

"Are you fucking crazy?" a woman shouted behind her.

"It was an accident," a man said defensively.

Nicole glanced to the side as a football rolled to a wobbly halt a few yards away.

"Accident, my ass. You did that on purpose." The woman on the bench set her book aside, rose, and stomped toward her. "Are you okay?"

Nicole started to nod but stopped when the slight movement magnified the pounding in her head. "Yeah. What happened?"

Lips tight, expression furious, the woman bent, took Nicole's hand in her gloved one, and pulled her up. "That asshole hit you in the head with the football. He threw it right at you. I saw the whole thing."

A football? *That's* what had hit her? It has felt much harder than that.

The asshole in question loped toward them, his friend approaching from the other direction. "It was an accident. I swear," the taller one said.

"Bullshit," the woman snapped before facing Nicole. "I saw the short one nod in your direction. That shit was deliberate. It was an assault, and you should file a police report and press charges."

The shorter one had nodded at her?

Suspicion rose. Though her head ached, Nicole studied the duo.

"Assault?" the taller one blurted in disbelief.

"Police report," the other one bleated.

She'd seen the tall one before.

Where? Here on campus during one of her runs?

No. At one of the parties she'd attended. He and another guy had hit on her. Aggressively. Had it been the shorter one?

She couldn't remember. But the tall one...

Yeah. That was the asshole she'd had to shut down forcefully. In front of his buddies. Who had laughed their asses off.

Anger rose. Nicole bent and picked up the football. Looking over the tall one's shoulder, she called, "Over here, officer."

Eyes widening, both men swung around.

Nicole drew her arm back and fired off the football, putting all the muscle she'd honed training in special ops and as a Second behind it.

The ball slammed into the back of Tall Guy's head. Stumbling forward, he barked, "Ah! What the fuck?"

The woman burst out laughing.

Tall Guy took a menacing step forward.

Nicole shifted into a fighting stance. She didn't doubt that she could take this asshole down. And in the unlikely event that she couldn't, all she had to do was hold him off until the special ops jogger turned around and headed back. The special ops "couple" should be up ahead, around a curve, and would come running if she sounded an alarm.

The woman pulled what looked like a small pepper spray canister out of her pocket. "Oh no, you don't. You stay the hell back."

Nicole's right palm began to tingle and burn. From scraping it on the pavement?

She risked a glance down. The skin around the abrasions glistened, as did her fingers. Not with blood. With something clear.

Frowning, she rubbed them together. They were wet.

From the football?

No. North Carolina hadn't had rain in weeks. They were going through yet another historic drought, and water restrictions forbade lawn watering and the use of sprinkler systems, so the football had to be dry.

And yet her hand was moist.

Her palm burned.

The woman took a step toward Tall Guy and started ranting about grown men having the mentality of juveniles.

Nicole had touched the woman's glove when she'd helped her up. Had it been wet?

She couldn't remember.

The skin all over her body abruptly flushed with heat. Her head swam as the campus tilted around her. Nicole staggered. *Oh crap.*

With a startled yelp, the woman hastily grabbed Nicole's arm to steady her. "Hey, are you okay?" She sent the men another scowl. "Way to go, assholes. You probably gave her a concussion."

The woman's glove was definitely wet.

Nicole tried to shake off her hold as the dizziness increased.

The woman turned back to her. "It's okay." Swiftly raising the small canister in her free hand, she sprayed a puff of something moist in Nicole's face.

That was *not* pepper spray.

"It's okay," she said in a soothing voice. "You're going to take a little nap now."

Nicole's knees buckled.

One of the men caught her before she could hit the ground.

"Find her phone," the woman ordered as Nicole's eyelids grew heavy.

A large hand delved into her pocket and yanked it out.

"Put it in here so she can't be traced."

"Hey," a man called from what sounded far away. "Is she okay?"

"Yeah, is she okay?" a woman seconded. "What happened?"

Though she found it hard to focus, Nicole thought it might be the special ops couple.

"She got hit in the head with the football," Canister Lady called back, "and she's feeling a little woozy. We're going to take her to the hospital and have them check her out, make sure she doesn't have a concussion."

"You need any help?" the man asked.

"No. We're good. Thank you."

Oh. Right. She was supposed to let them take her.

Ignoring the deep-seated urge to fight, Nicole forced her limbs to go limp.

Her eyes closed.

These had damned well better be the people who kept trying to get their hands on Becca.

Darkness fell.

Sean stared at the map on his cell. A little phone icon kept him apprised of Nicole's location.

He smiled. If she saw him, Nicole would probably think he eagerly waited for her to return with Taco Tuesday goodies, but he really just wanted to keep an eye on her. Cliff had given them the best news earlier. Aidan would take Nicole's place as Becca tomorrow, so she would once more be safe. They just had to get through one more day and night.

Nicole's phone jumped ahead as the app updated her progress. Then jumped ahead again.

Sean wished he could join her on her afternoon runs. He had been on his high school track team and enjoyed it. Then college and Krysta's vampire-hunting endeavors had eaten up the spare time he would've usually spent running, and he'd had to give it up.

He didn't blame Krysta or resent her for needing him to linger nearby, ready to race to her aid when she hunted. At the time, they'd thought they were the only people who knew that vampires existed. So if Krysta hadn't killed them to keep their numbers in check, who would've?

Nicole's phone jumped ahead again.

Sean missed sunshine, too. When he'd decided to transform, he'd known he would but had thought it worth the sacrifice. He still did. And having to eschew the sun hadn't bothered him much until now.

How he wished he could be by Nicole's side, joking with her and making her laugh or just enjoying a quiet run as they passed from shade into sunlight and back again.

The app updated again, but her phone didn't move.

Frowning, he refreshed it.

No movement.

Had she stopped to talk to someone? One of Becca's friends, perhaps?

He supposed it was bound to happen. She'd been lucky to avoid them this long.

When her phone remained stationary, Sean stood and started to pace. Agitation thrummed through him. She was okay, wasn't she? All of the previous attacks had taken place at night and had been conducted by vampires. Vampires couldn't attack during the day. So, she had to be okay. Right?

Nicole hadn't reached the lunch truck yet. Sean had learned the locations of all of them.

Maybe she'd paused to take pictures of a squirrel or something. She was always showing him photos she'd taken of birds and squirrels and flowers and frogs.

Her phone icon abruptly went dark, indicating she was no longer online.

What the hell?

His phone rang, startling Sean so much that he nearly dropped it. He glanced at the screen.

Darius, one of the special ops soldiers on campus, was calling.

*Oh shit.* "Yeah?" he answered.

"They took the bait," Darius said without preamble.

His stomach sank. "Who did?"

"Unknown." He sounded a little breathless, as if he were running and talking simultaneously. "Two males, one female. They camouflaged the kidnapping so students who saw it wouldn't intervene. Our sniper has eyes on them. They're heading toward the parking lot closest to the dorm. We're on our way there now."

Sean put the phone on speaker and tossed it on the bed. "Are you going to take them into custody?" He shoved his feet into boots.

"That isn't the mission. The mission is to follow them discreetly and step in only if Nicole's life appears to be in danger."

"Fuck the mission," Sean snarled, and crossed to the mini-fridge. "Get them before they leave. One of the telepaths can read their minds and tell us what we need to know."

"Those aren't my orders."

"I don't give a fuck. Do it."

"These people may not know any more than the vampires did," Darius continued doggedly. "Reordon's orders were explicit: Let them take her and step in only if she requires our aid."

Sean grabbed Nicole's backpack and yanked the modified mini-fridge's door open so hard it almost fell off. "Where are you?" With a burst of speed, he stuffed all but one bag of blood into the largest compartment, added a cold pack, then zipped it and looped it over a shoulder. He raised the last blood bag to his lips and sank his teeth into it.

"Approaching our vehicle." Keys jingled in the background. The chirp of the alarm shutting off carried over the line seconds before a door opened.

"Don't leave," Sean ordered, tossing the empty blood bag aside. "I'm on my way."

"What?" Darius blurted. "You can't—"

"Just keep your ass there!" He redirected the Find My app to Darius's phone. Thankfully, Reordon had given him every special op agent's cell number so he could locate them in an emergency.

Leaving Becca's dorm room, Sean headed for the side entrance that got less traffic. Bright sunlight spilled through the glass door at the end of the hallway. As soon as the app found Darius, Sean stepped outside, glanced around to ensure no one was looking, and shot off at preternatural speeds.

The campus took on a surreal strobe-light quality as he raced in and out of sunlight and shade. Students walking to class only noticed a breeze as he zipped past. Sean's skin began to tingle as he reached the parking lot and spotted the network's black SUV.

He reached it just as the engine started. When he tried the back door, it was locked.

Darius swung around in the driver's seat and gaped at him. Both the woman in the passenger seat and the man in the back jumped and drew weapons.

"Open the fucking door," Sean snarled.

Darius hit the unlock button on the door console.

As soon as Sean heard the telltale *thunk*, he yanked the door open and ducked inside.

"Are you out of your freakin' mind?" Darius snapped.

Sean slammed the door. "Yes. Where are they? Have they left yet?"

The woman—Iris, if he remembered her name correctly—lowered her weapon and shot Darius a triumphant grin. "Ha! I told you they weren't acting. He's totally in love with her. You owe me fifty bucks."

In the rearview mirror, Sean saw Darius roll his eyes as he put the SUV in reverse and backed out of the parking space. "If this op ends up FUBAR, it's on you, Sean."

"I'm okay with that." He grimaced at the sunlight that streamed through his window. "Catch me up."

Iris gave him a rundown of what had happened. Sean seethed when she told him the asshole had hit Nicole in the head with a football. Her returning the favor wasn't enough. When Sean got his hands on him, that bastard was going down.

A screen in the SUV's console displayed a map much like a sat nav would, a blinking dot showing them Nicole's current location.

Sean scooted to the middle of the seat so he could monitor it *and* avoid the sunlight that kept trying to sear him. Feeling eyes on him, he glanced at the soldier beside him and found him smiling. "What?"

"Nothin'," he replied. "It's just... You're my third immortal."

Sean stared at him. "What?"

"I've only ever met two Immortal Guardians, Aidan and Seth. You're my third." He thrust out a hand. "I'm Rick. Nice to meet ya."

Sean shook his hand. "Sean."

"Don't mind him," Darius said over his shoulder. "Rick's new."

"He's one of the *gifted ones* Gershom took but didn't turn," Iris added.

Rick's smile broadened into a grin. "Do you know Dana?"

"Yeah," Sean answered absently.

"We were roomies for a few hours at the base. I had the privilege of getting my ass kicked by her before we escaped."

Sean had no idea what to say to that. "Okay."

Darius laughed.

It sounded like a fun story, but all Sean could think about was Nicole.

The kidnappers drove a dark gray SUV. Darius remained far enough behind it that Sean only glimpsed it twice. When they turned onto a less-traveled road, Darius dropped back even more.

"Don't let them get too far ahead," Sean told him.

"If I get any closer, they'll make us," Darius responded, unperturbed.

Sean ground his teeth. "Damn Reordon for agreeing to this."

"Seth agreed to it, too," Darius pointed out.

Iris sent him a look of sympathy. "She'll be okay, Sean."

"You don't know that."

"They can't use her as bait if she's dead."

"But they can hurt her and threaten to torture her to gain Nick's swift cooperation," he countered.

None of them could deny that, so they opted to remain silent.

Sean didn't know how far they drove, but at least thirty or forty minutes passed.

"Looks like they're heading to a small airport," Darius murmured.

Iris frowned at the map on the screen. "Is it one of the network's?"

The network owned airports?

"No."

Oh, *hell* no! Sean wasn't letting Nicole get on a plane with assholes who may intend to do more than hit her in the head with a football. He opened his backpack, drew out a bag of blood, and sank his fangs into it.

Rick's mouth fell open. "Holy hell. You *do* drink blood."

Darius glanced at them in the rearview. "They don't drink it. Their fangs act like needles and carry the blood directly into their veins."

When Sean sank his fangs into a second bag, Darius's eyes narrowed.

On the third bag, he swore. "Whatever you're thinking about doing, don't."

"I'm not letting her get on a plane with them. We don't know where they'll take her."

"That's the whole point," Darius reminded him. "We need to find out who's running the show. She's still wearing her watch, so we'll track her the whole way."

"And if they ditch her watch?"

"We'll use the tracker Dr. Lipton implanted in her wrist to keep tabs on her."

"And if they get that one, too?"

"They won't."

"You don't know that. These aren't vampires. This wasn't a hasty snatch-and-grab. This was a shrewd, well-orchestrated plan that enabled them to take her in broad daylight on a school day on a college campus full of thousands of students without raising alarms. We don't know how technologically advanced these people may be."

Iris shared a look with Darius. "I don't know. Whatever they knocked her out with sure seemed advanced. One little spritz and she went down. And I think there might have been something on that woman's glove, because Nicole kept looking at her hand after the woman touched her."

A long moment passed.

Darius swore. "Reordon's going to have my ass for this," he muttered. Then he met Sean's eyes in the rearview. "Okay, what's the plan?"

"I'm going with her."

Darius stared at him. "You're just going to show up at the airport? You don't think that'll look suspicious?"

"I'll tell them we had a lovers' quarrel and I tracked her with her watch. If they've been surveilling us, they know I've barely let her out of my sight this past week." Fortunately, he still sported the tattoos, and he'd applied the blond hair wax when he got dressed.

Darius shook his head. "You think they'll let you on the plane with her?"

"If they don't want me making a very loud public scene, they will."

"How do you even expect to reach them? I'm sure all passengers have to pass through the FBO."

Rick frowned. "The what?"

"Fixed Base Operator," Darius supplied, "otherwise known as a terminal."

Sean pointed at the map. "It doesn't look like *they* are."

The vehicle carrying Nicole paused only briefly before circling around to the back of the airport.

Darius frowned. "Whoever is behind this must be as wealthy as Roubal if they can bypass the usual checkpoints."

Iris nodded. "Either that or someone in the SUV is well known there."

"And you don't have that luxury, Sean," Darius pointed out.

"No, I don't," he agreed. "But I do have preternatural speed. No one will see me until I hit the tarmac. Let me out at the end of the drive."

Instead, Darius pulled over to the side of the road half a mile early. "If you run that distance, the sun will blister you. Take the SUV as far as you can." Putting it in park, he turned to the others. "Iris, stay where you are. Anyone who sees you will assume you're his wife or girlfriend dropping him off for a flight. Keep us apprised and—if all goes well—circle back to pick us up."

She nodded.

Darius and Rick thrust their doors open and stepped out.

Sean swiftly ducked out his door and jumped into the driver's seat. "Tell Reordon I shoved you out and took the car."

194

Darius shook his head. "Nope. I lead the team. I make the decisions. Just keep Nicole safe and use that enhanced hearing of yours to pick up every piece of information you can." He closed the door. "You know they won't let you take your phone."

Sean had no difficulty hearing him through the raised window but lowered it a crack so Darius would catch his response. "Seth can track me. Give me time to get on the plane before you call Reordon."

Nodding, Darius stepped back.

Sean put the SUV in drive. But before he could floor it, Darius leaped forward and banged his palm against the door several times.

Sean frowned at him. "What?"

"Don't forget to call her Becca. I know you're upset, so I just thought I should remind you."

*Sheesh.* It was a good thing he had. Sean's thoughts were so scattered that he probably would've blown it and called her Nicole. "Thanks." He stomped on the gas pedal.

Iris said nothing as they raced forward. The little tracking dot on the map halted. Sean's heart pounded as he quickly swung onto the airport's drive. He didn't slow down until he approached the parking lot.

Fewer cars occupied it than he'd hoped. At an airport this size, most probably belonged to employees.

Sean pulled into a space near the others and cut the engine.

A small plane taxied into view on the runway.

"Is that them?" he asked with a touch of panic. Were they already on the plane? They couldn't leave *that* quickly, could they?

"No," Iris said. "They're still stationary."

He glanced at the dot, which didn't move as the plane took off. "Okay, I'm out."

"Good luck. I'll be here if you need me."

"Thank you."

Memorizing Nicole's general location, Sean ducked out of the SUV, closed the door, and took off. The men posted at the checkpoint the vehicle carrying Nicole must have used didn't even look up as he flew past with every ounce of speed he possessed. It took him only seconds to reach the back of the building, where he found a row of hangars and a single runway. Multiple bright white airplanes—ranging from small two-seaters to sleek jets that could carry twenty people—waited in front of the hangars.

Pausing in the shade of the FBO, Sean searched the lineup until he spotted the dark gray SUV parked at the far end near one of the larger jets. Two figures stood on either side of the lowered stairs. Both were big guys, like bouncers at a club. Neither wore pilot uniforms.

Four people emerged from the SUV and headed toward the gleaming white jet. Nicole walked unsteadily beside another woman, who kept an arm wrapped around her. To conceal a weapon pressed to her side, perhaps? They had also removed Nicole's ponytail tie, leaving her long hair to hang down and hide her face. She moved slowly, almost shuffling her feet in a manner that indicated she might still be groggy from whatever sedative they'd administered, while two men brought up the rear.

Sean loped toward them. "Oi!"

The two men in the back—one tall and one short—spun around as the others stopped.

"Oi! Becca!" Thanks to the blood he'd infused himself with, his skin didn't pinken beneath the sun's rays, which puffy clouds dimmed now and again.

"What the hell is this?" one man muttered.

"It's her boyfriend," the woman said, her face creasing with displeasure.

"How did he find us? We ditched her phone."

The woman skimmed Becca with a gaze and swore. "She has one of those damn smartwatches."

Sean slowed to a determined walk as he neared them. Ignoring the others, he focused on Nicole and continued in a British accent, "Are you having a laugh? We have one little row, and you run off to your mum and your new dad? That's bollocks!"

Interminable seconds passed while Nicole stared up at him, weaving slightly on her feet.

The tall man with blond hair and an athletic build wrapped a hand around her biceps. He must be the ass who'd hit her with the football.

A shorter, leaner man with light brown hair closed in on her other side.

"George?" she said finally.

Sean silently breathed a little sigh of relief. The effects of the sedative must be wearing off. He didn't think she would've remembered his fake name if it weren't. "Yeah. What are you doing? And who are these blokes?" He nodded at the men. "They look a bit dodgy if you ask me. Are they Nick's men?"

Everyone perked up at the name.

The woman stepped around the men. "Yes. They're Nick's."

Sean gazed past her at the jet and whistled. "You told me he owned a jet, but I didn't expect it to be so big."

"Do you know Nick?" the woman asked.

He snorted. "Of course I know him. I plan to marry his step-daughter. Nick and I are tight." Sean returned his attention to Nicole. "Look, I know my hovering is making you barmy, but can you blame me? I'm worried about you. You've had two blackouts that the doctors can't explain."

Nicole just groggily blinked up at him.

Sean frowned and reached out to touch her face.

The tall guy grabbed his arm.

Sean looked at the hand gripping his forearm, then at the guy who stood about three inches taller than him. "You're gonna want to remove that hand, mate. Otherwise, you won't be gettin' it back." He nodded toward the ass and asked Nicole, "Who's this prat?"

The woman smiled. "As you said, he's one of Nick's men. During her run, Becca was hit in the head with a football."

"What?"

"It was an accident. But she was on the phone with Nick when it happened. And he wants us to take her to get checked out."

"Not without me, you're not." He addressed the ass again. "And I'm serious about the hand. What's that saying you Americans are so fond of? Move it or lose it?"

"Kent," the woman murmured, steadfastly keeping her smile. "Let the man go."

Kent waited several seconds—each one of which ensured he would get a massive future ass-kicking—and let go. But he didn't release Nicole's arm.

Sean cupped her face in both hands. "Are you okay, luv?"

"She's fine," the woman said. "Just a little out of it. She had another blackout after the football hit her."

"She doesn't *seem* fine. Are you sure it's safe for her to fly?"

"Yes. If you give us your number, we'll keep you informed—"

"Bugger that. I'm comin' with."

Kent took a step toward him that Sean supposed was meant to be menacing. "No, you're not."

"You think so?" Sean got up in his face, not at all intimidated. "Well, there's gonna be a bit of a barney if I don't." He motioned to the FBO behind him. "The kind this hoity-toity place might frown upon, especially when I tell them I'm here to protect my fiancée, who clearly has a concussion. Maybe I'll tell them she isn't here of her own free will. Maybe I'll tell them you *gave* her the concussion. What do you think they'll make of that?"

"Kent," the woman said, her smile tight, "stand down. George... That *is* your name, isn't it?"

"Yes."

"George, Mr. Belanger didn't mention you accompanying us. I'm afraid we can't let anyone on the plane without preapproval."

Sean drew out his cell phone. "No worries. I'll call Nick and get it."

"You have his number?"

"Yeah."

The woman placed a hand on his phone to keep him from making the call. "You know what? That won't be necessary. As you said, you're close to the family. Becca isn't objecting. So you may accompany us. But you'll have to turn your phone's cellular service off, shut it down, and let us hold on to it during the flight. It messes with the pilot's instruments, and we can't risk you forgetting and making a call."

His skin began to prickle as he turned off his cell and handed it over. Giving Kent a shove to dislodge his hold on Nicole, he took the man's place at her side and wrapped an arm around her. "Shall we go then?"

After giving Kent a pointed look, the woman turned and led the way to the stairs.

Sean urged Nicole to climb them in front of him so he could catch her if she tripped on a step and fell. She didn't seem to be too steady on her feet but made it safely inside.

The two pilots in the cockpit barely spared them a glance as they conducted whatever tasks pilots must prior to takeoff. The interior of the jet was the height of luxury. A couple of inches above six feet, Sean could walk down the center aisle without ducking.

They passed through a swanky galley into the passenger area. The most comfortable seats he'd ever seen flanked a center aisle. Two of them faced the back of the plane. Two more faced forward, creating a little conversation area. Behind those, more opulent furniture created a larger gathering space. A long sofa and two chairs formed a U around a sleek coffee table. Across from them, two men occupied cushy chairs parked on either side of a large-screen television. Both men wore blazers that gaped a little as they rose, revealing holstered weapons.

These guys looked like hired guns.

*Experienced* hired guns.

Beyond the TV area lay a hallway with an open door on one side that probably led to a bathroom. The short hallway ended at a second open door that revealed...

He stared. Was that a king-sized bed?

Kent, his buddy, and the woman crowded in behind him as Sean guided Nicole down the aisle.

Pausing, Nicole turned and started to say something. When she looked past him, her eyes widened.

Something hard connected with the back of his head.

Pain careened through his skull.

Sean staggered forward a step. Fury rising, he was about to spin around and go medieval on Kent's ass—he just *knew* that was the bastard who hit him—when Nicole touched his arm and gave her head a barely discernible shake.

Oh. Right. He was supposed to be human.

*Damn it.*

Forcing his body to go limp, Sean gritted his teeth as the floor rushed up to meet him.

# CHAPTER TWELVE

N ICOLE CRIED OUT AS Sean collapsed like a ton of bricks, his poor head thudding against the floor. Her thoughts were so muddled by whatever the hell that woman had sprayed in her face that she almost slipped and called him by his real name. "George!" It *was* George, wasn't it? What the hell had been in that spray?

The pilots spun around in their seats.

"This doesn't concern you," the woman snapped. "Just get us out of here."

As they turned away, she slammed the cabin door.

Kent wouldn't let Nicole lean down and touch Sean. Grabbing her arm in a meaty fist, he shoved her into the nearest seat and reached for the seatbelt.

Nicole batted his hands away, knowing he was the kind of asshole who would touch more than the seatbelt if given the opportunity. "What are you doing? Don't touch me! Get away from me!"

The woman stepped over Sean. "I'll do that. You take care of George."

Kent's resentful scowl confirmed Nicole's guess as he reluctantly backed away.

The woman took his place and swiftly buckled Nicole's seatbelt.

"What's happening?" Nicole asked, her thick tongue making her sound as drunk as she felt.

"Everything's going to be okay, Becca." Those words would be a lot more reassuring if she hadn't delivered them without emotion. "I work for a very important man who is interested in getting in touch with your new stepdaddy."

"Nick?"

"Yes. And you're going to help us do that."

"Why didn't you just call him?"

"Because we haven't been able to obtain his phone number. And he hasn't returned to his home in Houston in months."

They'd been surveilling Nick's house? Surely they must know Roubal then.

Marge held a hand out to Kent. "Give me her phone."

He handed it over.

Marge held it out to Nicole. "Unlock it."

When she reached for it, Marge shook her head. "No. I'll hold it. I know these phones can summon emergency services, and we can't have that, can we? Just unlock it."

Nicole tapped in her password.

Marge turned the phone so she could view the screen.

Kent looked at it. "What are you doing?"

"Disabling the lock screen feature, turning off cellular, and turning on airplane mode so she can't be tracked."

A moment passed. "There it is. Nick Belanger's number. Her mother's, too."

Nicole's personal cell phone, which had a slew of phone numbers the network wanted to keep private, was actually back at Sean's house. The one she'd carried as Becca held far fewer numbers, mainly those that belonged to Kayla, Nick, *George*, two members of the special ops team, several restaurants that delivered, and a dozen or so burner phones the network had listed under random names these idiots would mistake for friends.

Marge tucked the phone into a blazer pocket. "Take care of the boyfriend."

Kent grabbed one of Sean's arms, hoisted him up, and dropped him in the chair across from Nicole's.

Sean's head lolled. Was he really unconscious?

He sure looked like he was, but she didn't think a blow to the head delivered with human strength would really knock an immortal out.

When Kent released Sean so he could buckle the seatbelt, Sean slumped forward and smushed his face into the other man's chest.

Swearing, Kent righted him. But as soon as he let go and looked away, Sean slumped forward again. This time, his face landed in the curve of the man's neck, almost like a lover nuzzling him.

Kent jerked away and shoved Sean back against the chair with a little more force. After holding him there for several seconds, he cautiously let go.

Sean remained in place until Kent turned his attention to the seatbelt. Then Sean slumped forward again.

"Damn it!"

Despite her pounding head, Nicole fought the urge to laugh. Sean was definitely awake.

"Oh, for Pete's sake!" Marge blurted. "Let me do it."

Kent held Sean in place while Marge buckled his seatbelt. Then the two of them followed the shorter guy to the large seating area behind Nicole.

Though Sean didn't fold forward this time, his chin almost touched his chest. As she peered at him, she could've sworn his lips twitched.

Unbelievable. Even when she was drugged and in enemy hands, he could make her smile.

Nicole wasn't sure how much time passed before the jet taxied onto the runway and took off. The ground beneath them fell away, and soon they soared through puffy white clouds.

Sean used the motion and pressure of takeoff as an excuse to tilt his head back against the seat.

Grimacing at the increased pressure in her ears, Nicole studied the light that passed through the windows. Thank goodness she and Sean were on the shady side. If sunlight poured through their windows the way it did through those on the opposite side of the aisle, Sean would've pinkened, then blistered with a sunburn. And the ruse would've ended abruptly.

Her head began to clear. If the sun shone on the other side of the jet, that meant they were traveling south. Or maybe southwest?

"It's Marge," the woman said behind her. "We have her."

Was she talking to the ringleader?

Nicole wondered absently if Reordon and the network could uncover the head honcho's identity simply by finding out who owned this jet and seeing if the pilot had filed a flight schedule with the FBO.

"There was a complication. Her boyfriend showed up just as we were boarding the plane," Marge continued. "She had one of those smartwatches, and he followed us."

Fingers snapped. Then the shorter guy appeared at Nicole's side. Looking up at him, she feigned lingering drunkenness. "What—?"

Without saying a word, he grabbed her arm, yanked it up, and started prying her watch off with clumsy fingers. As soon as he freed it, he dropped the watch to the floor and stomped on it with enough relish to hint that he expected some kind of reaction from her.

Nicole feigned dismay and mumbled something about it having been a birthday present.

Smiling with malignant pleasure, he took a moment to ensure Sean didn't have a smartwatch, too, before he returned to the others.

"No," Marge said. "Apparently, they had a lovers' quarrel, and he assumed she was running home to Mommy. He thinks we work for Belanger and that this is *his* jet. ... I don't know. ... I know nothing about him other than that he's been sticking pretty close to her since she returned to the dorm. ... She doesn't appear to remember anything of the previous attacks. And I don't think Belanger filled her in. She believes she's been having blackouts. ... He's here on the plane with us. ... It was unavoidable. He threatened to make a scene if we didn't let him accompany us. But there *is* an upside. He claims he's tight with Belanger. He and the girl are engaged. So it looks like we now have twice the bait. ... Yes, sir. ... That's what I was thinking. ... Yes, sir."

Kent and the other guy murmured to each other.

"Yes, sir. I'll call you as soon as we land."

Rustling sounded.

"Is he pissed?" Kent asked.

"Well, he isn't happy," Marge replied. "He isn't convinced that the girl knows nothing of Belanger's *uniqueness*. He thinks the boyfriend could help us there."

Kent chuckled. "Torture the Brit in front of her, and she'll spill everything she knows."

"Exactly. Now get your ass on the internet and see what you can find out about George."

"Hey," Kent called. "What's your boyfriend's last name?"

Nicole opted not to respond.

A sigh sounded. Soft footsteps approached. Then Marge stood beside her. "Enough of the sedative should've worn off by now for you to have an inkling of the position you're in," she stated matter-of-factly. "As long as you cooperate, I'll be your friend. Refuse, and Kent and Rylan will be your new friends. Piss me off, and I'll join the pilots in the cabin and ignore whatever sounds come from back here while Kent and Rylan convince you to play nice. My employer only told us to bring you in alive. He didn't specify what condition you should be in."

"Davies," Nicole blurted, borrowing the name of one of the dorm residents. "George Davies. The third."

Rylan snorted a laugh. "More like turd."

Marge frowned. "Oh, would you grow the hell up?"

Kent laughed. "Ask her where he's from."

Marge stared down at Nicole. "Well?"

"London," she improvised.

Marge cast Sean a glance. "You forgot to restrain him, Einstein. He's going to be a problem when he wakes up. Bind his hands."

As Marge rejoined the others, a new voice muttered, "Amateurs. Here. Use these."

Kent arrived and slipped some white zip ties onto Sean's wrists. After tightening them enough to cut off the circulation to Sean's hands, he left.

Minutes ticked past. Since Nicole no longer had a watch and could spy no clocks within view, she didn't know how many. The sounds of an Avengers movie filled the cabin. *Endgame* was her guess. Nicole listened to the scenes play out and tried to use that as a time estimator.

Half an hour?

An hour?

Marge spoke suddenly. "Have you found anything?"

DIANNE DUVALL

"Yeah," Rylan replied sullenly. "We found out there's a shitload of Georges in England."

"Doesn't his last name narrow it down?" she asked impatiently.

"No," Kent said, "because there's a shitload of Davies, too."

"Well, use her social media profiles to figure out which one it is," she ordered.

"We tried," Rylan said. "But Becca doesn't post any personal information on her profiles. Just a bunch of cutesy cat videos and shit like that."

Kent laughed. "Did you see the one with the cat attacking the alligator?"

"Yeah. That was hilarious."

Marge released a long-suffering sigh. "Just stay focused and keep looking. I'm sure our employer has a team working on this, but it would be nice if we could find something they can't."

Nicole thought it interesting that she didn't mention their employer by name. Was that for her and Sean's benefit? Or did the others not know whom they worked for?

"We're on it," Kent promised.

"I'm going to go make some calls in the bedroom," Marge announced. "Leave the girl alone until I say otherwise."

That sparked a few grumbles, but these guys seemed to knuckle under pretty quickly whenever Marge told them to do something. She was clearly the highest-ranked member of the team.

A door closed.

Kent and Rylan muttered a few disrespectful comments they were too afraid to say to her face. The other men remained quiet and just kept watching the Avengers movie.

Another half hour crept past.

Sean's boot moved.

Nicole glanced at it before peering at his face.

His eyelids were parted just enough for her to glimpse a hint of his brown eyes. As soon as he saw her looking at him, he winked.

Since her back was to the others, she gave him a faint smile.

Movement in his lap drew her attention. Though his wrists were tightly bound, the fingers of his right hand formed the sign language letters O and K.

Meeting his gaze, she gave a slight nod. "My head hurts." Nicole spoke so softly that the others couldn't hear her over the engine noise. But Sean should catch her words. "And my mind is still sluggish."

His jaw tightened. Amber light brightened his eyes before he closed them.

After a few seconds, he cracked his lids just enough to show his eyes no longer glowed.

"We gotta narrow this down," Rylan muttered. "This is taking forever. Try his phone again."

"I can't," Kent grumbled. "It's password protected."

"Hey!" Rylan called. "What's the password to your boyfriend's phone?"

Nicole said nothing.

"*Hey!*" he shouted. "Becca! I'm talking to you. What's the password to George's phone?"

"I don't know," she lied. While *her* phone was a plant given to her by the network, Sean's wasn't. Sean's contained the phone numbers of every Immortal Guardian stationed in North Carolina; their addresses; and the numbers of their Seconds, Chris Reordon, and all the special ops team members. She couldn't let these people get their hands on that information.

"What?" Kent called back.

"I don't know," she repeated, louder this time.

"Bullshit."

"No, it isn't," she retorted. "I never asked. I didn't want George to think I don't trust him."

"Then when's your boy's birthday?"

They wouldn't believe her if she feigned ignorance of that, too. Sean had said they were engaged. Couples that close would know each other's birthday, so Nicole pulled a random date out of the air. "April fifth."

"What year?" Rylan asked.

Her mind blanked.

"What year?" he repeated with more force.

She performed a quick calculation that would make Sean a little older than he was and blurted a year.

207

Mutters sounded.

A few minutes later, Kent appeared at her side.

Nicole looked up at him. "What?"

"This is bullshit." He thrust Sean's phone toward her. "Unlock it."

She shook her head. "I told you—"

"You're lying," he accused, expression darkening. "Every girl-friend I ever had gave me shit if I didn't tell her my password. They assumed I wouldn't do it because I was texting another woman."

"Because you were," Rylan called jovially.

Kent's face lit with arrogant satisfaction. "Hell yes, I was." Then he shoved the phone at Nicole. "Unlock it."

"I'm not lying. I—"

Kent took her hands in a bruising grip and forced them around the phone. As soon as she held it, he grabbed her face with one hand. His thumb dug into her right cheek. His fingers dug into her left as he leaned in close. "Unlock his phone," he ordered, his voice low, "or I will fuck you up."

Nicole's heartbeat quickened. If this asshole hurt her in any way, Sean would tear him limb from limb, and things would go sideways. Fast.

Pasting a terrified look on her face, she spoke in a tremulous voice. "Marge said—"

His grip tightened painfully. "Marge is sleeping and won't hear a thing."

Was she really? Or was he bullshitting?

Nicole opened her mouth and called, "Mar—!"

The hand on her face swiftly shifted to cover her mouth. "You stupid bitch," he hissed. "If you want someone here to be your friend, let's see how much you like being mine." His gaze dropped to her chest.

As soon as his free hand reached toward her breasts, Nicole clenched Sean's phone tightly and drove it up into Kent's chin as hard as she could.

Kent grunted as the device made contact. His head jerked up. Stumbling backward, he raised a hand to his mouth.

"Kent?" Rylan called, sounding more alert. "What're you doing? You okay?"

When Kent drew his fingers away from his mouth, they were slick with blood. "I bit my thongue," he cried incredulously. Face mottling, he glared down at her. "You bith!" Drawing back his arm, he swung.

Nicole tried to dodge to the side, but the seatbelt left her little maneuvering room. Pain exploded through her head as his fist made contact. It wasn't as hard a hit as it would've been if she hadn't tried to avoid it, but it still hurt like hell and rang her bell.

"Damn it, Kent!" Rylan hissed.

Momentarily stunned, Nicole raised a hand to her head. She'd thought he meant to slap her. Instead, the bastard had punched her!

Her eyes widened.

Wait. He had punched her?

She glanced at Sean

His brown eyes flashed with amber fire. The muscles in his arms bulged. The zip ties snapped and fell away.

*Oh crap.*

Sean rocketed from his seat. Several thuds and yelps sounded before Nicole could even register that he and Kent weren't beside her anymore. She turned to peek around the high back of her chair.

Kent was down on his hands and knees in the aisle, blood gushing from his nose and mouth as he wheezed and gasped for air. Sean tore through the rest of the cabin like the Tasmanian Devil. One of the unnamed hired goons collapsed to the floor in front of the big-screen television, his face a mangled mess from Sean's punches. The other slumped onto the sofa.

Neither moved, but she didn't think they were dead.

While explosions played out on the television screen, Sean knocked out Rylan, who had leaped to his feet.

Kent drew a handgun from the back of his pants.

Sean pounced and knocked it out of his hand.

*Wow.* Sean proceeded to beat the crap out of the taller man.

No match for Sean's enhanced speed or strength, Kent couldn't even call for help. It was like watching one of David's cats toy with a mouse it had caught.

*Well,* she thought with satisfaction, *the dumbass shouldn't have laid a hand on me.*

Sean yanked the battered man back against his chest and sank his fangs into his neck. Kent's eyes, already beginning to swell, widened as much as they could, then closed. His struggles ceased.

Nicole unbuckled her seatbelt and rose. Still clutching Sean's phone, she stepped into the aisle. When a sudden bout of dizziness struck, she grabbed the seat headrest with her free hand to steady herself.

Sean dropped Kent, stepped over his prone form, and strode forward. As soon as he was within reach, he swept her into a tight hug. "Are you okay?" he asked hoarsely.

The raw emotion in his voice made her want to cry. Wrapping her arms around him, she rested her head on his chest. "Yes."

"You're sure?"

She nodded. "I didn't expect him to punch me. I thought he would slap me."

Loosening his hold, Sean allowed just enough space between them to look down at her. "I should've taken him out sooner."

"That wasn't the plan."

"You getting hurt wasn't the plan either," he countered furiously.

No. But they'd all known it was a possibility. "Honestly," she said, hoping to quell his anger, "I expected Rylan or one of the others to step in." When he opened his mouth, she held up a hand. "Quietly, please. We don't want to wake Marge. And my head is killing me."

Worry furrowed his brow. "Marge isn't sleeping." Gently taking her by the chin, he encouraged her to look away so he could study the side of her head. He brushed the hair above her ear up without touching the place where Kent's fist had made contact. "He didn't break the skin. But this is going to swell."

"It was more of a glancing blow."

"If I had my blades, I'd cut his fucking hand off."

She smiled.

Releasing her chin, he tunneled his fingers through her hair and felt the back of her head.

When he touched the place where the football had struck her, she winced. "Yeah, that hurts."

Several more curses poured forth. "There's a lump. Do you have a concussion?"

"I don't think so. I'm a little dizzy. But that's probably from whatever drug they gave me, because I'm still not thinking quickly."

He cupped her face in his hands. Smoothing his thumbs over her cheeks, he studied her carefully. "Your pupils are dilated."

"That explains the blurry vision."

The amber light in his eyes brightened. "I'm going to kill him."

"Who, Kent?"

"Yeah."

"Well, you won't hear any objections from me. If Marge hadn't insisted on buckling my seatbelt, he would've groped me. I saw it in his eyes."

A growl escaped Sean as he turned to face the downed man.

Nicole grabbed his arm. "Hold on there, tiger. That can wait. Right now, we have a situation." She motioned to the unconscious men, all of whom still lived. "We've gone and messed up the plan again."

"*We* didn't." He pointed at Kent. "*He* did."

"True. So what now, *George*?" She forced a smile. "By the way, could you have worked *any* more Britishisms into your speech?"

He laughed. "No. Those were all I had."

She would've shaken her head if it didn't ache so much. "Where did you even learn so many?"

"Network headquarters. One of the med techs is British. And Bastien spouts them every once in a while."

Nicole took in the splayed bodies and spattering of blood. "Well, crap."

"No one will blame us for this."

"I know." Even the special ops team had been told to step in if it looked like she was in danger. "Wait. Marge isn't sleeping?"

"No. After she left, Marge made some calls, just like she said."

"You could hear that over the engine noise and the television?"

"Yes."

She studied him. "And?"

"They weren't going to torture me to get you to talk."

"Good."

DIANNE DUVALL

"They were going to torture *you* to get *me* to talk."

"What?"

"I was more convincing than I thought when I told them I was tight with Nick. They figured I knew whatever you did and thought hurting you in front of me would get them the answers they needed faster."

She scowled. "So they thought *I* would be okay with them torturing *you* but *you* wouldn't be okay with them torturing *me*? What kind of crap is that?"

"That isn't all."

"What else?"

"While they waited to see if Nick would meet them at a designated rendezvous site, they intended to study you like a lab rat to see if you're like him."

"If I were like Nick, the drug they used wouldn't have affected me."

"They don't know that. They know it wouldn't affect a vampire. But all they know about Nick is that he doesn't age and hasn't gone insane the way vampires do."

"So they know vampires go crazy?"

"Yeah. They think Nick might be infected with a different strain of the same virus. One that behaves differently. One that's a success. They're speculating that it was created in a lab. They think that the one the vampires have is the flawed first effort and the one Nick got is the prize."

She frowned. "Poor Becca. Thank goodness they took me instead."

He sent her a half smile and gave her cheek an affectionate stroke. "Yeah. You kick ass."

"I didn't today," she said with a grimace.

His smile widened. "Are you kidding? You made that bastard bite through his tongue and would've taken him down if I hadn't butted in."

"Damn straight." She said it for Sean's benefit but seriously doubted it. That drug had really done a number on her. "So now what?"

The door to the bedroom opened. Marge emerged, her head down, staring at her phone. "You need to turn the volume down. Or better yet, turn the TV off. What have you found on—?" She glanced up. Eyes widening, she stopped short.

Sean grinned and tossed her a wave. "'ello, luv," he said, his British accent back in place.

When the woman gaped at the four downed men, Sean shrugged. "Sorry for the mess." He pointed at Kent. "That prat there tried to put his hands on Becca. I couldn't allow that, so I taught him and the other blokes some manners."

Marge hastily reached into her jacket.

Crossing the cabin in a flash, Sean grabbed her hand and confiscated a 9mm. "I'm going to have to take that." He snatched the phone from her other hand. "Your phone, too."

"How did you do that?" she whispered. "How did you move so fast?"

"*I'm* asking the questions now. And I'll tell you what you told Becca. If you cooperate, I'll be your friend. If you don't..." His expression turned so menacing that even Nicole felt a chill. "Well. Dead women don't need friends, do they?"

Swallowing hard, she shook her head.

"Who's your boss?"

"If I tell you, he'll kill me."

"Perhaps," he responded darkly. "But he'll probably be quick about it—a shot to the head or some such. *I*, on the other hand, will draw it out. Everything you and your people planned to do to Becca to make me talk?" He stepped closer to her, so she had to crane her neck to look up at him. "That's nothing compared to what I'll do to you."

Her face paled. "I don't deal with him directly."

"Bollocks. I heard you talking to him."

"That wasn't him. It was his henchman."

"And the henchman's name is?"

"Alan Danvers."

"And who's your boss?"

"I told you. He'll kill me if I tell you."

"So you want *me* to kill you instead?" Sean shook his head. "I thought you were smarter than that."

She swallowed hard. "He'll kill Kent if I tell you."

"Good. Kent deserves to die."

She stiffened. "Kent's my son."

Nicole stared.

"Bollocks," Sean protested again.

Though she trembled, Marge raised her chin. "It's true."

"Well, you did a piss-poor job of raising him."

Her lips tightened. "Maybe, but I'd die to protect him."

Sean tilted his head to one side. "If you'd die to protect him, then I'm guessing you'll tell me the truth to keep me from torturing his sorry arse."

She paled.

"And you should know..." Sean leaned in closer. "I don't make threats I won't follow through on."

"I can't," she insisted.

Sean remained silent for a moment. "Take your blazer off."

She paled. "What?"

"Take it off."

Hands shaking, Marge discarded her blazer. Beneath it, she wore a sleeveless blouse.

Sean set the phone and gun on the coffee table. Straightening, he parted his lips and let his fangs descend.

Her eyes widened once more. "Oh shit."

When she stumbled backward, Sean grabbed her arm to stop her. Dipping his head, he sank his fangs into her neck.

Marge winced and struggled briefly before the chemical released by the glands above his fangs kicked in. It didn't take long. Her eyelids drooped as she stood meekly in his grasp.

Sean lifted his head. "Who do you work for?"

"Work for?" she repeated groggily.

"Come on, luv. You know you want to tell me. Who do you work for?"

"Augustus Benford."

Triumph lit Sean's features. "Wait here." Leaving her, he returned to Nicole's side and abandoned his British accent. "I have a new plan."

"You do?"

He gave her shoulder a squeeze, then slid his hand down past her elbow. Raising her forearm, Sean gently ran his fingers over the inside of her wrist.

"What are you doing?"

"Feeling for the tracker."

Nicole pointed to a spot on the back of her wrist where she'd worn her watch. "It's right there. I watched Melanie implant it."

"There's no mark."

"Seth healed it afterward so there wouldn't be."

Parting his lips, he let his fangs descend again. "This is going to hurt a little."

Her pulse fluttered nervously. "Okay."

Raising her wrist to his mouth, he dragged one sharp fang across her flesh.

Nicole winced as a shallow cut opened.

Sean swiftly lifted his head. "Sorry."

Nodding, she tried not to wince as he applied pressure to her skin and—as gently as possible—forced the tiny tracker out of her flesh. "You know that's the only way the network can track me without my phone and watch, right?"

"I know." He pinched the tracker between his thumb and forefinger. "Put some pressure on that to stop the bleeding."

She started to do as he suggested but realized she still held his phone. "Here."

Taking it, he stuffed it in a back pocket and headed back to Marge.

Nicole covered her wrist with the tail of her shirt and applied pressure.

"Open your mouth," he ordered.

Blood trailed down Marge's neck from the puncture wounds. After an owlish blink, she parted her lips.

Sean placed the tracker in her mouth. Grabbing a bottle of water off the coffee table, he handed it to her. "Swallow it."

Weaving on her feet, Marge took the bottle from him, tilted her head back, and gulped down several swallows.

"Show me," Sean said when she returned the bottle.

She opened her mouth.

Nicole couldn't see inside it from her position. "Did she swallow it?"

"Yeah."

Marge's eyes rolled back in her head as her knees buckled.

Sean caught her and turned to settle her in one of the cushy seats.

Nicole cast the cockpit door a nervous glance while he buckled the woman in. "Did biting Marge make her compliant like that?" The vampire victims Nicole had seen firsthand had all been unconscious or dead. She hadn't realized they could become that malleable when under the influence.

"Yes. It will also ensure she won't remember what happened. If we're lucky, the last thing she'll be able to recall is heading into the bedroom." He picked up Marge's phone. "Good. The screen hasn't locked yet."

"What are you doing?"

"Disabling the lock screen and turning the cell service off." Once done, he pocketed the phone. Squatting beside Rylan, he grabbed the unconscious man's arm, drew his wrist to his mouth, and sank his fangs in.

Nicole cast the cockpit another look. "Do you think they heard anything?" Sean's brief battle with the men hadn't been a silent one. Marge had blamed the noise on the television. Had the pilots done the same?

Sean dropped Rylan's arm. "I don't think those pilots are new to trips like this. Neither of them protested when Kent bashed me in the back of the head. I assume it was Kent?"

"Yes."

"I'm sure they're paid well enough to keep their attention and thoughts on flying the plane and let whatever happens in back happen."

"What total A-holes."

"Yeah." He drew the other blazer guy's wrist to his lips.

Nicole took a step toward him. "Sean? Are you okay? Did they hurt you? You're taking a lot of blood." She hadn't thought he'd sustained any injuries during the fight. But if he needed this large an infusion...

He didn't respond until he dropped the man's arm. "I'm not injured. The virus used all the blood I infused myself with earlier to keep the sun from roasting me. So I'm tanking up."

"Tanking up for what? What exactly is the plan, Sean?" Fight their way free from whoever would be waiting for them when they landed?

He rose and strode toward her. "I think we can salvage this." Taking her hand, he drew her into his arms, lowered his head, and took her lips in a deep, devouring kiss that instantly kicked her heartbeat into overdrive.

Wrapping her arms around him, Nicole kissed him back for all she was worth, happy he was okay and so grateful that he was there with her, even if it meant Reordon might go ballistic.

"You scared the hell out of me," he whispered. "When the special ops team told me you'd been taken..." His brown eyes brightened again with amber light.

Her heart melted. "I know. I'm sorry."

He kissed her again, softer this time. "Don't ever scare me like that again."

"I'll try not to."

Smiling, he released her. "Okay. Here's the plan." Sean took out his cell phone and held a button down to get it to boot up. "Once the cellular is back on, I'll call Seth. He'll pick up Aidan and teleport him here to the plane. Aidan will take your place as Becca. I'll resume my role as the dashing love interest, George Davies."

"Very dashing."

He motioned to the unconscious men. "Seth can heal these assholes and alter their memories. Then he can teleport you to safety while Aidan and I continue to our destination."

She stared at him. "That's actually not bad."

He grinned. "I know. I'm brilliant, aren't I?"

Her lips twitched. "And so modest. There's only one problem, hotshot."

DIANE DUVALL

Glancing down at his phone, he unlocked the screen. "What's that?"

"When they torture Aidan-slash-Becca to get you to talk, won't they notice that his wounds heal almost as quickly as they inflict them?"

He waved away her concern. "I'll fold long before they do anything that would leave a mark." A second later, his face twisted into an anguished mask as he linked his fingers in a prayer position around his phone. "Please," he begged, folding forward. "Don't hurt her." His breath hitched in a sob. "I'll tell you anything," he cried in a spectacular demonstration of overacting. "*Anything.*" More sobs. "Just please don't hurt her." Straightening, he smiled.

Nicole grinned. "Okay. But you're going to have to dial that back a bit."

Laughing, he unlocked his phone.

A gunshot rang out.

Nicole jumped as blood spurted from Sean's chest.

Warm liquid splattered her face.

What the hell?

# CHAPTER THIRTEEN

P AIN ERUPTING IN HIS chest, Sean pushed Nicole down behind the dubious shelter of the seats and swung to face the threat.

A second gunshot rang out.

The bullet pierced his arm before Sean could dodge it and passed right through. Eyes widening, he glanced over his shoulder.

The bullet plowed into the door to the cockpit a few inches from the first... and stopped without penetrating it.

Oh. Right. Terrorism. The door must be reinforced with steel.

Only partly relieved, Sean faced forward.

The bastard he'd left unconscious on the sofa squinted up at him through two swelling eyes. One arm clung to the sofa's seatbelt while he aimed a 357 SIG with the other.

"Are you crazy?" Sean blurted as he raised his hands in surrender, his phone still gripped in one. "We're on a plane!" If he took a single step toward the man, he knew the idiot would shoot again.

Sean thought furiously.

"I saw what you did," the man said through puffy lips. "You're not gonna get me, vampire."

His finger tightened on the trigger.

*Oh shit!*

The gun fired. Sean dove toward Nicole as glass broke behind them.

A thunderous BOOM filled the plane a split second before hurricane-force winds tugged at him.

Two steps away, Nicole screamed as she rose off the floor and flew toward the broken window.

Sean locked an arm around her waist and grabbed a seat to halt their flight, thankful for his enhanced strength.

Laptops, water bottles, and everything else that wasn't fastened down flew past them. Kent, Rylan, and the other guard did, too, partially plugging the hole in the window.

Oxygen masks dropped from the ceiling.

The shooter clung madly to the sofa's seatbelt and fired his gun again.

Sean looked around frantically and spotted the emergency exit a couple of yards away. "Wrap your legs around me!" he shouted over the howl of the wind, and lunged toward it.

Nicole turned in his hold and locked her arms and legs around him as he grabbed the handle with his free hand. Muscles straining, Sean operated the lever and forced the door open.

Wind reached in and yanked them out of the plane.

Sean held on tight to Nicole and made damn sure they weren't sucked into the engine.

Icy wind buffeted them. The air was freezing! Cold enough to frost his breath and swiftly spawn frostbite.

In the blink of an eye, he called on his ability to alter his body temperature and heated up like a freaking furnace to warm Nicole as he tried to cover as much of her body as possible instead of adopting a spread-eagle skydiver's position.

Nicole whimpered as they free-fell through the clouds. "We don't have parachutes!"

Neither did Kent, Rylan, or the guards, all of whom plummeted toward the ground some distance away, having been sucked out of the larger opening he'd provided. The shooter was the last to fall.

He must not have been able to hold on.

Once Sean and Nicole passed through a bank of clouds, he got his first glimpse of the ground *far* beneath them. Time was short. Breathing grew difficult. Too little oxygen.

Nicole would pass out within seconds from hypoxia.

Heart racing, he peered over Nicole's shoulder at the phone he still held in a death grip. Careful not to let the wind drag it from his grasp, he dialed.

"Yes?" a deep voice answered.

"Seth!" he shouted. "Come now! Come now!"

Seth appeared beside them an instant later. His eyes widened as he seemed to hover in place for a second before gravity started dragging him down. By then, Sean and Nicole had fallen quite a bit farther than him.

Flattening his arms against his sides, Seth rocketed toward them headfirst.

Nicole's hold on Sean weakened as she began to lose consciousness.

"Hold on, honey," he urged.

"Love you," she murmured.

Just before Seth reached them, his form shifted into that of a massive dragon.

Sean gaped as the beast reached down and wrapped them in a huge taloned grasp.

Warmth immediately suffused them. Oxygen filled their starving lungs.

Nicole's hold tightened as she drew in great gulps of air.

When the dragon spread its wings, their descent halted so abruptly that Sean would have lost his hold on her if he weren't so strong.

Those wings swept down and up again to keep them stationary.

Nicole looked up to see what had halted their fall.

Her jaw dropped.

Sean had never seen her so flabbergasted and couldn't help but smile.

In the blink of an eye, the clouds above them changed, as did the countryside below.

Sean glanced down. They now hovered above David's backyard in North Carolina.

Beneath them, Sheldon was waving a large bubble wand in an arc. When the dragon's shadow fell upon him, he paused. The two toddlers chasing bubbles stopped and looked up. Both grinned and squealed with delight as the majestic beast slowly descended toward the lawn.

Sheldon grinned, too. "That. Is. *Awesome!*" he cried, as excited as the children.

The dragon gently lowered Sean to the ground and released him.

Still clinging to Sean's neck, Nicole let her legs slide down until her feet touched the ground. Her whole body shook violently against his. And when she pried her arms from around his neck and slid her hands down to his chest, she fisted them in his shirt as though she weren't confident her legs would support her.

Sean wondered if his face was as pale as hers. He felt pretty shaky himself. That had been close. *Too* close. If one of those bullets had hit her in the head...

If he hadn't caught her in time to keep her from being sucked out the window...

If he hadn't kicked off the wing to keep them from being drawn into the engine...

His hands trembled as he ran them up and down her back.

The dragon landed some distance away, its enormous wings brushing the trees on either side of the meadow.

Both children raced toward it.

"Baba!" Adira cried happily.

Making a chuffing noise, the dragon blew bubbles out of its nose.

Sean laughed, giddy with relief.

Giggling wildly, the toddlers danced around and climbed over the beast's massive talons and tail.

After observing them for a moment, Nicole looked up at Sean. "Did we die?" she asked cautiously. "Is this like 'An Occurrence at Owl Creek Bridge,' and I only *think* we got away?"

Smiling, he hugged her tight. "No. We didn't die. That's Seth."

The dragon looked over at Sheldon.

Sheldon jogged forward. "Okay, cuties. Step back and give Baba some room." Expertly fielding their protests, he shepherded the children away from the dragon.

As soon as they were clear, the dragon shifted into Seth's form, complete with clothing he teleported on so the little ones wouldn't see him naked.

Seth took a moment to kneel and hug the children. When he rose, he eyed Sean balefully. "Seriously? You jumped out of a jet without a parachute?"

"Dude!" Sheldon exclaimed, gaping at them. "That is *so*—"

Seth shot him a glare.

"Unwise," Sheldon said hastily. "That is *so* very unwise. Come on, kiddos. Let's head inside."

Seth waited until the three of them were alone, then focused a sharp gaze on Sean. "Well?"

Sean shrugged. "I didn't have a choice."

Shaking his head, Seth drew out his cell phone, dialed, and put it on speaker.

"Reordon."

"I'm with Sean and Nicole," Seth said without preamble. "Looks like the plan has gone balls-up."

Chris loosed an epithet. "What happened?"

"I don't know the details yet, but the two of them just bailed out of a jet mid-flight without parachutes."

More swears on the other end.

"Sean called me. I had to shift into the form of a dragon to catch them, so..."

"I'll have my guys watch for anything to show up on the internet," Chris said with resignation. "What about the plane? Did it crash?"

"Not that I know of." He looked at Sean. "Were the engines damaged?"

"No. They should be intact." Everyone who was ejected from the plane had missed them. "Chris can use the tracker Melanie implanted in Nicole to locate the plane. The leader of the group that took her was a woman named Marge. I cut the tracker out of Nicole and made Marge swallow it. Then I buckled her into a seat and intended to call you to help me salvage things. I just didn't have a chance."

"Did you get that?" Seth asked.

"Yes," Reordon said. "Anyone else still on the plane?"

"Just the pilots," Sean replied. "The others were sucked out with us."

"Seth, did the pilots see you shift?" Reordon asked.

"I doubt it. We were beneath the clouds, and they were above them, dealing with a catastrophic decompression."

"Okay. Give me a few minutes to put my team on this, then come get me."

"All right. See you in a few." He pocketed his phone.

Nicole crossed to Seth and gave him a big hug. "Thank you."

His face lighting with an affectionate smile, he hugged her back. "You're welcome."

As soon as she stepped back, Sean took her place and wrapped Seth in a bear hug. "Thank you. Is Nicole okay?"

Seth patted his back. "She's fine. You generated enough heat to stave off frostbite."

"But I couldn't produce more oxygen for her."

"I'm fine, Sean," Nicole seconded.

Stepping back, he studied her carefully. Color was creeping back into her pretty face, and she no longer trembled. Sean drew her into his arms. "I'm sorry," he whispered.

"It wasn't your fault." She hugged him back. "We made it out safely."

"Thanks to Seth."

Belatedly realizing that he probably shouldn't hold Nicole too long in Seth's presence, Sean released her.

Nicole turned a grin on Seth. "That was freaking awesome. A dragon? I thought I was hallucinating or something."

One shoulder lifted in a shrug. "I needed a form large enough to carry you both."

"As much as I loved the dragon," Sean said, "why didn't you just teleport us here in your usual form as soon as you caught up with us?" Chris probably already had his guys combing the internet for dragon-sighting posts and videos.

"Because we would've hit the ground here with the same momentum you would've hit it there had I not caught you and halted your descent first."

"Oh." That was disconcerting. "Thank you."

Seth's lips twitched as his dark eyes lit with amusement. "That was a first for me, by the way. I have never in all of my long existence had to rescue an immortal who jumped out of an airplane without a parachute." And Seth had lived so many millennia that he tended to enjoy things that surprised him or caught him off guard.

Such rarely happened.

Sean's skin began to prickle and burn. The virus must have used all the blood he'd taken to heat his body enough to help Nicole. He would have to thank Melanie later for making him practice that.

"Sean," Nicole said, "you need to get out of the sun." Before he could respond, she took his hand and pulled him after her toward the shelter of the back porch.

He supposed the lack of cloud cover meant that Seth wasn't pissed at them. Storms often gathered when the eldest Immortal Guardian's temper flared. "How cold was it up there, Seth?" It had taken a *lot* of energy to keep frostbite at bay. He'd basically had to turn himself into a furnace.

"Negative seventy degrees Fahrenheit or thereabouts."

Sean swore. Immortals could tolerate that. But Nicole couldn't. Damn, that had been close.

When they entered David's home, Sheldon was waiting for them with a bag of blood. "I thought you could use this."

"Thanks." His skin an angry red, Sean sank his teeth into the bag and siphoned the blood into his veins before he, Nicole, and Seth headed into David's study.

Seated behind his desk, David looked up with a faint smile. "Didn't expect it to be so cold up there, did you?"

Sean grinned. "No."

David motioned to the chairs that faced his desk. "Have a seat."

Seth addressed David over their heads. "I'm going to pick up Reordon." He vanished.

David smiled at Nicole. "Can I get you anything?"

"That depends. Has my hair turned white?"

He laughed. "No. It's still a lovely brown."

She smiled. "Then I'm good."

Chuckling, he shifted his attention to Sean and shook his head. "I should've known you wouldn't let them take her."

Sean straightened. "She's my Second. Of course, I couldn't let them take her."

"Yes," David replied, his dark brown eyes twinkling with amusement. "Because she's your Second."

Sean looked at Nicole from the corner of his eye and found her doing the same.

Did David know about them?

Seth abruptly reappeared with Reordon at his side.

Reordon eyed Sean with a combination of irritation and resignation. "You just couldn't stick to the plan, could you?" He and Seth sank into two chairs that—added to Sean's and Nicole's—formed a horseshoe in front of David's desk.

Sean stiffened, hackles rising. "Hey, *someone* had to guard Nicole's back. And your special ops team insisted on keeping their distance."

"Because I told them to," Chris said.

"Well, that was a bad call. There was no way I was going to let her get on that plane by herself. And it's damned lucky I didn't. That asshole tried to grope her and then punched her in the head."

Every face darkened with anger.

Seth's eyes acquired a golden glow, David's amber.

Nicole held up a finger. "*After* I delivered a wicked uppercut."

Sean smiled. "She did. She hit him so hard with my phone that he bit through his tongue."

"Good," David said with relish.

Seth nodded. "Tell us what happened."

Sean and Nicole gave them a quick rundown. Sean did most of the talking because Nicole's memory was foggy in places. He cast Seth a worried look.

*What troubles you?* the Immortal Guardians leader asked telepathically.

*Her memory is spotty. Is she okay?*

*Yes. She suffered a concussion, but I healed her when she hugged me. There will be no lasting damage.*

Sean sighed with relief. *Thank you.*

Seth winked. *I healed you, too.*

Oh. Right. He'd been shot twice. Fear for Nicole had completely driven that from his mind. *Thank you.*

Chris shook his head. "What a dumbass."

Sean frowned, thinking Chris referred to *him* until he realized Nicole had just mentioned the guard firing his gun.

"How are your wounds, Sean?" Chris asked. "Are you okay?"

Surprised, he nodded. "Yeah. Seth healed me."

"I think the third bullet that guy fired might've hit something explosive," Nicole added. "There was a deafening boom."

Chris shook his head. "That was probably the abrupt shift in air pressure."

Sean nodded. "I didn't see an explosion."

Chris leaned back in his chair. "Okay. You didn't screw up. Good job, getting you both out of there safely." The network head could be stubborn as hell. But if he was wrong, he wasn't averse to admitting it.

Sean had always liked that about him. "Thanks. However, I don't know how safe it was. If I had dropped my phone before I could call Seth, we would've been screwed."

"Sheesh!" Nicole popped him on the arm. "Don't put that in my head. I was just starting to relax and think of this as a wild adventure."

All laughed.

As the amusement died down, Sean studied the other men. "Full disclosure—if the gunman hadn't forced us to bail, I probably would've mucked up the plan one way or another once we reached our destination after hearing what they intended to do to Nicole."

Chris frowned. "What did they intend to do to her?"

"Torture her to get me to tell them everything I know about Nick."

Swears erupted.

Nicole frowned. "Is it weird that I find it insulting that they thought he would cave faster if they tortured me than I would if they tortured him?"

"Yes," the men chorused.

She laughed.

Sean didn't. "They also intended to turn her into a lab rat and run all sorts of tests on her to see if her new stepdad had made her immortal like him."

Chris reached into his front pocket to withdraw a small notepad and a stubby pencil. "So they think Nick can share his immortality with others?" He started scribbling.

"Yes. They believe he's infected with a different strain of the virus that infects vampires. They're assuming it was created in a lab."

"Well," Seth murmured, "we know now that it was. It just wasn't created in a lab here on Earth."

That had been quite a revelation. Evidently, aliens with a penchant for committing genocide had created the virus and released it on Earth, expecting it to kill everyone off and leave the planet ripe for their claiming.

"They think the vampire's strain was a first effort, which was fatally flawed," Sean explained, "and that whatever Nick has is the corrected and refined version. They can't wait to get their hands on it."

Leaning forward, David rested his elbows on his desk and laced his fingers together. "You aren't telepathic. How did you learn this? Were they speaking of it openly?"

That would've been a pretty clear indicator that they had no intention of letting *Becca* and *George* live once they were of no more use to them.

"No. Marge made some calls from the bedroom."

Seth's eyebrows rose. "The bedroom?"

Chris nodded. "It's not uncommon for luxury jets to include bedrooms. Most of the network's jets have them."

Seth seemed surprised.

"You didn't know?" Nicole asked curiously. Like Sean, she'd probably thought Seth knew *everything* about the network.

"No. I teleport wherever I need to go."

"Me, too," David said.

She smiled. "Lucky you."

"Anyway," Sean continued, "Marge was arranging for *Becca* to be transferred from the plane to a place she referred to as *the lab*. It sounded a lot like the place Ami was held in."

Seth and David's countenances darkened. Both men loved Ami like a daughter and hated remembering the pain and suffering she had endured at the hands of so-called scientists and doctors.

"Two vehicles were supposed to meet us at the airport and take us there directly."

"Do you know what airport?" Chris asked.

"No. But before we jumped, I got the impression that we were close to our destination."

Chris checked his phone. "According to my latest alert, the plane will land soon. We don't know yet if that was its original destination or if it's making an emergency landing somewhere else. The pilot didn't file a flight plan and avoided controlled airspace whenever possible."

Nicole met Sean's gaze. "Sounds like you were right. This wasn't the first time they've done something like this."

Sean fought the urge to take her hand. "After I knocked everyone unconscious, I planned to call Seth and have him teleport Aidan in and Nicole out, then heal everyone and alter their memories so we could continue the operation."

Seth nodded. "Smart thinking. That would've worked."

Too bad the idiot with the gun had screwed everything up.

"Well, all is not lost," Chris said. "We're keeping tabs on the plane now, thanks to Nicole's tracker. Her cell phone is offline."

"And probably scattered among the other debris that flew out of the plane," Sean said.

Chris nodded. "Henderson sent a team out there to search for any objects or debris that fell. It was a rural area, which should make it easier. They'll collect the bodies, too, if possible. Nicole, I'm sorry they hurt you. Thank you for refusing to give them Sean's passcode. There are a lot of numbers and addresses on his phone that we don't want them getting their hands on."

"That's what I was thinking."

Sean frowned. Was *that* why she'd refused to give them his passcode? Because his phone—unlike hers—had the numbers of... every freaking immortal in the area? He swore. "I *did* screw up."

"No, *I* did," Chris said. "I should've anticipated that you'd intervene and given you a dummy phone. I didn't listen to my gut."

Sean frowned at him. "What did your gut tell you?"

"That you wouldn't let them take her."

"Because Nicole's my Second?"

The network head's lips curled up in a wry smile. "Sure. Because she's your Second."

Sean looked at Nicole and saw the same question in her eyes.

Did they all know the two of them were lovers now?

"Do you think Marge survived?" Nicole asked, changing the subject.

"Yes." Chris seemed confident that it was true.

"But she wasn't wearing a mask," Nicole reminded him.

"I know," the network head acknowledged. "The first thing the pilots would've done after donning their oxygen masks would be to descend as quickly as possible to 10,000 feet so there would be more oxygen for anyone still on board. She might have suffered frostbite or incurred a few injuries if something hit her on its way out the door. Otherwise, she should be fine."

Sean stared at him. "How do you know all that?"

He shrugged. "Before I became head of the East Coast division of the network, I worked in special ops and was a team leader. I wanted to be prepared for any eventuality, so I learned how to fly helicopters and pilot just about every kind of plane."

David smiled. "I don't think there's a land, air, or sea vehicle Chris can't operate. He can even captain one of those small subs that marine biologists use to study oceanic creatures."

Nicole blinked. "Wow."

"I'll second that," Sean said. Chris went above and beyond no matter *what* job he performed.

"After today," Nicole mentioned, "I wouldn't mind learning how to fly a plane."

"Me either," Sean added.

"I can arrange that," Chris offered absently as he wrote on his notepad. "So, as it stands now, we know nothing more than we did before they kidnapped Nicole, and we're waiting to see where they take Marge?"

"Actually," Sean said, "we know quite a bit more. I had a little talk with Marge after I kicked the other guys' asses. She told me the name of her boss and someone she referred to as his henchman."

Chris stopped writing and looked up. "Do you think she told you the truth?"

"I'm pretty sure."

Nicole nodded. "I don't think she was lying. She thought Sean was going to turn the tables on her and torture her son to get answers out of her."

Seth frowned. "Who is her son?"

"Kent, the man who punched me."

Chris shot Sean a look. "Did you torture him anyway?"

Sean frowned. "I didn't get a chance to. But I *did* kick his ass."

Lips twitching, Chris returned his attention to his notepad and held his pencil poised over it, ready to write. "What are the names she gave you?"

"The henchman she claimed to deal with is Alan Danvers. And the ringleader is Augustus Benford."

"Augustus Benford?" Chris repeated.

"Yes."

Seth studied Chris. "It doesn't sound familiar to me. Do you know him?"

"I know *of* him." Chris set the notepad and pencil down and picked up his phone. "He and Roubal fought together in Vietnam and kept in touch over the years. So far, we have found nothing to suggest a close relationship between the two. They weren't best buddies who got together often or anything like that. They invested in some of the same stocks. But that's not uncommon with men of their means." His thumbs danced over the phone's screen, but Sean couldn't tell whether Chris was looking something up online, making notes, or sending a text. "The special ops team Sean ditched earlier followed the dark gray SUV that was used to transport Nicole to the airport after it left. It led them to a location marked *Private Property*." More tapping. "We've been unable to determine who owns the building on it. It doesn't show up on any maps we've searched." He shook his head. "If it's one of Augustus Benford's holdings, we should've already found it in our investigation. The fact that we *didn't*—and the difficulty my team is having digging up information on it *and* this group—leads me to believe that Benford has far more resources at his disposal than we suspected. Even Roubal wasn't this secretive."

Seth nodded. "It only took the network a few hours to conclude that Roubal was involved with Kayla and Oliver's kidnapping and provide us with likely locations to search."

"Exactly." Chris tapped some more on his phone. "We found multiple business and personal properties owned by Benford. But

I don't remember seeing anything near the airport the private jet is currently headed toward."

"That may not have been their original destination," Seth murmured. "Do you have the plane's location?"

"Yes." Chris tapped the screen several times before turning it so the rest of them could see it. "They're landing here." He pointed to a blue dot on a map.

"Show me a satellite view," Seth ordered.

Chris switched the map to a satellite image.

"Zoom out."

Chris did.

"All right." Seth rose. "I'll head over and see what I can learn from them." He glanced at David. "Care to join me?"

Nodding, David rose and glanced toward the door.

A moment later, Darnell entered. His face and smooth, brown head carried a faint sheen of perspiration. His muscled chest rose and fell beneath his T-shirt as if he'd been exercising vigorously. In one hand, he held a katana with a blunt edge.

He must've been training Seconds.

"Yes?" he asked.

"Seth and I are going to check out a lead on the group pursuing Becca. Would you have Zach and Jared field our calls?"

"Sure." Nodding a greeting to the others, he crossed to a desk that was nearly as large as David's. After laying the sword atop it, he seated himself behind it. "Where's Leah? Should I send calls requesting a healer to her?"

Seth shook his head. "She's checking on her shop today, so only call her if the others aren't available." Leah had been the proprietor of a children's clothing, book, and toy store before she'd been swept into the Immortal Guardians' world.

"Will do." Darnell stared at his computer screen as his fingers flew over the keyboard. "Anything else?"

Chris held up a finger. "I may need you to help us gather more information on Augustus Benford."

"Because?"

"He may be the ringleader and is more secretive than Roubal was."

"Okay."

Sean glanced from Chris to Darnell. "Are you a cyber sleuth, too, Darnell?"

Chris snorted. "Are you kidding? Darnell can do more on a computer than anyone else on the network's staff. When David asked him to serve as his Second, I offered Darnell a ten million dollar signing bonus to stay on at network headquarters."

Darnell grinned. "I turned him down."

Stunned, Sean stared at him.

"See what you can find," Seth requested with a smile.

Then he and David left to do some intelligence gathering of their own.

# CHAPTER FOURTEEN

NICOLE'S KNEE BOBBED UP and down after Seth and David's departure. Energy thrummed through her. She didn't know what fed it: the bitter cold she'd been subjected to, the healing energy Seth had infused her with, or the adrenaline rush that lingered after *jumping out of a freaking jet without a parachute*. But she couldn't seem to sit still.

Sean's knee began to bob, too.

*We're so alike*, she thought with an inward smile.

His big hands curled over the arms of his chair. One index finger tapped an impatient beat. And he kept sending her little glances from the corner of his eye.

Nicole couldn't tell what he was thinking. Sean steadfastly kept his expression blank so Reordon and Darnell would read nothing in it. She wasn't sure that was necessary though. While spilling the tale of their adventure to Seth and David, she'd gotten the distinct impression that her intimate relationship with Sean was an elephant in the room that caused more amusement than alarm or disapproval.

Childish giggles sounded behind her.

Turning in her chair, she glanced toward the doorway.

Roland Warbrook walked by, a grin creasing his often dour features as he dangled his son, Michael, upside down.

She smiled. Roland was one of those austere sorts who tugged at her heartstrings, because his demeanor always changed—his face lighting up in such an adorable, swoon-worthy way—whenever he was with his wife and child.

"Roland," Chris called.

Backtracking, Roland halted in the doorway, turned his grinning son upright, and settled him on his hip. "Yes?"

"Would you teleport Sean and Nicole home? We're done here, and they could use a break after what happened."

He arched a brow. "What happened?"

"They were forced to bail out of a private jet at 40,000 feet without a parachute."

Roland whistled. "Sure. Let me return Michael to his play with Adira first." He continued up the hallway.

Nicole smiled at Sean. "He's such a sweetheart."

Every male in the room guffawed.

"What?" she protested. "He is."

"You know he can hear you, right?" Sean asked with a grin.

She winced. "Damn it. I forgot."

Roland returned. "Ready?"

"Yes." Nicole rose. "I'm sorry we interrupted your playtime. Thank you for taking us home."

His lips turned up in a rare smile as he offered her a slight bow. "It's my pleasure."

Moving to stand beside her, Sean whispered in a loud aside, "I think Roland may be suffering from oxygen deprivation, too. He's being nice."

The elder immortal cuffed Sean on the side of the head.

Nicole laughed.

"Do you even know where we live?" Sean asked.

Roland gripped their shoulders. "Yes. Sarah and Marcus forced me to learn the addresses of every immortal stationed in the area."

Sean pursed his lips. "And did you tell the other immortals where *you* live?"

If he had, Nicole hadn't gotten the memo.

"Hell no," Roland replied drolly.

She and Sean laughed. Then David's study faded to black.

Weightlessness engulfed her. Though such rarely bothered Nicole during teleportation, today it was too reminiscent of what she'd felt when they'd been yanked out of the plane. Unexpected panic filled her. As soon as they materialized on the front porch, she grasped Sean's hand and fought to keep her breathing even.

Roland's brow furrowed with concern. "Are you all right?"

She forced a smile. "Yes."

"Are you sure? Perhaps I should've driven you."

"No." Nicole beat back the fear. "I'm good. Thank you."

Nodding uncertainly, he vanished.

Sean's hold on her hand tightened.

When Nicole looked up, her heart gave a funny little leap and began to pound loudly in her ears.

Sean's eyes glowed bright amber as he studied her with an intensity that drove all thought from her head. "I could've lost you today," he professed, his voice hoarse with the emotion he'd refused to display in front of the others.

She nodded, unable to find her voice.

It had been a close call.

*Too* close.

They fell into each other's arms, their lips merging in a long, desperate kiss. Fire licked through her, speeding her pulse.

"I could've lost you," he repeated, the words tortured.

"I could've lost you, too." She parted her lips, inviting him in, reveling in the stroke of his tongue and the heat it inspired.

Sean slid his hands down her back, then curled them over her bottom and lifted her up. "Wrap your legs around me."

Nicole didn't hesitate, locking her ankles behind his back. Both moaned when her core settled over the hard ridge his pants restrained. He felt so good, and she needed him so much.

Clicks sounded beside them as locks turned. The front door opened.

*Oh crap.* Nicole dropped her legs to the front porch's planks and swiftly placed some distance between her and Sean.

Cliff stood in the open doorway. "Oh my," he said, deadpan. "What is this? Sean and Nicole kissing on the front porch? Do my eyes deceive me? I must be mistaken. Surely they would never break the rules."

Emma stepped up beside him and viewed them with exaggerated shock. "Sean and Nicole kissed?" Like Cliff's, her voice was almost robotic in its lack of surprise. "Surely you are mistaken. It cannot be. Whatever can this mean?"

When Sean burst out laughing, Nicole joined him.

"All right, all right," he said. "We get it. You aren't surprised."

Cliff shook his head. "You two becoming more than friends was the worst-kept secret in North Carolina." Stepping back, he and Emma gave them room to enter.

Nicole frowned. "How did you know about us?" It wasn't as though they had made out on David's couch or something. "And do Seth and David know? Because I got the distinct impression they do, which I don't get because we were just friends until this past week."

Cliff closed the door. "Don't you ever check out the Immortal Guardians betting book?"

Sean cast her a confused look. "Immortals have a betting book?"

"Yes." She thought about it for a moment. "At least, it *used* to be a book. Or probably a *series* of them, considering how long some of these guys have lived and their propensity for gambling. But I *think* now it's less a book and more an encrypted online database. I haven't accessed it myself, but I saw Tracy look something up in it once. Immortals and their Seconds both bet in it."

"A *lot*," Cliff added.

Sean's brow creased with puzzlement. "Seriously?"

She smiled. "I know. It's weird, right?"

"Very weird. Is it like sports betting?"

Cliff rolled his eyes. "It isn't just sports. Those guys bet on *every*-thing."

Nicole nodded. "When Tracy accessed the database, she was looking up when Seth would kiss a woman and when he would fall in love again."

Disbelief swept Sean's features. "Immortal Guardians bet about *that*?"

She grinned. "A *lot* of them. Darnell won both bets."

"A little friendly advice," Cliff said. "Don't bet against Darnell."

Sean frowned. "What does the Immortal Guardians betting book have to do with *us*?"

Nicole wanted to know that, too. She had placed no bets in it. And Sean hadn't even known it existed.

Cliff grinned. "Darnell bet you two would fall in love."

Her jaw dropped. People were betting about *her* and *Sean*? "What?" While she didn't particularly like that people were wagering over her personal life, the fact that she rated high enough to be mentioned in the book at all made her feel even more like she was part of the Immortal Guardians' family. "When?"

"When what?" Cliff asked. "When you would fall in love?"

"No. When did he place the bet?"

"The day you became Sean's Second."

*Unbelievable.*

Cliff locked the front door. "What happened today anyway? Darius called and said there'd been a change of plans, which I took to mean that Sean had somehow jacked up the operation."

Unoffended, Sean laughed. "You know me well."

Cliff shrugged. "I figured you would do anything to keep Nicole safe, so it did *not* surprise me to hear you'd gone after her when the bad guys nabbed her. Last I heard, though, you two were on a plane."

Sean gave them an abbreviated account of the day's events.

Emma drew Nicole into a hug, her pretty face full of concern. "I'm so glad you're okay."

Cliff nodded. "Good thing you held onto your phone."

Sean laughed. "Yeah."

Cliff studied them both. "I'm guessing by the clinch I interrupted on the front porch that you two could use some alone time."

"Yes," they blurted.

When Cliff and Emma regarded them with knowing amusement, heat crept into Nicole's cheeks.

Cliff laughed. "Okay. We'll stay out of your way."

"Actually," Sean said, "we're done for the day and don't plan to hunt tonight. Would you two like to take a break from babysitting us and head home for some quiet time of your own? Seth and David are following the bad guys to see what they can learn. If they call a meeting, I'll let you know."

Cliff looked at Emma. "I can go with that. What about you?"

Sliding an arm around his waist, she smiled. "Sounds good to me."

"Okay," Cliff agreed.

Nicole tried not to grin, but her lips refused to cooperate.

Emma grabbed her purse and keys. "There's some eggplant parmesan in the fridge if you get hungry."

Cliff retrieved a duffle bag, his steps a little lighter than usual. "We'll see you tomorrow."

"After dinner," Sean said.

Cliff laughed. "Okay. See you then."

As soon as the door closed behind the couple, Sean drew Nicole into his arms.

Her pulse picked up. Heat flared between them as their lips touched in a gentle kiss that soon deepened and set her heart to hammering.

"Should we lock the door?" Emma asked outside.

"Yeah," Cliff murmured, his voice rife with amusement. "They won't remember to do it."

Chuckling, Sean raised his head.

Cliff's and Emma's voices grew fainter as they walked down the path, climbed into their car, and drove away.

Quiet fell. "Did you mean it?" Sean asked softly.

Nicole stared up at him, uncomprehending. "Did I mean what?"

"When we were falling..." he clarified. "Did you mean it when you said you love me?"

As they'd hurtled toward the ground, death had seemed imminent. And in what she'd thought would be their last moments together, Nicole had wanted him to know how much he meant to her. "Yes," she vowed softly. "I love you, Sean."

Amber light flared to life in his eyes. "I love you, too." His lips touched hers, the contact conveying such immense tenderness that tears welled in her eyes.

She pressed a palm to his stubbled cheek. "As more than a friend?"

Though he turned his head slightly so he could nuzzle her palm, his bright eyes held hers. "As my everything."

Her heart swelled. So much emotion choked her that she couldn't find her voice and could only nod, hoping he would understand that she felt the same.

His lips brushed hers, the touch gentle despite the depth of feelings it carried. Sliding her hand around to cup his nape, Nicole drew her tongue across his lower lip.

He groaned and deepened the contact, crowding closer and tightening his hold on her.

Sean loved her.

He *loved* her.

Jubilation filled her, accompanied by red-hot desire. Rising on her toes, she wrapped her arms around his neck. Sean palmed her ass and aligned their hips, pressing her against the long, hard length behind his fly. *Oh yeah.* She wanted that. Wanted to feel him plunge inside her, driving deep, no-holds-barred. Wanted to feel his hands rove bare skin.

Pulse racing, she combed her fingers through his thick hair, fisted the soft locks, and gave them a tug.

Sean swore. Lifting her, he turned and pressed her back against the nearest wall.

Nicole wrapped her legs around his waist and ground against his hard cock. Both moaned as they strained together. Her breath shortened as he slid a hand down over her ass. All the while, his tongue danced with hers, stroking and teasing, stoking the fire.

"Sean," she breathed, wishing they were naked.

He slipped his hand around to her front. Dropping her hands to his shoulders, she placed some distance between them, eager for him to touch her breasts. Instead, she felt a hard tug on her shirt as a rip sounded.

Breaking the kiss, she looked down.

Her shirt was gone, torn away.

She met his heated gaze. "That was Becca's," she said absently, not really caring.

"I'll buy her a new one," he vowed, his voice rough with desire. Her sports bra followed. Then he palmed one of her breasts. Lust shot through her as he circled the sensitive peak, caressed it, pinched it.

He trailed a series of passionate kisses down her throat to her other breast. When his lips closed around the stiff peak, she moaned. He stroked it with his tongue, sending darts of desire

240

straight to her clit. Fisting his hair once more, she urged him closer, writhing against him. He sucked hard.

"More," she begged. He nipped her with his teeth. "Yes."

Sean raised his head, eyes blazing. "I need you naked," he growled, the intensity in his face stealing her breath.

The foyer abruptly blurred around her. Cool air brushed her hair back as he clutched her tighter and raced down the hallway. His erection rubbed against her with every movement, ratcheting up her desire. She needed him. Naked. Inside her. Right now.

Then they were in his bedroom, standing at the foot of his big-ass bed.

She'd make a joke about his feet not hanging off the end but wanted him too much. "Do that thing I've heard immortals can do."

His eyebrows rose. "Which one?"

"The one where you strip us both bare in less than a second."

Eyes brightening, he blurred. She felt another tug and heard more cloth ripping. When he stilled, they were both naked except for their shoes.

Sean gave Nicole a sheepish smile. "I didn't know how to get your shoes off without tossing you on the bed."

Her face reflected so much hunger as her brown eyes roved his form that he almost wished he had taken her against the wall of the foyer. Then he'd already be balls-deep inside her.

"I'm okay with that," she murmured.

Despite the need that rode him, he chuckled. "Okay with what? Us keeping our shoes on or me tossing you on the bed?"

"You tossing me on the bed." Reaching out, she curled her delicate hand around his hard cock.

Sean's knees damn near buckled at the inquisitive touch. He hadn't expected being immortal to increase the intensity of sex so much. He shuddered as pleasure rocketed through him. "I feel so much more now," he told her softly.

241

She circled the sensitive crown of his cock with her thumb. "Is it the enhanced senses?"

He nodded, having trouble finding his breath at the moment.

A twinkle of mischief entered her eyes. "So you feel *this* more?"

He groaned as she squeezed and stroked him, inciting a roaring conflagration of need.

Growling, he took her in his arms again, lips devouring, hands exploring until they were both frantic for each other. A fantasy surfaced. One he'd woven around her more times than he would ever admit since their little masturbation conversation. Spinning her away, he drew her against him, her back to his front.

"Sean," she whispered.

Dipping his head, he kissed her neck. A little shiver shook her as she reached up to cup the back of his head. He palmed her breasts. So perfect. So beautiful. The pink tips tight and eager for his touch.

He heard Nicole's breath shorten as he fondled her. Her pulse quickened. Moving restlessly, she arched her back and rubbed her ass against his hard cock. Moaning, Sean squeezed her breast and slid his other hand down past the triangle of curls to brush her clit.

Her hips jerked as she moaned. Tilting her head back, she met his gaze and drew him down for a ravenous kiss.

"You're so wet for me," he uttered hoarsely, and dipped a long finger inside her.

"Yes."

He added a second, thrusting in and out in a rhythm he would soon mimic with his cock. All the while, he stroked her clit with his thumb and continued stroking her breast. Moaning, Nicole rocked against him, writhing in his arms, breath shortening until an orgasm crashed through her. Sean clenched his teeth as her warm channel pulsed round his fingers.

He needed to be inside her. Now.

Urging her forward, he bent Nicole over the foot of his big bed. The mattress was so high that her toes barely touched the floor as he pressed a knee between her thighs and nudged her legs apart. "I love your ass," he murmured, smoothing his hands over it as his cock pressed against her clit.

Her breath quickened.

Fisting his cock, he pressed it to her slick entrance. Sean groaned as he pushed forward, an inch at a time, slowly stretching her, drawing out the pleasure. "Nicole." Her hands curled into fists around the covers as she pushed back against him, drawing him in deeper. He gripped her tighter and hoped like hell he wouldn't leave bruises. He wanted to go slow, to rebuild the heat and drive her to another orgasm before he came. But she made it hard. Made *him* hard. Or hard*er*. Rolling her hips as he withdrew almost to the crown and pushing back against him when he eagerly thrust deep again.

Unable to hold back, Sean abandoned all control and took her hard and fast. He just wanted her. So much. All of her.

Leaning over her, he slid a hand beneath her and cupped her breast. She moaned, the light muscles of her back flexing as she met him thrust for thrust. He slipped his other hand beneath her stomach and drew it down until he could stroke her clit in tune with his thrusts.

He even loved the sounds she made, the moans and gasps and cries, the way she called his name with such hunger. Their breath came in gasps, the pleasure increasing as he thrust harder and faster until she cried out in ecstasy, bucking beneath him as her inner muscles clamped down around him. Sean shouted with his own release, which seemed to go on and on as she milked him with those rhythmic squeezes. Then her lean muscles relaxed as she went limp, panting.

Breathing hard, Sean kissed the back of her neck. Sliding his hands out from under her, he braced his forearms on either side of her and leaned down. He tried not to settle too much weight on her, but he needed to be close. As close as he could get. Once more, he had nearly lost her. It made him want to wrap himself around her and never let go. "Don't ever scare me like that again," he pleaded softly.

Tears filled Nicole's eyes. How she loved him.

Still trying to calm her breathing, she covered one of his hands with hers. Part of her wanted to promise she wouldn't. But times had become more dangerous for immortals and their Seconds in recent years. "I'll try not to."

Sighing, he nuzzled her hair. "Have I told you lately that I love your scent?"

She smiled. "No." And she couldn't help but revel in the realization that his breathing was as labored as hers. Sean was a fantastic lover, his touch the perfect balance between rough and tender. And damn, he made her body hum. Even if her experience with men hadn't been limited, she knew with certainty that no one else could've brought her as much ecstasy as he did.

"I want to try something," he whispered.

And something in his voice sent a naughty thrill through her. "Okay." With Sean, she was up for anything.

Withdrawing, he turned her onto her back.

Fighting the urge to stretch like a cat, Nicole smiled up at him. His hair was mussed, and his eyes bore that wondrous amber glow. "Hi, handsome."

"Hi yourself," he returned, standing between her thighs.

Nicole was a little surprised that she didn't feel self-conscious, splayed out before him as she was. But this was Sean. *Her* Sean. Not just her lover. Her best friend. "What's on your mind?"

He winked. "This." His cock sank deep. Then his handsome form blurred.

Pleasure shot through her. Sudden. Intense. Eyes widening, she cried out as another orgasm took her.

Heat filled her, letting her know he had come, too.

Her heart racing, she stared up at him in astonishment when he stilled. "What the hell was that?"

He laughed. "I'm going to call that Immortal Guardian perk number one."

She grinned. "That's one hell of a perk."

"Agreed." Taking her hand, he tugged her upright.

Limp as a noodle after three orgasms, she leaned into him for several long minutes. "I don't know what you're thinking," she muttered, burying her face in his chest hair, "but all I want to do now is sleep."

Wrapping his arms around her, he rocked her slightly from side to side. "Are you sure? I was thinking about having a shower and then seeing how much of Emma's eggplant parmesan we can eat."

Her stomach rumbled at the thought of it. Straightening, she met his warm gaze. "Forget what I said. Let's do your thing."

Laughing, he scooped her up in his arms and carried her into the adjoining bathroom.

Hours later, Sean sprawled on his back, sated and relaxed, staring up at the ceiling and could think of no other place he would rather be. Nicole lay snuggled up to his side with her head resting on his shoulder. As he idly toyed with her hair, a phrase from one of his sister's favorite chick flicks came to mind.

*Jerry Maguire.*

*Sheesh*, Krysta must've watched that movie at least forty times. It had driven him crazy. But one line in it resonated with him: 'You complete me.'

Sean thought that summed up his feelings for Nicole nicely. She completed him. It was that simple. When she had spent those two weeks away in Becca's dorm, he'd felt as if a piece of him were missing. Even with Cliff and Emma there to keep him company, the house had felt empty. Everything had seemed duller, as if some of the color had leached from the world.

Sure, everything still existed in shades of gray. But he enjoyed it so much more with color.

With *her*.

With Nicole.

When he pondered the how's and why's of it, he couldn't pinpoint precisely when his feelings for her had changed.

*Hmm. Had* they changed? Or was this where they'd been heading all along, from the moment he'd first met her?

It didn't matter. Nicole was his best friend. Sean would do anything for her. Had he been alone on that plane, he would've taken however many hits and bullets necessary to complete the mission and find out whom they were dealing with. But when that bastard had started shooting...

A bullet causing explosive decompression hadn't been Sean's only concern. He had been terrified that the asshole would shoot Nicole. If a bullet had hit her in the head...

As he'd once told her, Seth's incredible healing ability didn't extend to resurrection.

"Nicole," he said softly.

"Hmm?"

"I love you."

Raising onto an elbow, she smiled at him, her lovely face full of tenderness. "I love you, too."

He combed his fingers through her tousled hair. "I don't want us to be apart anymore."

"I don't think you have to worry about that. If Seth, David, and Chris can't find what they need, Aidan will pose as Becca and—"

"I wasn't talking about the op."

She tilted her head a little. "What do you mean?"

"I mean, I don't want us to keep pretending we're just an immortal and his Second."

Face somber, she studied him. "You want to go public, let everyone know we're lovers?"

He nodded. "I know how much your career with the network means to you. If there are any negative repercussions, if Chris gets a bug up his butt or anything else comes up, then we can call Alena Moreno and—"

"Who?"

"Alena Moreno. She's the head of the West Coast division of the network."

"Oh. Right."

"I chatted with her once and don't think she would have a problem with arranging a transfer for us."

Surprise lit her features. "You'd do that? You'd move away from your family?"

His mother, father, and sister all resided here in North Carolina, and Sean was close to all of them. "To be with you? Absolutely."

Smiling, she gave him a quick kiss. "That means so much to me. But I think the cat's out of the bag regarding our relationship status. Everyone we talked to today acted like they'd already guessed."

"Full disclosure: Bastien, Zach, Roland, and every other immortal who attended Cliff's barbecue knows about us, too."

She stared at him. "They do?"

"Yeah. And they basically said that if we run into trouble, they'll have our backs."

"Awww. They did? All of them?"

He nodded.

"That's so sweet." Her eyes sparkled with mischief. "So, you were talking about us?"

He smiled. "I was worried that pursuing anything more than friendship with you would jeopardize your career."

"I was, too. But, Sean…" All laughter left her expression. "Your dad's vision."

"What about it?"

"What if I'm not the woman he saw you spending the rest of your life with?"

"You are."

Dropping her gaze, she started drawing circles on his chest with an index finger. "You asked him?"

Slipping a finger beneath her chin, he tilted her head up so she'd meet his gaze. "No. I don't have to. I don't *need* to. You're it for me, Nicole. If you aren't the woman he saw me with in his vision, then his psychic ability must have been wonky that day, because I don't want to be with anyone but you." He drew a hand over her hair. "You're my best friend. When I have news, you're the first person I want to share it with. When I hear a funny joke, you're the first one I want to tell because I love to make you laugh. When I'm troubled, you're the one I want to turn to. And if *you're* troubled, I want to do everything I can—beat the bad guys, move mountains, defeat dragons, whatever it takes—to make everything better."

She leaned into his touch. "Even if that dragon is Seth?"

"Even if." His lips turned up in a self-deprecating smile. "Although Seth would totally kick my ass if I ever went toe-to-toe with him."

Her expression softened. "I feel the same way."

He grinned. "You feel Seth would kick my ass?"

She laughed. "Yes. But I was actually saying that I feel the same way about *you*, Sean." Leaning down, she touched her lips to his in a loving kiss. "You're it for me."

His heart began to pound as she stroked his stubbled cheek. Rolling them to their sides, he snuggled her closer, their legs entwining. Some of her hair fell forward and obscured her expression. Wanting to catch every nuance of her reaction to his next words, he brushed it back and cupped her cheek. "Will you marry me, Nicole?"

Those beautiful brown eyes widened a fraction then filled with tears as she nodded. "Yes."

He kissed her. "Did I ask too soon?"

"No," she assured him with a smile. "This has been almost three years in the making."

"True." He kissed her again. "I'm sorry my proposal wasn't more romantic. I promise I'll do it again. We can dress up, have a fancy dinner, and—"

She pressed a finger to his lips. "You did it right, Sean. It was perfect." Replacing her fingers with her lips, she whispered. "*You're* perfect."

Rubbing noses with her, he whispered back, "I'm glad you finally noticed."

Laughing, she shoved his shoulder.

Sean grinned and hugged her tight. He would've never thought a day that had gone so horrifically wrong could end up feeling so right. Closing his eyes, he sighed in contentment. They would have one hell of a story to tell their grandchildren.

He stiffened. His eyes flew open as dismay shot through him.

"What is it?" Nicole asked, sensing the change in him.

Stricken, he met her gaze. "I can't give you children." Immortal males' sperm died as soon as they ejaculated. And even if they found a way to keep his sperm alive long enough to fertilize an egg...

The fetus would be infected with the virus. And they had no idea what effect the virus would have on a baby.

"I know." She said it matter-of-factly and evinced none of the disappointment he felt.

"That won't...?" He swallowed. "You'd be okay with that?"

"Yes." He must not have hidden his doubt well, because she shook her head. "I've never really been able to imagine having children, Sean. You know my history. My mom and dad weren't exactly stellar examples of parenthood."

Her mom and dad had sucked. They'd shown her no love and had kept such an emotional distance from her that she may as well have been their employee.

One slender shoulder raised in a slight shrug. "What kind of mother would that make me?"

"A great one," he answered with complete confidence. "A fantastic one because you'd give our children everything your parents denied you." But what kind of father would *he* be, unable to go outside during daylight hours, killing vampires for a living? How would he even explain his profession to his children? *You see, kids, Daddy uses these sharp knives and swords we're always telling you not to touch to stab, kill, and behead vampires. That's right. Daddy cuts off their heads. It's a brutal and bloody business, but it has to be done.*

Nicole toyed with the hair on his chest. "Actually, instead of having children, I was thinking..."

He heard her heartbeat pick up. "Yes?"

"How would you feel about us being the next Immortal Guardian power couple?" She darted him an uncertain look.

His heart stopped, then started beating the hell out of his ribs. Was she saying...?

"How would you feel about transforming me?" she clarified.

She *was*. Awe engulfed him. "You'd transform for me?"

"For *us*," she corrected, "so we could be together forever."

"And have a greater chance of surviving future unplanned skydiving excursions?" he quipped.

She smiled. "Yes."

Sean rolled her to her back and did his damnedest to kiss her senseless. Only when she hummed her approval and wrapped her legs around him did he break the contact. "There's nothing I want more than to spend eternity with you."

She grinned. "Because you've finally realized that *I'm* perfect?"

"Hell, yes, you are," he said with a laugh. But she was far too vulnerable as a mortal. He sobered. "You've had too many close calls since I met you. I never want to lose you, Nicole."

Her smile waned. "Would *you* be okay with not having children? If I transform, even artificial insemination with donor sperm will be out of the question."

"As long as I have you," he vowed, "I'll be okay." He kissed her. "*Better* than okay."

"Maybe one day," she proposed, "if you convince me I wouldn't suck as a mother, we can follow Roland and Sarah's example and adopt a *gifted one*."

Fatherhood had certainly brought Roland joy. And since he seemed fond of Nicole, perhaps Roland could offer Sean a few tips on balancing such an unusual profession with being a dad.

Sean nuzzled her tempting lips. "You'd have to convince me I'd be a good father first. But there's no need to rush. We have plenty of time." He kissed her. "We'll have eternity together."

A tender smile lit her features. "Eternity together. I like the sound of that."

# CHAPTER FIFTEEN

T ESSA STROLLED DOWN A deserted sidewalk on UNC Chapel Hill's campus.

Few students were out and about. She couldn't decide whether they were all inside, studying their butts off because final exams were next week, or the cooler weather had caught them off guard and driven them to seek warmth indoors. A cold front had swept through and lowered temps more than the meteorologists had predicted. After a long summer loaded with record-breaking temperatures and a warmer-than-usual autumn, the chilly breeze felt positively frigid to some.

Fortunately, Tessa could control her body temperature.

An imposing figure sauntered along beside her, his strides shortened to accommodate hers.

She glanced up at Jared from the corner of her eye.

Why did so many people think large men were awkward and clumsy? If anything, the ancient immortal possessed a certain natural grace. Or maybe confidence lent his movements the smoothness that somehow conveyed both casual disregard and indomitable strength.

Anyone studying Jared might think he paid little attention to his surroundings. Yet his sharp gaze missed nothing, and she knew well the power he wielded.

As usual, he was quiet in her company. Tessa couldn't decide how she felt about that. The guards at network headquarters often complained about his loquacious nature, claiming he talked their ears off.

Was there something about her that dissuaded conversation?

Did he mistake her quiet nature for aloofness or unwelcome?

Others had in the past. It sometimes seemed as if the more time people spent staring at their phones instead of interacting with others, the less capable they were of identifying or understanding something as simple as shyness.

Not that she was shy, per se. She was just often more content to let others do the talking.

Habit, Tessa supposed. She learned much more about people by observing them while they chatted than by jibber-jabbering herself. If one paid attention, it rarely took long to determine who was honest and who talked out of their butts. Who was manipulative and who was kind. Who delighted in tearing others down and who took pleasure in lifting them up.

Those were all essential details to know when you had a unique ability that would endanger your life if someone chose to deceive you and expose it.

"Thank you for hunting with me," she said.

"It is my pleasure," her partner responded with a slight bow.

She'd noticed *that* about him, too. Jared often reverted to more formal speech and mannerisms while in her company. "I was restless," she confessed.

"I was aware." Of course he was. Jared missed very little. "Does hunting help?"

Guilt suffused her. "Yes. Hunting with Sean was a welcome distraction. It helped me forget for a time." Forcing a laugh, she looked away. "That makes me sound as crazy as the vampires, doesn't it?"

"No." Jared didn't prevaricate either, something she admired. He was what her brother would've called a straight shooter and spoke his mind.

On this, however, she disagreed with him.

Stuart and the other vampires at network headquarters had an excuse for wanting to hunt. The virus chipping away at their minds also fueled a growing thirst for violence. Now that Cliff no longer battled insanity or needed the outlet, Bastien periodically took Stuart hunting with him to reduce the frequency of the psychotic breaks the young vampire suffered and give him an outlet for the vicious impulses the insanity spawned.

"Are you sure?" she countered. "What does wanting to go out and kill vampires for a distraction say about me?"

He clasped his hands behind his back. "It says you care about the safety of others more than you do your own. That you will risk your life to keep others from losing theirs to predators they have no hopes of defeating." He hesitated. "And it says grief is eating you up inside, that you're hurting and desperately need a respite."

Tears welled in her eyes.

"Guilt is, too."

Yes, Jared missed nothing. Guilt over giving her loyalty to the man who had eviscerated her brother in front of her constantly gnawed at her. Yet she couldn't view her actions with the positive context he'd applied to them.

"We all have regrets," he murmured.

When she looked at him, his gaze seemed far away, as if he saw the past rather than the placid campus around them. "Even you?" She found it hard to imagine someone of his age and wisdom making the mistakes she had.

His lips turned up in a smile that bore no mirth. "Oh yes. Several millennia's worth."

Would she say the same thousands of years from now?

Shivering at the depressing thought, Tessa hoped not.

Long minutes passed as they meandered down the path.

"When I wish to forget those regrets for a time, do you know what one of my favorite distractions is?" he asked casually.

"Movies?" she guessed with a smile.

He grinned with boyish enthusiasm, the expression taking years off his face and making him look almost as young as some of the university students. "Yes."

Oddly, it lightened her spirits. She studied him curiously. According to the accounts she'd heard, Jared had lived in almost total isolation for thousands of years. "Did you only discover movies recently?"

"Oh no. Films have long been my secret obsession. Many years ago, when rumors surfaced that someone had discovered a way to create moving pictures, curiosity drove me to slip away from the Others and see for myself."

253

She grinned, imagining him sneaking out like a teenager despite the thousands of years he'd lived.

"Did you know that when movies first got going during the silent era, the industry was full of women writers, directors, and producers?"

She looked up at him in surprise. "Really?"

He nodded. "Oh yes. Far more women directed films then than today. Lois Weber was even Universal's highest-paid director at one point and launched her own production company, signing what was then considered the most lucrative deal in the industry with Paramount. The films were quite progressive, too, as some would say today. Not at all what you would expect." Warming to the subject, he regaled her with descriptions of early movies that sounded nothing like the black-and-white movies she'd watched with her great-grandparents.

Tessa smiled as he grew more animated, that odd reserve falling away. Before long, she chatted as fervently as he did, her troubles forgotten as he entertained her with tales of furtively attending movie screenings, even though he was supposed to avoid all inter-actions with humanity.

She grinned when he admitted that he'd once hidden in the rafters of a warehouse to watch the production process and, when he got hungry, zipped past craft services to steal treats meant for the actors. She laughed when he told her he'd once shifted into the form of a cow so he could appear in a western.

"I told myself that I wasn't technically breaking the rules," he said with a grin, "because I was only interacting with other cows, not with humans."

Tessa was still laughing when his cell phone chimed.

"Forgive the interruption." He drew it from his back pocket. "I'm fielding some of Seth's calls tonight."

She nodded.

"Yes?" he answered.

"It's Gerard," a male cried in a French accent. "Caleb needs help. We came up against a larger group of vampires than usual and—"

"Are you fighting them now?" Jared cut in.

254

"No. We managed to defeat them. But Caleb nearly lost an arm and a leg. Both are barely attached."

"It's only a flesh wound," Caleb called in a British accent in a tribute to Monty Python's *The Holy Grail* that made her smile.

Jared glanced at Tessa, his reluctance clear.

She motioned for him to go.

"I shall be there shortly." As soon as he pocketed his phone, he reached for her shoulder. "I'll return you to network headquarters first."

Shaking her head, Tessa backed away from his touch. "No, thank you."

"You aren't supposed to hunt alone," he reminded her gently.

"I'll be fine. I've hunted with Sean often enough lately to handle myself with any vampires I may encounter." She motioned to the quiet campus. "And it looks like nothing is happening here anyway."

"Nevertheless—"

"I'll be fine, Jared." Touching his arm, she gave his big biceps a friendly squeeze. "Really."

He glanced down at her touch. And she could've sworn a flash of gold lit his eyes for a heartbeat before they returned to a brown so dark that it was nearly black. "I don't believe you've ever called me by my name before."

Surprised, Tessa released him. "I haven't?"

He shook his head.

Was that why he was often more reserved around her? "Well, I'll be fine, Jared. I was thinking about heading to Sean's place anyway, to see how he and Nicole are doing."

"Shall I teleport you there?"

"No. I'd rather run it. I want to be outside a little longer."

He frowned uncertainly. "Are you sure?"

"Yes. Go heal Caleb. His joking around doesn't mean he isn't in pain."

He took a step back. "You have my number?"

"I don't think so." After removing her cell phone from an inner pocket of her coat, she unlocked it and handed it over so he could add his name and number to her contacts list.

Jared studied her as he returned it. "As you will. Where is the nearest area without security camera coverage?"

She pointed to the building next to them. "Behind that building, under the trees."

Offering her another of those charming half-bows, he tapped the screen of his phone, brought it to his ear, and strode away.

"Yes?" Gerard said.

"It's Jared. Stay on the line." All the eldest immortals—Seth, David, Zach, and Jared—could trace phone signals to their sources and teleport directly to anyone they spoke to.

Tessa would love to know how that worked.

Jared glanced back at her when he reached the corner of the building.

Smiling, she tossed him a little wave.

His lips curled up in an answering smile as he slipped out of view.

Tessa's smile lingered as she turned away and studied the pretty campus. Her spirits felt lighter tonight. Lighter than they had in a long time. She even laughed again, imagining Jared turning into a cow and moseying into a herd so he could be in one of his beloved movies.

She would wager a month of her former earnings that he had done so more than once.

Quiet embraced her. Or as much quiet as there could be with her enhanced hearing carrying a cacophony of nearby conversations to her ears.

Tessa had intended to do as she'd told Jared: run to Sean and Nicole's house and check on them. And yet, how long had it been since she'd been alone?

Not alone in her apartment with guards outside and vampires roaming the hallways, able to hear everything she said or did outside the bathroom. But alone-alone.

When she thought about it, the answer surprised her: not since Gershom had transformed her.

Perhaps she should take a moment to enjoy it.

Tessa meandered along the path until she reached a bench. A dusting of sunflower seed shells littered the pavement in front of it, where an industrious squirrel must have coaxed a meal from someone.

Sinking onto the bench, she leaned back, sighed, and let peace infuse her.

For once, tortured memories didn't inundate her. Instead, her thoughts kept returning to Jared. She liked him more without the careful reserve. His face and voice animated, he had imparted a history of filmmaking that had utterly captivated her.

Was that all she had to do to get him to talk her ear off? Bring up films?

She grinned. Maybe she should talk him into having a movie night with her. She could have the network deliver some fun snacks to her apartment, and the two of them could kick back and relax on her sofa while they watched his favorites on her big-screen TV.

A gentle mist began to fall.

Smiling, she turned her face up to the sky. Even this was nice.

*Splat.* A large raindrop plonked onto her forehead, breaking apart into droplets that bounced into her eyes.

Grimacing, she wiped them. Another sizeable drop splooshed on top of her head. Her shoulder. Her other shoulder.

*Hmm.*

The sky opened up, a wall of water racing down to pound the ground. *And* Tessa.

She laughed as it instantly drenched her hair, water rolling down her face and dripping off her nose and chin. The long coat she wore kept her back and shoulders dry. The network always provided immortals and their Seconds with top-quality garments. But everything exposed where the coat parted in front already looked like she'd gone for a swim. Even her feet soon sloshed in her sneakers as rain pounded them and her socks wicked up the moisture.

"I guess I should've worn boots tonight," she murmured, unperturbed.

Feeling cozy and warm while sitting in a chilly downpour was surreal.

Nice, but surreal.

Tessa glanced around. If any vampires hunted tonight, this would probably send them hightailing it back to wherever they stayed. Not that she needed to hang around and wait for any. She wasn't required to hunt yet and didn't feel the need to, thanks to the distraction Jared had provided.

She might as well head for Sean's place.

Rising, Tessa stepped onto the sidewalk and launched into a comfortable jog.

She had never run in the rain before. Either she had been too cold or her parents had called her inside so she wouldn't get muddy and track it all over the house. She found it rather freeing. Exhilarating. And far more entertaining than running on a treadmill in the sterile lab on sublevel five.

She should mention it to Bastien. She didn't know the immortal black sheep well, but his dedication to helping the vampires housed at network headquarters was heartwarming. A run in the rain might be a fun diversion for Stuart, Miguel, and the other vamps.

Water swiftly pooled on the sidewalk, creating satisfying splashes with every footfall. *One should never be too old to play in the rain*, she thought with a grin. Which, of course, brought Jared to mind. He was one of the oldest beings on Earth. Did he ever play in the rain?

He'd lived such a strangely isolated life that she doubted it.

Then again, he *had* appeared in movies as a cow, she thought with a grin.

The sky lit up as branches of lightning crawled through the clouds above. A long, loud rumble of thunder followed.

Tessa continued at a mortal's pace, enjoying the novelty of it. Sean would be awake until dawn, so there was no rush to reach his place.

"Hey!" a voice called behind her.

She glanced over her shoulder.

A lanky, waterlogged fellow waved and started loping toward her. He was at least twenty yards away and didn't look familiar.

Tessa faced forward and kept moving.

"Hey!" he called again. "You okay?"

She glanced around to see if he was talking to someone else, calling out to a friend or something. But they appeared to be the only two people out and about.

Slowing, she turned to face him. "Me?"

"Yeah!"

Tessa stopped and scrutinized him as he approached.

His hair was cut short on the sides and left long enough in front for sodden strands to fall just below his eyebrows. The darkness, heavy rain, and its saturated state made his hair color difficult to determine. But she thought it was light brown or dark blond. He wore a Duke University T-shirt with a light jacket, jeans, and sneakers that looked brand new.

Water splashed with every step as he caught up to her in a slouchy jog. "Hey," he repeated, breathing hard. "You okay?"

She eyed him warily. "Yes." No blood stained his clothing, and he didn't reek, leading her to believe he wasn't a vampire. The deluge currently pounding them could've cleaned him up though.

"I saw you running and... thought maybe something had happened," he said between gasps. "That someone had scared you or something."

"No. I'm fine."

He squinted up at the rain, then glanced around and motioned for her to follow him off the path to the shelter of a large oak tree. "Oh, man." Bending forward, he planted his hands on his knees. "I gotta start working out. I am *so* out of shape."

As Tessa joined him, she kept her eyes and ears open for any movement in the shadows that would hint he was a vampire and hadn't come alone.

Though the tree's canopy was dense, droplets still made their way down through the branches, dwindling to a drizzle by the time she felt them.

Peeling off his jacket, he held it out. "Here. Take this. I don't have an umbrella, but you can hold this over your head."

"No, thank you." When lightning flashed again, she pointed up at the tree. "You know, I don't think this is the best place to stand during a thunderstorm."

At first, he didn't seem to comprehend his mistake. Then his eyes widened. "Oh. Right." He motioned to a building nearby that had an overhang in front. "Let's go."

Tessa followed him to the slim shelter offered by the overhang in front of the building's entrance.

"Do you live on campus?" he asked. "Would you like me to walk you home?"

"No, thank you. I'm fine." She couldn't seem to get a feel for this guy.

"It's okay," he assured her. "I'm a safe mate."

She studied him. A safe *mate*? Was he a predator of the human kind then? One who liked to prey upon women who were out alone at night? "What?" If so, perhaps she would scare the living hell out of him to get him to change his ways.

"I'm a certified safe mate."

More like a certified nutjob. "Safe *mate*?"

He grinned. "Not mate, as in lover or partner. Mate, as in friend."

Tessa tensed when he reached into his back pocket.

Instead of a weapon, he produced his wallet, drew out a business card, and handed it to her. "It's a thing my girlfriend and some of her friends started. I *told* them mate was a bad choice, but the only alternative they could think of was escort. And they thought that sounded worse."

She took the card. SAFE MATES was stamped across it in fancy lettering.

"Anyone who is nervous about walking home alone or walking to their cars alone can call that number, and a volunteer like me will quickly arrive and escort them. The girls vet all of us guys and make sure we aren't assholes. And it's a free service." Again, he smiled. "Although we do take donations. Not in person, online. The back of the card tells you how you can do that, but you really don't have to pay anything. And *anyone* can call us, not just girls. There's a lot of hate going around, so we escort guys, too. Bullying sucks."

If this was legit, it sounded pretty cool. "Are you armed?" she asked curiously.

"Only with pepper spray." He shrugged sheepishly. "To be honest, I'm not much of a fighter. But we figured guys would be less likely to mess with girls if they had male escorts. And if some bullies or hater assholes are looking to wail on a guy, we figured we could provide safety in numbers." He motioned to the sidewalk they'd left. "When I saw you running, I thought maybe someone had scared you or tried to hurt you. That's just where my mind goes now. Dangerous times, you know?"

Tessa nodded. "Well, thank you for checking on me. But I'm fine."

"Good to hear. You want me to walk you to your car or dorm or wherever? I'm already out and soaked."

"No, thank you. I'm meeting someone."

"You sure you don't want to use my jacket as an umbrella? You can return it tomorrow to me or my girlfriend. Whichever you're more comfortable with."

Smiling, she shook her head. "I don't think my boyfriend would appreciate me showing up with another guy's jacket."

He tugged the jacket back on. "No offense, but if your boyfriend would rather you get sick from the rain and cold than cover yourself with another guy's jacket, then your boyfriend sucks."

She laughed. "Maybe." Tessa made a point of looking at her watch. "I have to go."

When she held out the business card, he waved a hand. "Keep it. Just in case you or a friend might need it. I'm TJ, by the way."

"Cassie," she lied. "Have a nice night, TJ." Stepping out into the rain, she smiled at him. "And steer clear of the trees."

He laughed. "I will. Stay safe."

"You, too."

Tucking the card in her coat pocket, Tessa jogged away.

The clouds above lit up as jagged bolts of lightning carved paths through them. A second later, thunder boomed so loudly it sounded like an explosion. Jumping, she laughed at herself and glanced back.

TJ stood under the overhang, squinting up at the sky. If he thought to wait out the rain, he would be there awhile because the storm seemed to intensify rather than letting up.

He must've drawn the same conclusion. Hunching his shoulders, he darted out into the rain and loped away, heading straight across the sidewalk and disappearing behind another building instead of turning right and following her.

Good.

Facing forward, Tessa picked up her pace. Wind whipped her. Big drops pounded her. Her shoes produced greater and greater splashes as they hit the pavement, delighting the child in her.

Exhilaration brought a smile to her dripping face as the pleasure she'd taken in the run before TJ's interruption returned. Her body remained toasty warm throughout. Even her fingertips were warm, something that continued to amaze her.

A lightning bolt arced down from the sky and pierced the trees in the distance, so bright it nearly blinded her.

That *must* have touched down somewhere.

Her smile faltered. Could Immortal Guardians survive lightning strikes?

*Hmm.* No one had mentioned that, so Tessa thought it best not to test it. Slowing, she took stock of the security cameras—something Sean had drummed into her on their hunts—then slipped behind a building into the nearest blind spot.

She'd give Jared a call. He wouldn't mind teleporting her to Sean's, and she didn't want him to pop in somewhere cameras might catch it.

More light flashed. Sharp pain pricked her upper back.

Crying out, Tessa froze.

Had lightning just struck her?

No. That would've hurt like hell, even as an immortal. This had felt more like the hard jab of a needle.

She sucked in a breath. A needle?

Reaching over her shoulder, she clawed at her back until her fingers encountered something cold and hard. After yanking it out, she stared at the long tranquilizer dart.

Weakness seeped into her.

*Oh crap.*

Tessa threw the dart down and shot away with every ounce of preternatural speed she possessed, her only thought to avoid capture. In this rain, even Immortal Guardians with senses more acute than a vampire's couldn't track her if she got far enough ahead of them to leave their sight. And so much water pooled in the grass and on the pavement that she doubted anyone hunting her could find her footprints.

Leaving the campus, she zipped across a street with no traffic and plunged into trees.

Her heart pounded heavily in her chest as she forced increasingly sluggish limbs to help her flee. *Jared*. When Tessa reached into her coat to retrieve her phone, she stumbled and nearly fell. Her head spun. Her movements slowed. Only one drug could take down an Immortal Guardian, and it was doing its damnedest to incapacitate her.

Tessa doggedly continued forward, moving at mortal speeds now, never looking back. Her fingers grew so clumsy that it took her three tries to unlock her phone. She scrolled through her contacts until she found Jared's name.

A heavy weight slammed into her back. The phone flew out of her hand as she tumbled forward. Her elbows and forearms hit the ground. Then she and the heavy body atop her slid forward several yards, floodwater spraying up as if she were a surfboard. Her right sleeve tore. Stinging pain erupted in her forearm. Stones and lumps in the uneven ground bruised her flesh. Her chin hit something hard as murky water invaded her mouth, nose, and eyes.

Tessa coughed and choked as they skidded to a halt. Gritty water obscured her vision.

"Damn, you're fast," a voice said in her ear. "I did *not* expect you to run."

*Sonofabitch*! It was TJ!

Curling her fingers into the mud, Tessa prepared to lurch up and throw the bastard off. *Safe mate, my ass.* Icy fear filled her when she couldn't raise her head more than a few inches, let alone the rest of her body. She was so weak! And she grew even weaker as TJ planted his hands on her back and pushed himself up to straddle her.

The last of her strength dissipated.

Her arms went limp.

Tessa's face sank beneath the surface.

Muddy water invaded her mouth and nose as darkness claimed her.

# CHAPTER SIXTEEN

N ICOLE SMILED AS SEAN loaded his plate with a second helping of eggplant parmesan. "Worked up an appetite, did ya?"

He grinned. "In the most amazing way possible."

"Hell yes."

After adding some of Cliff's chunky pasta sauce, Sean winked. "I also figured I should load up on carbs to refuel me for the rest of the night."

She pointed her fork at him. "I agree with that assessment. Eat up."

He laughed.

They had made love again after his proposal.

A thrill danced through her. Sean had proposed!

Then they'd enjoyed a long, leisurely soak in his whirlpool tub, laughing and talking while rain drummed on the roof and windows. A doozy of a storm had rolled in, creating so much thunder that she'd been tempted to call David's place and see what Seth and Leah were up to.

Much to Seth's dismay, his ability to control the weather got away from him whenever he and his mischievous wife engaged in passionate endeavors. It had become fodder for many jokes and a great deal of teasing in the Immortal Guardians' family.

Since Cliff and Emma wouldn't return until tomorrow, Nicole and Sean had donned less clothing than usual after their bath. Sean wore a pair of boxer briefs and a T-shirt that showed off a muscled form drool-worthy enough to appear in an underwear ad. Nicole wore a tank top and pajama shorts. She didn't think herself nearly as drool-worthy, but Sean sure seemed to like it.

Stomach still growling, she shoveled another forkful of pasta into her mouth. Sex with Sean had left her ravenously hungry.

"You're so beautiful," he murmured.

Cheeks as full as a chipmunk's, she covered her mouth and laughed. As soon as she finished chewing and swallowing, she shook her head. "And you're crazy as a bag of ferrets."

Sean grinned. "Crazy for *you*."

Nicole liked this flirtatious version of him. She liked *everything* about him and found it hard to believe that he wanted to marry her. That he wanted to spend eternity with her.

That he loved her.

Sean had seen her at her worst. Many times. After living together as long as they had, he could enumerate every one of her imperfections and knew well her stubborn streak.

Yet he loved her.

Did Sean know he was the first person to make such a claim? The first person ever to love her?

They chatted between bites. Neither mentioned work or their impromptu skydiving. Instead, they just let the conversation take them wherever it willed. Sean relayed much of the little chat he'd had with Cliff, Bastien, and Zach at the barbecue.

Both were laughing when a loud pounding shook the front door.

Instantly sober, they looked at each other, then shoved their chairs back and ran for the armory. Sean got there first and returned in a blink. "Here." With a katana in one hand, he offered her a tranq gun and a 9mm with the other.

"Thanks." One challenge Nicole had faced during her special ops training was learning how to shoot accurately with a weapon in each hand, something that required her to strengthen her arms and spend what felt like thousands of hours practicing.

But she'd aced it.

Taking the tranq gun in her left hand, she palmed the 9mm with her right and followed Sean to the front door.

More pounding threatened to break it.

"Are you getting that feeling?" Sean dipped his head and looked through the peephole.

"No." She bit her lip. "This may not be the best time to tell you, but I often don't if *my* safety is at risk."

He gave her an incredulous look. "Are you kidding me?"

"No."

Scowling, he motioned for her to lower her weapons. "We're gonna talk about this later." Unlocking the front door, he tugged it open.

Jared stood on the front porch. Though sheets of rain poured down behind him, not a drop of water dotted him. He must've teleported. Clasping his hands behind his back, he issued them a nod. "Forgive me for interrupting. I thought I would drop by and see if Tessa is ready to return to network headquarters."

Sean sent Nicole a look full of confusion.

She frowned. "Tessa isn't here."

Jared's eyebrows rose. "She's already left then?"

Sean shook his head. "She was *never* here. We haven't seen her tonight."

A ripple of apprehension passed over Jared's handsome features, furrowing his brows. He glanced away. "When we were at Duke, she told me she intended to visit you," he murmured. "Perhaps the rain changed her mind."

Sean propped his katana in a corner and opened the door wider. "Would you like to come in?"

Jared didn't respond. Reaching into his coat, he drew out his cell phone.

Nicole shivered as a cold, damp breeze buffeted her. With it came a feeling of foreboding.

Jared's fingers flew over the phone's screen before he brought it to his ear. He frowned. "She isn't answering."

Nicole looked from one man to the other as concern welled within her. "Maybe she's in the shower? She could've headed back to the network when the rain started."

Jared dialed another number. "Todd, is Tessa at network head-quarters?" Whatever Todd said lured a curse from Jared as he disconnected the call. "I'm going back to Duke."

Sean took a step toward him. "Do you want me to—"

Jared vanished.

"—go with you?" he finished.

Nicole met his gaze. "Arm up in case he needs you."

"You, too." Sean slammed the door and darted into the armory. By the time Nicole caught up with him, he wore hunting blacks and was pulling on his coat.

Nicole always kept it loaded with weapons and was pleased to see that Cliff had done the same in her absence. "Do you think Tessa's okay?"

His brows drew down. "I don't know. She *should* be. She's gotten better about not letting vampires circle around behind her when she fights more than one or two at a time. But—"

"It's weird that she isn't answering her phone."

"I'm more concerned about her not being here after telling Jared she planned to drop by. Tessa knows how important it is for new immortals to make their whereabouts known at all times. I had to do the same after I transformed. Before you became my Second, someone *always* had to know my whereabouts. Krysta. Étienne. Melanie. Bastien. Richart. The one time I forgot, Reordon and Seth gave me an ass-chewing that ensured I wouldn't make the same mistake again. It's a rule you just don't break."

Nicole exchanged her tank and shorts for bikini panties and a sports bra, topping them with a pair of black cargo pants and a long-sleeved turtleneck. Every Immortal Guardian's home armory included both weapons and hunting garb so they could gear up faster in an emergency.

Sitting on the padded bench, she tugged on boots and swiftly laced them up.

"Are you getting that feeling?" he asked again.

"No. But that doesn't necessarily mean anything, because I don't know Tessa well."

"And it doesn't warn you when *you're* the one in danger?" His words carried a bite that left no doubt of the anger that roused.

"Right."

"I was going to head to Duke to help Jared look for her," he said, temporarily dropping the subject, "but I don't want to leave you alone."

Shaking her head, Nicole rose and donned a two-gun shoulder holster. "Jared can search the entire campus in the time it would take you to run there."

"Good point. Call Cliff."

Nicole hurried to the kitchen, retrieved her phone, and called Cliff.

"Hey, Nicole," he answered genially.

"Hey. Sorry to cut your evening short, but we may have a situation."

"Hang on." His voice lowered. "Get dressed."

"Okay," Emma murmured in the background.

Cliff switched to speaker phone. "What's up?" he asked, all business now. Rustling ensued.

"Jared just came by. He said he wanted to see if Tessa was ready to go back to network headquarters. Apparently, she told him she was heading our way. But we haven't seen her."

"I assume you checked with the network?"

"Yes. Todd said she hasn't been back since she left with Jared."

"Where was she the last time Jared saw her?"

"Duke."

He swore. "Okay. I'm going to have Aidan teleport me to you."

"Us," his wife corrected. "He'll teleport *us*."

"I don't want to put you in danger," he told her.

"I've trained with weapons, honey," Emma said, "and can handle myself in a fight. I'm going with you."

More curses. "We'll be there in a few."

Nicole looked up at Sean as she pocketed the phone. "You heard that?"

"Yeah."

"Can Emma really handle herself?" Emma worked a desk job at network headquarters, arranging transfers for Immortal Guardians and their Seconds. That didn't exactly prepare one for battle.

He nodded. "Cliff said that after mercenaries attacked the original network headquarters, she wanted to get as strong as possible so she could help others if it happened again."

Nicole had been there that morning. Though she had worked hard with the other soldiers and guards to evacuate the building, some employees hadn't made it out safely.

"Part of the ground floor collapsed on her," Sean continued, "and she couldn't get out. By the time Cliff found her, mercenaries were already infiltrating the building. And a couple of Emma's work friends were dead. She doesn't want a repeat of that, so she started lifting weights and worked with every hand-to-hand combat instructor at the network."

"Really?"

"Yeah."

She smiled. "That's awesome. Go, Emma!"

Jared appeared beside them.

Nicole jumped and let out a startled squeak.

Water flattened his midnight hair to his skull, sluiced off his coat, and puddled on the floor. "She wasn't there. Is she here? Did I miss her?" Gone was his usual reserve. He now looked frantic.

Nicole shook her head. "We still haven't seen her."

"Seth!" he shouted.

Seth appeared beside them. "A little louder next time?" he drawled, then frowned when he noted Jared's waterlogged form and realized Nicole and Sean had geared up for battle. "What happened?"

"Tessa's missing," Jared blurted. "I was with her at Duke but got called away to help Caleb in Toronto. She said she was going to run here to see Sean and Nicole. I planned to join her but got another call, then another and another."

"We haven't seen her," Sean added. "She never came by."

Jared's Adam's apple bobbed up and down in a hard swallow as he stared at Seth. "She isn't answering her phone. Is she dead? Did vampires kill her?"

Seth closed his eyes.

Silence reigned, broken only by the storm that raged outside.

Nicole held her breath.

When Seth concentrated, he could sense every Immortal Guardian on the planet and determine each one's location. It was why—unlike Zach and Jared—he didn't need to follow a phone signal to teleport to them.

His brow furrowed. "I can't sense her."

Anxiety flooded her.

Jared stared at Seth as if he didn't want to believe it. "She's gone?" he asked in a soft, tortured voice.

Seth opened his eyes. "No. I would've felt it if she died. I just can't sense her. Something is blocking me."

Aidan abruptly appeared, his hands on Cliff's and Emma's shoulders.

Both mortals were armed and garbed like Seconds.

Aidan took in everyone's expressions. "Tessa's missing?"

Seth nodded. "I'm going to Duke with Jared. She was last seen there." He motioned to Nicole, Sean, Cliff, and Emma. "Take them to David's place. Have Darnell call a meeting. Then round up every Immortal Guardian and their Second in the area."

He and Jared vanished.

"Huddle up," Aidan ordered, face grim.

Nicole swiftly took Emma's hand while Sean gripped Cliff's shoulder.

The room darkened and fell away as weightlessness engulfed her. This time, it didn't frighten her. She was too worried about Tessa.

Seconds later, Nicole found herself back in David's office.

Darnell sat at his desk, his brown eyes glued to the large desktop screen while his fingers flew over the keyboard. Unlike Nicole, he didn't jump at their abrupt appearance. But he rose when he saw their expressions. "What happened?"

"Call a meeting," Aidan told him. "Let everyone know I'm coming to get them."

Darnell snatched his cell off his desk. "I'll send a group text." His thumbs darted over the screen. "Done."

Aidan teleported away and returned a second later with Dana at his side. Dipping his head, he pressed a quick kiss to her lips, then vanished again.

Dana swept them all with a worried look. "What happened?"

Darnell nodded, seconding the question.

"Tessa's missing," Nicole told them. "And Seth can't sense her."

Dana paled. "Does that mean she's...?"

Darnell shook his head. "Seth would've felt it if she'd died." He turned to Nicole and Sean. "Fill me in."

Dana left them and went to arm up in the armory while they gave him a swift rundown.

"Has anyone contacted Chris yet?" Darnell asked.

Nicole glanced at Sean. "I don't know. I don't think so."

Darnell reached for his phone again.

Sean met her gaze and jerked his head toward the door.

Nicole followed him to David's enormous living room, which—for once—was empty.

"Aidan is teleporting everyone directly to the armory," Sean said. "Do you have enough ammo?"

"Enough ammo for what?" she replied helplessly. "We don't even know what or whom we're dealing with. The last we heard, Seth was following Marge while David monitored the airport. The bad guys think Becca is dead. So what the hell could've happened to Tessa?"

Pulling her into a hug, Sean rested his chin on her head. "I don't know. Honestly, I'm hoping she just snuck away to visit her family or something." Since Tessa's family believed she and her twin brother had both died in an accident, that would be a huge no-no.

"Seth could find her if she had," Nicole pointed out.

He sighed. "I know."

Richart suddenly appeared, his arm wrapped around his wife. As soon as Jenna stepped away, he teleported away again and returned with Krysta. Left. Came back with Étienne. Left. Popped back in with Sheldon. Then teleported once more to retrieve Étienne's Second, Cameron. The immortals all wore wet coats, having been out hunting. The Seconds sported the usual black cargo pants and shirts but lacked weapons.

Staggering sideways, Richart started to topple.

Jenna leaped forward to steady him. "Honey?" Wrapping an arm around his waist, she steered him toward the kitchen. "Come on. Let's get you some blood."

Younger teleporters ran out of energy faster than the elders did.

Sheldon and Cam nodded to Nicole and Sean as they headed past them to join the others in the armory.

Sean released Nicole but kept an arm around her, needing her close.

Krysta eyed the two of them, her sharp gaze noting every point of contact. "Tessa's missing?"

They nodded.

She looked up at her husband. "Let's get some dry clothes and arm up for bear. We don't know what we're dealing with, and I want to face it with more than swords."

"Agreed."

The couple darted away.

Jenna and Richart emerged from the kitchen and followed the others, the latter walking a little steadier while he held a bag of blood to his lips.

Nicole looked up at Sean. "I hope Tessa's okay."

He pressed a kiss to her forehead. "Me, too."

Seth stood beside Jared, an unrelenting downpour assaulting them. "This was the last place you saw her?"

Jared nodded. "You're sure she isn't dead?"

"I'm sure. Calm yourself." Resting a hand on Jared's shoulder, Seth infused him with peace. "You need your wits about you." He had never seen Jared so rattled.

"The rain had not yet begun." Some of the anxiety left the Other's voice. "The campus was quiet, with few out and about. She said she was going to Sean's place. I offered to teleport her, but she wanted to run. It soothes her the same way it does the vampires. And I thought she would enjoy the freedom of it. She hasn't been alone since joining us, always watched or escorted by others, but..." His eyes flashed golden with regret. "I should have insisted."

Seth patted his shoulder. "Your eyes are glowing." While Jared closed his eyes and struggled to keep his emotions in check enough to reduce their luminescence, Seth studied the buildings and light posts around them. The campus was darker than usual, the heavy rains defeating the many lights that usually brightened it. He had been here so often that Seth knew the locations of most of the security cameras. "You searched the campus?"

"Yes. North to south and east to west."

"Any signs of a scuffle?"

"If there *was* one," he said with a despondent shake of his head, "the rain washed away any evidence of it."

*Imhotep*, Seth called telepathically.

*Yes?*

*I could use your postcognitive abilities.*

*As you will.*

*I'm on my way.* Seth stepped into the security cameras' blind spot and teleported to Imhotep's home in Egypt.

Sun blazed through the windows, a startling contrast to the darkness Seth had left behind.

Imhotep awaited him, having swiftly donned his hunting togs. His Second, Amun, stood beside him.

Seth nodded to Amun. "I shall return him shortly." Resting a hand on Imhotep's shoulder, he teleported him to Duke. "Tessa is missing."

Imhotep's brow furrowed. He had guarded Tessa a time or two when she first joined them and had spoken highly of her.

Seth led him to Jared's side. "Jared last saw her here a few hours ago. The rain is keeping most students and employees inside, so I'm hoping you'll pick up something." Postcognitive abilities could be tricky. Using them to view the past was similar to collecting forensic evidence. If events had just transpired and no one else had crossed the scene, Imhotep could see what happened as clearly as if he were watching a video he'd just rewound. But the more time passed and the more traffic disrupted the scene, the muddier the view became. It was easier, for example, to identify the footprints of a killer in a deserted area than to do the same on ground that hundreds of people had since trodden upon.

Imhotep stared at the sidewalk for a long moment. "I see her." He walked along the path, his gaze focused in front of him as if he were following someone. Stopping at a bench, he nodded at it. "She sat there for a time until it began to rain." He stepped back as if he wished to give her room to rise and move past him.

A moment later, he jogged away at mortal speeds, conscious of the cameras.

When Jared would've followed him, Seth threw an arm out to halt him. "The less we move about, the less we'll disturb the scene."

Jared regarded him with dismay. "I ran all over campus, looking for her."

That would likely make Imhotep's work more difficult. "You didn't know."

Tense silence fell.

Thunder roared. Lightning flashed.

"Where were you when I summoned you?" Jared asked.

"At the facility where they took the woman on the airplane." He didn't elaborate, knowing the immortal grapevine would've informed everyone in the area of the day's events.

"Do you know if this is related?"

"Tessa disappearing?"

"Yes."

"I heard no mention of it."

Jared fidgeted. "How can you be so calm?"

"I'm not calm." Worry gnawed at Seth. "I've just been here before." Tessa wasn't the first Immortal Guardian to go missing. Such had happened too many times to count over the millennia. It was why he had started assigning every Immortal Guardian a Second. Before the invention of telegraphs, ham radios, phones, and finally cell phones, Seth often hadn't known until weeks or months after the fact if an immortal went missing unless a telepathic immortal contacted him. And younger telepaths had a shorter range, so they would have to relay that message from immortal to immortal until it reached Seth.

If those who were missing had Seconds, the Seconds could narrow down the last known locations of the immortals and launch their own searches until Seth arrived.

Jared cast him a penitent look. "I wish I had defected when you did."

He'd had strong reason not to. "You're here now. That's all that matters." Seth refused to dwell on the many lives that could've been saved if Jared and the rest of the Others had joined him and watched over his Immortal Guardians. Doing so would not alter the past.

Leah's voice filled his head. *Seth?* she asked tentatively.

*Yes?*

*I can feel your turmoil. What's happening?*

*Tessa is missing.*

*Oh no! Can I do anything?*

*Where are you?*

*Fussing over Caleb. He nearly lost an arm and a leg earlier tonight.*

Warmth filled him. His Immortal Guardians all adored Leah, who shone in her new role as matriarch of the group. *Meet me at David's when you're finished. I've called an emergency meeting and will head there as soon as Imhotep has gathered as much information as possible.*

*Okay. I love you.*

*Love you, too.*

A spray of water raced toward them, then veered behind a building. Seconds later, Imhotep rounded the corner and joined them, his countenance grim.

"What did you learn?" Seth asked.

"Jared said she intended to run to Sean's house. I believe she began doing so at a mortal's pace, but a man waylaid her up there." Swiveling, he pointed up the path.

"Waylaid?" Jared blurted. "By whom?"

"A vampire she thought was a student."

Jared frowned. "I wouldn't have expected her to fall for such a ruse."

Imhotep shrugged. "He was good. Nothing in his speech or mannerisms gave her reason to doubt him. Yet she remained wary. They spoke briefly. Then she left. The vampire headed off in a different direction but changed course once he was out of sight. She stopped." He met Jared's gaze. "To call you. I saw your name on her phone. But before she could, the vampire came up behind her."

"She didn't hear him?" Jared asked.

Imhotep shook his head. "The rain made too much noise, drumming on the roofs, hammering cars and dumpsters, and splashing in puddles as the campus flooded." He held up a cylindrical object with a fluffy red end. "He shot her with this. It took me a while to find it. It floated some distance away after she yanked it out and dropped it."

Seth took the tranquilizer dart. "Is it the sedative?" He sniffed it but smelled only rainwater and mud.

"Yes. She reacted wisely and raced away as fast as she could. Too fast for the vampire to catch her at first. If the drug had not tugged at her, she would've lost him. She passed the stadium, crossed Cameron Boulevard, and tried to lose him in the trees. But her declining speed enabled him to keep her in view. She was trying again to call Jared when the vampire caught her and took her down. I found this in the floodwater." Imhotep held out a cell phone with a cracked surface.

Taking it, Jared turned a tortured gaze on Seth. "I should've been with her. I never should have left her."

Seth shook his head. "We didn't anticipate this." He held up the dart. "Roubal didn't have the tranquilizer, so we assumed that whoever we're dealing with now didn't either." He turned back to Imhotep. "What happened next?"

"The vampire called someone. An SUV with dark windows pulled up. He got inside with Tessa, and then they drove off. I followed but lost them when they reached 15/501."

If the rain and the late hour hadn't kept pedestrians inside, Seth knew Imhotep would've lost them long before that. "What direction were they heading?"

"North."

"Thank you."

"Anytime, my friend."

After pocketing the dart, Seth rested a hand on Imhotep's shoulder. "I'll return momentarily." He teleported to Egypt, bid Imhotep good day, then returned to Duke.

Jared stood in the same place he'd left him. "I shouldn't have left her alone," he said as soon as Seth reappeared.

"Caleb needed you. David and I were both away, and Zach—"

"*She* needed me more!" he roared.

Seth kept his voice tranquil. "You didn't know that."

Jared shook his head. "What is the use of having precognitive abilities if they don't warn me about what's coming?" His visions were far stronger than Seth's and almost always came true.

"I wondered the same thing when my wife and children were slain," Seth murmured absently.

A stricken look crossed Jared's features. "You think they'll kill her?"

"No. If this vampire worked for the same group as Reed, they need her too much. Either Reed told them she's an immortal, or they think she's a vampire friend of Becca and their only remaining link to Nick now that they believe Becca is dead. Regardless, we'll get her back."

Jared's hands curled into fists as his eyes blazed with golden light. "I'll kill them all when we do."

"I understand your thirst for vengeance, your desire to punish," Seth said slowly, "but you will do this my way." When Jared shot him a glare, Seth held up a hand. "You *will* do this my way, or you will remain behind."

"You think you can stop me?" he growled.

"Yes."

Knowing Seth really *could* stop him didn't reduce Jared's ire.

"To be an Immortal Guardian," Seth reminded him, "you must maintain the delicate balance we always have. If you can do that, follow me to David's. If you cannot, return to the network and sit this one out."

Leaving him to decide, Seth teleported away.

Sean eyed the men and women gathered around David's long dining table. Ami sat beside Marcus, catty-corner to Seth's empty chair at the foot of the table with a baby monitor in front of her.

Little Adira must be sleeping. Roland and Sarah sat beside them with a second baby monitor.

Darnell and Chris Reordon sat at the opposite end by David's empty seat, scrutinizing the screens of a couple of laptops. Darnell shook his head and pointed. Nodding, Chris started to type.

Krysta claimed the seat beside Sean near the middle of the table. Once she greeted him and Nicole, she fell quiet and kept sending him glances from the corner of her eye.

"What?" he blurted when it worked his nerves.

"Nothing," she answered quickly.

Étienne snorted as he took the seat on her other side. "She feels guilty."

Krysta shot him a scowl. "Don't tell him that."

Puzzled, Sean studied his sister. "Why?" Had she done something he hadn't heard about yet?

She loosed an exaggerated sigh. "Because *I'm* usually the one who does reckless shit, like jumping out of an airplane without a parachute."

He quirked a brow. "Or leaping into the air and grabbing the landing skid of a helicopter as it takes off?"

Her husband's lips curled up. "Then killing the pilot before he can land?"

She grimaced. "Yes."

Sean smiled. "It sucks, doesn't it? Being on the other side." Worrying from the back seat.

"Yes!" she exclaimed. "It sucks balls! Don't ever do that crap again."

Amusement dawning, he shook his head. "I'll tell *you* what you told *me.*" He assumed an exaggeratedly penitent expression. "I'll try."

Krysta bit out several curses.

Laughing, Sean nodded hello to Jenna and Richart as they sat on Nicole's other side. It looked like Nicole and Darnell were the only Seconds seated at the table. Everyone else who claimed a chair was an Immortal Guardian. The rest of the Seconds formed an oval around them. All bore grim expressions and stood with their feet braced apart, arms crossed over their chests.

279

Zach teleported in with Nick, Kayla, and Becca. Sean was a little surprised to see the teenager joining them. Had she insisted they include her? Or had Nick and Kayla been too afraid to let her out of their sight?

Seth appeared and seated himself beside Leah at the foot of the table. Rainwater drip-drip-dripped from his shoulder-length hair. Taking his wife's hand, he brought it to his lips for a kiss and looked around. "Where's David?"

Darnell glanced over at him. "He went to the airport here in North Carolina to see if any unplanned flights left tonight."

"The one Sean and Nicole departed from?"

"Yes."

Jared appeared and sank into the only other free chair. Like Seth, he looked as if he'd just showered with his clothes on.

Sheldon darted into the kitchen. When he returned, he handed Seth a towel and tossed the other to Jared.

"Thank you." Seth drew the soft cotton over his hair and down his face.

Jared did the same, his face set in stone.

Sean stared at him. The smiling, loquacious movie buff from network headquarters had morphed into a silent would-be executioner who looked ready to attack.

David joined them, his clothing as saturated as the others', droplets of water dripping off the ends of his dreadlocks.

Sheldon trotted into the kitchen once more and returned with another towel.

Taking it with a smile, David sank into his chair. "Thank you."

All quieted.

Chris held up a finger and met Seth's gaze. "Before we begin, I think you should bring Henderson in on this. I already gave him a heads-up."

Leah patted Seth's hand and rose. "I'll get him." She vanished. A few seconds later, she reappeared with Scott Henderson, head of the Midwest division of the network.

Holding a briefcase that looked as battered as Reordon's, Scott nodded. "Evening, everyone."

Aidan retrieved a chair and nudged it in beside Chris and Darnell.

"Thank you." Henderson seated himself and drew a laptop out of his case.

Once everyone was settled, Seth met David's gaze. "What did you learn?"

# CHAPTER SEVENTEEN

D AVID LEANED BACK IN his chair. "Another flight left earlier tonight. Like the first, it was unscheduled. No one at the airport knows how many were aboard. An SUV with dark windows bypassed the terminal and drove into a hangar. All passengers boarded before the private jet exited. But the fact that Danvers called the terminal supervisor ahead of time and insisted he keep all eyes indoors leads me to believe they had Tessa."

"Did anyone know its destination?"

David shook his head. "The pilot filed no flight plan."

Nick huffed in disbelief. "How many jets does this bastard own?"

His eyes still on his laptop, Chris said, "Five. Benford usually keeps one here in North Carolina for personal use, another in Texas for family use, and three more in California for charter. But two months ago, he moved a couple of the California jets here to North Carolina, likely to aid him in his quest to get his hands on an Immortal Guardian."

One of the Seconds muttered, "What the hell do rich people have to complain about?"

Another snorted. "I know, right?"

David ignored them. "I teleported to the other airport and read every mind. It took some time to find someone who saw the identifiers on the tail of the last jet to land. They were the same as the numbers on the jet that departed here. But again, no one could confirm how many passengers disembarked. Nor did they know where the passengers went after they left."

Seth leaned back in his chair. "I think it's safe to say that the same people who kidnapped Nicole now have Tessa."

Murmurs of agreement rumbled all around.

Nicole looked from face to face. "What about Marge? What happened to her?"

"They took her to an advanced research facility," Seth said, "in an isolated location in Texas used to study diseases and develop pharmaceuticals. Based on what I heard, Marge is about to become the subject of their latest study."

Sean shook his head. "Seriously, what is up with Texas? The facility they tortured Ami in was there. Gershom infiltrated a top-secret military base there. Now this?"

Chris dragged his gaze away from his screen. "It's a big damn state with a lot of land to get lost in and plenty of places to hide things."

Henderson nodded. "Real estate is also more affordable there."

"And it's home to the largest medical city in the world," Chris added.

"Where's that?" Krysta asked.

"Houston," Nick, Kayla, Henderson, and Reordon replied.

Chris spoke. "Scott and I have been coordinating our efforts to investigate Augustus Benford, his holdings, and his relationship with Roubal. The link to Roubal still doesn't appear to be a strong one. And we found no digital communication between the two in the weeks that led up to Roubal's untimely demise."

"Our investigation," Henderson picked up, "led us to several shell companies, one of which handles all business and transactions conducted by the research facility. Several months ago, the facility beefed up security. Corporate espionage is on the rise in the pharma industry, so they already had fairly decent security before. But now it's so tight that you'd think every employee was carrying the nuclear football."

Becca bit her lip. "I don't know what that means."

"It's the president's emergency satchel," Henderson elaborated. "The president of the United States is always accompanied by a military aide who carries the case, which would enable the president to launch a nuclear attack while away from fixed command centers like the Situation Room or the Presidential Emergency Operations Center."

"In other words," Chris added, "security at that facility is even tighter than at network headquarters."

Multiple whistles of awe filled the room.

The network did *not* skimp on security.

"I parked Rafe outside the facility," Henderson continued.

"Who's Rafe?" Sean asked.

Nick answered. "He's an Immortal Guardian stationed in Texas. I've hunted with him many times."

"According to Rafe," Henderson said, "no cell phones or smart watches are allowed on the premises. Every employee received a photo ID tag and a personal code when hired. To get past the first level of security, they must show the guards their ID and enter the code into a touch screen after walking through a metal detector to ensure they aren't carrying hidden phones or other recording and listening devices. They must then undergo a second security check that requires fingerprint scans, and they can't leave without passing through the metal detector again. *No one* can take *any* work home with them."

Sean frowned. "Is that normal?"

Henderson shrugged. "The fingerprint scans aren't. And many pharma companies are laxer about employees taking work home with them. But if you're in pharma and are onto something big like a cure for cancer, the last thing you'd want is for some employee to take a laptop containing twenty years of research with them to the airport and have someone use the airport's public network hub to hack it and enable a competitor to come out with a cure six months later based on your research."

"Or," Chris added, "have an employee take his work home, absently toss some papers in the trash, and have the same thing happen after a competitor engages in a round of sneaky dumpster diving."

Henderson nodded. "And bypassing the security protocols on the wireless routers used in most homes is easy for those in the know, providing access to all home computer systems that use it."

"Some companies," Chris went on, "will learn the names and home addresses of competitors' employees for just those reasons."

Most of those present looked as stunned as Sean felt upon hearing that. It was like something you'd see in a freaking James Bond movie.

Seth, David, and the other ancients seemed unsurprised.

Henderson reached into his satchel and drew out a stack of papers. "Rafe also believes there are soundproof rooms in parts of the building that boast the highest security and safety protocols. He said there were several instances in which conversations he listened to shut off abruptly when a door closed."

Chris nodded. "The same way they do when network employees enter restrooms." All restrooms at network headquarters in North Carolina were soundproofed to keep the vampires housed below from complaining about having to listen to employees evacuate their bladders and bowels all day.

Nicole frowned. "What kind of research do they usually do there? When they're not hunting immortals, that is."

Henderson glanced at Seth. "You want to take that one?"

He shook his head. "I was focused on those surrounding Marge."

"Right. Well, Rafe skimmed through as many employee minds as he could. Their biggest project is an effective treatment for Alzheimer's."

"A treatment or a cure?" Nicole asked.

Henderson's lips curled up in a cynical smile. "A treatment. Costly medication that patients will have to take every day for the rest of their lives will earn Benford far more money than a cure will."

She frowned. "That sucks."

"That's business. Benford didn't dive into the pharmaceutical industry out of the goodness of his heart. He's in it for the money."

"Why?" Sarah blurted. "He's already a multibillionaire. What more could he possibly want that he doesn't already have?"

Henderson shrugged. "The ability to brag about being the wealthiest man in the world."

"*And* immortality," Seth added. "Reed hand-delivered a vampire to them for experimentation. The vampire was told they would make him human again and had no idea what was in store for him."

"That's messed up," Sean murmured.

"Yes, it is," Seth agreed. "He was newly turned and fully lucid. But after just a few weeks in their *care*, he lost his sanity, which led them to believe the madness strikes so quickly that they must get their hands on an Immortal Guardian. Otherwise, any fountain of youth serum they concoct will turn their influential clients into bloodthirsty monsters who must be slain. The purpose is to *lengthen* their life spans, not *shorten* them. Reed also gave them the sedative that was used to capture Tessa."

Sean caught Seth's eye. "Do they know what happened to Reed, that he's dead?"

"Gary, the second vampire who tried to nab Becca, told them an Immortal Guardian killed him. But Gary wasn't playing with a full deck. He'd be lucid one moment and violently psychotic the next. According to their thoughts, most preferred to deal with TJ."

"Who's TJ?" Sean asked.

"The vampire who captured Tessa. The doctors prefer to deal with *him* now because they believe Gary killed Reed so he could reap more of the benefits."

"What benefits?" Nicole asked.

"Reed told the lab that he and his crew would only hunt immortals if Benford compensated them for the risks they had to take. I believe he had lost touch with Gershom by this point and wanted a little financial security. The doctors working on the serum don't know what fee the vampires demanded, only that Benford paid them weekly. They did, however, know that the vampires were promised a cash bonus of two million dollars upon delivery of an immortal *and* guaranteed a dose of the final serum once it's developed."

"How will that help them?" Krysta asked. "They're already infected."

Seth dipped his chin in a nod. "Yes, but the doctors told them the serum would banish the madness, their need for blood, and their photosensitivity while leaving them with all the perks of infection."

Stunned silence gripped the room. No one moved or spoke for a long moment as they let the implications sink in.

A serum like that would be a serious game-changer.

Melanie sat forward. "Do they believe that's possible?"

"Unknown."

She flattened her hands on the table. "Okay. I don't know what the plan is, but I want to be on the front lines. I need to get in there and see what they've been doing. I want to see their research."

Bastien frowned. "I don't imagine they have much. It sounds as if they knew nothing about the virus or vampires and immortals until a few months ago. They're probably just talking out of their asses."

She looked up at him. "If there's even a chance that they aren't..."

Chris shook his head. "I agree with Bastien." That had to be a first. "I think they're bullshitting and telling the vampires what they want to hear to keep them on the leash."

Melanie whirled on him. "You *think*. You don't *know*. *I* need to know."

Bastien draped an arm across the back of her chair and rested his fingers on her shoulder. "Sweetheart—"

"No." A hint of desperation entered her earnest expression. "I need to know if they've found something I'm missing, Bastien."

"How could they? You've been studying this virus and its effects on the brain ever since you finished medical school."

"And I still haven't found either a cure or a way to halt or reverse the progression of the brain damage it causes in humans," she countered, voice rising. "In the greater scheme of things, I'm new to viral research *and* the study of cognitive diseases. Some of those researchers may have decades more experience than I do."

Chris shook his head. "Network doctors worldwide have been studying this virus for over a century, Melanie. They haven't found the answer either."

"Besides," Bastien added, "you heard Henderson. The doctors in that lab aren't interested in finding cures. Their focus is on developing drugs that treat the symptoms."

"Yes. Drugs that mitigate the symptoms of cognitive decline. And the cognitive decline in vampires is their primary problem. It's what costs them their sanity, their identity, and ultimately their lives. If *anything* in that lab's arsenal can help Stuart and the others, I want to get my hands on it." She swung on Chris. "Delete *nothing* until I examine it." She speared the rest of them with a look that promised dire retribution if they didn't obey her will. "And don't destroy *any* computers, laptops, tablets, or hard drives. Period. I need the information they may hold. That is *non*-negotiable."

Chris and Henderson shared a look.

"That," Chris said at length, "changes things."

David tilted his head to one side. "How so?"

Leaning back in his chair, Chris rubbed his stubbled chin. "Considering how high-tech that facility is and how extensive their security, I worried they may have a remote monitoring service the way we do here in North Carolina. The security feed of every camera at network headquarters isn't just monitored by our guards onsite. It's also monitored at two undisclosed remote locations to prevent telepaths from simply seizing control of the guards' minds and making them ignore any threats the cameras catch."

Almost everyone present darted Aidan surreptitious glances. The ancient Celtic immortal had once incurred Chris's wrath—which had lingered long—by doing just that and breaking into network headquarters shortly after Sean and Krysta had joined the Immortal Guardians' ranks.

Noticing the looks, Aidan crossed his arms over his broad, muscled chest and glared a warning.

"To avoid that possibility," Chris continued, unphased, "I thought I could have Seth pop in and hit the facility with a targeted EMP that would cut the power and take out all electronic devices, including their security system and backup generators."

Henderson nodded. "That would eliminate the risk of exposure by cutting all modes of communication and preventing cameras from catching you zipping around at inhuman speeds with glowing eyes."

Chris held up a finger. "But it would also wipe all the hard drives."

"*Hell* no," Melanie blurted. "I'm not kidding. I want every shred of data they have."

Cliff stepped forward between two Seconds. "I agree. We don't know how long they've had access to vampires. If Roubal is behind this, it hasn't been long. But if Gershom instigated it..." He shook his head. "Gershom liked to play the long game. For all we know, he could've hand-delivered a vampire to them a year ago—or five years ago—and then had Reed deliver a second one to them more recently, along with the tranquilizer and a little extra info on immortals. Plus, if Benford has *this* facility working on the virus, who's to say he doesn't have another one doing the same?"

Henderson pursed his lips. "We've found nothing to indicate that, but it *is* a possibility."

Chris sighed. "Tessa mentioned Reed was away, possibly working on some special project for Gershom, when we struck Roanoke and the base in Texas. It could've been this, but we weren't able to obtain telepathic confirmation of that."

Because Nick had killed Reed before they could.

A heavy silence fell as all eyes went to Nick.

Henderson broke it with a clearing of his throat. "I had Rafe draw a map of the facility, based on what he saw in employees' minds. We're having a hard time getting our hands on the building specs but hope to have those soon. Until then, Rafe's drawing will give us a general idea of where the soundproof rooms are. If the vampire they've been studying is still alive, he'll be in one of them. They'll hold Tessa in the other. Since they're hoping she's infected with a modified variant of the virus, they won't want to risk any cross-contamination." He gave David and Chris each a piece of paper, then handed a stack to Darnell.

Darnell took a sheet and passed the stack along. Once the immortals each had a copy, Sheldon took the remaining pages and handed them out to Seconds.

Chris held up his copy. "Rafe confirmed that this is where they studied the virus they extracted from the first vampire Reed took them. We just can't confirm that Reed did it on Gershom's orders."

Sean glanced at Nicole. If only they'd been able to interrogate Reed before Nick killed him.

Brow furrowing, she looked at Seth. "Do you think Gershom knew you were going to defeat him and wanted to start another ball rolling?"

Zach snorted. "Gershom was too arrogant to envision his own defeat."

Seth studied the map. "I agree. However, I see no other explanation for how these people got their hands on the sedative."

Roland scowled. "At the risk of repeating myself—"

Chris pointed at him. "Do *not* say it. *All* network employees are thoroughly vetted. *None* have betrayed us, not even those I transferred to shitty positions after they tried to kill Cliff."

All eyes shifted to Cliff, who shrugged. "Can't blame them for wanting me dead after I hurt so many during my worst psychotic break."

"I can," Emma declared with a scowl.

"I can, too," Bastien and Melanie added.

"I can and did," Chris professed. "And even those guys haven't betrayed us."

Seth held up a hand to calm flaring tempers. "For now, we'll operate on the assumption that Gershom gave them the sedative so we can move on and decide how to liberate Tessa."

Jared frowned. "We'll liberate her by going in tonight, won't we?"

"We have not yet formulated a plan," Seth reminded him.

"We don't need a plan," Jared snapped. "We just go in, grab her, kill everyone who hurt her, and get out."

Roland smiled. "I like this man."

Marcus snorted. "You would."

Seth shook his head. "This isn't a mercenary compound, Jared. It isn't a military base chock full of heavily armed soldiers. It's a pharmaceutical research facility. Most of its employees are conducting research meant to *help* people. Members of the maintenance staff who clean the place every night are just working to support themselves and their families. They are nonviolent and aren't there with malicious intent. We can't just rush in and start decapitating people left and right when our targets are the few who are holding Tessa."

Cliff held up a finger. "And those who tortured the vampires they experimented on."

Jared threw up his hands. "Then we rush in, kill those few, retrieve Tessa, and let the rest of the employees sort out the aftermath."

Chris let out a huff of disbelief. "We don't want them sorting it out, Jared. You heard Melanie. Our goal here isn't just to rescue Tessa. It's also to find out how much these people know, determine whether their source was Roubal or Gershom, and see how many others they've shared that information with."

Unphased, Jared said, "Then tell us what to steal and whom to question, and we'll get it done."

"Oh please," Chris rebutted. "You *can't* get it done. You aren't tech-savvy enough to get it done. None of you immortals are. We need access to their network, which has multiple tiers of protection. We need to search their hard drives and cloud backups, comb through their research data and their contacts. And all of that will take time. This place already had tight security before. With an immortal in custody, they will be on even higher alert. If you zip through their security checkpoints and start breaking shit up and blowing it to smithereens, we'll never get what we need."

A muscle in Jared's jaw twitched. "Tessa comes first."

Though pissing off someone with Jared's power was imbecilic, Sean felt the need to point out, "Tessa would want us to get what we need."

Nicole rested a hand on his thigh under the table. "I agree."

Jared's eyes glowed gold with anger. "When she's being tortured?"

"It's too soon for that," Melanie inserted. "The first thing they'll do is secure her and take blood samples. Right now, they have no reason to suspect her DNA is more advanced than that of an ordinary human or the vampires they've studied. They think she's infected with an alternate strain of the virus, one that doesn't cause brain damage. So they'll focus on comparing the virus she's infected with to the one they extracted from the vampires to see how they vary. When it becomes clear that the viruses are the same, they'll then want to determine if there's something unique about *Tessa* that makes it behave differently and will sequence her DNA. Since *her* DNA is far more complex than a human's, sequencing it will require multiple samples and take longer than usual."

"How long?" he demanded.

"Up to two weeks, depending on their speed and performance, maybe longer. In the meantime, they'll run a full blood panel to check for all the usual things doctors do during annual physicals. After discovering she doesn't host a different variant of the virus,

291

they might also question whether Reed was right about her being an immortal rather than a vampire like the others and wonder how they can prove it."

"How *can* they prove it?" Jared pressed.

She shifted, her look turning uneasy. "Until they finish sequencing her DNA, there aren't a lot of options on that. The easiest way would be to deny her blood or drain her."

If Jared could pale, Sean thought he would've been as white as a sheet upon hearing that. Jared sent Seth a look of panic.

"They are unlikely to resort to that before we get to her," Seth assured him. "Chris, Scott, what do you propose?"

A hush fell as the two network heads considered possible courses of action.

Henderson tapped a finger on the table, his head tilted to one side. "I think we should approach this from a corporate espionage perspective, rather than as a military incursion. It will preserve the data needed for their other research, prevent unnecessary deaths, and keep our identities safe. If we do this right, we'll be able to accomplish all of our goals without them even knowing with certainty whether immortals are responsible or one of their competitors."

Seth met David's gaze and held it long enough for Sean to assume they were conversing telepathically. A moment later, he nodded. "How do you suggest we proceed?"

Chris retrieved his trusty notepad and stubby number two pencil, then started writing. "I propose we choose a doctor who works days and have an immortal shape-shifter impersonate him. Scott's crew is already compiling a list of employees and their home addresses. The shape-shifter won't have to be spot-on the way we believed Becca's should be. He'll just need to fool the guards. And since the guards only see the doctors twice a day, as they arrive and as they depart, they're unlikely to notice minor discrepancies. Once we choose a doctor, we'll get our hands on his fingerprints. Seth can take my team to the doctor's house—preferably one who lives alone—to collect those. While he's there, Seth can pluck the doctor's security code from his mind. My team will apply the fingerprints to the shape-shifting immortal's hand. And that, along with the code and badge we'll modify, will get him through security."

Sheldon whistled. "That's some serious Mission Impossible shit there."

Sean nodded. "Except unlike Ethan Hunt and his team, immortals don't need makeup and masks to look like someone else."

Jared scowled. "Why can't he rush through security with enhanced speed? He'll be too fast for the cameras to catch, and everyone else will just feel a breeze."

"The alarm will go off," Chris responded without looking up from his notes.

"If the alarm goes off and they don't see anyone, they'll just assume it was a malfunction."

Chris's writing paused as he looked up. "You think they'll believe a malfunction with the security alarm happening the same night they kidnapped and captured an immortal being is a coincidence?"

Silence.

"We don't know their lockdown procedures," Chris continued, "or what weapons they may have in their arsenal. We've been in places before that were outfitted with booby traps designed specifically to halt immortals in their tracks."

Henderson nodded. "And this place *is* a pharmaceutical company. They've had the sedative for an unknown amount of time. For all we know, they've found a way to administer it as an aerosol. Even worse, what if they've developed a drug that's poisonous to both vampires and immortals?"

Melanie's brow furrowed. "I agree. We should play it safe on this."

Chris's phone buzzed with an incoming message. After reading it, he tapped a response and set the phone back on the table. "I suggest the shape-shifter we send in also be a teleporter. Once he reaches an interior room with no occupants, he can then teleport out, collect the rest of the team, and teleport back in. We'll dress some team members as maintenance staff and cleaning crew, who rarely garner attention. The uniforms are pretty generic, and the network keeps a variety on hand at all times."

Of course, they did. Because Chris thought of everything.

"Since security is so tight, any employees on-site will be less likely to raise a red flag if they see an unfamiliar face, because they have no reason to believe anyone could sneak in. One team will retrieve Tessa and take care of the vampire if they still have one in custody. The other will hack their system, retrieve the data we want, and then plant a virus that will erase everything related to vampires and immortals while leaving the rest of their data intact. Once done, they'll rendezvous at a designated place where the shape-shifter will teleport them out."

Jared turned to Seth. "Is that really necessary?"

"I believe so," the immortal leader responded. "We need to know definitively if this was Roubal's brainchild or if this is Gershom's Plan B. And I don't want any employees who are working in other departments to be harmed or their research destroyed."

Sean thought it was a sound plan. But clearly Jared disagreed.

"Why can't you just command everyone to fall asleep, sabotage their security measures, and force them to tell you what you want to know?"

That *did* sound less labor-intensive.

"Because we must maintain a balance," Seth reminded him, an edge of warning entering his deep voice as he caught and held Jared's gaze. "As you already know."

Once more, a hush descended.

"I don't understand," Becca said tentatively. "What balance?"

Kayla turned to her daughter. "Becca—"

Seth stayed her with a slight wave of his hand and turned a kind look upon her daughter. "There was a time long ago when those of our ilk—the first generation of Others that came before Zach, Jared, and me—walked openly amongst humans. When they shared their *magic*—as it was called then—with humans, such chaos and destruction resulted that the world had to be wiped clean to... reset things, if you will."

"The Great Flood," Sarah murmured.

Nodding, Seth motioned to himself, Zach, and Jared. "When *our* generation of Others was born, we were cautioned not to interfere with humans in any way, to keep ourselves apart so humanity could progress at its own pace. It's why Jared and the Others were so furious when I defected and married a human woman. They feared history would repeat itself. But I was very careful—I have *always* been careful—not to overstep my self-imposed bounds. Only once have I failed in that."

The day his wife and children were slain. Sean didn't know what had happened that day, but rumor labeled it catastrophic.

"I used my gifts," Seth continued, "to *help* humanity, not to corrupt them. And I often did so in secret. When vampires appeared on the scene, humans were no match for them. Had *gifted ones* suffered the same mental deterioration as vampires, mankind would've long since gone extinct. But *gifted ones* instead became immortals. So I banded them together, declared myself their leader, and trained them to hunt and slay vampires. We *restored* the balance."

"What kind of balance?" Becca asked. "I'm still not sure I understand."

"The kind that keeps us from conquering the world."

Zach smiled darkly. "Which we are more than capable of doing."

Seth tipped his head in acknowledgment. "The hunter who sits up in a blind and shoots a defenseless, unsuspecting deer while it feeds below has an unfair advantage. There is no balance. The deer has no chance of survival."

Sheldon muttered, "Unless the hunter is a sucky shot."

Seth's lips twitched. "We immortals must never set ourselves up as the hunter in the blind."

Becca glanced around the table. "What exactly do you think will happen if you do?"

"Armageddon," Zach supplied.

She blinked. "Seriously?"

The immortals in the room—all of whom already knew this—nodded.

Seth gave her a gentle smile. "It's why we take pains to even the field when we engage in battle. Our exceptional speed and strength, coupled with our gifts, give us an unfair advantage over humans. When we fought mercenaries or blitzed their bases, they always dramatically outnumbered us. And though the network's human special ops soldiers matched the mercenaries in weaponry and machinery, we immortals only carried our swords and blades. They had greater numbers. We had greater speed. They had automatic and semiautomatic weapons and grenades. We had incredible strength and regenerative capabilities."

He turned to Jared. "If we just barge in there and fell everyone with our gifts as Jared here desires, there will be no balance."

Jared's jaw jutted forward. "You forced information from the mercenary minds when you and your immortals attacked their bases."

"I didn't get anything out of them that torture wouldn't have also elicited. And that was different. *Their* actions—had they succeeded—would've put all of humanity in danger."

"And this won't?" Jared countered.

"No. The purpose of this is to make Benford wealthier."

"And enable him and his richest cronies to live forever," Jared pointed out disparagingly.

"Something we can remedy with our blades if it comes to that," Seth reminded him. "But Benford doesn't plan to share immortality with the masses. This won't launch wars or kick-start Armageddon. Again, these aren't mercenaries intent on developing an army of supersoldiers they can hire out to the highest bidder. They're doctors. Medical researchers. We don't need to kill everyone to keep them from telling tales, because most of them don't know what is transpiring in those soundproof rooms."

Jared glowered. "And those who do?"

Seth shrugged. "Those who do and who harm Tessa to achieve their end are fair game."

"They're mine," Jared growled.

"As long as you abide by the plan," Seth granted. "If you don't, I'll summon the Others to restrain you until we're finished. We *must* maintain a balance, Jared. You know that. It's why you hunted me for years after I defected. It's why you tortured Zach. We have to meet humans on their terms as much as possible, especially after what happened the night we defeated Gershom. That was an immense exhibition of power. Now more than ever, we must do nothing that may spark repercussions."

Jared couldn't deny it and did *not* look happy. "This all sounds as if it will take days to accomplish. Days of Tessa being at those people's mercy."

"Actually," David inserted, "we need to get it all done in a matter of hours. The jet that carried Tessa to Texas was refueling when I left and will head back to North Carolina later tonight. In the morning, two new pilots will fly Benford to Texas. No doubt he wishes to see the immortal firsthand and light a fire under the researchers' asses. He would've gone tonight, but he'd chartered the other jet to a friend who left for Alaska this morning."

Chris turned to Henderson. "Where are your men on finding a doctor to impersonate?"

Scott messaged someone on his phone, which buzzed with a response a second later. "They're narrowing it down now. They should have a name and address any minute. But we still need to get our hands on the fingerprints."

"Really?" Sean asked. "Shape-shifters can't produce the right fingerprints?"

Aidan shook his head. "Those details are incredibly hard to replicate. Even after all the time I've spent with Becca this past week, I couldn't replicate her fingerprints or signature if I tried."

"So." Seth swept them all with a glance. "Who will perform the impersonation?"

"I will," Jared blurted.

Seth scowled. "Hell no. You're too hot-headed and keep wanting to toss out the rules."

"Shall I do it, then?" Aidan asked.

He shook his head. "The task will include erasing knowledge of vampires from the minds of the doctors while doing as little damage as possible." Seth turned to Zach. "You're particularly adept at that *and* have mind-controlled others in the past without remorse," he added dryly. "If you do it, do you think you could rein in your violent tendencies and not kill everyone?"

Zach looked at his wife.

Smiling up at him, she nudged him with her shoulder and nodded.

He turned back to Seth. "Yyyyes?"

Sean and Nicole laughed, as did several others.

"Well," Seth said, "that doesn't inspire confidence."

"Shall I do it?" Roland asked.

"Absolutely not," Seth objected and grimaced. "You once suggested we mind-control the doctors at the base that held Dana and convince them they were proctologists who could find the answers to all of life's mysteries up each other's asses."

More laughter.

"I'll do it myself," Seth announced. "Zach, you'll have to field my calls."

"All of them?"

"Yes, unless Jared—"

"I'm going with you."

Seth speared him with a warning glare. "Not unless you give me your word that you will *not* disrupt the mission and will do as I say."

"You have my word," Jared vowed.

"Fine."

Leah smiled. "I'll help Zach field your calls."

Seth leaned over and pressed a quick kiss to her lips. "Thank you. David, will you keep an eye on Benford and the goings-on here in North Carolina? If he's working in cahoots with someone else, he may be quick to let them know he's on his way to see an immortal."

"Of course. I will apprise you of anything pertinent I see or hear."

Henderson's phone buzzed. He glanced down at the screen. "Okay, we have a guy. A doctor. My special ops team is assembling outside of Houston and will head to his home shortly. Should I have them call you, Seth, when they get there?"

"Do it," he commanded.

Henderson tapped a message on his phone. "A second team is assembling at network headquarters—the ones who will pose as maintenance and cleaning crew members. Rafe already went through our wardrobe stores and picked out uniforms identical to those he saw at the facility."

Darnell looked up from his laptop. "I want in on that team."

Chris nodded and turned to Henderson. "We need him on this. Trust me."

"I'll go, too," Melanie added.

Henderson nodded. "I assumed as much, Dr. Lipton. Rafe will tell you if you'll need to change your mode of dress to blend in."

"Okay."

"If she goes, I go," Bastien insisted.

Chris grunted. "No shock there. Add Bastien to the list."

That made four immortals, if one counted Jared's unpredictable ass.

Sean frowned. "Can I go as backup? Tessa was there for me and Nicole. I want to be there for her, too." *And* if things got hairy, he wouldn't mind getting a little payback for those assholes hiring the vampires who nearly killed Nicole. Twice.

Nicole shot him a look, then addressed Chris. "If Sean goes, I go."

"No way!" Sean protested. *After everything she'd already been through?*

She rolled her eyes. "I'm former special ops, Sean. I'm who Chris used to send on these missions."

"She is," Chris confirmed. "Nicole excels at this sort of thing. If *I* were going, I'd want her at my back."

She smiled. "And there should be a mortal for every immortal on the team. You guys may kick ass, but you suck at navigating modern technology."

"Agreed," Chris said emphatically. "So Sean and Nicole will be on the team."

His voice dripping with sarcasm, Henderson asked, "Are any of *my* guys going to be on the team?"

Chris grinned. "You can always add Rafe." Turning in his chair, he searched the Seconds until he spied Cliff. "Cliff, how would you feel about going? You've proven you're adept at spotting fail-safes or booby traps, and you're a lot handier with a computer than the elders."

His expression reflecting both surprise and pleasure, Cliff opened his mouth to respond but hesitated and glanced down at his wife.

Emma's brow furrowed as she slipped her hand into his.

Seth sent her a gentle smile. "No harm will come to him. You have my word."

Smiling tentatively, she nodded.

Cliff brought her hand to his lips for a kiss. "I'll do it."

Leah frowned as she studied them all. "That's eight people."

"Twelve," Henderson muttered. "I'm sending my best two hackers and my two head researchers along."

She nodded. "Okay. So, how big is their maintenance staff? I mean, won't a party that large draw notice?"

Henderson shook his head. "It's a four-story building, roughly thirty-five or forty thousand feet. We just need to make sure everyone has proper uniforms and credentials."

She glanced at Seth, then back at Henderson. "Will they? It's awfully short notice."

"Yes, ma'am," Henderson replied, no doubt in his tone. "My guys are already working on it."

A trebly version of Skillet's "Monster" filled the air.

Seth drew his cell phone from a back pocket and answered the call. "Yes?"

"Hello, sir," a deep voice said. Sean and the other immortals unabashedly eavesdropped. "This is Lorenzo. Henderson said I should call you when my team and I are in position outside the doctor's home."

"Excellent. One moment, please." Seth swept them all with a glance. "Is that everything?"

A rumble sounded as everyone murmured yes.

Seth rose and stepped back from the table. "Aidan, teleport all participating parties to network headquarters in Texas. Sheldon, I need you to step in for Darnell and redirect all my calls to Zach and Leah. David's, too. David will be monitoring Benford, so don't bother him unless you have to. Everyone else, hunt in pairs and be hypervigilant. Seconds, keep close tabs on your immortals. I don't want anyone else to go missing."

He vanished a second later.

"You heard him," David said. "Let's get moving."

# CHAPTER EIGHTEEN

B ECAUSE THE STATE WAS so large, Texas boasted three network
hubs: one outside of San Antonio, another in Houston, and a
third up by Dallas.

Nicole stood in what some referred to as the wardrobe department of the Houston headquarters, waiting her turn for Henderson's crew to tell her what she should wear.

Beside her, Sean whistled.

She glanced up at him. "What?"

His head swiveling this way and that, he took in the rows and
rows of clothing. Some garments were folded and stacked neatly on shelves. Others adorned hangers on long racks. "It's like
something you'd see backstage at a theater. Or maybe at a film
production company."

She smiled. "You've never seen their costumes before?"

"No."

The network kept a wide variety of emergency responder uniforms in stock. Police. Deputies. Constables. Paramedics. Firemen.
FBI. CIA. DEA. All excellent reproductions, but totally fake. If
immortals made a mess, things often worked out better when network employees hit the scene first and acted as authority figures.

The massive wardrobe included clothing suitable for other pro-
fessions and occasions as well. Doctors. Nurses. Postal employees. Delivery persons. Waiters. Waitresses. Janitors. Maids. Military
uniforms. Suits. Slacks. Skirts. Jackets. Formalwear. Beachwear.
And everything in between.

"Next," a burly man called as he waved them forward. "Sean and
Nicole?"

"Yes," they answered.

A woman beside Burly Man stared down at an electronic tablet. "Cleaning crew. He's immortal. She's mortal."

The man swept his gaze down Sean's form, turned away, plucked a stack of fabric from a shelf, added shoes, and topped the pile off with a folded cloth bag. "Here you are." After thrusting them into Sean's arms, he did the same for Nicole, adding a bulletproof vest. "Go through those doors. You can change in there."

Clutching her bundle to her chest, Nicole led the way into the changing room.

There wasn't much to it, just a large room with benches along one wall and partitioned stalls attached to another. Anyone wanting a little privacy could duck into one of the latter and draw a curtain.

Darnell passed them on his way out of the room. Clad in dark slacks and an untucked beige oxford shirt, he looked handsome as hell.

Bastien stood in front of a curtained stall, facing the room with his feet braced apart and his arms crossed over his chest. Already changed, he now wore black slacks and a muted green oxford shirt. He'd left the top button unfastened and rolled the sleeves halfway up his muscled forearms. Instead of combat boots, casual dress shoes now graced his feet.

Over by the benches, Cliff and a man Nicole didn't recognize had stripped down to their boxers.

"Damn," Nicole said as she watched Cliff tug on a pair of navy pants. "Cliff is ripped." He had packed on some serious muscle.

Cliff tossed her a grin over his shoulder.

"I'm right here, you know," Sean grumbled.

She laughed. "And *you're* ripped in a way that I find utterly irresistible. But you already know that."

"Hell yes, I do," he said with a roguish smile.

The man next to Cliff blurred. When he stilled, he wore navy pants, a white short-sleeved sport shirt, and an aqua-colored smock with pockets on the front.

"I'm guessing that's Rafe," she said.

Glancing at them, he nodded. "Nice to meet you."

"Nice to meet you, too. I'm Nicole. This is Sean."

Rafe motioned to the bundles in their arms. "Looks like you'll be joining me on the cleaning crew."

"Yep."

Sean frowned as Cliff drew on a pale gray dress shirt and dark slacks. "You get to pose as a researcher?"

Tilting his nose up, Cliff arched a brow and feigned arrogance. "Apparently, I look smart."

Nicole grinned. "You *are* smart." Now that Cliff no longer battled insanity, Chris had been lobbying hard to get him to accept one of the higher-up positions at network headquarters in North Carolina. Right now, Cliff worked with the vampires on sublevel five, counseling them and helping them find productive ways to combat growing aggression and—for those who heard them—quiet or subdue the voices in their heads. But she suspected he would catapult high up the ranks once Chris wore him down.

Sean nudged her. "Let's get changed."

"Okay."

A habit from her special ops days, Nicole started toward a bench. Reordon had placed her on teams that were given only minutes to dress and prepare for action so many times in the past that she didn't think much about changing in front of others. Since she always kept her bra and panties on, Nicole figured her teammates didn't get an eyeful of anything they wouldn't see at a beach or swimming pool anyway. But Sean snagged her elbow and guided her over to a stall instead.

Biting back a laugh, she indulged him and ducked inside.

When he tried to join her, she gave him a hard push. "Sean, we can't both change in here. You're huge. And I don't want to get elbowed in the face. Get your own space."

Grumbling something under his breath, he backed out, closed the curtain, then dropped his pile on the floor just outside. A second later, he toed off his boots.

"Bastien tried to do the same," Melanie said in the next stall, her voice full of amusement.

Laughing, Nicole swiftly doffed her clothes.

The navy pants fit well. So did the bulletproof vest, white shirt, and aqua smock. Network employees in the wardrobe department never failed to impress her with their ability to accurately assess a person's size. Though she would rather not forgo her boots, Nicole replaced them with serviceable and very generic-looking black sneakers.

Even those fit perfectly.

She didn't bother to fold her clothes before stuffing them—and her shoes—into the cloth bag provided. Once done, she thrust the curtain aside.

Standing with his back to her, Sean glanced over his shoulder.

She grinned. "I half-expected you to be bent over, mooning me."

Laughing, he shook his head and stepped aside. He had already replaced his hunting blacks with navy blue pants, a white sport shirt, and an aqua smock identical to hers, all of which seemed to accentuate his broad shoulders and muscled chest.

Feigning irritation, she motioned to him. "How can something that makes me look frumpy make you look positively edible?"

He snorted. "If you think you look frumpy, you haven't looked in a mirror."

Melanie exited her stall and joined Bastien beside them, wearing slacks, a button-down shirt, and a white lab coat.

"What do we do now?" Sean asked.

All watched Nicole expectantly.

"Follow me." She led them to a wall composed of wooden cubes stacked floor to ceiling. A small white strip adorned the lower edge of each with a whiteboard marker attached to it via hook and loop tape. Once she placed her bag of clothes and shoes into a cube, Nicole wrote her name beneath it with the marker. "So we can find our stuff easily when we return."

While Sean, Melanie, and Bastien followed her example, she glanced around. Cliff and Rafe had left while she changed. But others had taken their place. Two men and two women garbed in cleaning crew uniforms sat on benches, tying their shoes. A fifth figure...

Nicole stared.

"Is that Jared?" Sean asked beside her.

"I think so." The elder immortal had altered his appearance enough that she hadn't recognized him at first.

Instead of his usual six feet ten inches, he now stood at five feet nine inches or thereabouts. Crow's feet marred the skin beneath and beside his eyes while deep lines bracketed his mouth. Adding to his aged appearance, a plethora of gray hair peppered his short raven locks.

"Shape-shifting is so cool," she murmured.

Like Melanie, Jared wore slacks, an oxford shirt, and a lab coat. He also still wore a scowl, which she suspected wouldn't go away until Tessa returned to her network apartment.

When Nicole led the exodus from the changing room, the woman waiting outside the door handed her a black elastic hair tie. Melanie and Bastien received the same.

Nicole finger-combed her hair back from her face and used the elastic band to confine it in a ponytail. "How do I look?"

Sean smiled. "Beautiful."

Knowing he was biased, she turned to Melanie. "Doc?"

Melanie finished pulling her hair into a ponytail and moved to stand in front of Nicole. "Looks good." She tidied the sides a bit. "What about mine?"

Nicole smoothed a few strands that wanted to poke out. "You're good."

Sean looked at Bastien. "Do you want me to pretty up *your* ponytail?"

The immortal black sheep snorted. "Anyone who doesn't like my hair can kiss my ass." He turned to the woman holding the hair ties. "Where's the armory?"

"This way, sir." Spinning on her heel, the woman strode away.

Several minutes later, Nicole stuffed multiple EpiPen-like autoinjectors full of human sedatives in her pockets. She would've preferred 9mms and extra mags, but they were supposed to go in quietly and attract as little attention as possible.

When the woman caught her gazing longingly at the semiautomatics, she smiled. "Don't worry. You'll have two carts loaded with cleaning materials. Each will also contain hidden compartments that house a substantial arsenal should you need it."

Nicole smiled with relief. "Here's hoping we won't."

More team members joined them.

Darnell was notably absent. Perhaps he was already hard at work, knocking down firewalls or whatever security the facility's servers had in place with a network hack.

Nicole shot the breeze with the others, focusing on Rafe and the four new-to-her network employees who would accompany them. Knowing your team was always a good thing. You worked better as a unit when you did.

Rafe asked them how Nick and Kayla were holding up. Nicole liked him. He seemed genuinely furious that someone was targeting his friend's stepdaughter.

Personality-wise, the four network employees were what some would've deemed computer geeks, but they sure didn't look like it. Instead of the stereotypical pasty complexions and scrawny or doughy bodies often bestowed upon nerdy types in movies and TV shows, these tech geniuses bore trim, athletic builds and toned muscles.

Perhaps the network in North Carolina wasn't the only one that required all employees to exercise and train in self-defense to keep their bodies at optimum performance in case an emergency should arise.

An older man entered, interrupting their chitchat long enough to stand each one up against a white wall and take their picture.

The woman from the armory brought in a basket full of walkies and handed them out.

Jared paced. "What's the holdup?"

Tyler, one of the tech wizzes, watched him curiously. "It takes a little while to reproduce fingerprints and apply them. It isn't something you can rush."

The other techs—Seong-Su, Ashley, and Amani—launched into an enthusiastic explanation of scanning and re-creating fingerprints using gelatin, a topic that fascinated Nicole.

Sean nudged her with his elbow. When she looked up, he smiled and whispered, "This is so cool."

Grinning, she nodded and wished *she* were the one who got to use someone else's fingerprints. She would love to see that entire process in action.

A man with graying blond hair suddenly entered. "Okay. Let's do this," he said in a familiar baritone voice that bore a British accent.

Her eyes widened. "Seth?"

He nodded. Thanks to his extraordinary shape-shifting abilities, his six-foot-eight-inch form now topped off at five feet eight. Narrow shoulders had replaced muscular ones. And his trim waist now bore a paunch that poked out between the lapels of his lab coat. His dark brown eyes were now blue and bracketed by lines and bags that hinted at years of too little sleep. Wire-rimmed glasses perched on his nose.

He arched his brows. "Everyone ready?"

Answering with various affirmatives, they crowded around him.

"I'm going to teleport all of us to a temporary FOB that Henderson and his crew have set up. From there, I'll drive to the facility in a car I borrowed from the doctor I'm impersonating and pass through security. As soon as I'm able to enter one of the building's empty conference rooms, I'll return to the FOB and teleport you and your gear inside. Any questions?"

Head shakes.

"All right. Grab a shoulder. I'd grab yours, but I'm trying to use my hands as little as possible because I don't know how easily these false fingerprints will come off." When he held up his hands, Nicole could discern nothing odd about his fingertips. Whatever magic Henderson's team had worked blended in well.

Seconds later, they all stood inside a large army-green tent. Through the open entrance, Nicole spied dense, dark forest. Warm, humid air wafted inside, ushering in a few mosquitoes.

Grimacing, Nicole swatted one. Clearly, cooler temperatures had not yet reached the outskirts of Houston.

Tables laden with computer equipment lined the walls of the tent with diligent employees parked in folding chairs before them. Though she didn't look to confirm it, Nicole knew multiple solar generators rested along the tent's exterior, silently powering everything inside.

Many heavily armed, black-clad special ops soldiers filled the tent and mulled around outside the entrance. Henderson apparently wasn't taking any chances with backup.

Striding into the tent, Henderson swiftly divided Nicole and the others into three teams. "Okay. I texted everyone the specs of the building. Rafe, Seong-Su, and Amani, you're Green Team. Your job will be to copy every bit of data stored in their system and in the cloud on the other research they're conducting. I want everything you can find on every project, no matter how benign or unrelated it may seem. We've used green to highlight the data entry point you should focus on."

Rafe and his team members drew out their phones and stared down at them, nodding as he continued.

"That area of the building shouldn't have much activity this time of night. Rafe will hear everything taking place on your floor and give you a heads-up if someone approaches. A tip for the immortals and others who have never used this sort of subterfuge: Act like you belong there and most won't question your presence. If you're posing as members of the cleaning crew and hear someone coming, your best options are to either engage in rabid gossip while mopping or drink a soda and look like you're slacking off while you discuss last night's football game. The first will generate disinterest. The second will—at most—spark disapproval, especially if you hurry to put the soda down and start cleaning as if you don't want to get in trouble. Both will lead whoever sees you to dismiss you as employees."

He glanced around. "Where's Jared?"

Jared raised a hand.

A slight smile curled Henderson's lips. "Sorry. I didn't recognize you at first. Jared, you, Cliff, Ashley, and Tyler are Yellow Team. You'll infiltrate the soundproof lab we believe they studied the vampires in. We don't think they currently have one in custody but couldn't confirm that. Either way, the lab *will* likely be active if they're pulling double duty to run tests on Tessa."

Jared took a step forward. "I want to be on the team that rescues Tessa."

Seth shook his head. "I need you in the other lab. You'll have to sedate whomever you find in it fast enough to keep them from sounding the alarm. While Cliff and the others retrieve data from their computers, I want you to peruse the thoughts of the researchers and see if you can find something of use they might not have mentioned in their notes: the source of the sedative, hypotheses or half-formed ideas on methods they can use to prevent the madness the virus inspires, anything that Melanie may find useful."

"Rafe can do that," Jared countered.

"Rafe can read minds, but he can't exert control over them should that become necessary. He's younger."

And Nicole suspected Seth didn't want Jared in the room if they found Tessa in unexpectedly dire conditions. She hadn't realized Jared and Tessa had become friends, but they must have. He looked like he would burn the entire building to the ground if she suffered any harm.

Henderson glanced from Seth to Jared, as though waiting to see if Jared would complain further, then continued where Seth left off. "Melanie, Bastien, Darnell, Sean, and Nicole, you're Red Team. You'll infiltrate the soundproof lab Tessa is being held in with Seth. We expect that to be a hive of activity and a mother lode of information. They'll want to learn everything they can before Benford arrives in the morning. Seth won't cause a stir when he arrives. The doctor he's impersonating has been called in and was getting ready to head back to work when we caught him. Melanie, Bastien, and Darnell all look like researchers, so it will take a moment for the others to question their entry. Sean and Nicole, though, may spark irritation and objections. That should buy you time until you're all inside with the door closed."

"After that," Seth picked up, "we merely have to incapacitate everyone and keep them from triggering the alarm. If possible, I'd like to question them *before* they're tranqed. Darnell may need special codes or passwords to retrieve the information Melanie wants from their computers. And getting those will be easier if I listen to their thoughts while he asks instead of sifting through every thought and memory in their head. But tranq them if you feel you must. Darts will work faster than autoinjectors, but I want you to be armed with both."

A special ops soldier shouldered his way through the crowd and held out a box full of tranquilizer guns specially designed by the network to fire up to five darts.

Nicole took one and tucked it in her smock's pocket. Sean did the same.

"Nicole," Seth continued, "once we're inside and have everyone under control, I want you to man the door and tranq anyone who opens it before they can shout a warning that one of the guards patrolling the building may hear. Henderson, did you send them the specs?"

Nicole's phone buzzed with an incoming message.

"Just sent it," the network head told him. "I've highlighted Seth's designated room with red, Jared's with yellow, and—just a reminder—Rafe's with green."

Nicole opened the enclosed images on her phone and thumbed through them, leaning toward Sean so he could study them with her instead of looking at them on his own phone. She and Sean would accompany Seth to a room on the fourth floor. The same floor as Jared's. Rafe's was on the second floor.

"Once the op begins," Henderson told them, "we'll shut down landlines, internet service, and cell service. If we need to communicate with you, we'll use the walkies."

"Any questions?" Seth asked. When no one voiced any, he nodded. "I'll leave now and return once I've made it into an interior room."

Henderson looked around. "Randy, show Seth to the car he'll be driving." He held a set of keys out to a man covered in tattoos.

Randy took them and motioned for Seth to accompany him. "This way, sir."

Henderson addressed the rest of them. "Red, Yellow, and Green Teams, stay with me. Security monitors, remain at your posts. Everyone else, out."

Murmurs arose as an exodus began.

Henderson crossed to a trio of techs seated in front of computers. "Have you recorded enough security footage to loop it?"

"Yes, sir," a man responded.

"Any flies in the ointment?"

"No, sir."

Sean nudged Nicole and raised his eyebrows.

Leaning closer, she whispered, "He means anything that might tip off bored security guards that they're watching the same footage they saw an hour ago. Something out of the norm, like someone tripping as they exit the elevator and face-planting on the floor or someone surprising a fellow employee with a big birthday balloon. Anything you wouldn't expect to see twice."

"Ah."

A network employee approached them and handed each an ID badge that doubled as a security card. "Clip this to your smock," she instructed. "We encoded them with the same information on the Doc's security badge, so it should get you into every room on the fourth floor. Rhodes, would you bring them their gear?"

Gear?

A man pushed a rolling cart full of cleaning supplies over to them.

Nicole grimaced at it. "Are there really weapons hidden inside that?"

Rhodes grinned. "A hell of a lot of them. Don't let anyone else near it." He delivered a second cart to Rafe's group.

Nicole, Sean, and the others spent the next few minutes acquainting themselves with all the deadly goodies hidden inside their carts. Hopefully, they wouldn't have to use them.

Henderson pointed to a computer screen. "There's Seth's car. Once he's inside, distracting the guards, loop the security footage."

Footage from an exterior security camera showed a quiet, inactive parking lot peppered with vehicles. Seth's car pulled in and parked. Nicole watched Seth tromp across the parking lot, irritation etched into every feature. She shifted her attention to a monitor that displayed interior footage from the lobby. Everyone seemed to hold their breath as Seth entered the building and exchanged a few words with the security guards. Nicole and Sean tensed as they waited to see if the scanner would accept his fingerprints.

Both smiled when Seth passed through without incident.

A few minutes later, he reappeared in the tent. "All right. I perused the thoughts of the guards on duty. Most have been on the company payroll for years and, thanks to the security upgrades recently implemented, expect no problems. They mostly focus on individuals entering and exiting the building and pay little attention to what goes on *inside* it. So we should be good. Let's go."

Seth teleported them to a sleek, modern conference room.

Sean glanced around. A large-screen monitor for presentations dominated one wall. A table with multiple chairs led away from it, leaving enough open area for the cleaning carts that accompanied them. Gray curtains lined two walls, hiding what Sean suspected were windows.

He wondered idly if that was to minimize employee distractions or to ensure no one outside the building could see in and steal information, since corporate espionage was so prevalent.

"Okay." Seth motioned to one set of curtains. "A hallway divides this floor into two sections. Jared, you and your team will find what you seek on this side of the hallway. Red Team, we'll handle the other side. Green Team, take the elevator at that end"—he pointed—"down to the second floor and follow the diagram Henderson sent you. I hear no activity in the hallway up here, so you're good to go. Remember, we're trying to do this without triggering any alarms or drawing unwanted attention. Rafe, summon me if you need me."

Nodding, Rafe grabbed a cart and led Seong-Su and Amani from the conference room.

Seth turned a stern look on Jared. "Stay focused. Keep your team safe. Find out what you can. I'll keep you posted on Tessa."

Face grim, Jared left with Cliff, Ashley, and Tyler.

"That's a powder keg waiting to explode," Bastien muttered.

Melanie bit her lip. "Jared led such an isolated existence before joining the Immortal Guardians. I don't think he's ever been in a situation where a friend's life has been in danger before." She looked at Seth. "Has he?"

Seth shook his head. "The last friend he lost was me, millennia ago, and he was too pissed at me for defecting to care."

Bastien grunted.

"Let's go." Seth headed for the open doorway.

Melanie, Bastien, and Darnell followed.

Grabbing the cart of cleaning paraphernalia, Sean pushed it after them with Nicole at his side.

They exited into a large, shared community space. A long, curvy sofa slithered through the center. White tables of varying heights and widths appeared in pockets here and there, with chairs or bar stools pulled up to them. One wall was curtainless glass and offered a view of the parking lot. A carpet of live plants adorned a second. A third was glass like the first and revealed a hallway beyond.

Seth led them out into the hallway. Another shared community space or lounge lay on the opposite side. In its center, a round, glassed enclosure offered a patio with several tables and chairs. Large potted plants proliferated beneath open sky where there ordinarily would've been a ceiling.

"Mental note," Sean mumbled, "if we need to make a hasty escape, the lounge's access to the roof is an option."

The other immortals nodded.

The rest of the hallway bore stark white walls without windows. Both the floor and ceiling were white, too, lending it a clinical feel that the more colorful lounges had lacked.

When they reached the lab door, Seth paused and eyed them all. "Secure all employees. Sedate them if you have to. If any fight back, try not to kill them. We aren't here for that. We just don't want them sounding the alarm." Tugging his ID card off his shirt, he swiped it through the card reader. A click sounded as the door opened a crack.

Seth pushed the door open.

Sean and Nicole held back, allowing those posing as doctors to enter first. When he followed, Sean found himself in another white hallway, facing a wall of windows interspersed with glass doors. The door up on the right opened onto a sizable lab that reminded him a little of Melanie's at network headquarters. At least half a dozen people inhabited it, some bustling about with harried expressions.

*The bulk of their research is being conducted inside this larger lab. Tessa is being held in a smaller lab beyond it on the far right,* Seth told them telepathically, drawing their gazes to a solid wall beyond the researchers. *Bastien, Melanie, and Darnell, join me in the primary lab. Sean and Nicole, take care of anyone you find in the other rooms. Once you're done, Nicole, I want you to return and guard the main door. Sean, join us inside.*

The primary room held another electronic lock. Seth swiped his card. As soon as he pushed the door open, Melanie began to talk.

"All I know is he told me to get my ass down here as quickly as possible," she said.

Bastien offered a disgruntled, "He told me the same," as they entered.

The doctors inside turned at their entrance.

A woman with graying red hair pulled back into a ponytail exhibited relief when she spotted Seth. "Albert. It's about time you got here."

The man beside her scowled. "What the hell took you so long? And who are they? Do they even have clearance?"

The glass door swung shut behind Seth and the others.

Sean turned his cart and strolled down the hallway with Nicole. Scuffling erupted behind them.

Thanks to the hallway's glass walls, he could see inside each room before they reached the doors. The first narrow lab they passed boasted two long white desks, many shelves, and medical equipment similar to Melanie's.

No one inhabited it.

A woman wearing a white lab coat, blue gloves, and safety glasses occupied the next. Her dark blond hair twisted up into a messy bun, she focused on removing liquid from a beaker with a pipet and depositing samples into a series of tiny tubes. Catching movement from the corner of her eye, she glanced over at them, looked away in dismissal, then spun back to frown at them.

Sean pushed the door open. "Hi. Where's the vomit?"

Her expression blanked. "What?"

Stepping inside, Sean made a show of examining the floor while Nicole entered behind him.

"Hey. You aren't allowed to be in here," the woman said belatedly.

He nodded. "We're just here to clean up the vomit. Someone called and said they wanted it mopped up ASAP. We'll leave as soon as we're done. Where is it?"

"No one vomited in here."

Sean propped his hands on his hips and frowned. "This isn't the... what was it he called it... the catamaran lab?" He looked at Nicole. "I know the word I'm looking for isn't catamaran. But now that it's in my head, I can't stop thinking it. What did he call it? Whatever it was started with a C."

Nicole feigned thought as the door swished shut behind them. "Catalytic converter?"

"No. That's a car part."

"The one they keep mentioning thieves targeting on the local news?"

"Yeah."

The woman made a huffing sound of irritation. "Look, there's no vomit in here. If you don't leave, I'll have to call security. Who even let you in?"

Sean turned back to her. "I think his name was Al." The name on Seth's ID card read Albert. "I'm pretty sure he said we were supposed to go to the catalytic something."

"Catalyzing growth lab?" she suggested.

Grinning, he snapped his fingers. "Yes! The paralyzing growth lab."

"Oh brother," she muttered, and pointed. "It's two doors down."

Nicole turned to Sean. "By the way, now might be a good time to tell you I'm a sympathetic vomiter."

"Come again?"

"I'm a sympathetic vomiter. If I see or smell vomit, my gag reflex kicks in and I puke my guts out."

"You're kidding, right?"

"No." She sent the woman a hopeful smile. "Maybe I could wait in here with you while he cleans it up?"

Scowling, the woman carefully set her tools down. "*No*, you can't wait in here! I'm working. And I'm still not sure you're even allowed to—"

A dart struck her in the chest.

Half a second later, her eyes closed and her forehead hit her desk.

Sean stared at the woman, then turned to Nicole, who now held a tranquilizer gun.

Both burst into laughter.

"That was freaking awesome," she said. "I did *not* expect her to pass out so quickly."

Trying not to laugh loud enough to draw attention, Sean said, "It was like a cartoon character or something."

"I know."

*Focus*, Seth suddenly commanded in their heads.

Lips twitching, they hurried out the door and down the sterile hallway. The next lab was a little larger, with two long tables loaded with equipment. Both inhabitants were already looking toward them.

Had they heard their laughter?

He and Nicole used a shorter version of the same vomit excuse to tranq them while they were seated at their research stations.

A slender man with a blond comb-over full of highlights worked in the last lab.

When Sean and Nicole entered, he gave them no chance to speak. After sizing Sean up, he turned a furious gaze upon Nicole. "Who the hell are you?" he demanded. "You don't have clearance to be in here. Your ass is so fired. Don't *ever* interrupt my work. *No one* interrupts my work. I—"

Sean shot him with a tranquilizer dart.

The anger on the jerk's face drained away as his eyelids closed.

Neither Sean nor Nicole stepped forward to break his fall when he toppled to the floor.

"What an asshole," Sean muttered.

She nodded.

"Did you see how he sized me up and then started bitching at *you*?"

316

"Yep. Classic bully move. Only attack those who appear defenseless."

"What an asshole," he repeated.

She grinned. "I love you."

Irritation falling away, he smiled back. "Love you, too."

Leaving the unconscious man on the floor for Seth to examine later, they hurried up the hallway once more. Nicole stationed herself just inside the main door, tranq gun in hand.

"Be careful," Sean whispered.

"You, too."

He stole a quick kiss, then headed into the primary lab.

# CHAPTER NINETEEN

MELANIE AND DARNELL EACH sat before a computer, their fingers dancing over the keyboards. Four men and one woman lay unconscious on the floor. The last woman—the one who had looked relieved upon seeing Al—sat in a chair, restrained only by Bastien's glower as he stood before her with his feet braced apart, arms crossed over his broad chest. Her pretty face creased with anxiety as she alternated between trying to see what Darnell and Melanie were doing and sending Bastien wary glances.

"Everything okay in here?" Sean asked as he joined them.

Bastien nodded. "This wise doctor is giving us everything we need. Did you tranq everyone else?"

"Yeah. The guy at the far end might have hit his head kind of hard when he fell," Sean said, unconcerned. "He was an asshole."

The woman snorted. "Does he have blond highlights in his hair?"

"Yeah."

Her lip curled in a sneer. "That's Orson. He *is* an asshole. The kind that would've enjoyed hurting the girl in there if Silvy and I hadn't kept him away from her."

Sean arched a brow. "You mean hurt her more than *you* did? Or more than you intended to?"

Her face blanched. "I just set up an IV and took some blood samples. And she was unconscious for most of it."

"Because you drugged her." Crossing his arms, Sean matched Bastien's stance.

The woman offered no response as her gaze slid away from his.

At least she seemed contrite. Most of the bad guys they dealt with lacked anything resembling a moral conscience.

Bastien nodded toward the door at the opposite end of the lab. "We've got this. Go help Seth."

Worried about what he might find within, Sean left them and headed toward the *mystery room*. All the other labs in this space boasted at least one glass wall. The fact that this one didn't made it stand out as one in which they wished to hide something.

Or someone.

The mystery room was bigger than he'd anticipated. Two rows of lab stations extended from a center aisle like spider legs. Rows of chairs did the same behind them. Everything was white: the walls, the floor, the ceiling, the furniture. And the place bore a sharp antiseptic scent that made his nose twitch. A glass wall beyond revealed the area in which they held and studied...

*Tessa.*

His heart thudded with dread. She was so pale. Strapped to something that resembled an operating table, her slender form sported only a generic hospital gown. Multiple tubes were taped to her hands and arms. No blanket covered her bare legs to stave off the cold. And even with his body's ability to control his temperature, Sean knew it was damned chilly in this room.

Tessa's eyes remained closed with nary a flicker of movement behind her lids as Seth leaned over her.

Back in his usual form and garb, having shed his Albert guise, Seth gently brushed her hair back from her face and spoke her name.

She didn't move.

Sean forced his feet to carry him forward. "Is she okay?"

Lips tight, Seth waved a hand. The manacles sprang open. "She's drugged. In their exuberance, they came damned close to over-dosing her."

Sean swore. Too much of the sedative killed vampires. Would an overdose do the same to an Immortal Guardian? He couldn't remember. "What can we do?"

"She needs blood. They have greatly depleted her supply and didn't give her more because they wished her to remain weak. Reed and the other vampires told them immortals are stronger." Seth carefully removed the needles and tubes from her hands and arms, healing every wound they left behind. Afterward, he drew an autoinjector from one of his pockets. "I'll wake her with Melanie's antidote. Once she rouses, I want you to give her blood."

"Okay."

Sean moved closer to the bed.

Seth flipped the lid open and pressed the autoinjector to Tessa's thigh.

A few seconds later, her lashes fluttered and rose.

Tessa stared at the bright lights above, her gaze unfocused.

"Tessa?" Seth stroked her hair again.

Blinking sluggishly, she glanced over at him. "Seth?"

He nodded. "You need blood. I want you to take Sean's."

She opened her mouth to speak. Closed it. Blinked.

Her gaze returned to the lights above, then took in the room around her. "I don't think so."

Sean shot Seth a look. Tessa wouldn't take his blood? Why?

Seth's brow furrowed as he studied her.

"No," she said, still groggy and disconnected. "I'm okay."

Seth's features abruptly smoothed out with relief. "Jared is talking to her telepathically."

Oh. Good. For a moment, Sean had feared she wasn't quite there.

"Yes." Her voice grew stronger. "I'm just a little out of it."

*Stop distracting her, Jared*, Seth said, his telepathic voice reaching Sean, too. *Let us take care of her.*

Tessa focused on Seth.

"Take Sean's blood," he coaxed.

Forcing a smile, Sean extended his forearm. "Bon appétit."

Her lips quirked at the corners as she sat up with Seth's aid. "I suddenly feel like we're in a low-budget vampire movie."

He chuckled. "Yeah. This is so weird. I've never given another immortal blood before."

"Have you ever taken blood from a live person?"

"No."

She shook her head with a smile. "That's even weirder." Clasping his forearm with icy fingers, she sank her teeth in.

It hurt more than he'd expected. Étienne had bitten him when he'd transformed Sean, but Sean had no memory of that thanks to the GHB-like chemical the glands above fangs released under the pressure of a bite. Fortunately, the virus rendered him immune to the chemical this time, so Tessa feeding from him wouldn't leave him loopy.

Seth glanced to one side as if he heard a noise.

Sean followed his gaze and listened carefully but heard nothing aside from the activity of their teams here on the fourth floor and down on the second. That and the conversations the guards and maintenance staff in the rest of the building conducted.

Seth's brow furrowed. "David is having a hard time locating Augustus Benford."

So that's what he'd heard. David was so powerful that he could speak to Seth or anyone else telepathically even if hundreds or thousands of miles separated them.

"He isn't at his home," Seth continued. "Neither is his driver. His Carolina office hasn't seen him since this morning. He hasn't appeared at the airport. And no one seems to know where he is right now."

Sean frowned. "Do they think something's happened to him?"

"No. David just can't find anyone who knows the man's current location."

"Could he already be on his way here?"

"If he is, he took someone else's jet. David said the one that brought Tessa here won't land in North Carolina for another twenty minutes."

When Tessa would've removed her teeth from Sean's wrist, Seth motioned for her to continue.

A hint of weakness crept in, the kind Sean usually felt as a result of blood loss when wounded. It wasn't debilitating. But if she kept going, it might slow him down a bit.

Clicking sounds suddenly filled the lab. They seemed to come from Seth's vicinity and... the floor at Sean's feet?

Sean looked down, searching for the source.

The clicks repeated, more coming from the other room.

*Click-click*. Pause. *Click*. Pause. *Click-click-click*.

"There's a red moon tonight," Nicole said conversationally out in the hallway.

DIANNE DUVALL

Sean frowned.

"How's the weather?" Henderson's voice emerged from multiple sources simultaneously.

The encrypted walkies.

Sean dug his out of his smock but didn't press any buttons, because he'd failed to ask Nicole their various functions.

Seth and Tessa stared at the walkie in his hand.

"Clear skies here," Nicole replied. "How is it there?"

"Looks like it's gonna rain cats and dogs," Henderson drawled. More clicks followed.

"Seth." Nicole spoke out in the hallway without raising her voice or opening the door, knowing every immortal in the building could hear her. "Read Henderson's thoughts. Something's up."

Frowning, Seth looked in the FOB's direction.

Bastien entered the room, one of his hands still curled around the biceps of the doctor who'd called Orson an asshole.

Before Bastien could speak, Seth held up a hand to halt him.

A long moment passed.

The doctor looked around, her brow furrowing with confusion.

If she hadn't seen Seth abandon his disguise, she probably wondered where the hell Albert was and how Seth had come to be in here without her noticing.

Seth swore and turned to Bastien. "What is it?"

Bastien nodded at the woman. "She claims she has information."

A door opened in the primary lab. "Here," Nicole said, beyond his sight. "I don't know the details, but if Henderson says it's gonna rain cats and dogs, you need to arm up."

Seth speared the doctor with a look. "Speak."

Fastening her nervous gaze on him, she straightened her shoulders. "I heard you say you don't know where Augustus Benford is. Orson told us earlier that Benford is on his way here."

Seth studied her. "Do you know when he left North Carolina?"

"No. But we're supposed to find out everything we can about—" Her gaze flittered to Tessa, and her eyes widened upon finding her sitting upright with her teeth sunk into Sean's wrist. The doctor swallowed hard. "About the woman before dawn."

Which wasn't more than an hour or two away at this point.

Seth loosed an irritated growl.

David abruptly appeared beside him.

The doctor jumped. "Holy shit," she breathed as she gaped up at him.

Ignoring her, David turned to Seth. "What's up?"

"According to the doctor here, Benford will arrive at dawn. But we have bigger problems. Henderson said a large team of heavily armed men is moving toward our location as we speak."

Multiple engines reached Sean's ears, approaching the building at a fast clip.

"Mercenaries?" David queried calmly, his gaze going to an exterior wall.

"Most likely."

"How many?"

"Two dozen. Maybe more."

"What?" the doctor blurted incredulously.

As soon as Tessa withdrew her fangs from Sean's wrist, he shot past Bastien and returned to the main room.

Nicole was bent over, opening a compartment in the cleaning cart to reveal a small arsenal.

Melanie zipped over, grabbed a couple of shoto swords, then returned to her seat and laid them on the desk beside the computer. Focusing on the screen once more, she resumed typing. One window after another opened.

Sean tucked a 9mm into his smock and slipped on a harness that settled two sheathed shoto swords on his back. He usually preferred katanas. But in an enclosed space indoors, the longer blades might be a hindrance. "Darnell?"

The only other mortal in the room didn't move. "I already have two 9mms under my lab coat and extra mags in my pockets," Darnell murmured distractedly.

Nicole swiftly donned shoulder-holstered 9mms equipped with 33-round magazines. Sean grabbed several extra mags and stuffed them in her smock pockets.

Seth, David, Tessa, Bastien, and the doctor entered.

Seth eyed Darnell and Melanie. "Where are we on copying their data?"

Darnell never looked up. "I need you to buy me some time."

"Me, too," Melanie added.

Seth turned to David. "Go take Jared's place in the other lab so he can spirit Tessa away. He's driving me crazy."

Shaking his head with mild amusement, David vanished.

"What the hell is happening?" the doctor whispered shakily as she looked wildly from one to the other. "Are you... are you messing with my head? Did you drug me?"

Jared zipped into the room and halted two feet from Tessa.

The breeze created by his swift arrival blew the hair back from her face and startled a yelp from the doctor.

After several rapid blinks, Tessa looked up at him.

"Are you sure you're all right?" he asked, his sharp gaze taking in every aspect of her appearance.

She smiled. "Yes. I'm feeling better every second."

Jared turned to the doctor Bastien still restrained. His eyes flashed bright gold as his face darkened with fury. "You're the one who drugged her?"

Fear widening her eyes, the doctor plastered her side to Bastien's, then tried to slip behind him.

When Jared took a threatening step toward her, however, Tessa hastily grabbed his arm. "Don't."

Jared swung a confused gaze upon her.

Tessa studied the woman. "She was kind to me. One of the other doctors intentionally hurt me, tightening the manacles too much, jabbing me multiple times with the needle instead of inserting it in my vein."

"Fucking Orson," the doctor muttered.

"This woman verbally bitch-slapped him and forced him to leave, then loosened the manacles a bit and inserted the rest of the needles herself."

Jared's countenance remained dark. "Seth said she nearly over-dosed you."

The doctor stopped trying to disappear behind Bastien as alarm entering her features. "What?"

Spinning on her, Jared snarled, "You could've killed her!"

The doctor looked at Tessa in horror. "I'm so sorry. TJ said the dart barely slowed you down when he tranqed you. He said it was so ineffective that he had to knock you out and told us immortals required twice the normal dosage."

Tessa scowled. "He didn't knock me out. He nearly drowned me while he waited for the sedative to kick in."

The doctor shook her head, her face full of dismay. "You roused shortly after they brought you in, so I thought he was right and... I-I just..." Rubbing a hand on her thigh, she swallowed hard. "I was afraid if you struggled, it would give Orson the excuse he needed to hurt you more."

Jared remained unforgiving. "You're still complicit. You knew they brought her here against her will, and you did *nothing* to free her!"

Anger entered the woman's face, surprising the hell out of Sean. Though Jared was usually a happy-go-lucky kind of guy, he could be damned intimidating when he was angry, especially to mortals who hadn't spent time around more powerful beings.

"What *could* I do?" she countered with a frown, her voice rising. "If I called the police to tell them she was being held here... sure, they would've shown up. But as soon as they saw her glowing eyes and the other doctors finished giving them an earful about her being immortal, they would've carted her off to another lab. A government lab. One that would focus on *weaponizing* her differences instead of finding ways to *help* people with them."

"How will enabling Benford and his ilk to live forever help people?" Jared countered, taking a menacing step toward her.

She didn't back down, daring to step toward *him* instead. "It won't. But discovering why she and others like her—others like *you*—don't suffer cognitive decline as she ages will help millions!"

Seth held up a hand. "Jared. Let it go. Dr. Baker is only here because her mother has Alzheimer's and her father is showing signs of dementia."

Melanie turned her swivel chair so she could study the doctor. "Did she hurt the vampires?"

"No," Seth said the same time the doctor said, "Yes."

All looked at her.

"One of them." Her gaze flitted to Seth. "The cameras record video twenty-four hours a day, but they don't record audio. During Cole's last lucid period, I was intentionally careless with my equipment and *accidentally* left a scalpel within his reach. With the camera behind me, I whispered for him to take it, then turned my back to fetch an alcohol swab. The scalpel was gone when I faced him." Tears welled in her eyes. "I thought Cole would use it to free himself. They didn't use metal manacles then. They used heavy canvas restraints he could cut through. I told him he could escape through the roof if he made it to the lounge at the other end of the hall. But he didn't. He slit his wrists while we were all in the conference room."

Approaching vehicles swung into the parking lot.

Sean nodded toward the front of the building. "We don't have time for this. They're here."

Melanie turned back to the computer. "Don't kill Dr. Baker. She's coming with us."

Nicole backed toward the door. "What do you want us to do with the mercenaries?"

Seth closed his eyes.

A long moment passed.

A muscle jumped in his jaw.

When he opened his eyes, they bore a luminous golden glow. "Their orders are to bring down every hostile they encounter with bullets." Telepathically, he continued. *TJ has been outside, downwind, listening all along. He saw Henderson's team erect the forward operating base and texted Benford. Benford put the mercenaries he'd hired for protection on high alert and conveyed the location of the FOB to them so they could bypass it without detection.*

Nicole smiled darkly. Henderson had detected them anyway.

*The moment we infiltrated the building,* Seth went on, *TJ texted Benford again, and Benford gave the mercenaries the green light to move in. Though most intend to shoot us until we go down, some are armed with tranq guns. Any mortal hit with a dart will die from an overdose.*

Sean sent Nicole a look of alarm.

*Both Benford and the mercenaries consider humans collateral damage.*

"So do we shoot to kill or tranq them?" Nicole asked as adrenaline surged through her veins.

"Whichever will keep them from killing *you*," Seth said. "I want you and Sean to protect and retrieve Green Team. I'll help you when I return."

"Where are you going?"

He narrowed his eyes and responded in their minds. *To deal with TJ. Don't worry about the guards on the first floor. Their eyes are on the mercenaries in the parking lot, not on the monitors.*

He vanished.

Jared took Tessa's hand. "I'm getting Tessa out of here."

They vanished.

Nicole left the primary lab and crossed the hallway she and Sean had explored earlier. Planting her back against the wall, she eased the door open.

"It's empty," Sean said as he joined her.

"What?"

"The hallway. It's empty." Smiling, he tapped his ear. "Super hearing. Remember?"

"Right." She sent him a rueful smile. "For a minute there, I slipped back into special ops mode. Most of the time, it was just us mortals working together to eliminate human threats while you immortals took care of the vampires."

Smiling, he tugged the door open and waited for her to exit. "Well, now you have me."

The wide corridor that divided the fourth floor into two halves was indeed empty. The elevator doors remained closed, the directional triangles above them dark.

She glanced at the other end of the hallway.

The door to the lab that Yellow Team occupied was cracked. Cliff leaned against the jam, a 9mm in one hand while he propped the door open with his foot.

Nicole motioned to the lab they'd just left. "There are more weapons in the cart. Arm up. We're heading down to protect and retrieve Green Team."

Sean zipped over to the elevator and pressed the button.

Nicole backed toward him as she addressed Cliff. "We'll block the elevators, but they'll still be able to use the stairs, so stay sharp." Spinning, she jogged down to join Sean in front of the elevator.

*Ding.*

Feet braced apart, Nicole drew a 9mm and aimed it at the elevator seam.

The doors slid open.

Empty.

Lowering her weapon, she stepped inside and pressed the button for the second floor.

Sean smiled as he joined her.

"What?" How did he lighten her spirits with just a smile?

"You look fierce," he professed, his expression rife with admiration. "I love that you kick ass."

Fighting a grin, she narrowed her eyes in warning. "Well, don't get distracted, or I'll have to kick *yours*."

He laughed.

*Ding.*

Nicole again raised her 9mm and braced for battle as the elevator doors slid open.

At the far end of the hallway, Rafe stood in an open doorway near the latter and gave Sean and Nicole a brief salute.

Holstering her weapon, Nicole stepped out but extended an arm back through the elevator's doors. "Find something to keep these open." She looked around. "There. Use that sofa."

The layout on this floor wasn't very different from that on the fourth. A smaller community lounge spread across both sides of a central corridor, providing employees with a couple of sofas to relax on, a few tables, and some chairs. The hallway beyond looked pretty generic. Just white walls and solid doors.

Sean grabbed a sofa and shoved it toward the elevator, moving it with as little effort as someone else might a tricycle.

Nicole kept the elevator doors from closing while he positioned the sofa half in and half out of it. Once he finished, she lowered her arm.

Unlike the top floor, this one boasted two elevators. But Rafe had already blocked the other one with a high-backed chair.

Nicole pointed to a door on the other side of it labeled STAIRS. "Pile some crap against that door to buy us some time."

"Yes, ma'am," Sean said with a grin.

Shaking her head, she strode toward Rafe. "Everything okay here?"

"Yes."

She poked her head in the doorway.

A security guard lay unconscious on the floor several yards away. Two men in slacks and rumpled oxford shirts sprawled beside him in the same condition. Blood marred neither their forms nor the floor, so Rafe must have either tranqed or bit them.

Seong-Su and Amani sat side by side at a long table across the room, a briefcase full of computer hardware open between them. Cords stretched from the case to the two computers the duo manned.

"You almost done?" she asked.

Amani shook her head. "We need more time."

Seong-Su nodded, never taking his eyes off the monitor. "There's a shitload of data here. Transferring it is taking forever."

Though the delay grated (Nicole would *really* like to avoid a firefight if possible), she understood. The network—and all of its employees—stored nothing in the cloud. They couldn't risk the kind of data breach that might occur if an engineer at a public cloud server pulled down a firewall when pressured to provide faster delivery and then forgot to lock up again. So anytime she upgraded to a new computer, she had to copy everything onto an external hard drive and bounce it onto the new computer instead of transferring it via the cloud. Sometimes it took hours.

Hours they didn't have now.

Moving to stand behind the tech wizzes, she peered over their shoulders.

That was moving a *lot* faster than it did for her at home. It must be whatever they'd plugged into the computers, because they had already copied many terabytes of information.

Rafe spoke from his position just outside the room. "Mercenaries are entering the building."

Wishing she had preternatural hearing, Nicole patted Seong-Su's shoulder and headed for the doorway. "Finish up as quickly as you can. We'll hold them off."

Sean strode up the hallway toward her. "It sounds like they're tranqing security and any personnel they come across. A few mercs wanted to shoot them instead, but Benford didn't want to kill off the staff. Replacing them would take too long. So he's hoping to pass this off as a gas leak that made everyone pass out."

Nicole arched a brow. "And if the mercenaries start shooting us? What's the plan then?"

He shrugged. "There've been almost six hundred mass shootings in the United States this year. No one will question it if they claim this was another."

Rafe shook his head. "All they'd have to do is say *disgruntled employee.*"

Unfortunately, that was true. Sighing, Nicole headed up the hallway. About midway, she found a restroom. "Once they realize they can't use the elevators, they'll take the stairs. I'll duck in here and pick them off as they climb over the crap you piled in front of the stairwell."

The elevators emitted periodic beeps when the doors couldn't close.

She ignored it.

"Rafe and I can handle the mercenaries," Sean said.

"Rafe should stay with Seong-Su and Amani," she countered. "We don't know how well-trained these guys are. As long as Rafe remains out of sight, the mercs won't know what room their targets are in."

Rafe leaned inside the room he guarded. "Work faster. Don't open this door for any reason. When you're finished, say *done.* We'll be able to hear you, even over the gunfire." Closing the door, he strode toward them. "Sean and I will handle the mercenaries."

Nicole rolled her eyes. "Fine. I'll draw their fire to this side of the building so they won't accidentally shoot Amani or Seong-Su through the walls. Rafe, if these guys get frustrated and start spraying the place with bullets, get your ass back in there; grab Amani, Seong-Su, and their gear; and get them out of here however you can. If there aren't any mercs below, break a window, jump, and run. If there are—"

"Don't worry. I'll get them out," he promised.

Sean grinned. "He's older than me and has done this a time or two, you know."

Nicole sent Rafe a sheepish smile. "Sorry. Force of habit." She jerked a thumb toward Sean. "This guy likes to throw himself headlong into danger."

Rafe smiled. "So I heard." News of their airplane exploit had traveled fast. "If I had a Second like you, I'd throw myself into danger for her, too."

Her smile broadened.

Suddenly, Sean looked toward the stairs. "Here they come."

Nicole backed into the restroom and propped the door open with her butt. Drawing a 9mm, she kept her finger near the trigger as she watched the stairwell door.

Thuds sounded as boots tromped up the stairs.

The stairwell door opened a crack.

Through the chairs and tables Sean had piled up in front of it, Nicole saw a small mirror poke out.

Aiming at it, she fired.

Her bullet shattered the mirror before whoever held it could get a good look.

Swears erupted. The door swung open.

"It's blockaded," someone snapped. "Buy us some time."

An arm appeared and blindly tossed a small object inside.

Nicole didn't even have time to call a warning. Spinning into the bathroom, she dropped her weapon, covered her ears, opened her mouth, and squeezed her eyes closed.

The flash-bang detonated in the lounge with a thunderous *boom*. The bathroom door bounced open and hit the wall.

*Sean.*

Immortals were not immune to flash-bangs. Their significantly enhanced hearing and vision actually increased the effectiveness of such weapons. It could be excruciatingly painful for them.

Ears ringing, she swiftly retrieved her fallen weapon and returned to her position in the bathroom doorway.

A man dressed in black and wearing body armor stepped into view. While two others started shoving and tugging at the furniture barricade, the first raised a 9mm.

She risked a glance at Rafe and Sean. Both were bent at the waist and staggered as they held their ears and blinked furiously.

The mercenary started shooting. Blood spurted from Rafe's back and Sean's hip.

Nicole opened fire, hitting the man's vest, then the unprotected flesh above it.

Blood gushed from his neck as the merc dropped his weapon and stumbled backward.

Nicole didn't wait for him to fall. She had to keep those bastards too busy to shoot Sean and Rafe again. So she targeted every mercenary who stepped into view. A second and a third man collapsed. Then a fourth. But each made progress in knocking down more of the barrier before they fell.

Behind them, dark figures hurried past and continued up the stairwell.

"David," she said, knowing he and the immortals above would hear her, "you've got incoming. Some are bypassing us and heading your way."

Her 9mm continued to bark bullets.

Recovering from the flash-bang, Rafe and Sean sent the intruders snarls of fury.

Nicole stopped firing as the two immortals dove toward the door.

Yeah. They were pissed.

Sean didn't even wait for the men to get through the barrier. He just reached over it, yanked a mercenary across the top, and vented his anger upon him with shoto swords.

Rafe did the same.

The fight eventually dislodged enough furniture for more bodies to stream through the door. Wide-eyed mercenaries fired

9mms with mags as long as hers. Panic filled more than one face as they took in the immortal pair's speed, strength, fangs, and glowing eyes.

Maybe no one had briefed them regarding the incredibly powerful beings they would face.

More and more began to fire wildly. A few did their damnedest to slip past Sean and Rafe in search of other targets.

Nicole shot anyone who succeeded, targeting body parts that weren't protected by helmets and vests.

Bullets tore through the wall beside her. Ceramic tile shattered behind her.

How many mercenaries *were* there?

Bodies carpeted the floor at Sean's and Rafe's feet, yet more kept coming.

One mercenary did as she'd feared and started spraying the floor with bullets, no doubt believing doing so would increase his chances of hitting the immortals that zipped about.

Pain ignited in Nicole's arm when a bullet passed through it. A second hit her in the thigh. As her leg buckled, a third grazed her side just below the edge of her vest.

Swearing, she dropped to her knees. Her breath came in ragged gasps as she fought back the pain and gave the wounds a quick glance. They hurt like hell, but it didn't look like they'd struck bone or major arteries.

Agony burned through her arm when she tried to raise it, so she passed the 9mm to her left hand and targeted the idiot shooter. Tile shattered above her head an instant before she returned a flurry of fire.

The man jerked backward as a bullet hit his shoulder. A second and third hit his vest. The fourth tore through the carotid artery in his neck.

Good thing she'd practiced shooting with both hands.

Nicole's injured leg ached unmercifully. Her arm throbbed. Warm blood stained her sleeve and slithered down to drip off her elbow.

Cursing, she gritted her teeth and shot the next mercenary, then the next.

"Nicole!" Sean shouted.

"I'm okay!" she called back. "Mind your six!"

She shot a mercenary aiming at his back before Sean could turn around.

"Define okay!" he called back.

If her arm and thigh didn't feel as if someone were holding a blowtorch to them, she might've laughed. "Okay enough to kick your ass if you don't stay focused!"

At last, only a couple of mercenaries remained. Confident that Sean and Rafe could handle them, Nicole rested her weapon on her uninjured thigh and tried to breathe through the pain.

# CHAPTER TWENTY

R AFE PLANTED HIMSELF IN the door to the stairwell while Sean dropped the last mercenary and looked up the hallway.

He'd heard Nicole grunt and swear earlier. She'd said she was okay, but he wanted to confirm it with his own eyes. Unfortunately, all he could see from this angle were her knees.

His heart sank.

The navy blue fabric covering one was darker than the other and glistened with moisture.

*Oh shit.*

Sean raced up the hallway. The many wounds he'd incurred protested as he knelt before her. Fortunately, most were already healing.

Blood ran down one of Nicole's slender arms and dripped onto the floor. More stained her shirt and smock on the same side at her waist.

Panic gripped him. "Are you okay?"

She responded with a series of curses so foul they could've made a sailor blush.

Relief rushed through him, driving him to smile. "*Now* who's crazy as a bag of ferrets?"

She laughed, or tried to. A grunt of pain cut it off.

Sean checked the wound on her arm. It was a straight through-and-through that had missed both the humerus and her brachial artery. "Feel better now that you got that off your chest?"

"No, damn it."

He stole a quick kiss. "I love you, kick-ass cranky puss."

She tried to smile, but it looked more like a grimace. "You'd better."

He checked her thigh next. That bullet had passed through as well, damaging muscle and tendon. Though it had missed the bone, it had come alarmingly close to nicking her femoral artery.

Sean flattened his hand over the wound. Healing warmth built in his chest and flowed down his arm into her thigh. "What about the blood on your side? Is that from your arm?"

"No. A bullet caught me just under the edge of my vest."

They had shot her three times? "How bad is it?" Even with his gift pulling double duty healing the gunshot wounds he'd received, Sean could heal her leg and arm. But blood loss weakened him and may make mending more serious injuries difficult. He shifted his healing touch to her arm. "Did it hit any major organs?"

"I don't think so."

"You don't *think* so?" he parroted incredulously. "Seth!"

Seth appeared beside him.

Sean finished healing Nicole's arm and shifted to the side to give him room. "She's hurt, and I'm running out of energy." When dizziness made the hallway around him spin, he braced a bloody hand on the floor to hide it.

Seth knelt in front of Nicole to assess her wounds.

Sean met her gaze.

Clenching her teeth against the pain, she jerked her head toward the opposite end of the hallway. "Go check on Seong-Su and Amani. Make sure they aren't injured. The asshole who shot me was firing blindly."

His eyes widened. *Crap.* He'd been so concerned about Nicole that he'd almost forgotten about them.

Rising, Sean raced up the hallway and burst through the door.

Amani and Seong-Su both grabbed 9mms and swung around in their seats.

Sean quickly threw up his hands in surrender. "It's okay. It's just me."

Relaxing, they turned back to their respective computers.

"Is it over?" Amani asked.

"For now." Sean didn't know if more mercenaries would follow. "Are either of you injured?"

"No," they replied absently.

"Are you almost done?" he asked hopefully.

"Yes."

Satisfied, Sean hurried back to Seth and Nicole.

Seth's hand covered the wound on her torso. Pain creased her features as the flesh knitted itself back together and healed.

Though Sean kept his expression impassive, inwardly he growled with fury. Those bastards had hurt her!

Nicole glanced up at him. "It's not that bad, Sean."

*Hmm.* Had he *outwardly* growled with fury?

She consulted Seth. "Is it?"

"The arm wasn't," the immortal leader announced impassively. "But Sean's thoughts tell me the bullet that passed through your leg came dangerously close to nicking your femoral artery. And *this* one damaged your kidney."

Sean glared at her for underplaying it.

"What?" she demanded. "I didn't know."

"Too bad. You get no pizza tonight."

Her laugh twisted into a grimace as Seth's hand began to glow. A muscle in her cheek jumped as she ground her teeth together. Soon she blinked furiously to dispel the tears that rose in her eyes.

Sean rubbed his palms against his thighs. Not being able to touch her and comfort her was killing him.

Then the creases in her forehead and lines of agony in her face smoothed out as her face lit with relief.

Seth withdrew his touch and rose. "All healed."

Sean held a hand out to Nicole and helped her up. "How are things upstairs? Is Cliff okay?"

"He's good," Seth said.

Nicole smiled. "What about Darnell?"

"He's fine. Neither received so much as a scratch," Seth told her. "When we return to network headquarters, make sure you visit the infirmary. You need a transfusion to replace the blood you've lost."

"I will. Thank you."

Nodding, Seth gave Sean a quick inspection. "Any wounds you want me to heal?"

"No." Now that he'd stopped healing Nicole, his injuries mended quickly. "I'll be as good as new once I score a quick infusion."

That Nicole needed blood worried him though. And his mind was full of what-ifs that soon made him tremble.

What if that bullet *had* nicked her femoral artery?

What if that mercenary had tossed a grenade instead of a flash-bang?

Yet again, Sean had come terrifyingly close to losing her.

Too shaken to worry about Seth watching them, Sean drew Nicole into a tight embrace and rested his chin on her hair.

"I'm okay, Sean," she assured him softly, and wrapped her arms around him.

Closing his eyes, he shook his head. "If one of those bullets had hit you in the head..."

She gave him a squeeze. "It would've bounced right off. You know how hard my head is."

Chuckling, he held her as close as he could without harming her. His eyes met Seth's over her head. *I can't lose her*, he thought.

*You won't.* Smiling, Seth clapped him on the shoulder. "Don't worry. Once she transforms, she'll heal as quickly as you do. Even faster if you ask Roland or Aidan to transform her for you."

Sean sucked in a breath. Was he saying...?

Stiffening, Nicole turned her head against his chest so she could look up at Seth. "You would be okay with that? With me transforming? With us wanting to spend eternity together?"

"Of course," Seth said simply.

They stared at him.

Her hold loosened. "Reordon specifically told me to steer clear of intimacy as a Second, that sex was not part of the job. Many, many times."

Sean nodded. "Me, too. He basically said *Keep your hands off her or else.*"

Seth shrugged. "Chris's mother was sexually harassed by an employer, so he tends to be more protective of women who work for the network. And unlike me, he didn't have prophetic visions of you two falling in love."

Shock tore through Sean. "You what?" He and Krysta were still new to the Immortal Guardian family. Sean wouldn't have thought

338

he rated high enough to land in one of the illustrious leader's visions.

Slipping out of Sean's embrace, Nicole gaped up at them. "Who did what now?"

Seth laughed. "A prophetic vision showed me the two of you would fall in love."

Sean exchanged a disbelieving look with Nicole. "When?"

"The night Étienne and Cam brought you and Krysta to David's place after your rental home was destroyed and I shook your hand for the first time."

"That long ago!" he nearly shouted.

"Yes."

"Why didn't you tell us?" they demanded simultaneously.

Amusement lit the immortal leader's face. "For the same reason that Sean's father didn't. So you wouldn't question whether getting together was *your* idea or ours."

That wouldn't have been a problem for Sean, but when he looked at Nicole...

She bit her lip as uncertainty furrowed her brow. "I hate to admit it," she said slowly, "but I could see myself wondering somewhere down the line if you would've chosen to be with me if your father or Seth hadn't told you we were meant to be together."

The confession spawned neither anger nor resentment. He'd been privy to his father's visions his entire life and was accustomed to them. He knew they didn't *cause* events to happen. They merely foretold them. *And* his parents and grandparents loved him and had always ensured he knew just how much he meant to them.

Nicole's hadn't. Sean was the first person in Nicole's life who had truly loved her. So he could understand how part of her might've wondered if he hadn't pursued her simply because a vision had told him to. "But now you *won't* question it?" he asked.

Smiling, she shook her head. "I won't."

He brushed her lips with a kiss. "Then take pity on me and transform as soon as possible. If I weren't immortal, I swear the last few weeks would've aged me forty years."

She laughed.

Amani stepped into the hallway. "We're done," she announced.

Seong-Su followed, carrying the bulky briefcase.

Rafe joined them, looking a little worse for wear. Multiple bullets had hit him. And his wounds weren't healing as swiftly as Sean's.

Seth took a minute to heal Rafe, then motioned the tech whizzes forward. "I hear no more mercenaries. Let's reconvene on the fourth floor and let the network move in so they can start cleaning up this mess."

Sean surveyed the downed men, bullet-hole-riddled walls, and blood splatter. It was quite a mess. But the network excelled at taking care of such things, particularly when Seth aided them by altering a few memories.

"I'll teleport Amani and Seong-Su," Seth said. "You three clear both elevators for the network then take one up and join us."

Sean nodded. "See you in a few." Keeping an arm around Nicole's shoulders, he headed for the elevator.

Seth waited in the *immortality lab*, as Henderson called the sound-proof room doctors had shackled Tessa in.

All was quiet. Not just here, but throughout the building.

Henderson's massive cleanup crew here in Texas impressed Seth as much as Reordon's in North Carolina did. All facility employees on the lower floors were unconscious. Most now bore wounds they hadn't when the battle had ended. Bruises, for the most part. Nonlethal injuries that would explain their lack of consciousness without tranquilizer darts raising questions.

Henderson had gone with the simplest explanation for the violence: a mass shooter, namely Dr. Orson, had loosed his vengeance upon them all. An examination of Orson's mind had uncovered acts in the man's past that had eliminated any guilt Seth might've otherwise felt over framing him. Dr. Orson now lay dead in the outer lab, the result of what authorities would ultimately deem a self-inflicted gunshot wound.

The other primary lab researchers—none of whom had borne the concern and guilt Dr. Baker had over the inhumane treatment of the vampires and the abduction of Tessa—had replaced the mercenaries whom Seth, David, Bastien, and Cliff had slain up here. All had been rewarded for their lack of ethics with nonlethal gunshot wounds and new memories of how events had transpired. Every spec of blood spatter on the fourth floor now bore the doctors' blood rather than that of the mercenaries killed in the fray or the wounded immortals.

The blood on the second floor had been replaced with that of guards authorities would praise for valiantly attempting to stop the shooter. The memories of *all* employees would reflect the cover story.

Henderson's crew had since withdrawn to the FOB.

Sean, Nicole, Bastien, and the others were all back in North Carolina.

Only Seth remained.

Crickets chirped. Other insects hummed and buzzed, unconcerned by the night's chaos.

David abruptly appeared.

When Seth cast him a questioning look, he shrugged. "I thought you might like some company."

Seth nodded. "How are Nicole and Tessa?"

David lowered himself onto the chair beside Seth's and stretched out his long legs. "Tessa is nestled in a spare bedroom at my place, with Leah fussing over her."

A smile full of affection curled Seth's lips as he pictured it.

"Nicole is trying to convince Sean to wait until tomorrow to pester Aidan or Roland into transforming her."

Seth laughed. "They'll have better luck if they ask Aidan."

"Such was my thought," David responded with a chuckle. "Roland *does* seem to like Nicole, though, so he may make an exception."

"As long as the others don't start calling him The Transformer again?"

David grinned. "Just so."

Engine noise disrupted the usual night sounds, produced by a vehicle approaching at high speeds.

Both looked toward the front of the building.

Seth delved into the minds of the drivers. "Benford, his henchman Danvers, and six armed guards."

David nodded.

Neither moved as the car parked in front. Doors sprang open.
Shoes pounded the pavement. Then bodies tromped through the
front doors.

Swears erupted when the newcomers spotted the fallen guards
and employees.

"How do you want to play this?" a man asked. "You want to call
911?"

"And tell them what?" Benford snapped. "That the mercenaries
I hired accidentally shot more people than I told them to?"

Seth listened to their progress as they made their way to the
elevator. Instead of taking stock of the rest of the building, they
took it straight to the fourth floor.

*Ding.*

More swears.

"Why the hell did they shoot the researchers?" Danvers demanded.

"I thought you said they were professionals," Benford growled.

"They are. They do shit like this all over the world."

More curses. "Do you know how hard it will be to find replace-
ments who won't leak what we're doing here?" Benford snapped.
"And where *are* the mercenaries? Did they cut and run after they
fucked up or something?"

"No," Danvers grumbled. "I'm telling you, these guys are professionals."

"He's right," a third man muttered. "That one there looks like
he shot *himself.* I don't know what went down, but we don't fuck
up missions. Our guys must be canvassing the second and third
floors." *Click.* "Saturn, this is Titan. Over."

Silence.

"Saturn, this is Titan. What's your 20? Over."

More silence.

"Saturn, this is Titan. Radio check. Over."

A long pause ensued.

Someone shifted.

"Let us take point," Titan uttered.

Footsteps tromped up the hallway.

A security lock clicked when someone swiped their card and typed in a passcode.

The door to the outer lab opened.

More swears. More footsteps.

Then six mercenaries entered the *immortality lab*. Spreading out, they aimed their weapons at Seth and David, who lounged in chairs near the glass room in which Tessa had been restrained. Like the others, these wielded semiautomatic handguns. But assault rifles dangled down the backs of four of them.

Danvers entered next, followed by Benford.

As soon as Danvers saw Seth and David, he drew a 9mm and aimed it at them.

Benford planted himself at the center of the horseshoe of assholes. Lips tight, he reeked of arrogance and false power. "Who the hell are you?" he demanded.

Ignoring him, Seth smiled at the mercenaries. "Thank you, gentlemen. You may lower your weapons."

After exchanging confused looks, they opted not to comply.

Seth rose, as did David.

The mercenaries tensed.

"Hands in the air! Hands in the air!" one shouted, his voice identifying him as Titan.

Seth and David merely smiled. And their complete lack of concern clearly rankled the other parties.

"Who are you?" Benford demanded again. He looked past them to the empty glass room. "Where's the girl?"

Seth arched a brow. "Do you mean the girl you kidnapped from a college campus in North Carolina and brought here against her will so you could use her as a lab rat?"

Not even a smidgen of doubt or indecision flickered across the mercenaries' faces. And a quick examination of their thoughts revealed duplicitous natures. None of them cared if some unnamed college girl got hurt as long as they got paid.

They were no better than the bastard who'd hired them.

"Where is she?" Benford shouted.

DIANNE DUVALL

"Dead," Seth lied, "like the other college students you kidnapped." Benford believed Becca and George were both dead. And Seth opted not to refer to the other victims as vampires.

No mercenaries wavered.

"Bullshit!" His face mottling with fury, Benford pointed at David and ordered, "Shoot him." He directed a smile full of satisfaction at Seth. "You'll talk, or he'll bleed."

Before Titan's finger could tighten on the trigger, Seth swept forward, knocked everyone except Benford unconscious, and returned to his original position beside David.

The old man started violently and gawked as his henchman and the mercenaries he'd hired to protect him all collapsed to the floor and lay motionless. His face blanched. His heart pounded in his doughy chest. And his blood pressure spiked as he returned wide eyes to Seth and began to tremble. A true coward, he didn't lunge for a gun to fight back. Lulled by decades of bullying and intimidating others with financial threats and hired muscle, he remained too frozen in place by utter terror to move.

Disgust filled Seth as he perused the man's thoughts. This man bore no honor at all.

There *was*, however, hope for his grandson, whom Benford thought of as a worthless "do-gooder" who had been the only member of the family with the balls to question his grandfather's ethics. Seth made a mental note to ensure that Benford's will would leave *all* of his business holdings to the grandson he had formerly omitted from it.

"Wh-Who are you?" Benford stuttered.

Seth offered him a smile that bore no warmth. "You may consider me a protector of the young woman you hunted like an animal."

Confusion entered the man's pale eyes. "Rebecca Dorman?"

"Yes. Tessa, as well."

"You're Nick Belanger?" Benford studied him.

"Oh, no. I'm not Nick. I'm far more powerful than he is."

David stepped up beside him. "And far more deadly."

Benford nearly wet himself.

Seth walked a slow circle around the scoundrel. "You've terror-ized these women and the vampires you purchased in a blatant search for immortality."

Benford neither acknowledged nor denied it, perhaps unsure which would condemn him more.

Stopping in front of him, Seth stood only a foot away. "Well, now you've found it." He rested a hand on the man's shoulder. Warmth flowed from him into the old man, healing some of the damage wrought by age and decades of excess and self-indulgence.

Benford sucked in a breath. His posture straightened. Wonder filled his features as his aches and pains vanished, erasing all the fear. "What is that?" he whispered.

"A taste of what you seek." Seth infused him with a temporary surge in strength that would make him feel thirty years old again. Once done, he backed away to stand beside David.

Benford stared down at his body in amazement. After clenching and unclenching hands that no longer ached with arthritis, he jumped up and down experimentally. A jubilant laugh burst from his lips. "This is amazing." He touched his hair, which was a little thicker now, then did several jumping jacks. When he didn't lose his breath or grow weary after only a few, he stopped and stared at Seth with awe. "Am I immortal now?"

Seth and David looked at each other, then burst out laughing.

"Hell no," Seth said.

His face full of excitement, Benford took a step toward them. "Make me immortal. I'll pay you anything."

Seth shook his head. Men like this would never understand that some things were more valuable than wealth. "Money means little to us."

Feigning consideration, David tilted his head to one side. "What would you do with immortality if we granted it to you?"

The man's mind instantly filled with how he would wield the power immortality would give him, the many ways he would abuse it and use it for his own gain.

David sighed as he met Seth's gaze. "It always saddens me to see how little progress humanity has made."

Seth nodded.

Benford's face twisted into a scowl. "What's that supposed to mean?"

"It means," Seth told him, "that we've lived for thousands of years and are tired of seeing men of your ilk hold humanity back. You've done enough damage as a mortal. Nothing you offer could coax us into helping you live forever."

"That's bullshit. Everyone has a price."

David shook his head. "Only if they've no care for the greater good."

Benford had the temerity to sneer at him. "The greater good? You sound like my loser grandson."

"Who will no doubt do far greater things with your fortune than you have," David replied calmly.

The man frowned. "What?"

Seth smiled. "Your life, I'm afraid, ends tonight. And thanks to us, your lawyer will find a notarized last will bearing your signature that leaves everything to young Vernon." Ironically, Vernon's parents had hoped that naming him after the powerful family patriarch—Augustus Vernon Benford—would ensure themselves a larger portion of the inheritance pie.

Instead, he was the only member of Benford's family—which included three children and six other grandchildren—worthy of the payoff and the responsibility that accompanied it.

"You're lying," the man blurted.

"I'm afraid not," Seth said.

Fury getting the better of him, Benford swung a clumsy fist.

Seth caught it easily. "You fool. You only *feel* immortal."

As soon as Seth released him, Benford lunged for Titan's abandoned 9mm.

Seth caught him by the throat with one hand before he could reach it. Ever so slowly, he applied enough upward pressure that Benford had to rise onto his toes to keep from choking. "You showed Becca, Tessa, and the vampires no mercy. So we will show *you* none."

"Don't," the man begged. "I'll give you anything you want."

"Information?"

346

A light of triumph lit the bastard's eyes. "What kind of information?"

"How did you learn about Nick Belanger?"

"A tip from a friend."

Seth peered into the man's thoughts and found the memory of a video, the image pixilated the way nighttime footage shot with a phone sometimes was. In it, Nick Belanger and fellow immortal Eliana walked together on University of Houston's campus. The footage followed and captured them as they confronted and fought a pack of vampires.

Where the hell had he gotten that?

He delved deeper into Benford's mind. The footage had come on a DVD in a package with Richard Roubal's address on it. "Richard Roubal told you about Nick?"

"You know Richard?"

"Yes."

"I thought he was out of his damned mind. He didn't even remember sending it to me."

Roubal had suffered from Alzheimer's, his symptoms worsened by cancer and the treatment he received. Seth had found negotiating the man's mind incredibly difficult.

"But my guys confirmed the video hadn't been altered," Benford continued. "Roubal said he was going to capture Belanger to study him but died before he could get it done." He smirked. "He probably would've fucked it up anyway. Roubal was a shell of himself by the time he kicked it."

Well, that was the last piece of the puzzle they needed.

Seth let Benford go.

The man's heels hit the floor with a thud. Staggering to one side, he drew in several deep breaths as his face filled with triumph. "You won't regret this." The idiot thought Seth had changed his mind and intended to make him immortal.

"No. I'm afraid I won't." Seth focused on the man's chest.

Benford paled as what felt like a fist tightened around his heart. Eyes wide, he grabbed his left arm. His face contorted with pain as his breath shortened. Bending forward, he gazed up at Seth. "Wh-Wha—?"

"You're having a heart attack," Seth informed him.

The man's lips moved, but no more sound emerged. In his chaotic mind, however, he shouted, bargained, and struggled to get the words out.

David shook his head. "He still thinks he can buy us off."

Benford's face reflected utter astonishment that he couldn't as he breathed his last breath.

Seth and David watched him fall.

"Roubal sent that video after we defeated Gershom," David commented.

"Yes." Roubal hadn't encountered Nick until a few weeks after the final battle.

"So, how did Reed connect with him? All arrows point to Gershom having sent him."

A troubling thought. "And yet, I didn't see Gershom's name or likeness anywhere in Benford's memories."

"Nor did I."

Seth sighed. "I wish we could've read Reed's thoughts. TJ was never part of Gershom's army." Seth's perusal of TJ's memories had revealed as much. "He met Reed after the latter lost contact with Gershom."

"So," David posed after a moment's thought, "*did* Gershom play a role in this?"

"I don't know. But if he did, that role ended when we defeated him."

"Are you sure? Zach communicated with Lisette through dreams while he was imprisoned. Could Gershom do the same?"

Seth shook his head. "He's too weak and buried too deep. I learned from Zach's trespasses and ensured Gershom could not do the same. He can take no more action against us."

"Perhaps he merely asked Reed to do a little research and find someone like Benford who would have the resources, desire, and lack of a moral compass to do whatever he could to create an immortality serum."

"And he just happened to choose Benford, who had a history with Roubal?"

David shrugged. "Benford owns one of the largest pharmaceutical companies in the country."

"And the largest Reed would find in North Carolina."

David considered the quandary. "Coincidence?"

Seth found a smile. "This wouldn't be the first time coincidence has wrought havoc in our world."

Chuckling, David shook his head. "No, it wouldn't."

Since Seth had appointed himself the leader of the Immortal Guardians, the chaos that simple happenstance could spawn had sometimes astounded him.

"If Gershom *was* involved," David asked as they strolled from the lab, "do you think this was the extent of his backup plan?"

Seth sighed. "I certainly hope so."

# CHAPTER TWENTY-ONE

N ICOLE GRINNED AS SHE raced through the trees. Somewhere up
ahead, Sean attempted to elude her, but she now had a nose
as powerful as an elephant's. And she *loved* Sean's scent. Even more
now that she was immortal.

They had wasted no time in asking Aidan to transform her.
Nicole would've preferred that Sean do it, but practicality over-
ruled that. Aidan was roughly three thousand years old and a healer. That magical combination would make Nicole faster, stronger,
and more resilient than she would be if an immortal as young as
Sean transformed her. It would also give her a greater tolerance
for sunlight.

And it had. She couldn't go out and sunbathe for hours on end.
But it took longer for Nicole's skin to pinken and burn than it did
for Sean's.

Nicole remembered little about her transformation. According
to Sean, once Aidan bit her, she got pretty loopy and said some
things Sean admitted he wished he could've caught on video.
Nicole vaguely recalled not feeling well the next day. She developed a high fever and vomited up everything Sean coaxed her into
eating or drinking. Even water.

Sean had been a real sweetheart, staying by her side, comforting
her, distracting her, and making her laugh. All she remembered
after that was waking up with a haggard Sean leaning over her and
discovering—much to her shock—that three days had passed.

Poor Sean. As soon as he'd realized she was lucid, he had crawled
into bed, curled his big body around hers, and held her almost
painfully tight for at least an hour, mumbling something about an
ice bath and her scaring the crap out of him.

Then he'd fed her *lots* of pizza.

She grinned.

Though there wasn't much of a breeze, the wind generated by her exceptional speed yanked Nicole's hair back from her face. Running this fast wasn't as easy as she'd expected. Nicole had nearly crashed into a tree the first time she'd raced through the forest. But she had since learned how to process visuals of her surroundings as quickly as she could run.

Tonight, Sean was helping her learn how to use her enhanced senses to track targets as part of her new vampire-hunter training.

Since she could run as fast as a three-thousand-year-old immortal, Nicole had given him a head start. But she was gaining on him and would soon—

She skidded to a halt. The thick trunks of towering evergreens rose around her.

Peering between them, she sniffed.

Sean's scent had abruptly grown fainter, not stronger as it would have if she were about to catch him.

Frowning, she turned in a slow circle.

That was odd. It seemed stronger behind her than it was in front of her. Had he doubled back?

She pondered it.

He couldn't have. She would've run into him if he had. And if he'd veered off and taken a circuitous route to bypass her, she would've smelled it *and* heard it.

Wouldn't she?

Swearing, Nicole sprinted back the way she'd come. Every half mile or so, she paused to sniff and listen.

Run. Pause. Sniff. Listen. Run. Pause. Sniff. Listen.

At no point did she unearth anything that suggested Sean had struck off in a different direction.

When she could barely detect his scent, she reluctantly conceded defeat and returned to the point at which she'd lost it. Frowning, she propped her hands on her hips. "Sean," she called, "where are you?"

"Up here." A smile tinged the deep voice that came from above.

Tilting her head back, she looked up.

Fifty or sixty feet up in the branches of a nearby tree, Sean grinned down at her as he hugged the trunk. "Hi there."

She smiled back. "Hi yourself."

As agile as a monkey, he began to climb down. "Did you know your eyes glow when you get frustrated?"

No, she didn't. She'd have to keep that in mind on future hunts. "How do you know it's frustration and not your gorilla-like prowess turning me on?" she countered. Sean was no longer the only one in this relationship whose eyes glowed when he became aroused. He had proven that shortly after her transformation by ardently making love with her in front of a mirror.

Nicole's pulse jumped just thinking about it. That man could heat her blood like no other.

A wistful sigh escaped her.

And immortal sex was the best.

Pausing in his descent, Sean jumped up and down on a thick limb, emitted several deep-throated hoo's, and beat his chest like a gorilla. "Is that what gets your motor running?"

Nicole laughed. "No. We'll have to chalk it up to frustration. Why are you climbing down, anyway? Why don't you jump?"

When he was about thirty feet up, he did just that. Stepping off a stout limb, he plummeted down and landed in a neat crouch a couple of feet away. So cool. "Because I'm not a fan of heights," he admitted with a sheepish smile.

She wasn't either and didn't look forward to learning how to land safely when jumping or falling from such heights. "How did you elude me like that?"

Propping his hands on his hips, he puffed out his chest, turned his head to the side, and assumed a superhero pose. "I'm just that good," he professed, oozing arrogance.

Nicole shoved him with a laugh. "Seriously, how'd you do it?"

Sean shrugged. "You assumed that greater speed would deliver an easy victory. Overconfidence in our line of work can sometimes bite you in the ass."

She would've made a jesting comment about using her new fangs to bite *him* in the ass if she weren't so embarrassed to admit that hubris had indeed misled her. "Yep. I screwed up."

Smiling, he grasped her hips and drew her closer. "I'd tell you *I* never screw up, but—"

"I used to be your Second."

"And came to my rescue how many times?"

"I lost count."

"Exactly. So don't sweat it." Dipping his head, he pressed his lips to hers in a slow kiss full of warmth and affection. "You've only been immortal for a few weeks. And unlike certain *other* new immortals, you haven't accidentally crashed through the side of a house or tossed someone up through a ceiling."

She laughed. "Who crashed through the side of a house?"

"Dana."

"Who got tossed through a ceiling?"

"Seth. *And* Aidan, I think."

"Oh my." She couldn't help but grin as she pictured it.

Lowering his head, Sean nuzzled her neck, his warm breath sending a delightful shiver through her. "Have I told you lately that I love you?" He trailed a path of nibbling kisses up to her ear.

"Yes." Gripping the front of his shirt, she leaned into him and drew in his scent. "Multiple times when you took me in the shower earlier." And as Sean had once told her, she felt *everything* more now that she was immortal.

"Thank goodness our room at David's place is soundproof."

They'd been staying there since her transformation so David could monitor her progress. And thanks to all the soundproofing packed into the walls, floor, and ceiling of their room, Sean had spent many, many hours showing her how her enhanced sense of touch could transform sex from awesome to absolutely mind-blowing. "Speaking of which..." Rising on her toes, she nipped his ear. "Are we far enough away to keep everyone from hearing us if we ditch these clothes and—"

"No," he groaned. But it didn't stop him from pressing her hips into his so she could feel how hard he was for her.

The light breeze picked up. "Mmmmm," she purred. "What is that delectable scent?"

"Me, wanting you," he growled. Slipping a hand under the hem of her shirt, he stroked her back, then caressed his way to the front and cupped her breast.

*So good.*

He stilled. "Wait." Lifting his head, he gave the air a sniff. "You mean *that* scent?"

"Yes."

Lips twitching, he shook his head. "It's dinner."

Her stomach gave a hearty rumble. "As much as I like where this is going..." she said, arching her hips into his.

"Let me guess. You're starving?"

She wrinkled her nose. "Yes."

He grinned. "Yeah. I was hungry twenty-four hours a day when I first turned. Running and training with the speed and strength we do burns a *lot* of calories."

Nicole waggled her eyebrows. "I know something *else* that burns a lot of calories." She meant the words to be flirtatious, still thinking about the awesome quickies they'd engaged in, but her stomach ruined it by growling again.

Laughing, Sean slung an arm around her shoulders. "Come on. Let's head back."

Half an hour later, Nicole plowed her way through a second plate of spicy lasagna, much to Sean's amusement. Every Immortal Guardian stationed in the area was present, and all were in high spirits.

Jared and Tessa joined the boisterous group seated around David's long dining table, as did Becca. The teenager seemed immensely relieved to no longer be a target and much happier now that life had returned to normal.

Tessa showed no signs of lingering trauma from her abduction. She had even begun to hunt vampires nightly.

Bastien finally managed to drag Melanie away from the wealth of information they'd stolen from Augustus Benford's company so they could join the festive supper. Melanie had worked tirelessly at the network, refusing to leave for days at a time as she desperately combed through every shred of data they'd retrieved on methods of forestalling cognitive decline.

Both Stuart and Miguel suffered periodic psychotic breaks that steadily increased in frequency. Nicole fervently hoped that something in the research they'd stolen would help Melanie save them. Both were good men and good friends. And, like Cliff, they clung tenaciously to their honor.

Perhaps the new set of eyes Dr. Baker brought into play would help. Benford's former employee had initially balked at joining the network. Not because she didn't want to help them. *Gifted ones'* advanced DNA and its effect on the virus fascinated her. And she wasn't averse to working hands-on with the vampires. But she wished to continue searching for an Alzheimer's cure for her mother.

When Seth and David told her they would use their healing gifts to do whatever they could to increase the duration of her mother's lucid moments and stave off her father's dementia, however, Dr. Baker agreed to study both Alzheimer's *and* the virus at network headquarters.

A sudden burst of guffaws drew Nicole's gaze to the rowdy group behind her. The Immortal Guardians' family in North Carolina had grown so large that Darnell and Sheldon had added a second dining table almost as long as the first to accommodate the Seconds and other mortal employees who wished to join them.

She grinned. Sheldon was recounting the tale of Seth appearing above David's backyard as a massive dragon with Sean and Nicole clutched in its talons.

Sean nudged her. "They'll be talking about that for ages."

"I will, too," Krysta said. Seated across from them, she narrowed her eyes at her brother. "I still can't believe you two jumped out of a plane without parachutes. The virus can only heal so much damage, you know."

"I know," Sean groaned. "You've made that very clear." Krysta and Étienne had given him a stern talking-to over the incident.

Nicole laughed.

The front door abruptly burst open, slamming into the wall with so much force that it sounded like a gunshot.

All conversation halted as everyone looked toward it. Several immortals rose and drew weapons.

Nicole palmed a knife, just as startled as the others.

Cliff ran in, tugging Emma behind him by their clasped hands. Both breathed hard, as if they'd parked at the end of David's long driveway and had run at top speed to reach them.

Tears coursed down Emma's cheeks.

Nicole's stomach sank.

"Bastien!" Cliff bellowed as they stumbled to a halt in the living room.

Bastien stood so quickly that his chair fell over. "What is it?"

Melanie rose, her face full of concern. "Cliff? What's happened?"

He turned at the sound of their voices. As soon as Cliff spotted them, his eyes filled with tears.

*Oh crap.* Had someone died? One of the vampires at network headquarters?

*Please, not Stuart or Miguel.* They'd both been struggling in recent months.

Bastien strode forward. "What is it? Tell me."

As Cliff met Bastien's gaze, his lips curled up in a tremulous smile. "Emma's pregnant."

Utter silence descended upon the group.

Then a rousing cheer swelled, loud enough to raise the roof.

Bastien raced forward and dragged Cliff into a hardy embrace.

Relief and happiness suffused Nicole.

The best friends clung to each other for many long moments while Melanie zipped forward to hug a grinning, weeping Emma.

When Bastien finally stepped back, his face was as tear-streaked as Cliff's and Emma's. "I'm so happy for you both."

Everyone present abandoned their dinner to crowd around the couple and express their joy. Nicole and Sean hurried over to give their friends exuberant hugs.

When Seth finally made his way through the throng, Cliff hugged him as hard as he had Bastien.

"Thank you," Cliff whispered hoarsely. "For everything."

Smiling, Seth clapped him on the back. "I'll always be here for you, Cliff. You and Emma are part of our family." When Cliff stepped back, Seth offered Emma his congratulations. "You just took the test today?"

Smiling, she nodded.

He motioned to her flat stomach. "May I?"

"Yes, please."

Seth rested his big hand on her flat stomach, fingers splayed a little.

Quiet fell as they all waited.

Nodding with apparent satisfaction, he withdrew his touch and stepped back. "All is well."

Everyone sighed with relief.

Seth raised his brows. "Would you like to know the sex?"

Emma stared at him. "You can tell that already?"

Nicole had thought couples usually had to wait a few months to learn that.

"Yes," he said simply. "It's in the chromosomes."

Cliff and Emma looked at each other, excitement blooming on their faces. Emma nodded. So did Cliff. Then they turned big smiles on Seth. "Yes!"

The Immortal Guardians leader smiled. "Then congratulations. You're having a baby girl."

Pure joy shining in his handsome features, Cliff whooped and swept Emma into his arms, lifting her feet off the floor and twirling her around. "We're having a girl!"

"*And...*" Seth said.

The couple looked at him.

His smile stretched into a grin. "You're also having a boy."

The look of shock that blanked the couple's faces nearly made Nicole laugh.

Cliff's hold loosened.

Emma slid down his front until her feet touched the floor. She looked at Cliff, then Seth. "We're having twins?"

Clearly enjoying their astonishment, Seth nodded.

Emma met her husband's eyes. "We're having twins."

"A son and a daughter," he whispered.

She nodded.

Drawing her into a tight embrace, he buried his face in her thick hair. "I love you so much, Emma."

She clutched him tightly, one hand fisting in his dreadlocks. "I love you, too."

The touching moment tugged at Nicole's heartstrings. After all the couple had been through, they were finally living their dream.

Bastien suddenly thrust a fist into the air and shouted jubilantly. "I'm going to be an uncle!"

Cheers and laughter erupted.

When Cliff released his wife, well-wishers crowded around to offer hugs and pats on the back.

Nicole smiled and swiped at damp cheeks as she watched.

Wrapping an arm around her, Sean pressed a kiss to the top of her head.

As grateful to have Sean in her life as Cliff was to have Emma, Nicole leaned into his side. "Now he has everything he wanted," she murmured happily.

Sean cupped her face with his free hand and gave her a tender smile. "And I have everything *I* wanted."

Her heart swelled with emotion. "I love you, Sean."

"I love you, too."

# FROM THE AUTHOR

T HANK YOU FOR READING *Rogue Darkness*. This was the first Immortal Guardians book that featured two relative newbies to the group. Sean and Nicole have such a playful, teasing relationship. I had a lot of fun writing their story and laughed quite a bit. I hope you had as much fun reading it.

If you enjoyed *Rogue Darkness*, please consider rating or reviewing it at an online retailer of your choice. I'm always thrilled when I see that one of my books made a reader or audiobook lover happy. Ratings and reviews are also an excellent way to recommend an author's books, create word of mouth, and help other readers find new favorite worlds to escape into.

# ABOUT THE AUTHOR

Dianne Duvall is the *New York Times* and *USA Today* bestselling author of the Immortal Guardians paranormal romance series, the Aldebarian Alliance sci-fi romance series, and The Gifted Ones medieval and time-travel romance series. She is known for writing stories full of action that keeps readers flipping pages well past their bedtimes, humor that readers frequently complain makes them laugh out loud at inappropriate moments, strong heroes who adore strong heroines, lovable secondary characters, and swoon-worthy romance. *AudioFile Magazine* declared *The Segonian* (Aldebarian Alliance Book 2) one of the Best Audiobooks of 2021 and awarded it the AudioFile Earphones Award for Exceptional Audio. Audible chose *Awaken the Darkness* (Immortal Guardians Book 8) as one of the Top 5 Best Paranormal Romances of 2018.

Reviewers have called Dianne's books "fast-paced and humorous" (*Publishers Weekly*), "utterly addictive" (*RT Book Reviews*), "extraordinary" (*Long and Short Reviews*), and "wonderfully imaginative" (*The Romance Reviews*). Her audiobooks have received multiple AudioFile Earphone Awards for Exceptional Audio. One was nominated for a prestigious Audie Award. And her books have twice been nominated for RT Reviewers' Choice Awards.

When she isn't writing, Dianne is active in the independent film industry and has even appeared on-screen, crawling out of a moonlit grave and wielding a machete like some of the psychotic vampires she creates in her books.

For the latest news on upcoming releases, sales, giveaways, and more, please visit **DianneDuvall.com**. You can also connect with Dianne online:

360

**Subscribe to Dianne's Newsletter**
eepurl.com/hfT2Qn

**Follow Dianne on Amazon**
www.amazon.com/Dianne-Duvall/e/B0046IHUO6

**Follow Dianne on BookBub**
www.bookbub.com/authors/dianne-duvall

**Join the Dianne Duvall Books Group**
www.facebook.com/groups/128617511148830/

**Facebook**
www.facebook.com/DianneDuvallAuthor

**Instagram**
www.instagram.com/dianne.duvall

**Twitter**
twitter.com/DianneDuvall

**Pinterest**
www.pinterest.com/dianneduvall

**YouTube**
bit.ly/DianneDuvall_YouTube

Printed in Great Britain
by Amazon

26273955R00212